Spitting from high places

by ***Verna Bednarski***

White Mountain Publications

ISBN: 1-894747-19-4
Printed in Canada

White Mountain Publications
A Division of White Mountain Investments Ltd.
www.wmpub.ca

Cover Design: Johanne Loach of *Johanne's Photography*
www.johannesphotography.ca and Deborah Ranchuk

Library and Archives Canada Cataloguing in Publication
Bednarski, Verna, 1943-

Spitting from high places / by Verna Bednarski.

ISBN 1-894747-19-4
I. Title.

PS8603.E426S65 2006 C813'.6 C2006-903593-8

The characters in this novel are fictional.
Any resemblance to persons now living, or dead, is coincidental.

Chapter One

Pat shoved the slim spade into the soft earth and drew up another bit of soil which she gently deposited near the fresh hole she had created. She quickly wiped her sleeve across her forehead to remove the perspiration that had formed and then using the spade as a lean post she glanced carefully around her. Her backyard was quite contained, completely surrounded by bush and trees. She didn't think anyone could see her, but you never knew. Better to be a bit cautious. Pat reached back and pulled her sweat pants out of the crack of her bum. "Oh, that feels better," she sighed. She reached over and extracted another pink petunia plant from its container and gently placed it into the freshly dug hole, pulling and patting the dirt around it.

"There, the middle of June and the planting's finished." She looked around at her garden with satisfaction. She used to maintain just a spring and fall garden, but now that she didn't have the cottage at the lake any more to look after, she was busy transforming the various beds into ones with summer blooming plants: zinnias, marigolds and asters. Before it had been daffodils, crocus, iris, and for the fall, mums. Planting mums seemed to her almost a waste of energy as they never survived the winters. Sometimes the flowers had hardly opened up before the snow came in the fall pounding the plants to the ground; and the poor sad flowers lay withered in the crisp fall air.

Things had changed somewhat after Earl had died seven years ago. Pat kept their home in Trenton, Ontario along with their cottage. She had tried to keep the cottage going for a few years, mainly because she thought her children would come back to visit and bring their families. Her oldest son Jason lived right in the same town as she did, but he wasn't the outdoorsy type, and found that keeping up his modest yard in town kept him busy enough. The other two children only came up for short two or three day visits each summer, so it was hardly worth it, money or time wise to keep the place maintained. She had enjoyed it while Earl was alive. They would load up their truck every weekend with food and drinks and head off to the cottage. It was fun to putter around, cut wood, go for long walks in the woods, watch the wild life, sit in front of a roaring fire at night. She smiled at the memories. Unfortunately, in the last few years the lake had become almost like a subdivision of the town. There must be over fifty cottages now just at their end of the lake, and a lot of these were being replaced with permanent homes. It wasn't that far into town, and more and more young people were building out there. Everyone had two vehicles and the roads were plowed all winter, so it wasn't any hardship to live out by the lake. It wasn't the nice peaceful place it had been earlier, what with snowmobiles whining around all winter, and Sea-doos and boats zipping all over the lake. Even the back roads were overrun with quads or all-terrain vehicles. You hardly saw wild life any more, the odd rabbit maybe, chipmunks, squirrels, and raccoons. She had those in town, anyway. In the old days, there had been deer every day, the odd moose, bears and her favourite, wolves.

Actually, she quite liked her peaceful backyard. It was a small yard, but she had found it plenty big enough when she started cutting the lawn. "Maybe next year, I'll start getting one of the young fellows or girls to cut it every second week," she thought. It wasn't like she didn't have the money. She had invested the money received from the sale of the cottage wisely, and the interest on this investment supplied her with what she called, "a pleasant little surprise every year." The yard had a fence and was entirely enclosed by pine, spruce, cedar, oak trees and a couple of mountain ash. All kinds of shrubs mingled with the flowers. She had made a couple of rock gardens but they had slowly turned into annual flower beds as the years progressed.

She looked forward to every morning when she would take her cup of coffee and walk barefoot in the grass along the beds to look for some new little treasure that had managed to poke its head up through the earth over night. The grass was still wet with dew and some mornings it felt uncomfortable and cold, but most mornings it felt refreshing. A little towel hung on a hook near the back door, conveniently placed, so she could reach in and take it out to the patio to wipe her feet before she went back into the house. She considered this little trip in the morning part of her morning ablutions. It was as important to her as going to the bathroom, brushing her teeth, or combing her hair. Even when it rained she went out. She had a raincoat with a hood, and if it was cold out she would don her rain boots. If it wasn't, she just went barefoot.

Pat sat down on one of the little stools usually reserved for a plant. She sighed as she looked out over her garden. It was beautiful just as it was and by late summer it would be even lovelier. Suddenly, a strange feeling swept over her. She couldn't give it a name, sort of like homesickness, loneliness. The feeling wasn't all bad; it was a bit like the feelings she sometimes had when she was driving a car on a lovely day and it felt like it would be nice to be travelling to someplace far away. It was a sad feeling, but at the same time there seemed to be this little spark of, she really couldn't put a name to it, not hope, maybe excitement or expectation, for what she didn't know. It was 9:00 in the morning, and already you could tell that it was going to turn into a hot one later in the day. The little pink heads of the petunias that she had planted earlier were starting to droop. She made a mental note to come out with her watering can soon to give them a little drink. Good thing she had invited the girls to come over early, otherwise it would be too hot to sit outside. They could go into the house, she did have air conditioning, but so far she hadn't had the occasion to turn it on. It just seemed wrong somehow, to turn it on in early June. Not to worry, they could all pick their chairs up and go sit under the blue spruce in the corner. It was nice and shady there. Then again, Marie always made such a fuss about mosquitoes. If they sat near the flowers, she didn't like the bees. Marie didn't hate insects. This was evident by the interest she took in their habits. She knew everything there was to know about each little creature. She had learned most of this, not by first hand observation, but by reading books. As interesting as an insect was to her, good, bad or otherwise, she still didn't want to be bitten by it, and sitting where they were liable to be was just tempting fate.

Pat pulled off her gardening gloves. She hated wearing them when she worked in the garden. She much preferred the feel of the soil in her hands and anyway, the gloves made her hands feel stiff and cramped. It was either wear gloves or have dirty fingernails the rest of the day, because no matter how hard she scrubbed or how diligently she used her fingernail file she couldn't seem to get them clean again. "Oh, I'd better run in and turn the coffee maker on, plus I have to phone Louise."

Louise was the one friend of Pat's who always had to be reminded of dates. She often said, "Just refresh my memory, please."

Pat dashed into the bathroom, rinsed her hands under the tap and ran the brush through her dark short hair. A few strands stuck out to the side. She rubbed a little water on them to calm them down. Pat stood back and looked into the mirror, straightening her collar. She tipped her head to the right. Definitely older than she was ten years ago, but not bad considering she was approaching sixty-five this year. Her hair was really grey, but she managed to hide it successfully with several visits a year to the beauty parlor. She had her fair share of wrinkles, but for some reason they didn't bother her. She remembered her mother saying that "Wrinkles show that you have lived to laugh and laughed to live. Nothing is worse than seeing someone that you know is old and they don't have any wrinkles on their face to prove that they had any fun or cared about anything but themselves while they were on this earth." She smiled at her mother's witticism.

Pat's eyes were still one of her most attractive features, big and brown. Her dad had called her his little Spaniel puppy. *Little Spaniel puppy.* How she had loved those endearing words until one day she happened across a picture of a sad droopy little dog and some one had informed her that it was a picture of a Spaniel. She remembered she had hidden under her bed and cried and cried. Her father had finally placated her by hugging her and telling her he loved Spaniels and thought they were absolutely the most beautiful dog in the world.

Pat had hardly tipped the coffee into the coffee maker when the doorbell rang. She didn't stop what she was doing, because usually her friends just walked in right after they had pushed the doorbell.

"Yoooou, whoooo! Pat, where are you hiding?"

Pat recognized the voice. It was Louise. "One call I don't have to make," she thought.

A short chubby face rolled into the kitchen. Louise, with her teeny little steps always looked like she had little wheels fastened to the bottom of her feet. Her body seemed to roll wherever it needed to go. Louise loved food as was evident by the many extra pounds that were positioned all over her otherwise tiny frame. Her body movements, always quick and matter of fact, betrayed her facial expressions. Even though she was a little dour-faced, Pat liked Louise. She was good hearted, and would do anything for you.

"I wasn't sure if it was this morning we were supposed to come, so I just chanced it. Even if it wasn't the right day, thought the little walk over here might do me some good. Oh, goodness, I'm tired. I didn't get a decent sleep last night. I was supposed to go down and get a perm this afternoon," Louise reached up and pulled a handful of her straight stringy grey hair out to the side, "but I phoned up and cancelled my appointment. After I go over and tidy up Gary and Sarah's place, think I'll just lie down for awhile, see if I can't grab a couple z's this afternoon. Hate sleeping in the afternoon, because then I can't sleep at night, such a vicious circle!"

Pat looked over at her friend. She couldn't help but wonder why, if she was so tired, she felt compelled to go and clean her son and his wife's house. They were quite capable of cleaning their own house, and even if they didn't, so what? Louise not only cleaned their house, but she picked up their mail, often made them supper and left it in the fridge. Lately, it had been getting harder and harder to get Louise to do anything with her old friends. It seemed that she always had something to do for Gary and his family. If they went somewhere, she had to go with them. If they stayed at home, she felt compelled to stay home, too.

The aroma of fresh coffee wafted invitingly through the cozy kitchen. Pat reached into her cupboard and brought out two mugs. She was just turning to reach for the other four, when she heard gay chatter coming through the patio windows. The other girls must have met out front and decided to come in the back way. Pat yelled out the window, "Theda, tell the others to make themselves comfortable and we'll be right with them. Lou's here already." She turned to Louise, "Here, Lou, would you take these two cups? I can get the rest of the stuff on the tray. Just leave the door open a bit so I can kick it open. Thanks."

"Okay, but I'll get the door for you; sure there isn't anything else that I can take out for you?"

"Nope, way you go, I'll be there in a sec."

"Your garden is starting to look great, Pat, of course it always does. Wish I had a little more space to grow a few things. Living in an apartment has its drawbacks," sighed Marie. Marie was the scholastic one of the group. She would have been labelled a nerd by the younger set today. She always seemed to have her nose in a book. She pushed her long, grey-streaked hair away from her pale face. Large brown age spots intermingled with freckles speckled the back of her slim hands.

Pat looked over at Marie who was sporting a huge blue T-shirt that almost hung to her knees. The shape of the T-shirt itself was unflattering to Marie's fairly slim figure, but the blue certainly enhanced the blue of her eyes. "Thank you, Marie, it takes a little work and time, but I do enjoy it."

Marie's glasses dangled from the corner of her mouth. She withdrew them long enough to reply, "Time, that's something I don't seem to have enough of, so it's probably just as well that I live in an apartment."

Theda, looking slightly annoyed, sat down beside Marie. "What do you mean you don't have enough time, Marie, that's all you've got? You don't have a job or a family to look after, like, really, what do you do with your time? Oh, excuse me, I remember, you have your reading, you and your books, Marie, really!"

Theda was probably Pat's closest friend. Pat liked her, because she was always game to do anything, always made time for you, and if you asked her something, you knew you were going to get a straight answer. It might not be what you wanted to hear, but it was honest and you absolutely knew where you stood with Theda.

"What else is there to do in this town?" Marie came back in rebuttal.

Theda shook her short bouncy hairdo and laughed, "You could go out with somebody once in a while, after all, there are still a few men left in this town. I know a few who wouldn't mind leaving their slippers under your bed once in awhile."

"Oh, yeah, name me one. There's nobody, I repeat nobody that I'd even care to talk on the phone with, let alone go to bed with, not since..."

"Not since, since what, Marie?" Theda leaned over to her other friends, placing her hand over the side of her mouth, feigning a whisper. "She means, ever since Bob Conrad."

Everyone laughed, except Marie. Years ago, Marie had had a casual date with Bob Conrad. The two of them had gone to a musical presentation at the local playhouse, a coffee after and then he had left her on her doorstep, no goodnight kiss, not even a hand-shake. The next morning, Bob's cleaning lady found him collapsed on the kitchen floor. She had called the ambulance, and it had taken Bob to the hospital where he proceeded to die shortly after, the result of a massive heart attack. Poor Marie had taken quite the razzing from everyone, about how she had been in bed with him and had worn the poor man to death. One other story that circulated was that Marie had read Bob to death. Theda later admitted that she was the originator of that rumour. After that unfortunate experience with Bob, Marie never accepted another date.

Marie looked around at her friends and sadly shook her

head. “You people, honestly, how can you joke about someone’s death like that?”

“Yeah, come on, Theda, the poor guy’s not even here to defend himself, besides, I kind of liked Bob Conrad,” spoke up Pat.

Theda laughed, “I know he’s not here, but I can’t help myself. He was probably so bored that night that he decided to try to liven the evening up by killing himself. Knowing Marie, she probably brought along a book to read on their date. But you’re right, I shouldn’t be making fun of anyone’s death, and normally I wouldn’t, especially if I thought that he meant anything to you Marie. I won’t say any more. Consider it a dead issue,” stated Theda. Then she giggled, “A dead issue, that’s for sure.”

“Speaking of death, did you hear that old Mrs. Mercer died?” asked Marie.

“No! How old was she? She couldn’t have been…” Theda bit her bottom lip, closed her eyes and sat calculating for a few seconds. Suddenly she opened her eyes wide. “Holy shit, you know she was only about five years older than me!”

“Well, it’s to be expected, you know we’re all getting up there. You never know when it could be you,” offered Louise.

“I suppose you’re right. God, I hate this growing old. I’m afraid I’m not going to be too graceful about the whole damn thing,” said Theda. “I’m beginning to feel like a rusty old bike that everyone looks at and thinks *it must have been fun riding that when it was new*, but no one wants to now, because they’re afraid a wheel or the handlebars will fall off.”

Marie smiled, then turned to Pat, “How come Gwen and Edna didn’t come this morning?”

“Both had appointments, but they’ll be here later. Gwen has a doctor’s appointment, and Edna has something going on at the church. Not a ladies aid meeting, something more like, I think she referred to it as a fun Bible study,” replied Pat.

“A Bible study, oh goody! And if Edna’s there, I’m sure it will be a fun one at that!” said Theda sarcastically. She was not fond of Pat’s friend, Edna. This was one case where opposites did not attract.

Edna, in her own right, had no use for Theda who she thought was a coarse, vulgar person.

Theda quickly changed the subject, "So, what's the plans for this weekend, anybody doing anything exciting?"

"I'm going to the company picnic with Gary and his family," stated Louise.

"Yeah, what's new?" Theda mouthed to Pat who was sitting right beside her. "What about you, Marie, what's shaking?"

"Well, the librarian left a message that a whole new section has been added to the library since last week. Several articles on numerology, one about plants called *Outer Space and How Your House Plants React to It.* She put them aside for me, so I'll probably go over this afternoon and pick them up. That should keep me busy for awhile."

Theda rolled her eyes. "Okay, Pat, can you do any better than these two?"

"Probably not, I'll putter in the garden a bit, that's all. Oh, here's Gwen and Edna. Come on, you two, join the fun. We're taking turns telling each other about the exciting things we're going to do this weekend. We've already got a company picnic, a bunch of library books and exciting garden work. What can you add to make this list any more fascinating than it already is?"

A slightly heavy set, dark, weary-looking lady pushed open the back gate. This was Pat's friend Gwen. She was immediately followed by Edna, a slim, rather pinched-face creature.

Theda sat up bouncing on the edge of her chair with her hand raised in the air, "Oh! Oh! I know what they're going to do already. Gwen's going to stay home, play the piano and sing to herself all day, and Edna's going to go to church, Saturday and Sunday, Monday, too, if they will let her."

Marie got down on her knees, stretched her arms out in front of her and bowed low several times in front of Theda, "And what about you, *Oh, One of Many Bright Ideas*, what are you going to do that is different and far reaching?"

Theda laughed, "Please don't do that, it bothers me."

"Why, don't you like it when people bow down to you?"

"You can bow down to me as much as you want; I'm just afraid that someday, you won't be able to get up. And since you asked, I don't know. There's nothing going on in town that I care to go to. It's no fun going to any of the dances when you don't have a partner to dance with. I'm tired to death of dancing with other women. One thing I can't stand is dancing with another broad. I don't know, it just doesn't seem right or something. I wouldn't mind going if you could even just sit around and visit with people, but these disc jockeys they have nowadays play such crap music. It's so bloody loud you can't hear yourself think, let alone hear anyone else talking. God, we live such a sad life. Wish to hell there was something interesting or different to do!"

"Well, why don't you hop on the next freighter that comes along and hitch a ride to Hong Kong, or better yet, fly down to Houston for the weekend," spoke up Louise.

Pat laughed, "We could, but we don't have too many freighters coming through this town."

"Well, we still have railroads. You could ride the rails to Winnipeg," ventured Marie.

"Thanks heaps! We have railroads but no trains to go on them. Think again, girls."

"Well, you could go on some exotic boat cruise through the Mediterranean," added Gwen, one of the new arrivals who had pushed her matronly self down between Pat and Marie. She turned to Pat, "Okay, we've tried, now it's your turn, Pat."

Pat didn't reply. Everyone chattered gaily for a few minutes. Suddenly everyone stopped and turned towards Pat. "Yes, Pat, it's your turn to add to our wish trip. Yoohoo, Patricia, you with us?" Theda snapped her fingers under Pat's nose.

Pat snapped back from her reverie, "What, oh, I'm sorry, I was just thinking."

"What about?" asked Marie

"Oh, nothing earth shattering, just I guess you people talking about trips and stuff, started me thinking that maybe that's what I need to put a little pep in my life. A change is as good as a rest. We need something to look forward to like a little trip. You know, go into Toronto, do a little shopping, visit someone for awhile. I've still got a few friends who live just outside the city. It would be fun to see them again. Oh, who'm I kidding. By the time I weed my way through this garden, and I've got two weddings to go to this summer, there's not much time for anything else." Pat pushed at her watering can with her foot. "Never mind, it was just a thought," she sighed.

"I sometimes imagine travelling across the country in a nice trailer or something. Mel and I always talked about doing that, but he died two months after he retired, so we never even got to the planning stages," commented Louise.

"Excuse me people, but why do we have to just sit here and imagine any of this, why couldn't we go on a little trip of some kind?" asked Theda. "Doesn't have to be long or far," she finished.

"Oh, gee, Theda, at our age, I don't know, that would probably be biting off more than we could chew. I'm really quite content to do stuff around here. It's comfortable, I guess," said Louise.

"I have to agree with Louise, what's so wrong with this place?" spoke up Gwen. Gwen, with her little dour face, flashed an angry look at Theda, then immediately switched it to Pat.

Pat looked at Gwen and thought, *what is it about this lady that I like?* She rubbed around the corner of her eyes feeling the indentations where old and new wrinkles formed. No laugh lines on Gwen's face, only the little purse lines set around her tight little mouth and a permanent frown in her forehead. She could probably count the times on one hand when she had seen Gwen really laugh, a good gut-wrenching laugh, like Theda. Theda seemed to be laughing about something or other all the time. The only time Pat remembered seeing Gwen smile was just before she started to sing a solo in church. Then she looked happy.

"Nothing's wrong with this place, it's just goddamned boring, that's what it is! And Louise, what do you mean, at our ages? God! Now's the time to do something if we're going to do it, while we still can– before it's too late. You might not have noticed, people, but our friends are dropping off around us like flies! Soon it will be our turn." Theda wrapped her arms around herself and shivered.

"A trip costs money. Something we all don't have a lot of," volunteered Marie.

"What you talking 'bout, Marie? You've got more money than the rest of us put together. You can't take it with you, you know."

"I wasn't referring to myself exactly." Marie glanced uncomfortably over in Gwen's direction.

Theda caught her look, "Oh, sorry, I suppose you're right, but hey, listen, people, it doesn't have to cost an arm and a leg, and I'm sure we could cut some corners here and there to make it cheaper."

"Oh, I don't know. I hardly have the energy to get down here to your house, Pat. Can you just see me going on a trip?" spoke up Edna.

"Yep, once you turn sixty, it's downhill from then on," Louise sighed.

"What do you mean sixty? As far as I'm concerned, it was downhill right after forty," added Edna.

"Good God, ladies, come on, I know people who have been going downhill since they turned twenty. Well, I don't deny that we are going downhill, but we sure as hell don't have to jump on a roller coaster to do it. All I can tell you is, I'm going on a trip soon, and I don't care where or with whom, I'm just going. Anybody that wants to join me is welcome," stated Theda.

"Well, I'm going on a trip all right, a trip right down the street to my home," said Marie.

"Yeah, I have to run too, see you people soon. Thanks, Pat, for coffee," said Louise. Edna and Gwen simultaneously drained their cups and joined Marie and Louise as they made their way out the side gate.

When the gate clicked into place, Theda helped Pat gather up the empty cups. "I would think that you'd be the one person who would be game to go somewhere or do something different.

Pat, where would you like to go?" Before Pat had a chance to answer, Theda continued, "As long as it isn't on one of those old people tours where they cart you around in a bus and you spend half your time waiting to get on the bus, and the other half waiting to get off."

Pat looked over at her friend. Theda was about four inches taller than her and she still had a very attractive figure for an over-sixty broad. She still had naturally dark brown hair that had one distinguishing characteristic– a streak of pure white hair that ran from the side of her forehead just above her right eye. It petered out after a few inches. She had always had this feature, even as a teenager. Theda used to laugh about it saying if it had been another inch closer to the middle of her head, people would mistake her for a skunk. Pat laughed, partly at the recollection and partly at Theda's comment, "I know what you mean, and when you do get off, they line you up like a bunch of kindergarten children."

"I'm surprised they don't make you hang onto a rope so you don't get lost."

"Don't laugh, my parents went on a bus tour once to Peggy's Cove in Nova Scotia, and they did exactly that. I guess they didn't want any of them wandering too close to the water where a wave could dash up and drag one of them into the ocean."

"Well, we'll just have to think about it some, and come up with some suggestions. Do you think any of the others would come with us?"

"I wouldn't hold my breath waiting for any of them. If you could pry those books out of Marie's hands long enough for her to pack, you might get her to come."

"I know what you mean, and Louise would never leave her precious family for a day, let alone a week or two."

"Maybe Edna or Gwen would be interested."

"Well, Gwen would probably love to go, but I honestly don't think she could afford it. She really doesn't have much money. It's all she can do to just keep her head above water at the best of times. And if the truth be known, I could care less if Edna comes or not. In fact if you want me to be absolutely honest, I'd rather she didn't."

"Oh, Theda, I know she can be a bit of a pain sometimes, but deep down, she's really a kindly soul. She'd do anything for anyone, even you, if you needed her," commented Pat.

"Well, God forbid that I'd ever need her. Think I'd kill myself first. It isn't just her holier-than-thou attitude that I can't stand, it's the whole her, always popping pills for this ailment or that. Christ, she's always talking about drug addicts and what did she say the other day, something about them having or being a direct relative of the devil? Ever count how many pills she pops in an hour. I swear she must have taken six, if she took twenty, with the coffee you served her this morning! She's a walking drugstore if there ever was one," exclaimed Theda. "Like, what is, or should I say, are her problems, anyway?"

"You mean physical?" Pat shook her head, "I don't know, maybe high blood pressure, I've never asked. She really looks healthy enough most of the time."

"Well, on that cheery note, lady person, I must be running, since I still have a few errands to run before lunch."

Pat closed the door after she waved good-bye to Theda and walked over to the kitchen sink to rinse the coffee cups under the tap. Then she opened the dishwasher and arranged them on the rack before closing the door. She went back out onto the patio and stood thinking. Why do we necessarily have to go on a conventional trip. Why couldn't it be something simpler and cheap enough that everyone could go?

She slipped on a pair of old runners, and walked through her garden to the back of the yard to the old shed. Earl had kept a few odds and sods, and most of his big tools in this shed. There was something else he had kept there, carefully covered with a huge blue tarp. The old door groaned when she pulled it open. A puff of dust and stale air whooshed out. Pat peered in, then pushing aside a thick cobweb she stepped inside the shed. Slowly her eyes became accustomed to the dark. There was one lone window on the back wall, and with the door open there was enough light to see the interior.

She walked over to the huge blue tarp. It was tied down

in several places. After she had undone the slim ropes, she started to pull and fold the tarp at the same time. Before long, the tarp became too heavy, so she let it drop to the floor. There it sat. Earl's pride and joy. Why, she never knew, but because it was, it held a special place in her heart. God, it was ugly. She shuddered slightly, and tried to smile. Bottom lip tucked under her top teeth, she walked around the huge monstrosity. Monstrosity was exactly what it was. Even her children had nicknamed it *The Beast.* It's even worse than I remember. She reached out and rubbed her hand over the scraped, brown paint of the '82 Ford Club Wagon.

She felt where the big dint was in the bumper. Earl had just finished giving the children a stern lecture on driving defensively, looking out for the other guy, then proceeded to ram the right side of the bumper against the oak growing beside the driveway. She remembered that it had taken every ounce of her and her children's will power not to burst out laughing. One tail light on the other side was smashed. She had done that, with a bicycle no less. She had parked her bike to the side of the van and thinking she'd secured the kick stand she started to walk away. Suddenly she heard a loud crash. The kick stand had collapsed taking the bicycle with it. That's when the tail light was smashed. The other bumper was still intact, but looked rather crooked.

She walked over to the door, rubbed a little hole in the dust that had collected on the side window, held her hands up to either side of the window and peeked in. "The interior doesn't look too bad," she hummed to herself. She tried to open the door and was surprised that it worked. Hoisting herself up onto the first little step, she approached the driver's seat. Her eyes were beginning to adjust to the dimness. There was nothing wrong with the upholstery and the interior was spacious, easily enough room for three or four people and their luggage. I wonder if this baby will start. The keys were in the house, in Earl's top drawer. After seven years, it was still Earl's drawer.

Several hours later, it was mid-afternoon, and much too hot to be in the garden, so Pat had gone into the house and plopped herself in front of the television. She sat on the edge of the lounge folding clothes and watching a soap at the same time. She really didn't like soaps, but there wasn't much else on– talk shows and soaps, take your pick. She figured that the soap was the lesser of the two evils. Just as she was trying to decide whether to make the old worn out towel that she had extracted from the pile of clothes into an official rag, the phone rang. She threw the towel back on the pile, and reached over to answer it.

It was Charlie from the high school. Charlie was a distant relative, some cousin twice or thrice removed on her husband's side. The whole town was full of them. Pat quite liked this relative. He was a likeable, bright, young fellow, a teacher in the automotive department at the high school. Their school was one of the last in the area to teach shop any more and Charlie had a large class of young people that he taught how to fix and maintain a vehicle. There were as many girls in his class as boys, not because the girls were into women's lib, role reversal or wanted to be more independent, it was simply that Charlie was a hunk.

"Charlie, thank you for returning my call, hon, I have a favour to ask you. When you're free could you come over here? There's something I want you to look at in our old shed, preferably in the daytime."

Pat leaned back in her chair and laughed, "Of course I trust you, but that's not why I want you here in the daytime."

She enjoyed his flirting, even though Charlie was thirty years younger than Pat. She thought of him as sort of a favourite nephew, and besides he flirted with everyone. "There's no electricity out in that old shed, so that's why it has to be in the daytime, you nut! You can? Today, after classes? Oh, wonderful! Good, see you then."

Charlie and Pat stood on the patio appreciating Pat's garden. "Can I get you something to drink, Charlie? It's certainly hot enough to warrant one. Here, sit down, there's at least some shade over on this side."

"Sure, I'll have a drink. Just a beer, Pat. You'll join me? Something wrong with your air conditioner? Why don't you have it on?"

"Oh, Charlie, the middle of June is just too early to have the air conditioner on. If it was later in the month, I wouldn't mind so much. Besides it will cool off in the evening."

Charlie shook his head and smiled, "Pat, that's why you have an air conditioner. When it's really hot out, you run it, doesn't matter if it's July or December."

Pat looked at Charlie as she handed him his beer, "We're from two entirely different generations, Charlie, that's what the matter is."

She twisted the cap off her own bottle using the bottom of her shirt to cushion her hand. Then she tucked the cap into her pocket. "So, doctor, what's the verdict? Can we get it running again?"

"Can't say for sure just looking at it in that short a time. I'll have to take it out on the road for a spin. The bumper definitely has to be reattached. God, Earl just had it tied on with binder twine."

"Oh, I don't think he ever drove it around like that, he just sort of tied it up to make it look like it was all in one piece."

Charlie sat back in his lounge chair, rubbing the cool bottle across his forehead. "You know, Pat, I just might have a solution for you. Why don't you let me take the van over to the school? I can use it as a teaching tool, our very own vehicle, sort of like a body from the morgue. Being the end of the school term, the kids don't have much to keep them busy anyway. This would give them something to work on."

"Oh, I don't know."

"Look, trust me, it'll be fine. I always supervise everything they do. Plus, I can do a bit of tinkering on it, too. We'll do a good job for you, honest, and listen to this, this is the best part. It won't cost you a red cent. Free, do you hear, not a single solitary sou! Now, what do you think of that?"

"Oh, you do strike a hard bargain, Charlie, my boy, but all right, go ahead, do what you can."

Chapter Two

Pat stood up holding the small garden trowel in one hand. She arched her back and rubbed the small of her back with her free hand. "There, finally it's done. Okay, you little buggers, grow!" Her old Tilly hat hid half her face. It had been Earl's, and it was far too big. She knew it wasn't very attractive, but it did the job, and every time she took it off its hook, she was flooded with lovely warm memories of Earl. It was as if he suddenly materialized and put his big old arms around her just for an instant, and that instant was enough to keep her happy for several hours.

The serenity of her garden was soon disturbed by the distant ring of her phone. Pat reached over and picked up the portable sitting on the table. "Hello! Oh, hi, Theda. Yes, I'm here, probably all day. No, come any time. Sure, bring Marie with you, by all means. What's the matter, did she lose her library card? No, I'm not being catty. I don't know of too many times when she doesn't have her nose in a book, and when she doesn't there has to be a good reason, like the library has burned down...okay, see you both shortly then."

She set the phone down. Hmmmm, that's funny. Theda almost sounded excited, wonder what's up? She was glad that they were coming over, because she had something she wanted to discuss with them.

Pat had hardly put the gardening tools away when she heard a car pull up into the driveway. Two car doors slammed in succession. Theda had told her not to bother with coffee as she was picking up some Tim Horton's coffee for them all.

Theda and Marie whisked into the kitchen without knocking. Theda laid a bag and a box on the table. "Coffee's here, and doughnuts. If anyone wants some help yourself. Now let's get down to the chase." Theda handed Pat a coffee. "Pat, sweetie, we've decided to take you up on your offer."

Pat accepted the coffee and looked at her two friends with a puzzled look and asked, "What offer?"

"You know, silly, the trip, going away, doing something different and exciting," offered Marie.

"See the freaking world!" yelled Theda, her arms spread out wide in front of her.

"On a shoe string don't forget," added Marie.

Pat started to smile, "Well, people, it just so happens that I have a little plan of my own, so it sounds like we're all on the same wavelength. You remember that old van Earl used to drive when we went on vacation when the kids were still coming home for school breaks? Well, here's the plan." Pat explained what she was having done to the van. Marie and Theda kept butting in adding and taking away. One lone doughnut sat at the bottom of the twelve pack cardboard container. Pat looked at the doughnut then glanced up at her black cat clock hanging over the fridge, a rather ugly present from one of her children. The cat's tail swung from side to side as the seconds ticked by. The clock portion took up the whole of the cat's belly. "Oh, look at the time! I never noticed how late it had gotten. You guys want to stay for lunch? I've got some cold cuts and fresh buns."

"No, really, thanks, but I've still got a few errands to run. Didn't realize we'd blabbed so long. You stay if you want, Marie."

"No, I've got to go, too. So what have we decided so far?"

"Okay, this is it. I'm to talk to Gwen and Louise and what's her face," said Theda.

"If you mean Edna, I'll talk to her," said Pat.

"Ohhh, I was half hoping you'd forget. Are you sure you want her to come with us, Pat?" asked Theda with a rather hang doggy expression.

Pat laughed, "Look, she might not even come, and anyway, Theda, you're the only one who doesn't like her. The rest of us get on just fine with her. You can ask Gwen, but I doubt if she will be able to come though. You know her financial condition."

"Yeah, and I doubt if Louise will leave her precious family. We're lucky to get her away from them for a couple of hours, let alone a few days," stated Marie.

Pat nodded her agreement, "I know, but we have to at least ask them." She escorted her friends to the front door. As she stood waving goodbye to them, her mind was busy categorizing a huge jumble of thoughts and plans. They fell into three areas: immediate, should do soon, and can wait a bit. In the immediate list was phone Charlie and find out how he was making out with the van.

Charlie swung the vehicle into Pat's driveway. It bumped slightly, catching the edge of the curb making Charlie grimace. The van was rather a long vehicle. In fact it was longer than a lot of trucks. He'd have to take Pat out and let her drive around town a few times to get used to it. When he had phoned last night to tell her that the van was ready, she'd told him about her plans for her friends and herself. He thought the idea was great. The van was in good shape now, thanks to his mechanics class. The kids had accepted the challenge, and they were quite proud of their ability to turn what they referred to as *the old clunker* into something quite serviceable and *cool looking*. The only expense that Pat had had to incur was the price of four new tires as the old ones were pretty bald. Oh, yes, and Charlie had asked her to buy several tins of spray paint. The kids had gone out to one of the wrecking yards and they had managed to find a covering that fit over the signal light. The motor had been gone over with a fine-tooth comb, the bumper was secure now, and they had even managed to take out a few of the more noticeable dents. Charlie had left a few of the students alone one evening confident that they could put the finishing touches on the paint job. The next morning when he entered the workshop at the school he was quite impressed with the job they had done on the van. He just wasn't sure if Pat would be.

Before he even had time to let himself out the door, Pat came running out of the house smiling and waving at him. Suddenly she stopped dead in her tracks and stood, her mouth hung open, as her waving hand slowly lowered itself to her side. Adorning all the side of the van facing her was a pictorial.

At the extreme left hand side sat a crumpled up skeleton. Several skulls were positioned around the bones and from each, fiery reddish orange eyes glowed. Smoke and fire smoldered through the scene. The wisps of smoke continued along the side until they reached the front door where the smoke swirled into the frontal view of a human. The creature's legs were spread slightly more than shoulder breadth apart and its arms were raised to the sky. Both its fists were clenched. Golden tanned muscles rippled down all portions of its perfectly sculpted body. Black wavy hair caressed its shoulders.

"Magnificent!" thought Pat. "There's no doubt about the sex of the creature with that oversized penis dangling between its legs." Pat laughed to herself, "Well, dangling, was hardly the right word."

Charlie walked around to Pat. He was smiling, obviously enjoying Pat's discomfort. "How do you like it? Something else, isn't it? It's called *Rebirth.* The kids thought that the name was appropriate since the old van was just about on its last legs and they figured they brought it back to life."

"The name might be appropriate, but the uh...you know...hardly appropriate for a bunch of old maids. Who painted it? It's really quite good, except for the...you know..."

"Martha Svenson."

"Martha Svenson, the minister's daughter?"

"She is good, isn't she? A little lacking in proportions maybe. Oh, here comes Theda."

Theda had hardly parked her car in the street before she was up the driveway, standing by Pat and Charlie. "Holy old shit, Charlie, I love it! I absolutely love it."

Pat put her hand on Charlie's arm, "Charlie, look, I can go for the painting on a whole, but I'm sorry, your artiste is going to have to scale that…that rather impressive appendage down a bit; you know cover it with a loin cloth, a speedo or something. I can't drive anywhere with that. I'd probably be breaking some obscenity law or other."

"Cover it up? No way! Come on Pat, live a little. I've never seen anything like it!" exclaimed Theda.

"Exactly, and I doubt that you ever will. The man would need an elephant to…oh, you've got me started! Listen Charlie, it's got to be fixed," stated Pat.

Theda grabbed Pat's arm. "Wait, Pat, just wait. Okay I agree we should fix it, but please, please let me go home and get my camera. I've got to get a picture of it before you castrate him."

"Oh, for heaven's sake, go in my house, and on my desk is my camera. Use it. The faster you take the picture, the faster Charlie can take this back and get it repaired."

"I'm going to put it in your garage for the afternoon. I'll take it back tonight. I told Martha that I didn't think you'd go for it, and to tell you the truth, I don't think the principal of the school will be overjoyed if he finds out about it, so we'll have to try to keep it kind of hush-hush."

"You drove this thing through town, and you think you can keep it a secret!"

Theda returned with the camera and took photos from every possible angle. "Now, take one of me beside it." She handed the camera to Pat. She grabbed the camera back, "Better yet, here Charlie, you take it of both Pat and me. We can stand on either side of it and ogle it."

"The van, you mean," laughed Charlie taking the camera.

"Hardly, my boy, hardly," leered Theda.

Charlie snapped a couple of pictures, and then walked over to the van. He reached over to the bottom back corner, and using his fingernails, gently pried a tiny portion of the van's paint away. Then he walked along side the van, peeling the whole picture away in a flash. Both Pat and Theda stood with their mouths open. Charlie held the long peeled off portion in his hand, "It's just a plastic stencil. I'm sorry, I couldn't resist it. You should see your faces."

"What about Martha Svenson?"

"Martha Svenson couldn't paint a stick figure, and I really doubt that she's ever seen a...you know."

"Damn, I was going to commission the girl to decorate my bedroom. She could have made a fortune doing paintings like these."

By this time, the three of them were doubled over with laughter. Charlie finally took Pat's hand, "Come on, old girl, before you die on me. Come and look the rest of the van over. Look at this chrome. We cleaned it up and it's as good as new."

"Why is it five different shades of brown?" asked Pat.

"You wouldn't let us give it a paint job, remember, you thought it would change the character of it too much. We had to fix the rusts spots though, and Canadian Tire had a sale on car paint, these are the only shades of brown they had. Besides, it's not five different shades, it's only three. They don't exactly match the original, but voila! No more rust. Come on, you two, hop in, I'll take you for a spin. It runs like a top, you'll see."

"Hell, I'll be spending enough time in that contraption, you two go ahead. I'm going to get this film developed," said Theda, clutching the film cannister tightly to her chest.

"Oh, Theda, do you think you should have the film developed in town here? Those pictures are pretty risqué."

"Pat, I'll warrant they've seen just as bad if not worse. Don't worry, I'll make sure I give them my name for pick-up, not yours." Theda walked down the driveway giggling to herself. "Yeah right, sure I will."

Once they reached the outskirts of the town, Charlie pulled over and let Pat take over the driver's seat. Pat turned the key in the ignition. She glanced in the rear view mirror and to the side and turned the car onto the main road. The motor, that used to growl and grind and make strange noises, purred. "It sounds like a wee puss purring, Charlie, are you sure it's going?"

"We're moving aren't we? So, is everybody going as planned, Pat?"

Pat glanced over at Charlie, then quickly back to the road,

"Well," she sighed, "Gwen would like to come, but really can't afford it, and besides I guess her family really put up a stink when she suggested that she would like to go with us. Then there's Louise. Her family would let her go, but she won't let her family go."

"That's too bad. They both seem like fun people. Well, I shouldn't say that. Poor Gwen always seems so dour-faced; not really dour, more like sad. Yeah, that's it, just plain sad. Do you think she'd lighten up any if she went on a trip like you girls are planning?"

Pat shirked her shoulders, "I can't say for sure. All I know is Gwen is a really nice person and she deserves some fun for a change. Oh well, there's not much we can do about it. We're all getting together later on today to make more decisive plans. The major problem was transportation, and that's been solved, thanks to you, Charlie. Have I remembered to thank you? Thank you! Thank you! Thank you!"

Pat swung wide, remembering Charlie's warning about the van being a big vehicle, then pulled into her driveway. She let the van glide to a stop, put it in park and turned off the ignition. "Listen, buddy, how much do we owe you? We want to give you something for your trouble," offered Pat.

"Naw, the kids and I had a blast working on the van, and they learned a lot in the process. A copy of the pictures we just took would be nice. And when you get back from your wild adventure, I'll expect to be invited to one of your super spaghetti meals. Is that a deal?"

"Definitely, can't wait for either, the trip or the spaghetti meal. Look, not to change the subject, but I noticed you made a little addition in the back there." She turned in her seat to look into the back of the van.

"Yeah, I hope you don't mind, but I built that little storage area under the window. It's pretty sturdy. I had it anchored from the outside, so you could even stretch out on it and have a sleep if you want. You can do whatever you want with it, storage, sleep, you name it. Charlie had his hand on the door handle. "By the way, thought you might be interested, the word is out on the street about you girls."

"About us. What do you mean?"

"Well, half the people in town think you ladies are nuts to even think of going on a trip like this; the other half think it's just some crazy fantasy of some old…uhhhh…"

"Go, ahead, Charlie, say it– old women, right?"

"Well, that's not exactly what they called you."

"What do you think, Charlie, think we're crazy?"

"No, definitely not. I think it's a blast. I've told some of them that the worst that can happen is that the van could break down. If it does, you dump it and catch a plane or bus home. If you get in an accident, so what, you could just as easily get in an accident right here in town. No, Pat, I say, go for it girl, and I hope you all have a wonderful time."

Charlie leaned over and gave Pat a peck on the cheek.

Chapter Three

Theda plunked her beer bottle down on the table. Its contents foamed up and over the top, then ran down the side of the bottle forming a small puddle under it. Theda lifted the bottle, bent over towards the table, and slurped up the overflow. When she finished, she smacked her lips. "Look, guys, we knew from the start that Louise wouldn't come, so we can forget about her, but I really think Gwen would if she thought she could afford it. Damn it, people, there's no reason she shouldn't. What is it going to cost her extra? We have the room. We're already paying for the gas, and we're tenting all the way, so what's left? Her share of the meals and the odd piece of clothing maybe, and that's all. There's got to be a way to get her a little extra cash without making her feel that she's a charity case. I'd happily pay her share outright, but I know she won't let me."

Theda, Edna and Marie were sitting at Pat's kitchen table. Pat had a notebook open where she jotted down suggestions as the group thought of them. Edna took a sip of her tea and set the cup back down in its matching saucer. "Yes, I feel that it is important that no one feels like they are a burden to anyone," she sighed, "I'll say a special little prayer tonight when I'm in church."

Theda almost choked on her third swig of beer, "A little prayer, what good will that do? Besides, tonight is Tuesday. Christ, Edna, what are you doing in church on Tuesday? You already go twice on Sunday. Hell, I've even seen you in our church some days!"

"It never hurts to keep in close contact with our Saviour."

"Get any closer, Edna, and people are going to start talking. You'll smother the poor bugger!"

"Ladies! Ladies! Come on now, enough please, let's get back to the problems at hand, okay?" yelled Pat. She glanced threateningly at Theda.

"Pat's right. And getting back to Gwen, I heard via the grapevine that her son Phil is one of our staunchest critics. Something about 'those stupid old floozies trying to involve my mother in some cockamamie trip,' that's the latest I heard," reported Marie.

Theda roared with laughter, "Old floozies! Us? Never! Floozies maybe, but old, no!" She took another swig from her bottle.

"Listen, people, listen up, I have a plan. Tell me what you think, or if you have any other ideas let's hear them," ordered Pat.

The three women set their drinks down, leaned attentively over the table, and listened as Pat told them about her idea.

During the next two weeks, the four women were constantly dashing back and forth between each other's homes. Pat's phone seemed to ring every five minutes. Charlie came over four nights in a row and taught them how to change a tire, repair a broken fan belt, replace a fan belt, clean spark plugs, put air in a tire and check the oil. He explained what noises should be checked out and which ones could be ignored. Marie devoured voluminous quantities of magazines and books on auto mechanics. The last night of Charlie's instructions, everyone was assembled in Pat's garage. The van was parked out in the driveway.

"I thought we could store some of our stuff in here, later we can decide what we really have to take and what we absolutely don't need." Pat kicked at an orange and royal blue tent that was rolled up in the corner. "I managed to resurrect my son's old tent. There doesn't seem to be any holes in it and I aired it outside for a couple of days so it smells half decent. It will sleep four quite comfortably, so that takes care of our lodging."

Charlie nodded, "Good, and I brought this over for you. It's a thin tarp, but it's really pretty big when you open it up. There's a bag of small metal poles that all fit together to make four long ones. You only need to put this up if it looks like rain.

It will keep the initial onslaught off your tent. Oh, and the thing you should remember: whenever you stop to pitch your tent in a campground, look for the highest area. That way there won't be any floods or unpleasant surprises if it rains."

Theda threw her sleeping bag into the corner with the other three, "Ha! What about when we asked Merle about giving us the best physical defense course he could, did you see his face when we told him that he only had two weeks to do it in? I thought he was going to croak."

"I don't think we did too badly, learned a couple of things."

"I like the move when you grab the guy's ba...," snickered Theda.

"Theda, for heaven's sake, don't forget poor Charlie's here," laughed Pat. Charlie quickly put his hands over his crotch area and turned away from Theda.

Pat's ears perked up when she heard voices coming from her patio. "Oh, good, I think I can hear Gwen and Louise. Come on out here girls, in the garage," she hollered.

Gwen left Louise behind and ran across the front lawn waving a piece of paper over her head. She quickly skirted a flower bed, and stopped in front of the group. "You guys, look, look...." she said breathlessly. "This morning...lady phoned...won 50/50 draw...brought a cheque over...$300.00!"

"Who...where? You didn't tell us you'd entered a draw. You never buy tickets, Gwen."

Gwen was leaning over clutching her knees to catch her breath. "I didn't and when I asked her who did all she said was someone else might have put my name in for me. Can you believe it? I can't. If it would have been a couple hundred more, I could have joined you ladies on your trip."

Theda glanced over at Pat, and then quickly bent her head, suppressing a smile. She soon looked up and said, "Listen, I have an idea. I thought of this a while ago, and I think we should be able to fly with it. Why don't we have a garage sale? Go through our stuff. I'm sure we've all got gobs of things we don't need any more and anything we make on it, we'll use for, I don't know, gas or something like that, or repairs to the van while we're on the road. What do you think?"

"Hey! I'm for that," spoke up Louise.

"What do you mean, you're not even going on the trip, so what does it matter to you what we do?" queried Theda.

"I know, but I've still got a basement full of crap and corruption. I was going to donate it to some worthy cause, but I think this is as worthy as you're going to get. I don't mind helping you guys out."

"Count me in, too. I don't have much, but I'm sure there are a few things I can rummage up for you. I've got that cracked old Hummel in my window. Don't know why I keep it. It's been there forever," said Gwen.

Pat glanced over at Theda and winked, "Hummel, you say. Gee, Gwen, if it's old, I know a lady who collects these things for other people. She might give you a couple bucks for it, even if it's cracked. You'll probably get more for it through her than at a garage sale. Want me to give her a dingle for you?"

"You've got to be kidding, but sure, why not, go ahead. Nothing ventured, nothing gained."

"Good, I'll run into the house now, and give her a call, arrange a day that she can come over and look at it," said Pat.

Marie shoved an old green Coleman stove aside, and leaned against the wall, "Actually it will be good to give my place a good housecleaning. I've collected so much over the years. I still haven't gone through all my mom's possessions since she died. I just shoved them in the storage locker in my apartment building. It's been over ten years. Can you believe it?"

"I know, each generation gets saddled with crap from the previous one. My mother couldn't decide what to throw or give away, so she just left the decision up to me. I don't mind that we keep something that is pretty or valuable, or something special someone we loved made, but some of the stuff we save is pretty sad. Just because it was your mother's, or your father had it in his study for years. Hell, I saved a stuffed white owl that my father had in his den since the beginning of time only because it was my father's and I thought he loved it. I was reading some of his letters to mom and I found out that he hated the thing, and only kept it in his den because it was his father's before him. It didn't take me long after that to get rid of that ugly old moth-eaten thing," said Theda.

"I say, keep a clean cupboard," interrupted Charlie, "If you don't use it throw it. Personally, I can't see my family saving anything of mine when I croak. They'll probably just toss half of it in the garbage. I know I did when my parents died. It's sad, I know, but you can't be expected to save everything."

"Spoken like a man. You'll feel differently when you have a family, Charlie. Right now, you're young, footloose and fancy free, just living for the now. You'll change when you're older, I promise you," volunteered the usually quiet Louise, patting Charlie lovingly on the shoulder.

Charlie turned to Pat who had returned from inside, "I know when I'm not wanted. Listen gal, I'll be over at the school late tonight, but should be free tomorrow. If there's anything you need, call." He leaned over and gently kissed Pat on the cheek. "See you all, soon."

Pat watched Charlie drive off and then turned to the group. "Okay, two things, first of all, does anyone know where Edna is? She was supposed to be here tonight. I called her house and there's no answer."

"She's probably at church. You know her, probably praying for guidance, praying for a good trip," accused Theda.

"More like asking for deliverance from having to go on a trip with you, Theda," jokingly added Louise. "Really don't know where she is. I'll call her later, see if I can track her down. Remind her that she has earthly obligations, too. You said, Pat, that there were two things, what's the second?"

"Good news, Gwen, I managed to contact that woman who deals in Hummels. I told her what I could remember about it, and she is going to come over to your house right away, if it's all right with you?"

"Sure, why not. Look all of you, come on over to my place. I'll put the pot on while we wait for her."

"Okay, Gwen, you go on ahead and we'll join you in about five," said Pat.

Gwen turned and walked briskly down the street. Pat turned to the other women, "Okay, girls, listen up. This is how it's going down."

Fifteen minutes later four women arrived at Gwen's tiny house. Louise had gone home to set out lunch for her son's family. Theda gave the flimsy screen door a healthy rap.

"Come on in, I'm in the bathroom. Just got the coffee started. It will take a few minutes to perk," yelled Gwen.

Everyone pushed into Gwen's small kitchen. Two chairs were pushed under the miniscule kitchen table. "There are more chairs in the bedroom, or we can have our coffee in the living room if you prefer," Gwen yelled again.

Theda glanced through the doorway into the little living room, "I think there's more room in your van, Pat, than there is in this house," she whispered.

Gwen flushed the toilet, washed her hands, and then paused as she caught her reflection in the mirror. She backed away from the mirror as much as the tiny room would allow. Just then she heard Theda and Pat laugh. She could envision them. Theda's eyes always crinkled up when she laughed and Pat's face was full of what Pat delightfully referred to as her laugh lines. She moved closer to the mirror, raised both her hands to her face and ran her finger tips down both sides of her face. *No laugh lines on this puss.* She felt across her forehead trying to smooth out her frown. *Lots of lines here, but no one calls them laugh lines when they're on your forehead.* She laughed softly to herself and went out to join her friends. She edged her way through the kitchen and over to the window over the kitchen sink. She lifted one corner of her slightly frayed white lace café curtain and peeked outside towards the driveway. "Oh, is that your friend, Pat? Does she have a dark green car?"

Pat moved over and glanced out over the top of the bottom layer of curtain, "Yes, that's her all right. Get your Hummel, lady!"

Pat's introduced her friend to everyone. Her name was Helen Hipple. It was a small town, so they had all heard of her, but none knew her personally. Gwen took a chair and dragged it the short distance to the kitchen cupboards. Gwen and Marie had to shift their chairs together to make more room. Theda, tucked in the corner, obligingly tucked her feet under her chair. Pat remained standing, leaning against the fridge.

A little pair of diagonal shelves had been built at the end of the cupboards– a good place for knick-knacks or plants. This is where the Hummel sat. Gwen stood up on the chair and gently lifted the little cracked figurine down. Grasping the back of the chair with her free hand, she lowered her leg to the floor. She turned and set it down on the table in front of Helen. Helen's mouth opened in shock. She glanced up quickly at Pat, then back down at the figurine. She put her hand over her mouth stifling a giggle. It was obvious the little boy cradling a lamb in his arms had been broken completely in two at one time. Dry yellow glue had long ago oozed from the cracks. She quickly regained her composure, "Oh, excuse me, but I just can't believe it. I've been looking for this particular Hummel for years now, and I can't believe my luck. Imagine, practically sitting right here under my nose. Look, I can offer you four hundred dollars for it. I already have a buyer."

Gwen slapped both of her hands to either side of her face. "Four hundred, I can't believe it! Four hundred…girls, do you know what this means? I might be able to go with…" then she started to cry.

Helen looked over at Pat, "Could I trouble you for a glass of water?"

Pat reached over the heads of her friends to get a glass. She took it over to the little sink and turned on the tap. She kept her back to the others. No one noticed her reaching into her pocket.

She turned and handed the glass directly to Helen. Helen reached for the glass with both hands, took a sip and then pretended to cradle the glass in her lap under the table. Out of Gwen's view, she quickly slipped off the rubber band around the glass. She set the glass on the table in front of her at the same time as she reached down for her purse. “Listen, I’ll pay you now for the Hummel and I can collect from my buyer later.” She took the figurine of the little cracked boy and his pet and tucked it carefully into the depths of her huge purse. As her hand came out of the purse it held four one hundred dollar bills. She handed them towards Gwen. As Gwen picked up the bills one at a time, she didn’t notice that the last bill was a little damp.

“Thanks for the coffee, Gwen, don’t forget the garage sale this Saturday,” yelled Pat back at Gwen who was happily waving goodbye, the four bills fluttering like a hanky in her hand. “It will be at my place and even if you don’t have anything else to sell, just come, you can help us sell our stuff.”

“I wish she’d put that money away, Christ, she’s going to lose it before she even gets to use it,” complained Theda. As soon as they rounded the corner away from Gwen’s street, she added, “Okay, Pat, here’s my share for that stupid Hummel. God, I was sure Helen was going to blow it when she started to laugh. Okay, cough up, Marie, and you can get that religious nut of a friend of yours to hand over her share.”

“Don’t worry, warden, I’ve got it right here, and don’t worry about Edna. One thing, she’s not tight with her money, and I know she wants Gwen to come with us,” spoke up Marie, defensively.

“I think we’ve got her hooked now. After this garage sale, all we’ll have to do is reel her in,” chortled Pat.

Chapter Four

During the next few days, Pat and her friends dashed frantically around attending to the countless chores that had to be done before they could embark on their trip. They all wanted to leave their houses clean. Pat was concerned about her yard and enlisted one of Charlie's students to keep the grass trimmed and mowed. Charlie offered to check on her house and oversee the student's work. Theda and Marie updated their wills.

"I've been meaning to do that for years," said Theda.

Marie laughed. "Yeah, and when we discussed it, she persuaded me to make out my will too!"

Each one of the women had had complete physicals. Several had to stock up on prescriptions. A fund was set up for gas to which everyone contributed and when the fund was depleted, they would pay up again. Another fund was created for food when they were camping. If they ate in a restaurant, each person would pay her own bill.

"What if one of us gets sick on this trip?" asked Marie.

"Well, I don't know about the rest of you, but if I'm the one to get sick, I sure don't want to feel responsible for everyone else having to give up their trip for me," spoke up Gwen.

It was agreed that if someone became ill, the rest of the group would stay with her for no more than five days. If the person was in no shape to travel in the van, the rest would see that suitable travel arrangements would be made for that person to return home, whereas the rest of the women would continue on their trip without her.

A new tent was found, because, now, instead of four, there were five people going. It was small and would hold two sleeping bags. Each person was allowed to bring only the barest of necessities, which were to be packed into a small suitcase or duffel bag. Pat, much to her joy, had found an empty zippered pocket on the side of her duffel bag into which she immediately stuffed an extra couple pair of what she referred to as her granny pants—white cotton panties that completely covered both cheeks and all the necessary stuff in front.

"Just out of curiosity, has anyone wished any of you a bon voyage? I've met a couple people in the market that I know and they don't even say hello any more, just sort of look at me strangely and walk on past. I'm beginning to feel like I've committed a crime or something."

"I got a lecture on all the horrible things that could happen to us on this trip from Mr. Peterson, the old guy that works in the bank. The worst part was he was so loud. He had everyone standing in line behind me, nodding his or her head in agreement. The way he's got it figured is, all going well, we all should be sick, dead and buried before a week is up." laughed Theda. "I told him in a good loud voice 'Just give me my money and I'll thank you to keep your hands to yourself.' That sure shut him up fast, the old nosey bugger."

"Yes, and besides that, we could crash, or be robbed at knife point, beaten, raped…" added Marie.

At the word, raped, Theda smiled ecstatically, rolling her eyes.

"I just tell anyone who makes a negative comment about us or our trip to pray for us. That usually stops them from saying any more," volunteered Edna, popping a rather large green pill into her mouth followed by a good swig of water to help wash it down.

She swallowed, then continued, "Actually, I haven't told you this before, but Pastor Evingham is going to ask the congregation to pray for a safe journey for us, the Sunday after we leave."

"Oh, God!" moaned Theda.

"No, not God, Pastor Evingham, and I think it's very nice of him. We're going to need all the help we can get," retorted Edna.

"Pessimist!" hissed Theda.

At exactly 8:00 o'clock Monday morning, Pat stood by her door looking over her last check list. Lidsters are picking up the mail. Charlie's in charge of the yard. Mrs. Piermont is watering the house plants. The house is in reasonable shape, just in case I don't make it back in one piece. No one will be able to say, "Poor dear, she lived in such terrible filthy conditions. Someone should have done something."

The van had been packed the night before with everything but their individual suitcases or bags. Pat picked up her old gardening shoes, tucked them in the closet and closed the door. Happening to glance out the front door, she saw Marie sitting on the front porch. Pat laughed to herself. Marie had her nose deep in a book. Pat grabbed her wallet sitting on the hall bench, slipped her keys over the index finger of the same hand and bent down to grab her duffel bag. She pushed open the screen door with her hip. "Hi! Marie, I didn't know you were here already, why didn't you give a holler?"

Marie didn't budge or acknowledge her. Pat walked on over to the van and set her bag near the side door. Then she unlocked the door, put her foot on the bottom step and stretched across to insert the key in the ignition. Her back jeans pocket bulged where she had tucked her wallet. She breathed deeply. The morning air always smelled so good and fresh, that is before the exhaust fumes took over. She glanced over at Marie and then walked over to where she was sitting. She left the door to the van open. Charlie had said that since there wasn't any light that came on when the door opened, it was all right to leave it ajar. It wouldn't run the battery down or anything. Pat leaned over and peeked under Marie's book cover and read: *Five Easy Steps to Dismantle a Shotgun*. Pat laughed and shook her head. She was always amazed at her friend's diverse interests. Before she had time to make a comment to Marie, Theda arrived.

Theda hopped out of the car that brought her, turned around and yelled back at the driver, “Don’t run away, yet, I have to get my bag out of the back.” She pulled two bags out of the back seat, swung the door shut and yelled to the driver, “Thanks a mil, Paul. See you whenever. ’Bye now.” The car and its driver moved away down the street.

She turned and walked up the driveway, threw her one duffel bag near the van, and knelt down on one knee and started to open the other one. “Hey, girl, just a minute,” protested Pat, “We’re only supposed to have one duffel bag each, what gives?”

Theda’s eyes challenged her, “Hold on to your underpants, lady. I just brought an extra bag for all our estrogen tablets.”

Pat laughed. “That’s okay then. I just thought you were being obstinate. Edna and Gwen will soon be here. Edna called just shortly before 8:00. She was walking over to pick up Gwen. Louise is coming over, too, to say goodbye. Gee, I wish she would change her mind and come with us. Oh, well, I guess there’s no hope of that happening.”

Theda proceeded to flatten her one duffel bag, and then she rolled it up until it was only the size of a huge fist. She picked it up and pushed it in front of Pat’s face, “There, Miss Old-Meany-Pants, see, it will hardly take up any room at all. In fact, I’m going to put it into the bottom of my own bag. I thought we could all put our dirty clothes in it. Save us having to keep our dirty laundry in with our clean stuff all the time.”

“That’s a good idea and I want the record to show that I was the first to apologize. I’m sure there’s going to be many more before this trip is done.”

“Ideas?”

“No, apologies. Ah, there’s the others now. Good, we can start loading our bags.”

Fifteen minutes later the van was loaded, a bulging duffel bag under each seat. “Okay girls, if anyone needs to use the bathroom before we leave, this is absolutely the last call. I just have one last thing to check on, and I’ll be right out. Pat ran back into the house. The screen door whacked shut behind her. She checked that the instructions for watering the indoor plants were on the table with the watering can and towel to wipe up spills. She stepped out on the patio for a second and took a quick look around her garden. In two or three weeks, the flowers would be at their peak. "Oh, well, there's always something that will be reaching its peak, and if you stay at home always waiting for this *peakedness* you'll never get away and do anything different," she thought. "Perhaps I'll see something on our trip that is at its peak and it will make up for what I'm going to miss here." She took one last look, sighed and turned to join her friends.

By 8:45 a rather large group of people had assembled on Pat's lawn to say their goodbyes. Among them were neighbours, the odd relative and some friends. Gwen's family was there still trying to talk her out of going on the trip. Charlie stopped by, on his way to the high school.

Louise came on the run and quickly pushed her way through the others. She was carrying a huge box covered with a crisp white tea towel. She handed the box to Pat. "Here, you guys, I came to say good bye. Hope you all have a wonderful time, and thought you might enjoy these for your first coffee break."

Pat took the box and lifted the corner of the towel to have a little peek. "Oh, my gosh, but these smell so good!"

She looked quickly at the huge assortment of sugarcoated air doughnuts, muffins and various kinds of cookies. "Oh, Louise, you shouldn't have. I mean, I'm really glad you did, but… And the box is warm. Did you just make these?"

She wrapped her spare arm around Louise and gave her a warm hug. "Thank you so much. We really do appreciate this, and oh, I wish you could come with us, lady person. We're going to miss you, so much."

"You're welcome, and yes, I just made the buns this morning, so they are really fresh. The rest I made yesterday." She looked at her friends and bit her lip, "I wish I was going, too, but I just can't leave the kids. They would never be able to cope without me. They all depend on me so much, you understand. Anyway, I just wanted you to have something homemade for once on your trip."

"No, I don't understand," muttered Theda under her breath, "God, they're not kids any more."

Overhearing Theda's comment, Gwen responded, "Oh, well, you know, the fleas never travel far from the dog."

Theda looked at her inquiringly and shook her head, "What a comparison, Gwen, honestly!"

Gwen beamed proudly, "I thought so."

The women took turns hugging and whispering their good-byes to Louise. Gwen climbed into the van, wiping a few tears away with the cuff of her shirt before she sat down. Theda looked at her, "Oh, stop that, Gwen, or you'll get me going, too. Oh, oh, I forgot something. Get out Gwen, hurry up, get out!"

Gwen looked at Theda, "What's the matter?"

"Nothing's the matter, just get out."

As soon as Gwen was out again, standing beside the van, Theda raised her hands over her head and whistled loudly to attract everyone's attention. "Everyone! Your attention please! We have to christen this old boat before she sets sail.''

She reached down to a paper sack that she had placed on the grass and withdrew a good sized bottle of champagne. "Nice bubbly, and instead of wasting this by breaking the bottle on the front of the van and making a terrible mess, I have six plastic glasses. Louise, you're included in this. We're going to toast the van instead."

"None for me, thank you," said Edna sanctimoniously.

"Oh, for Qui-ryst's sake Edna, it's just a toast. Just take a little sip. It's not going to hurt you," said Theda impatiently.

Edna shook her head emphatically. "No!"

"Oh, never mind then, the rest of us will do the toast." She turned, raising her glass into the air, "God bless this van, and all who, uh…drive her and in her. To the van, our home away from home!"

"And here's to our trip, wherever we end up!"

"Here's to friendship."

"Hear! Hear! Here's to friendship!" they all raised their glasses towards Louise.

And so at 9:00 o'clock, on the third of July, the five women hugged Louise one last time then quickly scrambled into the van. Pat sat in the driver's seat. The rest claimed the first seat that was free. "Are we all comfortable and accounted for? We're off then, wave goodbye, girls."

Pat carefully backed the van out of the driveway and they were on their way. Everyone turned and waved to the people in Pat's yard. Pat kept glancing in her side's rearview mirror. She watched as Louise got smaller and smaller. Louise was quite a hefty lady, but somehow Pat thought she looked almost small and pitiful as she stood hunched over waving goodbye.

Theda broke the silence, "Where the hell are we going, Pat?" she yelled.

Marie laughed and added, "Are we there, yet?"

Pat responded with a hearty laugh, "I don't know and no we're not. I'm just pointing this van and it can drive itself, watch." She turned at the next street corner, folded her arms across her chest, and closed her eyes briefly. Several loud shrieks made her open them quickly. She grabbed the steering wheel and twisted it, narrowly missing a garbage man who had walked out between two parked cars. "Sorry about that, ladies, won't pull that stunt again."

Theda roared, "You'd have got twenty-five points if you'd have hit him, Pat."

The rest of the passengers giggled and laughed nervously, except Edna who was busy looking through her purse trying to make up her mind what colour of pill to take to calm her nerves; it could be either the yellow long one, or the fat red round one. The fat red one won out, and she popped it into her mouth.

The garbage man, with his pail of half spilled garbage strewn around him stood in the middle of the road shaking his fist. "Crazy old bags!!"

Chapter Five

Pat and her friends had planned on travelling approximately two hundred kilometres a day. That, it was decided, would allow them lots of time to stop and look at attractions on the way.

The first day on the road, Pat felt like she was driving in the city. It was stop and go all the way. They had stopped at nine different little curio shops, and two times for meals. They had had four coffee breaks, four extra pee stops, and by 6:00 at night they had only travelled sixty kilometres. The low number of kilometres travelled wasn't the only thing that bothered Pat.

The van at the best of times was very crowded with just their bodies and gear. When Pat looked in her rear-view mirror, she couldn't see the back of the van for all the packages and bags. They were everywhere. Each person had bought several articles at each of the stores at which they had stopped. There was everything, from birdhouses to porcelain dolls. There were two big bags of wool to make afghans, two large Gund teddy bears, which were an excellent bargain, a large stained glass Blue Heron, that Edna held in her lap so it wouldn't get broken. Marie had bought several large nature books for her coffee table along with two large rolled up posters.

Marie, who was riding shotgun, was the navigator for the day. She soon spied a respectable looking campground and pointed it out to Pat. They considered themselves lucky this time as the manager of the grounds only charged them for one campsite, but was allowing them to pitch both their tents. Pat parked the van in their space and left to find the bathroom. When she returned, the van had been unpacked and both tents were erected. The lone picnic table was totally concealed with their recent purchases. A pot of hot dogs bubbled merrily on the little Coleman stove that balanced precariously on the edge of two logs. Everyone was chattering to each other.

"Come on Pat, these dogs are ready to eat, grab a bun you peoples!" Theda was serving.

Upset, but trying not to show it, Pat walked over to the stove and picked up a hot dog, pushed it between the layers of the bun with her fork and then slapped almost half a jar of mustard on it. She bit into the dog thinking, *God, at this rate, we won't get out of the province this year, let alone next week. We can certainly forget about reaching the West Coast. Sixty lousy kilometres, and look at the van. It's already full to the brim with all the crap that they've bought.*

She took another bite of the hot dog. Mustard oozed out over her fingers.*One consolation, everyone seems to be having a wonderful time; no quarreling, yet. Theda and Edna have made the odd snipe at each other, but that's par for the course, nothing that makes it uncomfortable for the rest of us.*

She popped the last bite of her hot dog into her mouth. It had tasted good, really good. She continued to talk to herself: *What is it about hot dogs, when you cook or eat them outside they seem to taste a hundred percent better than when you eat them inside?*

She hated to throw a wet blanket on the group, but unfortunately, something had to be done, probably the sooner the better before it got completely out of hand. She looked around. Everyone seemed to be finished eating.

Edna was busy organizing all her pills. She had them separated into groups on a napkin. The napkin was spread neatly over an upright block of wood. Pat had never seen such a colourful hodgepodge. There were pills for every occasion.

She stepped carefully around the makeshift table and stood facing her friends. She cleared her throat, "Ladies, I have something to say."

The chattering continued. She raised her voice noticeably, "Excuse me, please, can I have your attention, just for a few moments?"

There was silence. "Thank you, I don't know how to put this diplomatically so no one's feelings will be hurt, so I'll just say it because it has to be said. Damn it ladies, we can't be stopping at every little junkie tourist trap we see! We've travelled all day and here we are in Cobourg, less than sixty kilometres from home. For all intents and purposes, we still haven't officially left home yet. We'll be lucky to reach Toronto in a week—a trip that should take less than half a day."

"Well, if you didn't want us to stop, why didn't you say something?" snapped Theda.

"Some of these stores are quite unique. We may not come across their like again," argued Gwen.

"So, tomorrow we'll make up the lost time," stated Marie.

The mass grumbling continued, each protest getting louder. "Just a holy old minute, please!" yelled Pat. She waited for the women to quiet down then proceeded, "You're right, we should have set some ground rules for this sort of thing before we left, but we didn't." She pointed over to the table, "Just look at this pile of stuff. If we buy one more thing, one of us will have to stay behind because there won't be room for her. Just think, we still have hundreds of kilometres to go yet. It just can't go on like this, I'm sorry."

"Holy Old Shit! I think this is the first time I've seen Pat really angry, and I hate to admit it but I think she's right. Let's calm down a bit, girls, and try to think of some way to get ourselves out of this mess," laughed Theda.

"I'm not mad, just…," proclaimed Pat.

"Oh, come on, admit it, you're mad. Say it. I'm mad as hell, and I don't give a da…" prodded Theda.

Pat laughed along with the others. As the laughter subsided, Edna came up with the first good suggestion. "Perhaps we could find someplace tomorrow to wrap all these things up and then we can send them home. I'm sure there's a bus depot around here somewhere. That will probably be the cheapest way to send them."

"That's what we'll do then, and from now on I suggest that we only stop at one store a day," said Marie.

"Only one store?" asked Gwen. "Couldn't we make it two or three? I love looking at all the different things."

"Excuse me, but if I remember correctly, Gwen, you didn't buy one thing today, so why should you care how many we stop at?" questioned Theda.

"I know I didn't. Like I said, I like to look."

Edna placed the last pill in its little white compartment marked Sat. "I think one is enough, and if there's a place that's looks interesting at the place we stop for the night, we can go to that one, too. How does that sound?"

"Yes, we'll just have to be a bit choosier about where we stop. Should we vote on this or something?" asked Marie.

"Okay, everyone agree with Edna's suggestion?" Theda peeked over at Pat grinning. "How 'bout you, captain, agreed?"

"Yes, yes, it sounds good to me, but there is one other thing though: if you buy something, I think it should be very small. If it is, say, over six by six inches and you really want it then it's your responsibility to make arrangements with the store to send it to your home. Most stores will do this, for a price. I know this is going to cost us all more, but I really don't see any other way. The van is big, but I'm sorry, it's not that big."

The next morning, after a tasty breakfast, a trip to the post office and the bus depot, the ladies finally pulled out onto the main highway. Everyone chattered contentedly as they watched the scenery sweep past the van's large windows. Gwen started to sing: "Oh, the old brown van, she ain't what she used to be, ain't what she used to be."

Marie and Theda joined her. They sang the song twice before Gwen broke off, "You know what, I think we should pick out a couple of songs, learn the words to them and have them as our theme songs for this trip. It would be fun."

Everyone agreed, "Good idea, but what songs will we sing?"

"I want to sing *Big Crap Van*," yelled Theda.

"I'm not singing any song with a title like that. What about something like *A Closer Walk With Thee*? I also like *Peace in the Valley*," declared Edna.

"Well if it has to be a hymny song, the one I like has a bunch of bum-bum-bums in it. I could do the bum, bums," said Pat. "I can't think of the name of it, but I know someone is born and there's a bunch of bum-bum-bums. Then the same person dies and more bum-bum-bums. I could do the bum-bum-bums."

"If it's the one I think you mean, it's bong, not bum," laughed Gwen.

"I still want to do *Big Crap Van*!" pouted Theda.

"Well Theda, to be honest with you, I've never heard it. Do you know any of the words; give us a couple lines?" asked Gwen.

"Know the words, of course I know the words. I need a little reggae beat here. Help me out Gwen."

Gwen smiled happily and expertly started humming a reggae tune, keeping time with her hands on the back of the seat nearest her.

Theda sang out, "Moo-van, Moo-van, in our big crap van! Pain-teed brown 'cause there weren't no tan... 'as one headlight, three tires good-one not so, such a pain. Crap van go'n' take us there and back again."

"Whoa! Stop!" interrupted Pat, "What's a 'Moo-van'? Some vehicle that transports cows?"

"Theda giggled,"It's not a Moo-van. It's mov*ing*. The van is moving, going someplace. Get it?"

Theda continued to sing the whole song. The tune was peppy and full of rather cute sexual inuendos. It also held more than its fair share of cuss words. Few of the women would have sung this song under normal circumstances, but seeing that they were travelling in a brown van, it seemed appropriate to choose the song as one of their official theme songs. Theda volunteered to write the words down that night when they stopped so the rest of the women could memorize them.

"I think it's a disgusting song. Don't bother making a copy for me. You won't catch me singing that. I don't want to even hear it," Edna's mouth tightened, she crossed her arms over her chest and turned her face away from the others.

Since everyone liked the bum-bums or bong-bongs, The Bum Bong Song, as it became known was also chosen. To placate Edna somewhat they also decided to include *Just a Closer Walk With Thee.*

"Good, then Gwen, you will be our choir director. We want this to be really good, so don't be afraid, if someone is too loud or out of key, you can tell her. We might even turn pro after this trip, who knows," declared Theda.

Gwen happily accepted the challenge. They continued down the road shouting and, in a couple of cases, screeching out their songs. "Okay, girls, that wasn't bad for a first time," Gwen said tongue-in-cheek. "Let's try it again, but this time, don't yell the words quite so much. Try just saying them softly, with a tune. We'll work on the volume later. Ready? A one, a two, a three." She signaled the start of the song with her hand.

Chapter Six

After a late lunch break, Theda stood outside the van stretching and twisting her waist from side to side. Then she worked her neck and shoulder muscles for a few seconds. Her duffel and camera lay at her feet. She yawned as she said, "Where is Marie? Everyone else took off for the bathroom, but I haven't seen her for a long while?"

"Oh, where do you think? She's in the van already, ensconced in one of her books," replied Pat.

"What's she reading this time? Lord, that woman sure likes her books. She just devours them. It's beyond me how anyone's brains can absorb that much knowledge. If books had calories, she'd be a three hundred and fifty pound genius by now," laughed Theda.

"I don't know. I didn't get a good look at the cover, something about *You and Your Car*."

"*You and Your Car*? Last night it was *Body Language: How to Decipher Evil Intent*, and the night before that it was *VCR: Friend or Foe*. Shit, the woman doesn't even own a VCR, so why read about one?"

Pat double-checked that she had her credit card in her wallet and then stuffed her camera into her duffel bag. She was about to put the bag in the van when the others started to return. "Oh, here's the rest of the crew now."

"Oh good. Now it's off to the big T.O."

"Busy road, hey? Have you ever driven in traffic like this before?" inquired Marie of Pat. "I've never seen so many cars and trucks." Pat was still doing all the driving for the group.

She loved driving, but had decided that once they passed Toronto this was going to change and they could all take turns driving.

"No, not really, Earl did most of the driving when we went anywhere. I remember him saying, just get in the middle lane and stay there. You couldn't go wrong if you did that. The only problem with that is, now the big trucks aren't allowed in the extreme left outside lane, so the hogs want the middle lane, too."

An hour later, the van zipped expertly in and out of the slower traffic. Pat had soon learned how to navigate through the heavy traffic making use of every lane, including the faster outside one. Her husband's old adage about staying in the middle lane had been chucked.

Pat spoke over her shoulder, "Marie, I've been thinking. We reserved that camping space on the other side of Toronto. The chap that took my reservation said he would save it for us until 6:00 o'clock. I hadn't planned on driving through the city, but this road seems okay. I think I can manage. It's 4:00 o'clock now, and if we take the route around the city I'm afraid we may not get there in time. What do you think?"

"Yeah, this road seems pretty good and we seem to be moving right along. At this rate we should be through the city in less than an hour. I say go for it, girl!" Marie turned to the others, "We've decided we're not going to go around Toronto, we're going straight through the city, guys. That way we can get to the campground an hour earlier."

"Sounds great, I'd love a shower right about now, and maybe we could wash a load of clothes; we're due you know," yelled back Edna.

"Yeah, some of us more than others," Theda whispered under her breath.

Everyone glanced at Marie who was wearing a dark grey pair of sweat pants, old Nike running shoes that had seen better days and a dark blue, long-sleeved sweatshirt that sported a picture of a mother loon and her two babies on it. Marie's friends often commented on her skimpy use of deodorant.

Marie happened to glance up just at that moment from her map and caught her fellow travellers looks. "Why is everyone looking at me?"

"God, Marie, didn't you bring more than one set of clothes? You've worn that same outfit everyday that we've been travelling," pointed out Theda.

"I beg your pardon, but I change my socks and underwear every day, and to answer your question, yes, I do have another set of clothes. Pat told us to pack light, so I did. And if you don't mind me adding a bit to this conversation, this is only our second day on the road for heaven's sake!"

"Well, I'm still going to pray for a laundromat," declared Edna.

"That's not a very Christian remark, dear lady," said Theda.

"You're right, it's not, but I never see you sitting directly behind her in this van," retorted Edna.

Theda stuck her tongue out at Edna then asked Marie, "Marie, could I change seats with you for a bit? I'll take over the map reading for you for awhile."

Marie obligingly moved to the back of the van taking one of her books with her. Two seconds after making herself comfortable, feet up on the seat, back against the side of the van, book balanced against her knees she continued to read, completely oblivious to the traffic outside.

Theda spread the map out over her lap, "God, two sets of clothes for a month's holiday and how can she read like that in a moving vehicle. Why doesn't she get car sick or anything? Don't get me wrong, I'm really happy that she doesn't get car sick."

Pat looked up and smiled at her in the rear-view mirror. They were making excellent time. "At this rate, we'll be there before you know it."

Suddenly, there was a huge backlog of vehicles. The traffic around them slowed down to a crawl completely hemming the van in on every side. Pat tried to nose out to pass a huge green and silver sixteen-wheeler, but the vehicles in the other lane ignored her attempt, so she pulled back behind the monstrosity.

"Guess I tempted fate by making that last comment."

Gwen rolled down her window a little more and poked her head out, she quickly brought it back, "I don't think it's worth trying to pass, Pat, there's cars to eternity up ahead. I hope there wasn't an accident."

An hour and a half passed, and the brown van and her crew were still inching their way through the huge city. Pat blew a puff of air out through her mouth, and just as she did the van jerked to life as spaces suddenly began to appear on either side of it. Pat signaled and pulled out to pass the huge transport truck. As fast as the traffic had slowed to a snail's pace, it started to move along normally again. She turned to Theda, "We must be almost through the city by now, what does it show on the map?"

"Map shows city almost gone. I guess that was the city rush hour. Lord, can you imagine doing this every day of your life. Yuck! Give me the backwoods anytime."

"Bad calculating on my part, I'm afraid," Pat glanced down at her watch, "We'll never make that campground in time now. Darn and phooey!"

"Oh, well, not to worry. We'll check anyway and if it's gone, we'll just have to get a motel room tonight, that's all. Not the end of the world," assured Theda.

A half hour later, just outside of Cookstown, Pat pulled up to the brightly lit office of the campground. She stretched briefly when she got out and then walked into the little building. The rest of the women sat in silence. Several of them yawned. Marie, taking advantage of the office's big neon light shining through the van window tried to finish the article she was reading. Gwen, leaning her head against the window, mouth open, was snoring softly. They could see Pat talking to the clerk. They saw him shake his head. Finally he reached for a phone.

"There mustn't be any place or she would have been out by this time."

"Come on, Pat, hurry up, even the motels will be filled up by the time we get to them," someone in the van said.

In about ten minutes, Pat came out of the office. As she climbed back into the van, she handed Theda a piece of paper,

"Here, hold this."

"What's the verdict, lady?"

"Well, this is the way it is. That was the manager of the campground. He let our space out two hours ago, and just now he was trying to find us a motel room. There isn't anything within a hundred mile radius of the place. Four or five big conventions in town, a school holiday this weekend and for some reason, he said half the States seems to be up this weekend. Anyway, to make a long story short, we can either drive for another hour or so, and take our chances then, or take this place he found for us," she nodded towards the paper in Theda's hand.

"I don't care where it is, just as long as it's a place to lay our heads. I'm so tired," volunteered Edna.

"I'm starved," added Marie.

Pat swung the van back out onto the highway and they backtracked for several minutes. "Okay, he said to turn off at this exit, and it should become Turner Road. Yes, there's the sign. What does it say next, the third turn on the right, Theda? Here I'll turn on the indoor light for a second, so you can see."

Theda squinted at the paper, reading it quickly, "Yes, the third. May I ask where we're going? This just looks like a bunch of farms back here? Sure don't see any motel."

"Did I say anything about a motel?" Pat pulled into the third driveway and slowed the van to a halt in front of an old farmhouse. An older man and lady who had been sitting on the verandah slowly got up. As they approached., the lady waved.

"Ladies, if I'm not mistaken, that's Mr. and Mrs. Hoeflicker, your hosts for the evening."

"In that old house? Pat, you've got to be kidding?"

"Well, not exactly in their house, more like behind or to the side of it. They're going to let us pitch our tents in their yard."

Pat leaned out the window, "Is this the Hoeflicker residence?"

"I can't believe it!" protested Theda.

"Shhhh!! Look, get over it. It's better than nothing. Besides, we pitch the tent and the manager of that campground said there's a Burger King about four minutes from here. Not only that, there's a laundromat in the next town we drive through tomorrow morning. We can throw a load of clothes into the machines. Then we can grab some breakfast, and by the time we're done the clothes will be dry. Come on ladies, let's go meet the Hoeflickers. They're waiting."

Mrs. Hoeflicker was busy greeting everyone as they tiredly dragged themselves out of the side of the van. A very grey and stooped Mr. Hoeflicker slowly made his way down the stairs of the verandah. As he came down the brick path he seemed to speed up considerably reminding Pat of a ball that had started rolling down a hill, and the further it travelled the faster it went. She thought he would slow down when he came to the side of the gravel road, but he didn't. The women stood watching, mouths agape, half expecting him to slam face first into the side of the van. Several inches in front of the van he came to a sudden and complete stop. He even had to take a step backwards so he would have room to turn around to face the women.

"Welcome! We were expecting you!" called out Mrs. Hoeflicker, cheerfully. "You'll have to excuse Jim, with his arthritis it takes him a little time to get going," she added fondly.

"Thank you for letting us camp here. Where can we set up our tents? First of all, before you answer that, these are my friends. There are five of us." Pat made brief introductions.

Mrs. Hoeflicker turned to her husband, "Jim, you just go back on up and sit down while I show the ladies where they can put their tent." With a sigh, Jim carefully turned, and methodically putting one foot in front of the other, made his way back to the verandah.

"No, actually, Jim," she yelled after him, "you can grab a few of the ladies' bags, whatever you think you can handle, dear, and bring them along."

Jim sighed again, louder this time, and turned to come back to the van.

Pat quickly ran over to him and touched his arm, "Mr. Hoeflicker, Jim sir, never mind, we can easily handle all this stuff. It just means a couple of trips. It's no trouble, really. You just go on up to the verandah there and plop yourself down on one of those comfortable looking chairs. Go ahead now."

Jim smiled, nodded assent and started back up the pathway. When he reached the set of three stairs leading to the verandah he paused and sighed again. Pat wanted to go over to help him climb the stairs but thought better of it. She couldn't help thinking that she was glad that there were only three steps and not six or twelve. She looked up at the old two-storey house and wondered how the poor man managed the stairs in there. Maybe he didn't, maybe they had a bedroom on the ground floor. She hoped so.

Pat and Marie followed the farmer's wife. She was a bit sprier than her husband, but not much. Mrs. Hoeflicker prattled on. "Poor Jim, his arthritis is just getting worse and worse. Doesn't seem to be anything they can do for him. Now me, I have it too, but they've been replacing my parts for the last ten years now. Come to think of it the warranty will probably soon be up on these hips. Had a couple fingers done last year." She held up two digits for the girls to see, and then used the same ones to point to a place not far from the back of the house. The other spot she showed them was much closer to the van. The grass all around the house was knee deep.

"Think we'll take the spot closer to the van, that way we don't have to haul stuff so far. It's getting dark out Marie, let's get back and get those tents up while we can still see."

Mrs. Hoeflicker stood and watched the women pull all their gear from the van and carry it over to the new campsite. When they were finished she walked over to Theda, and put her hand on her shoulder, "Okay, ladies, I'll leave you now. It won't be long before it will be too dark to see. I just wanted to tell you, when you go in that door there, the bathroom is immediately to your right." She pointed to the green screen door in the middle of the back of the house.

"We'll leave the door unlocked tonight so you can have access to the facilities any time. There's a toilet and a sink. There will be a light on in the hall. Just leave it on so you can see your way. I'm sorry I can't let you use the bathroom upstairs for baths, but we get our water from the cistern and it's been a terribly dry year so far, so we're a little low on water. The drought hasn't seemed to affect the flower beds much. The plants in them are growing lickety-split," she laughed, "especially the weeds. Darn things will grow any place, anytime, water or no." Pat looked back over Mrs. Hoeflicker's head to take in the garden in the backyard, but all she could make out in the gathering dusk were what she presumed to be flower beds.

"Thank you, very much. Now don't you worry about us, we'll manage nicely." She started to give an order, but at that moment a convoy of huge tractor trailers thundered by the yard. Up to that point they had heard the constant hum of traffic, which was expected and bearable, but when the huge trucks came by the whole world vibrated and you couldn't hear anything but their grinding gears and the roar of their motors. Pat waited a bit and then hollered, "Come on ladies, let's hustle and get these tents up quickly while we can still see."

Theda and Marie had already unrolled one tent and were ready to set it up where Edna and Gwen had stomped a section of the grass down.

Pat came up to them, "Look, I imagine the laundromat in town is still open, so while you people finish setting up the tents, I'm going into town and wash at least one load tonight."

"I'll come with you; we can pick up something for us to eat while we're in there. Better place your orders, girls," called Gwen. "No, don't bother, I'm afraid you're all going to have to settle for hamburgers because that's all I'm getting tonight."

Theda laughed, "You drive a hard bargain, Gwen, but you're the boss. Hamburgers, fries and soft drinks sound good."

Edna and Marie walked around to the back of the house. A huge porch light shone over by the big old barn. Moths and bugs zipped and swarmed around the bright yellow light casting weird and sometimes gigantic shadows over the barn yard. Mr. Hoeflicker was still sitting in his chair on the front verandah. He looked over at the women, "You're welcome to plunk your behinds down here, make yourselves at home." He made a motion with his pipe towards the other chairs near him.

"It's very pretty here, Mr. Hoeflicker. Unfortunately we can't see much right now. We'll be able to better appreciate it in the morning when the sun's up," said Edna. Just then a huge tractor trailer roared down the highway. Edna could see Mr. Hoeflicker's lips moving, but couldn't hear a word he said. Another huge vehicle followed close behind the first. Edna turned her head and moved a little closer to the old gentleman. "I'm sorry sir, but I couldn't hear what you said. That traffic gets pretty loud sometimes."

Mr. Hoeflicker waited then laughed, "You get used to it after you've been here a few years. It used to be a real pretty place years ago, before they expropriated our land to extend that damn highway. Guess it had to be done. Had to have a highway, so they had to take somebody's land for it. If it wasn't ours it would have been someone else's. Seem to notice the noise more at night, too. Night sounds always travel better anyway, and then that's when most of the truckers hit the road. It's funny, but if you ever get a quiet day, you know when it storms, or there's too much snow, then it seems strange not to have the noise. Like I said, you get used to stuff after awhile. It's like people who live close to the airport. After they've been there a year or so, they all get used to the take-offs and arrivals."

Theda came around the corner of the house just then. She didn't notice Mr. Hoeflicker sitting in the shadows, "I was just in the bathroom. God, when those big sucker trucks go by the whole damn building shakes! Think you're in the middle of an earthquake. Windows rattling all over. You'd wonder how the glass stays in the frames."

Theda laughed. "There's an old dog stretched out on the floor by the kitchen stove and when one of those trucks goes by, I swear the vibrations move the poor old thing from one side of the kitchen to the other."

Edna cleared her throat, and Mr. Hoeflicker laughed. Theda turned quickly, saw him and gave him a slightly embarrassed smile, and turned to her friends to whisper, "I didn't know he was sitting there."

Trying to change the subject she quickly added, "I hope

Pat and Gwen hurry up with those hamburgers, I'm starved."

The foursome sat quietly for a few minutes, listening to the traffic and watching the moths and bugs attack the light near the barn. They could hear Mrs. Hoeflicker bustling about in her kitchen. Soon, the screen door swung open. Mrs. Hoeflicker held the door open with her hip and, turning her body while she balanced a medium sized tray in both hands, she stepped out onto the verandah floor. The screen door slammed behind her. "Here, ladies, I have a fresh loaf of bread that I made this morning. Help yourselves to the marge and there's also a little jar of red currant jelly left over from last year. It's not much, but it should help to tide you over until your friends return with your food."

Mr. Hoeflicker rocked his chair forward and stood up. "Have to excuse me for a few minutes, I'll be back shortly."

The bread, cut into huge thick one-inch slices, sat on the plate invitingly. Theda, not one to stand on ceremony, reached and grabbed the closest slice, slapped some jelly on it and took an enormous bite. She closed her eyes as she chewed, "Oh, this is heaven, absolute heaven. Mrs. Hoeflicker, you are a doll."

By this time, the others had helped themselves. "The jelly is really good, too, what did you say it was?" asked Edna.

"Red currants, supposed to be real healthy for you, just chock full of vitamin C. I don't put half the sugar the recipe calls for 'cause I prefer my jelly and jams a little tart. At least this way it tastes like the fruit and not just a mouthful of sugar."

Just as the last mouthful of bread disappeared into their hungry mouths, Gwen and Pat pulled up in the van. "Hi, people, washings all done and here's your hamburgers. Come and get them while they're hot. Hey, Hoeflickers, bought you a couple hamburgers, too, if you want them."

"Well, thank you! Jeepers, don't know the last time I had one of these." Mr. Hoeflicker had returned by this time, his sparse grey hair was damp and freshly combed.

"Here, you two grab a seat," offered Marie pushing a couple of the chairs closer to the older couple.

"Oh, now, what kind of a gentleman would I be if I took a

seat and left so many lovely ladies standing? It wouldn't be very chivalrous on my part."

"Listen, if you want to know the truth, we've been sitting all day in that van. It feels good to just stand for a change. If we need to sit, we can use these stairs or the floor, so you just set yourself down and enjoy," replied Marie.

Mr. Hoeflicker eased himself slowly into the chair. He sighed contentedly. He was quite happy to have a place to sit. "Well, that's real nice of you, getting this food for us, too. We certainly didn't expect this treat. Thank you, ladies."

The hamburgers and fries disappeared quickly. Marie gathered all the cardboard containers, papers and serviettes and stuffed them into one bag. Pat licked her lips and wiped her hands on the legs of her jeans. "Do you mind if we go for a little walk after we're done here. We need to get a little exercise. Where's a good place to walk where we can't get in any trouble?"

"Well, it's pretty dark now." Only the tiniest edge of a sunset shimmered on the edge of the horizon. "I guess you could walk through the pasture over there. You have to make sure that it's the first pasture and not the one next because that's where the bull is. You'll have to crawl under the fence, because even if you managed to get the gate open I'm afraid you'll never be able to close it. Just be careful that you don't snag your clothes on the barbed wire," Mr. Hoeflicker said.

"They won't be able to see anything. In a few minutes it will be pitch black. I'll get the flashlight for them, and at least they'll be able to stay on the path," declared Mrs. Hoeflicker.

"Yes, and watch where you step, our cows aren't very well trained. They do their business wherever they pretty well please," laughed Mr. Hoeflicker jovially, pipe still in his mouth.

"The flashlight sounds like a good idea. I don't like the idea of walking straight into a cow, especially in the dark," giggled Gwen.

"Cows, what cows? Are there cows in that pasture now? If there are, I'm not going," protested Edna.

"Oh, come on, Edna, a cow won't hurt you, and we'll all be with you," volunteered Pat.

Mrs. Hoeflicker was standing with the flashlight. She handed it to Theda, "No, don't worry, they won't hurt you. Besides at this time of the night they usually all bunch up at the end closest to the barn. Paul, he's our young neighbour, actually owns the cows. He rents our pastures from us. He'll soon be coming over to feed them, so that's why they come right up here at the same time every night."

"Anyway, once you get through the pasture, you have to go under the fence again at the other end. There's a road there," Mr. Hoeflicker pointed with his pipe, "get on that road and it's not a far walk over to the main highway. There's a bridge across the highway. It's kind of fun to stand there and watch the lights of the traffic. When Sarah," this was the first time the women heard Mrs. Hoeflicker referred to by her first name, "and I used to walk over there, especially in the winter when it was snowing lightly we'd stand in the middle of the bridge. The snow made the lights all swirly and bright. It was fun, wasn't it, Sarah?"

"Yes, it was, dear," Sarah said reflectively, "very fun."

The group started out, with Theda in the lead holding the flashlight. "Oh, and another thing," yelled Mr. Hoeflicker after them, "depends when you come back. Just remember, the fumes you smell, not to worry. It's not a volatile mixture. The place won't blow up and burst into flames. It's just gas," Mr. Hoeflicker chortled gleefully as he bent over holding his side.

They all made it under the barbed wire fence without mishap and, thanks to the light given off by the flashlight, they soon found the path to take them directly across the pasture. At each step they took it seemed to get darker and darker. The light from the flashlight bounced from side to side as Theda walked. Suddenly, the beam fell on a rather huge rock. "Oh, my, what is it? Is it a cow? Let's go back," Edna grabbed Theda's free arm and hung on for dear life.

"Edna, let go of me, it's only a rock for heaven's sake!" Theda shook herself free of Edna's grasp. Just then, the flashlight caught the form of a little creature scurrying across their path in front of them.

"Ahhh! Did you see that?" Edna grabbed Theda again.

"Maybe the bull has escaped and he's in this pasture now," she screamed.

"Oh, yeah, Edna," sneered Theda, "Did you see the horns on it, and the ring in its nose? Cripes, it was all of two inches tall! Get a grip, woman."

The trek along the rest of the path was uneventful, and at the end of it, they all crawled under the fence and stood in the middle of a road. A bit of the moon had started to poke its nose up over the hills and with its help their eyes gradually became accustomed to the dark. Theda switched off the flashlight. They walked to the middle of the bridge. Even though it was close to 9:00 at night, the traffic was still heavy. A huge transport truck vibrated the bridge as it approached and then as it passed under the bridge, they heard a mighty swish and felt a huge suction as the huge truck drew the air away from them.

Gwen leaned out over the edge of the bridge. She was leaning so far over that her feet left the ground. "Gwen, be careful, you could fall," reprimanded Pat, "and if you do those trucks would squish you like a bug."

Gwen turned to Pat and pouted slightly, "I just wanted to spit."

"Pardon me?"

"I want to spit."

"I thought that's what you said. Well, my dear, be my guest. Go ahead and spit if it makes you happy."

"I want to spit on one of those trucks."

"Oooh, gross!" declared Marie.

"I'm going to, I'm going to spit. The next big truck that comes is going to get it."

It was only seconds before the lights of another huge truck bore down on the group standing on the bridge. They stood staring straight at the bright lights as the huge truck bore down on them. Just as the moment of impact seemed imminent, the truck disappeared under them. "Hurrah! Hurrah! I did it, I spit on him!" Gwen was dancing up and down.

"What a weird sensation!" yelled Theda, "Man, this beats

Disney World all to rat shit! Here comes another one guys, come on. This time I'm going to stand right in the middle." Theda stood with arms spread wide, "Come on you big bugger, come and get me, I dare you." The big truck lights beamed over the Christ-like figure of Theda and just as it seemed it would run over her, both person and truck disappeared in the darkness. Pat was relieved to hear Theda's voice over the traffic noise, "Oh, man, what a sensation!"

"Spitting is more fun. Why don't you try it?" argued Gwen.

"Oh, Gwen, please, the next time we drive under a bridge I'll be watching for a huge gob of spit to land on my windshield," Pat said disgustedly.

"I've heard of teenagers dropping rocks on windshields from bridges, but old broads spitting, nope, don't think I've heard of that," added Marie, "oh, look at that one coming! Look at the lights on it, looks like a Christmas tree!"

Theda yelled, "Hurry up, everybody, one last kick at the can, before we go!"

The five women lined up at the edge of the bridge like a group of men standing in front of urinals. They stood silently, waiting. Waiting, as the mighty truck roared savagely as it rushed towards them. A collective sigh of relief came only as the truck rumbled under their feet and away.

Theda, lighting the way with her flashlight, led the friends back down the road, under the fence and along the pasture path. They were nearing the end of the trail when the night air was filled with a heavy sulphurous rotten egg smell. Theda gagged, "Ugh, how disgusting! That wasn't here when we came, what gives?"

Pat laughed, "Theda, they always say the first one to comment on the smell is usually the one responsible."

"Oh, God, even I, at my worst could never produce something that overpowering."

"I think it's the cows. They're all at this end of the pasture, and I read that that's when the cows release all their gases. They've eaten all day and then they stand around at night and fart," offered Marie. "That's what Mr. Hoeflicker was joking about just as we started out, remember? Volatile gases."

"Well, if that's the case let's move it. Come on Theda, hurry up!"

"Hope that smell doesn't float up near the house or we'll all gag to death in our sleep."

Tucked snugly into their sleeping bags, Gwen and Edna fell asleep the minute their heads hit the pillows. A lantern light shone from Pat, Theda and Marie's tent.

"Boy! Gwen and Edna sure conked out fast tonight," Theda punched her pillow several times to make it more comfortable.

"Gwen wore herself out spitting on the trucks," laughed Pat.

"All I can say is that we're pretty desperate when we've got to get our jollies from spitting off bridges and pretending trucks are going to run over us," commented Marie.

"Come on, Marie, it was fun and we had some good laughs, what more could you want?" asked Pat rolling over on her side to face the other two.

"I thought it was a rush. Speaking of rushes, did you ever take drugs when you were younger?" inquired Theda.

"No, I never did. Guess I never really had the occasion to try them, or maybe we were born too soon. There wasn't the peer pressure to try them. When I went to university, I knew a few kids that always seemed to have a supply of something or other. Guess that shows how naïve I was, I didn't even know what drugs they even had. There probably weren't all the horrible kinds of drugs they have now. I remember signing up for some clinical study using LSD through the university. They were paying people so much an hour to take the drug and then they were probably conducting tests under the influence. I thought it would be a way to make some extra money. They never picked me. We had to go and write some silly test. It had the stupidest questions on it. One had to do with diarrhea. They asked how many times a week you had diarrhea. Then they would ask you some like and dislike questions. Then they asked if you don't have diarrhea, how many times a week do you wish you could have it. I guess I didn't know too much about diarrhea because they never chose me to be one of their guinea pigs. I think they paid me something like two or three whole dollars to take that test. I've read lately what LSD did to some people and I guess I should consider myself lucky that I wasn't picked."

"Why are we talking about diarrhea? Please, I want to go to sleep," yawned Theda.

Marie ignored her. "Sometimes you hear on TV or read about the rush people get when they take drugs; you know, they experience feelings that they have never had before. They enjoyed a whole range of intense emotions. I sort of felt some of that when we were standing there waiting for those trucks to run over us. Some of the feelings I had on that bridge were good; you know, the excitement of thinking something is going to run right over you and smash you to smithereens. I guess you could compare it to a ride at an amusement park. But then, I also felt really, really sad."

"Sad? Why sad?" asked Pat.

"Well, those truck lights reminded me sort of like life coming at you, really fast, and then wham, before you know it, it's all over before you even got a chance to experience any of it. I sort of feel that way right now, about life. The lights are coming at me, but they're getting awfully close and then WHAM! It's all over, just like that," Marie snapped her fingers.

"Speaking of lights, would you two can that stupid lantern, shut up and go to sleep," protested a sleepy Theda.

The next morning, everyone woke up early. A gentle mist had settled over the valley behind the barn. The sun was eating away at it bit by bit. The traffic was just a gentle steady hum. Theda shook her sleeping bag and placed it on the tent floor to roll it up nice and tight so it would slip into its bag easily. "You know what Marie was saying about the effect our little game on the bridge had on her and how time seems to be slipping by so fast? It made me think. From now on I don't want to miss out on anything. If there's something I want to do, dammit, I'm going to do it. Something I want to see, I'm going to make damn sure I see it. I'm not going to constantly put off today what I can do tomorrow. Life is not going to pass me by if I have anything to do or say about it!" She shoved her bag into its holder and gave it a couple of good thumps with her fists.

Pat pulled the draw-strings on her sleeping bag container and laughed. "Here I thought you were going to wake up all lovely and refreshed. Instead you've become all philosophic on us. What did we do to deserve this?"

Gwen poked her head into the tent. "Morning, girls, have a question for you. How long do you think it would take the five of us to weed those gardens in the back yard? I don't mean that we have to get every little weed out, just the huge big ones. I was walking around back there this morning, and there's some really lovely flowers planted there, but you can hardly see them unless you stand right over the beds. You can't even see the delphiniums and they're usually quite a tall plant. There are lupines by the dozens and lots of daisy type plants. It could be really pretty. And you…" Gwen kept going on and on, "should see the vegetable garden. Those poor little vegetables don't know what the sun looks like, the weeds are completely covering them. Not only that, those poohie old weeds are taking all the goodness out of the soil."

Pat stopped her, "I don't think I really feel like digging around in dirt and bugs right now. I did enough of that in my own garden before I left. Besides, I'd like to leave soon, put some kilometres between here and there."

"Yeah, Gwen, don't think every time you see someone who needs something you have to feel obligated to stop and help them. The world is full of those people, and if you stop for everyone, you'll never have any time for yourself," volunteered Theda.

Pat continued, "I agree, Gwen, I mean these people are very nice and all but…."

"I don't know, I just thought it would be nice to help the Hoeflickers out a little bit. I really don't think it would take us all that long, and I don't think you have to stop for every helpless person on the way, but once in a while it surely can't hurt," interrupted Gwen.

Pat looked at her friend, "What did the others say about your suggestions? If they agree then I will, too."

Gwen looked to her side and swallowed, "They weren't too keen on the idea either."

"I'm sorry, then, I'm afraid you've been outvoted this time. Come on get your stuff together and then we can load the…"

Just then, the screen door squeaked open, followed by a loud whack as it closed itself. Gwen pulled her head out of the tent, and Theda and Pat followed her out with their bags in tow. Mrs. Hoeflicker moved softly across the verandah floor. Then she picked her way carefully down the three little wooden steps, "Ladies, before you go, I want to give you these. Jim and I got up early and went down to the little pasture. We have three of the loveliest cherry trees down there. We were lucky that there were enough cherries on the lower branches that we could both reach them and we managed to pick enough to fill these two little baskets. We thought it would be a nice treat for you while you're driving. They're already washed and everything so you don't have to worry about that."

Pat envisioned the two arthritic old people toddling down that hill early in the morning, Mr. Hoeflicker with his cane, and Mrs. Hoeflicker probably holding him by one arm so he wouldn't fall or trip while they made their arduous way down the path to pick these cherries for them. She half groaned to herself at her own selfishness and then graciously accepted the baskets of plump red cherries. "Oh, how lovely, I forgot it's cherry season here. Oh, these look lovely. Would you look at the size of some of these. Thank you, so much!"

Theda took the cherries from Pat and added, "Yes, thank you. I absolutely love cherries. I don't think I got any last year. The season just crept up and before I knew it there was none left."

"Yeah, and they're always so expensive in the stores. This is great!"

Pat watched Theda take the cherries to put them in the van. She turned to the old couple, "Anyway, the man at the campground was going to charge us ten dollars a tent and we had two tents, so here's twenty dollars for you. You saved our skins last night. We would have had to drive forever last night to find any place to park," she handed the money to Mr. Hoeflicker.

The old man straightened himself up as best he could, took one surprisingly quick step towards Pat and tucked the money into her shirt pocket. "Thanks anyway girls, but Mother and I decided this morning while we were picking the cherries that we wouldn't accept any money from you."

Mrs. Hoeflicker came forward, put her arm through her husband's and smilingly added, "Yes, we've just enjoyed so much having you all here.You're fun company, just what we both needed. The laughter itself was worth the twenty dollars. You take that money and treat yourselves to something nice later on in the day when you're kind of tired, maybe an ice cream cone or something, and while you're eating it, think of us."

The women tried to make the couple accept the money, but the Hoeflickers held out stubbornly. Finally they gave up, gave the Hoeflickers each a big hug, and climbed into the van. The van rolled quietly down the Hoeflicker's driveway. Pat glanced out her side mirror and caught the old people's reflection. The old man, bent over, and the old lady, her arm linked in her husband's, were both waving with their free hands. Everyone waved back at them. Suddenly, Pat slammed on the brakes.

"What the hell was that for?" screamed Theda.

"What are you doing, Pat? Did you hit something?" demanded Edna.

"Oh, pooh…The poor cherries! Oh, look, everyone, the poor cherries!" sang out Gwen.

Pat turned and looked at her friends. They were all staring at the floor of the van. Pat lowered her gaze. Gwen was right, the poor cherries had spilled out of their little container and were rolling everywhere, under the seats, up against their feet, at the back of the van and to the front, anywhere a cherry could roll, it had. Pat gestured towards the mess on the floor, "Never mind the cherries, we'll clean them up in a minute. Once in awhile, we have to stop what we're doing and take the time to help others. And Gwen, I think you were right and this is one of those times.

What about it, what do the rest of you say?"

"They were awfully nice people, and so old."

"And they let us camp in their yard for free."

"Even gave us fresh buns and these cherries."

"Oh, the poor, poor cherries. Move your feet, Pat." Gwen was already down on all fours picking up the renegade cherries.

"Okay, count me in. It probably won't take us that long, if we all pitch in; maybe a couple of hours to pull the worst of the weeds," cheered on Theda.

When the van backed into their yard again, the Hoeflickers thought that the women had forgotten something. They were surprised that, when the van came to a complete stop, everyone tumbled out and Pat started to walk towards them. "There was something we forgot to do when we were here. It shouldn't take us too long, so I want you two to just go sit on the porch. No, better yet, Theda and Marie, grab those two chairs there and bring them out to the backyard. Mr. and Mrs. Hoeflicker, you can just relax there in the shade of those trees and watch us." The poor old couple, mouths agape, settled into the chairs placed on the lawn for them. Pat continued to issue orders, "Theda, you and Edna will be responsible for the vegetable plot, Marie…"

Theda started to protest, "Why me and Edn…?"

Before she had time to finish her sentence, Pat emphasized the first four words carefully, "Theda, you and Edna will be responsible for the vegetable plot; Marie, Gwen and I will do the flower gardens. Okay, remember girls, don't worry about the little weeds, but anything over six or eight inches yank it. Marie, you start at that end of this bed, I'll start at this end, and you Gwen can do that little bed over in the corner. If we finish before you we'll come over and help."

The women started to attack the giant weeds with a vengeance. A few perennials mistakenly made it into the giant weed pile that was forming. The Hoeflickers watched in amazement as their scrubby gardens were transformed before their eyes. Colours began to replace green. Purplish blue delphiniums provided the backdrop for bright splashes of red poppies, white daisies and yellow marigolds. Two large peony plants, each covered with huge massive rose blooms bordered the end of the large central bed. Before long, there were eight huge piles of weeds and three distinct beds of flowers.

Over in the vegetable garden, Theda and Edna were pleasantly surprised to find that when the weeds were pulled they were left with tidy little rows of vegetables. They could distinguish a couple rows of potatoes, a patch of corn, some carrots, beats, onions and some rather sad looking cucumbers. "These cucumbers look pretty straggly, don't you think, Theda?"

"Yes, they sure do, but you know they just might do better now, all those bloody weeds were probably just choking them, besides sucking up all the moisture. I think we're almost done. There are lots of little weeds here, but at least the vegetables will have a little chance now with those big suckers gone. I think we did a pretty good job, if I do say so myself." Theda went to high-five Edna, but Edna ducked, thinking Theda was going to hit her. Theda laughed, "I wasn't going to hit you, silly, I was going to high-five you. It's like clapping someone on the back to congratulate them."

Edna laughed nervously, then presented her hand to Theda, "Here, we'll just shake hands instead."

Pat walked over to Mr. Hoeflicker. Her arms held a huge bundle of weeds that she had gathered from one of the piles. "Where can we throw these weeds, Mr. Hoeflicker?"

Mr. Hoeflicker, took his pipe from his mouth and wet his lips with his tongue, "Just throw them over that fence, sort of around the base of those trees. They'll cover the ground like a mulch and keep other weeds and stuff from growing under it."

Thirty or so arm loads later, most of the weeds had been gathered and tossed over the fence.

"Hey, Edna and Theda seem to have disappeared. They were a here a few minutes ago. Where did those two characters go? Probably off somewhere killing each other." said Pat.

Edna and Theda's names were no sooner mentioned, than they appeared from around the corner of the house. "I heard that last comment, Pat."

"Ah, here they are. Where did you guys go? We weren't quite finished you know."

"Don't get your panties in a knot, Edna and I just went down to the cherry trees. We picked a couple of nice baskets for the Hoeflickers. We just picked ones that we thought were too high for them."

Everyone gathered around admiring the cherries. Theda slapped a couple of fingers that reached for the plump juicy fruit. "Get out of there, these aren't for the likes of you," she laughed, pieces of red cherry skin stuck in her teeth.

"Oh, I see that someone's been into the cherries big time. You could have at least tried to hide the evidence," suggested Marie.

Theda set the cherries near the Hoeflickers' chairs and looked out over the yard, "Wow, does that ever look nice now. Who would have imagined that all that beauty was hidden in that mass of weeds?"

Edna sighed, "There's a lesson in all this. Sometimes we have to look through, or under, things or people to find the true beauty around us."

Theda groaned, "Oh, God, there she goes again, another sermon from *Sister Edna of the Van.*"

Edna frowned and Pat laughed, "On that pleasant note, we'll take our adieu. Everyone into the van." Just then Gwen elbowed her way through the others and headed to the house with the two original baskets of ill-fated cherries, "and just where do you think you're going missy, lady?"

"I'm washing these poor, poor cherries. If you think I'm eating these after they rolled all over the floor next to your feet, Pat, you've got another think coming!" Gwen fixed Pat with a hard stare.

"Ooooh, touchy. Okay, be my guest, please wash them. Come on the rest of you, we can get in the van and wait for Gwen. Hop aboard, Sister Edna," Pat giggled.

Gwen returned from the kitchen, stepped into the waiting van and made her way to the back. She sat down and carefully arranged the baskets of cherries carefully beside her sleeping bag. "There, there, you poor little dears. Mommy will watch over you. We won't let that bad old Pat hurt you any more." She peeked over the back of the seat and winked at Pat.

Pat closed the van door and, amid enthusiastic farewells to the Hoeflickers, they finally headed down the driveway.

"Sister Edna, move your bum for a minute. You're sitting on my coat," teased Theda.

"I'm not even Catholic, so quit calling me that. The next person who calls me that, I'll Sister Edna them all right."

"Okay, we won't call you that any more, but I just thought of something else." Theda half turned to Marie, "You know, the whole time we were at the Hoeflickers, I never saw you with your nose in a book once."

"Let's face it, there wasn't time, was there?" Marie frowned thoughtfully.

"Here everyone, help yourself to the poor, poor cherries. Are they ever good!" Gwen smacked her lips loudly.

Chapter Seven

Two days had passed since the brown van left the Hoeflicker farm. Pat felt like they were making good time. Once they had escaped the strong tentacles of the city roads, the traffic moved quickly. They had taken turns driving, stopping at one-hour intervals to change drivers and stretch. Gwen, mouth open, her head leaning against the window of the van, snored softly.

Marie was sitting on the other side of the van across from Gwen where a little makeshift table had been pulled out. The little table was just big enough that she could assemble one of her puzzles on it. She wasn't reading quite as much as usual, but she seemed to have to do something to occupy her time, so the puzzles replaced the books. Theda turned around and watched as Marie quickly assembled the latest, a mountain scene. She smiled, wishing that she was just a little bit like Marie, content to just sit and do relaxing stuff, like reading or working on a puzzle. She turned back to keep her eye on the highway. She could never sit still or be quiet for even five minutes let alone a couple of hours to work on something as tedious or as stupid as a puzzle. She glanced back at Marie again and watched for a few minutes while piece after piece was made to fit together forming the center of the picture. Around and around Marie went, the tiny portion in the middle becoming more and more like a huge ball as each piece was added. Theda faced the front of the van and watched as real trees and rocks flew by the window. She thought about the puzzle for awhile and then she spun around and closely watched Marie work. Piece after piece notched together as Marie's flying fingers created the picture on the front of the box.

"Marie, I hate to interrupt, but you're half done that puzzle already and you only started it about half an hour ago."

Marie laughed as she continued to piece the puzzle together, "Oh, this is a small puzzle, only three hundred pieces. It's about the only size I can make in the van, the ones I like are too big for this space."

"I just noticed something else, most people pick out all the side pieces and put the sides together and then work on the puzzle from there, but you seemed to have started from the…"

"…middle? Yeah, I used to do the sides first, but that was too easy, so I look on the box and try to pick out the middle approximately and then work from there. It makes it a little more of a challenge."

"Jeez! Tell me, if you were going to do a puzzle of say, five hundred pieces and you did the edges first, how long would it take you to finish it?"

"I don't know exactly, probably about one and a half to two hours, I suppose. Why?"

"Hmmmm? Oh, nothing, I was just thinking, yeah, thinking," Theda raised her right eyebrow and smiled to herself. She glanced down at her watch and aloud she said, "Let me know when you're done, Marie, okay," and to herself she started muttering, *300 is to 500 as 2 is to x…no x is to 2, yeah, that's right, cancel the zeros.*

Three hours later Theda was driving through the small town of Blind River. Marie had long since finished her puzzle and had already taken it apart and put it back in its box.

"Look, mind if we stop in this little town? I just saw a decent looking bar back there!" yelled back Theda. "It's so damn hot, I'd love to stop and wet my whistle. There's a restaurant across from the bar, so if any of you don't want to come with me you can go in there instead."

"I don't mind stopping for a drink, but just one, okay. Edna doesn't drink, so she can be our designated driver when we leave, okay, Edna?" suggested Pat.

"Oh, I guess it won't kill me to come in with you girls since I don't have to order an alcoholic beverage," replied Edna.

Theda hissed to herself, *Alcoholic beverage, good God. I can just hear her placing her order to the bartender, 'Ah, yes, sir, I believe I'll have an unalcoholic beverage.'*

Theda parked the van and everyone got out assuming various postures on the sidewalk in front of the van. There was much stretching and rolling of shoulders, some rocking of heads back and forth; all efforts to try to soothe sore inactive muscles.

Theda headed straight for the bar. Marie started walking down the street, "Pat, tell the rest I'll join them in a few minutes. Just going to see if this little department store down there has something I need. Actually, go ahead and order me a light beer. Any kind, it doesn't matter."

Pat nodded and entered the bar. It took a few minutes for her eyes to accustom themselves to the dark interior. She heard Theda before she saw her. A couple of old seedy looking characters were perched on the bar stools, and at another table, three men sat sprawled on their chairs, talking among themselves. Theda was conversing with a couple of locals sitting near their table. Pat heard Theda laugh, "No, sorry guys, can't make your party tonight. I'm afraid we're travelling on just as soon as we finish this one drink. Maybe another time." One of the fellows already had his arm around Theda's waist. Her arm was resting on his shoulder. "Good, here comes our drinks, gotta go, guys. Nice talking to you."

"Boy, it sure doesn't take you long, does it?" Edna sneered at Theda as she passed near her.

Theda pulled her chair out, sat down and fixed Edna with a long stare. "Listen, Miss Holier-Than-Thou, lay off. If you can't even talk to people when you're on a trip, what the hell's the sense of going on one?"

"Oh, never mind," answered Edna.

The three men at the first table were getting louder. It was obvious that they had already consumed more than their fair share of liquor. The biggest one kept tilting his chair onto the back rungs. One of the others kicked at the chair knocking the big fellow onto the floor. They all roared with laughter, even the one who had been tipped over. He managed to right his chair and plop his big behind back down on it. He reached over for his friend's cigarette that was smoldering in the ashtray. His friend whacked him on the back of the hand, "Listen, idiot, keep your hands off my stuff. Try that trick again, and next time I'll pin your goddamn hand to the top of this table with my knife."

"What? Your trusty fishing knife, Harley? That what you're gonna use? Big fisherman didn't even catch so much as a minnow this time." Harley had a tiny dark moustache that trailed down the corners of his mouth. His little pig eyes darted from his large barrel-chested friend, then over to the women's table. The third man had hardly moved through the whole episode. He just kept puffing quietly on his cigarette. Every time he inhaled, he would blow the smoke out his mouth jutting his bottom lip out so that he could inhale the smoke a second time through his nostrils.

"Ah, nobody caught anything this time, least of all you, Mister Mouth. You were the one who was gonna whup our asses and catch more than the two of us combined. That's what you said. Ain't no fish up here in these lakes any more. Used to be lots of fish in these lakes, but no more. Have to catch something else instead. Maybe we can get us some Canadian Pussy instead."

Pat looked over at their table in disgust. "Must be bloody Americans."

Edna bent her head, and kept it bent as if keeping it that way would prevent any nastiness from penetrating her head.

"Where ever they're from, they sure aren't very nice men," said Gwen.

Just then, Marie entered the bar carrying a parcel. Pat waved her over to their table. "Want the keys, to put that in the van?" she asked.

"Nope, it's okay, it's not heavy or anything. Just don't let me forget it here. Got a couple more puzzles." Just then the big one at the noisy table smacked his hand on the top of the table.

"What they call them up here, Canucks? Canuck Pussy." He turned and ogled Marie as she edged past their table. "Here, pussy, pussy, pussy, are you a Canuck pussy?" He stubbed his cigarette out in the ashtray and then dropped in into his drink. He leaned back on his chair again and half turned to the girls, "Excuse me ladies, meow." Laughing uproariously at himself, he leaned forward, picked up his glass and took a deep drink, then suddenly stopped and spit out the cigarette stub." His two comrades, who had each just taken a drink, laughed spraying booze all over the table and each other.

"Aw, shit. I need a new drink, bartender!" Big One took out a wad of bills from his side pocket. Theda was quick to notice he peeled off five one-hundreds before he came to a twenty.

"What royal assholes!" Theda commented to her friends. Then she quickly turned and smiled at Big One, "Where you from, sweetheart?" He smiled back and returned his money to his pocket.

"Arkansas, pretty lady."

"Ain't no fish in Arkansas? You gotta come all the way up north here to catch our fish?"

"What you mean your fish? The United States owns over half of Canada already and in a few years it will probably own the other half, so the way I see it, that makes them my fish. We've been coming up here every year now for over fifteen years. Probably know more about this territory than you sweet things. But listen, girls I don't want to argue with you. How would you like to join us at our table?"

"I don't think so, we're not stopping long. You guys have a good day though, nice meeting you all." Theda leaned over the table and winked at Pat, "Did you see the wad he was carrying?" Then rather loudly, so that the fellows at the next table could hear, she added "What's that? No, I'm not kidding. Marie can so put a five-hundred piece puzzle together in two hours."

Pat reluctantly played the game, "I don't believe you. Nobody can put that big a puzzle together in that little time, nobody! Have another drink, Theda."

"Well, she can and that's that. I saw her do it once."

"When did you see her do it? Come on tell me, when?"

"I don't remember exactly when, but I just did."

Unknowingly, Gwen got into the act. "I think it would be next to impossible to do that. Really, Theda."

Theda felt a none to gentle jab at her shoulder, she turned, it was Big One, "Couldn't help hearinover, honey, but you're 'sagerating jist a little. Ya shouldn't do that."

"No, I'm not fooling. This is my friend right here and I bet you a hundred bucks she can do it."

One of Big One's friends snickered. "Aw, Smitty, go ahead, bet her, take a chance. Far as I can see it, you can't lose or are you SQUAWK, SQUAWK!" He tucked his hands under his armpits and flapped his arms.

Big One frowned, put down his drink, got up and walked the two steps to the women's table. Pat looked up at him. Suddenly, he looked very big and didn't look all that drunk any more. Theda started talking softly to herself, "God, I hope he isn't one of those guys who's just all wind and whistle, and appears more drunk than he is."

Big One staggered a couple of steps backwards then cocking his head to the side said, "Why dun't we make it two 'undred 'stead, maki' more trestin'?"

Theda breathed a sigh of relief, "Two hundred? Oh, that's quite a bit of money. Gosh, I don't know."

"Theda, what are you doing? Don't be an idiot. I don't know if I can do a puzzle in that amount of time or not," Marie was shaking her head. She pulled Pat by the arm, "Pat, stop her, please. This is getting out of hand."

"What's the matter sweetheart," one of Big One's partners, the one that wasn't Harley, asked Theda, "you chickening out?"

"Oh, all right, it's just that two hundred is such a lot of money. I don't even know if I have that much cash on me. Let me check." She pulled out her wallet and fingered the two twenty dollar bills she had, "I guess you're in luck, I just happen to have two hundred. Okay, it's a bet then."

Big One smiled, "Just let me reach into my pocket here and I will extract my roll of currency. Then I think that the proper thing to do would be to let the bartender hold both our monies. Agreed, sweetheart?"

Theda looked at Pat, then she leaned towards her, "How the hell did he get sober so fast? I think I smell a bit of a con here, but two can play at that game. Pat, I need two hundred dollars. I only have two twenties in my wallet."

Pat whispered back, "Well, you're out of luck. You're not using our money to place bets with. We need it for more important things."

"Give me the goddamn two hundred dollars. If you don't, I warn you, you're going to see shit fly like you never seen it before. That big bugger isn't fooling around. Fork it over now!"

"Theda, I don't think we should do this, what if I can't do it?" said Marie.

"You can. I know you can. I've watched you in the van and you're really good at putting puzzles together, exceptionally good. I don't know how you do it, but I trust that you can. Please Marie, just try, and if you can't and we lose the money, I'll pay you all back. What do you say? Please, Marie."

Marie nodded, "Okay, I'll try."

"Oh, boy, this is against my better judgment, and I'm warning you, Theda, this had better be the last time something like this happens, is that understood," warned Pat.

"Okay, okay, I promise, now give me the money."

Pat peeled off two hundred-dollar bills and handed them to Theda who turned and smiled at the three men. "Here's my money, gentlemen, but first, we have to have a few ground rules. First of all, we have to pick out a puzzle for Marie to do. She has a couple of them right here in this bag she could use." She lifted Marie's bag in the air.

"Let me see those," demanded Big One. After inspecting the boxes on all sides, he looked at Theda. "These are only three-hundred piece puzzles. You said she could do a five-hundred piece puzzle. Besides, how do we know she hasn't done these puzzles before."

"Look at the boxes, they haven't even been opened. Anyway, you're right, I did say five-hundred. Okay, this is what we're going to do. You go over to that department store, the one where Marie bought these puzzles, and you pick out a five-hundred-piece puzzle and bring it back here. And make sure that you don't open it."

"Any one we want?"

"Any one you want. 'Way you go, guys. We'll be waiting for you."

A narrow ray of bright light lit up the interior of the bar as the threesome left the bar by the front door.

Theda jumped up and ran over to Marie's table. "Marie, what do you need, anything special? You've got your glasses, good. Bartender, could we get a little better light over at this table, 'cause it's pretty dark in here?" asked Theda.

"Oh, I'm so nervous. What if Marie can't do it?" Gwen caught her breath before she continued, "I think that money was our gas money, wasn't it? Oh, dear."

The bartender came out from behind the bar, "Listen, I have a desk back here off to the side, it's got a good light, and I'll clean some of my stuff off. Your friend can do her work there if she wants."

"Great, thanks, buddy. Come on, Marie. Ah! Here comes the Mighty Trio back. Find a puzzle, fellows?"

"Oh, yes! We found a puzzle. Here it is. Five-hundred pieces and it's a doozie. Here you go little lady, *Sentinel of Stormy Seas*. It says here on the outside, *relative difficulty*. Whatever the hell that means, relative to what, a six-year-old, a blind person?" Big One handed the box to Theda. "Check it, it ain't been opened or anything. Just the way we bought it."

Theda turned the box over and inspected the tape around the bottom. It didn't look as if it had been tampered with. "Oh, my God, what kind of a picture is this anyway? It's all blues and greys, practically the same colour all over. How do you expect a person to do this in two days, let alone two hours? Look at this, Marie, it's horrible!"

"You're the one who said we could pick out any picture we wanted. Okay, everyone, let's synchronize our watches with the bartender."

"Fine," said Theda decidedly. "Marie's going to sit at that desk over there in the corner. That way, we won't bother her. Now, Marie, sweetie, can I get you anything, something to drink, something to nibble on?"

"Oh, yeah, like I'm going to have time to nibble!"

"Okay, so, are you ready? One of us will come around every half-hour and check to see how you're doing. Do your best." Theda patted Marie on her right shoulder, "Good luck, kiddo."

Marie could see the clock over the bar from where she sat. It read two o'clock. She picked up the box and stared at the picture on it. It was a picture of a grey lighthouse set on grey rocks being dashed by huge, cruel, greyish blue waves. The sky was a mass of swirling grey clouds. Marie smiled to herself.

The rest of the two groups made their way over to their respective tables and sat down. Gwen was facing the corner where Marie and her puzzle were ensconced. "What's she doing, Gwen, can you see her?"

"She just seems to be sitting there staring at the top of that box. She's not sorting or anything."

"Seems like your friend has hit a road block, ladies, wanna go help her?" laughed Big One's pal.

Theda snorted back at him, "Just wait, she'll get going in a second and then, watch out!" She waved her hand in the air, "Could we have another round of drinks here, please?"

Edna looked at her coldly, "I thought you were just having one drink."

"Aw, put a cork in it!" Theda retorted. "Gwen, Gwen, you can see her, what's she doing now?"

"She's still just looking at the top of the box."

"Oh God, oh God.... Marie, come on, honey, let's move, time's awasting."

Marie finally moved the box top to the side of the table and started to sort the puzzle. Side pieces made one pile and all the other pieces were sorted into several different piles. There was no hesitation as each piece was picked up, and then tossed to its respective pile. Hands flew back and forth like someone with a magic paintbrush dipping into this colour of paint and then that colour, creating a masterpiece on canvas. Not once in the next hour, did she look up or acknowledge her surroundings.

The hands of Theda's watch pointed to three o'clock. She

approached Marie, "Marie, do you need anything? Are you thirsty? How you doing? Tired?"

Marie didn't even look up from her work, "Leave me alone."

Theda made her way back to the table. "What did she say?" asked Pat.

"Told me to bugger off," laughed Theda, "not in so many words, but that's what she meant."

"You notice she never looks back at the box top while she's doing the puzzle. When I do a puzzle, I'm always looking at the picture to try to match a particular piece. How's she making out?" inquired Pat of Theda.

"Actually, not too bad. The sides are all finished, and everything else seems to be sorted now. I don't know what the hell she's sorting. All the pieces look the same to me, one freaking bluish grey mess of the same bloody blue colour. She's starting to put the various sections together. That's a good sign, don't you think?"

"Maybe the reason Marie doesn't refer back to the picture is because our girl has a bit of a photographic memory," thought Gwen out loud.

"Do you think? Maybe you're right. She is very clever, but I just thought it was 'cause she always has her nose in a book. I'm getting hungry, what time is it?"

"It's three-thirty. There's a plate of hamburgers and fries back at our table if you want them. Edna, what about you, want something to eat?"

Edna didn't reply to Pat's question. She was busy, both hands clasped in front of her, eyes tightly closed. She rocked back and forth in prayer. *Oh, God, she doesn't have much time left. I probably shouldn't be praying for something like this, but, oh never mind, just help Marie, please. I'm sorry I said never mind.*

Theda looked at her watch again – three-fifty – then over at the men's table. Big One winked, "Yo, ladies, it's almost four o'clock, getting worried yet?"

Theda stuck her tongue out at him, and then turned back to her friends, "Two hundred dollars, gone, just like that. Look, she still has one pile of pieces left. There's no way she can finish on time now. Shit, shit, shit!"

Marie stopped for a few seconds as she pulled her hair back with her hands and refastened a section that kept flopping across her eyes. Then she rolled her shoulders back and forth a few times, took a deep breath and went back to work.

Pat sniffed, "All that money, Theda. I mean it, if you ever, ever get us in a situation like this again, I'll personally murder you with my own two hands."

The bar clock showed three-fifty-eight. "Well, guess we might as well admit defeat. Can't be sore los..."

"Fit, you bugger, fit!" The whole room resounded to Marie's mighty whack as she hit the top of the puzzle with the flat of her hand. "I'm done, I'm done!"

Everyone in the bar rushed over to Marie's desk. There it was – *Sentinel of the Stormy Seas* – in all its blue and grey glory. Theda turned and hugged Big One and planted a kiss on his bushy cheek. "Oh, I'm sorry, I didn't mean to...oh, what the hell." And she kissed him again.

"Put 'er there, Pat!" She jumped up and double high-fived Pat.

Edna was pumping her clasped hands up and down in front of her. Gwen had the hint of a smile on one side of her face. Marie got up from the desk, walked past the groups of people to the door of the bar, opened it, took a big gulp of fresh air and then went outside.

Minutes later, the women were all back in the van with Edna in the driver's seat. Theda was fanning the bundle of bills. Suddenly, she whipped a twenty from the pack. "Don't worry, girls, this is my twenty. I'll be right back, just wait."

Theda strode up to the bartender, "Bud, a round of drinks for our fishermen. Keep the change. Oh, and tell them it's from the Canuck Pussies."

Edna backed the van out of its parking spot, drove down

to the end of the main street where she came to a complete stop at the highway, then expertly eased the van out onto the road. Theda looked over at Marie, “Holy crap Marie, you sure came through for us back there. What’s with you anyway, you have a photographic memory or something?”

“No, I don’t think so. It’s just when I look at something I can remember it.”

“Isn’t that what a photographic memory is?”

“I don’t think so, not really. I can’t just glance at something quickly and remember it exactly. I have to study it for a bit, but once I know it, I’ll remember it forever.”

“Is that why you sat staring at the picture of the puzzle so long?”

“Yes.” Marie yawned and stretched.

“One more thing, and then I’ll let you rest. When you sorted all those little piles, what were you doing?”

“Well, each puzzle piece has a distinct pattern that creates the colour running through it. That’s how you know it belongs where it does. I don’t try to solve a puzzle by looking at the shapes of the pieces, just the colours or those distinct patterns that run and blend into each other to create a picture.”

“Whatever, I don’t quite understand it. But when we get to the coast, you and I are going to hit one of the casinos. With your memory, lady, just think what we could do at Blackjack!”

“Forget it. That’s cheating.”

“You did it with the puzzle, so what’s the difference?”

“Well, with the puzzle, I was pretty sure that I could do it, but it wasn’t an absolute certainty. So there was still a chance to be taken by all parties concerned. But in cards, if you can remember all the cards that have gone, the other guy doesn’t have the same chance you do. That’s cheating since you’re not taking a chance on chance, so I won’t do it. Now, please, let me sleep for a few minutes.”

Chapter Eight

Louise picked up Gary's letter. Yesterday, the mailman had delivered one piece of her son's mail to her house by mistake so she would just run over right now and give it to him before he left for work.

Louise found Gary outside tidying up the inside of his car. She handed him the letter, talked to him briefly and then went into his house by the back door. Sarah, Gary's wife, worked four days a week. Today was one of her working days, so she was busy getting ready for work. Louise sighed when she saw the kitchen. No one had taken the time to clean his or her mess up from the morning breakfast. Oh, well, that's what she was here for, so she busied herself tidying the dishes. As she put the milk back into the refrigerator, she heard the front door slam. Louise thought to herself: *must be Sarah leaving for work.* Gary would have driven the car out to the front of the house by this time. She'll catch a ride with him. The kids had already left for school a half hour ago, so she was alone in the house. She quickly wiped the table and counter, rinsed the dishrag under the kitchen faucet, folded the rag neatly and draped it over the middle of the two sinks. As she was leaving Gary's house, she noticed the pink petunias that she had brought over yesterday for Sarah. They were wilting badly in the morning sun. By late afternoon, they would probably be dead. She found a little shovel and planted the sad little plants along the edge of the small vegetable garden. Then she turned the hose on gently and watered them generously.

After she finished watering, she wound the green plastic hose back up neatly onto its holder on the side of the garage and then hustled on home to make Gary the apple pie she had promised him.

As soon as Louise got home she checked her phone for messages. One, from the lady across the street, could wait. She probably just wanted her to come over for a coffee that morning. Another, from an old acquaintance who phoned once in awhile to visit, could wait, too. She was too busy today. She had to run out to the store after the pie was made. No, she could dash to the store as soon as she put the pie in the oven. She wouldn't be long. She had noticed that Sarah didn't have much butter left, so she would pick her up a pound, and might as well get her an extra loaf of bread.

Gary and Sarah were going out tonight to a card party at a friend's house. Louise had offered to babysit. Even though Paul and Sarah Jr. were twelve and thirteen, respectively, and quite old enough to fend for themselves, she enjoyed spending time with them. The kids usually spent most of the evening watching television. The odd time, Sarah gabbed to a friend on the phone. Louise wasn't into *Much Music* or the *Simpsons*, so she would find something to clean while the kids did their thing. Tonight would be a good night to tidy the bathrooms. There were two, the main one upstairs and a little powder room on the ground floor. By the time she did that and the kids had the snack that she had prepared it would be bed for them. Then she would cozy up with a blanket and watch a couple of shows until Gary and Sarah came home.

There weren't many shows that she enjoyed watching any more; most of them were full of shootings, swearing and car chases, not to mention all the sex they showed on the screen now. All the others seemed to be about either the supernatural or aliens of one sort or the other. Maybe if she was lucky there would be an old *Murder She Wrote* episode that she could watch.

Let's see, better check that I have enough flour. Louise had promised Sarah a pan of nice cinnamon buns for her bridge party tomorrow. She had phoned Sarah at work to ask her if she thought the buns would be too sticky to eat while they played cards. Sarah assured her that it was all right since no one ate until after the card games were finished.

Louise opened the top of the fridge and pulled out some hamburger, and then quickly checked to see that she had the rest of the ingredients for spaghetti sauce. Paul and Gary loved spaghetti, especially when the noodles were dripping with Louise's special sauce that she made from scratch. She would invite the family down for it tomorrow night. The phone rang. Louise picked it up, "Hello."

"You sound chipper this morning. It's Kate. Listen, I won't keep you long, just wanted to tell you that the Mansons are coming to town this weekend, and I know you and Mel used to be good friends of theirs before they left for Toronto. Thought maybe you'd like to join us for supper Saturday night. I wanted to have it Sunday, but they want to leave early in the morning to beat the traffic back. Tried to talk them into staying an extra day because they could go back Monday instead. The traffic wouldn't be bad then. Neither of them are working any more, so what's a day here or there. Oh well, whatever, that's their business. It will be nice to see them anyway, even if it's just for a short time."

"Oh, thank you, Kate, but I think Sarah and Gary have something planned for that day. I really am sorry. It would have been nice to see the Mansons."

"That's too bad. I'm sorry you won't be able to make it. Perhaps another time. Don't want to keep you; must run myself, bye."

Louise gently replaced the receiver, peeked at her watch then noticed the pile of mail that still needed attending to sitting on the counter where she had left it. She picked up the first piece that didn't look like a bill, stuck her finger in the corner of the envelope and ripped it open. *Oh, this looks like a wedding invitation. Let's see. Yes, the Petersons' daughter. Don't know why they even bother having a wedding since, goodness, she's been living with that guy Percy for almost ten years now.* It didn't bother her at all that the couple lived together without the benefit of matrimony. It was that when they did decide to get married, they made such a big fuss over the huge wedding. The expensive white dress, bridesmaids, the whole kit and caboodle. Nowadays, it wasn't uncommon for the couple's children to be part of the wedding party. These weren't children from previous marriages, these were the couple's children. Janice Peterson, Louise thought, was a lovely girl, hardly a girl any more. She must be thirty some, but the boyfriend was as creepy as they come. She couldn't for the life of her see what Janice saw in him. Oh, well, different strokes for different folks. *Have to check with Gary and Sarah, see if they received an invite too, if they didn't, I won't bother going.*

Louise pushed the mail aside, jumped up, and before long she had whipped a pie together. She threw it in the oven, grabbed her purse and took off for the grocery store. As soon as she came home, she checked the pie. The top was golden brown with thick steamy juice bubbling out of the cuts she had made in the crust. It was done, so she took it out and placed it on top of the stove to cool. She took her thick oven mitts off and tucked them back into the bottom drawer of her kitchen cupboard, then closed the drawer with her foot. She turned back to her few bags of groceries and started to put them away. She had just stacked the last two items – a can of corn and one of mushrooms – in her cupboard when she happened to glance at the time. *Heavens, I'd better get going, it's almost 12:15!* She quickly tested the top of the pie with the tip of her finger. She wanted it to be just the right temperature when she took it over to Gary. He liked his apple pie to be just hot enough to slowly melt a scoop of vanilla ice cream when it was plopped on top of it. He would be home for lunch at 12:20. Usually he got home at exactly 12:05, but when she had delivered the mail in the morning he had told her it would be later today because he had to drive someone else home first.

Louise set the warm pie on top of a tea towel and, while holding the pie, slipped off her slippers and tucked her feet into a pair of old scuffed penny loafers sitting on the rug by the door. She leaned over to push the door open with her elbow when she remembered, *Oh, darn, have to get the bread and butter.* Fortunately, the bread and butter were in a bag so all she had to do was slip one of her middle fingers in the grocery bag and lift it up. It could dangle under the pie. Finally she managed to release the catch on the door, pushed it open with her thigh and slipped outside, gently shoving her bum against the door to shut it. She walked the half a block to Gary's house. His car was already in the driveway. *That's nice,* she thought, *I'll get to visit with my son a bit while he eats his lunch. It's good that he can come home for lunch, gives him a nice break away from the office.*

Louise, carefully balancing the pie in one hand, softly hummed as she made her way to the back door of Gary's house. Just as she passed under the open kitchen window, she happened to hear Gary say, "My mother wouldn't do that. You're just complaining again, what's new?" She paused for a few moments, embarrassed to be eavesdropping on her son and daughter-in-law's conversation.

"What's new you ask? Well I'll tell you. Of course it isn't new, but your mother was here when I left for work this morning, as usual. Then I had hardly settled into work at the office and she phoned me there to make sure that I knew she would babysit the kids tonight. Gary, I've tried I don't know how many times to tell her in as nice a way as I can that the kids are old enough to look after themselves."

"What does it hurt if she comes here to be with the kids?"

"The kids don't even want her here. They want to be by themselves once in awhile. After all, they're kids. When she comes, she's always cleaning up one of our rooms. She makes me feel like we're slobs or something. To tell you the truth, I'm even sick of all the food she keeps bringing over. Doesn't she think I can cook anything by myself?"

Gary took another bite of his sandwich. "Why don't you just sit her down and talk to her about it?"

"Oh, sure, talk to that woman about anything. She's so set in her ways. There's only one way to do anything, one way to make a salad, one way to make a bed…" Sarah sounded exasperated.

"Okay Sarah, look, do you want me to talk to her?"

"If I thought it would do any good, I'd say yes. I sometimes wish she would just leave us alone for a few days. Even a few hours would be a treat. I shouldn't say it, but sometimes I wish that she'd have gone with the rest of those crazy old broads when they took off on their trip, give us a few days peace at least."

"I think you're being a little harsh. She is pretty good to us you know, Sarah, and she probably gets lonesome in that house all by herself, especially now with all her friends away."

"It's not my fault all her friends took off on her. Oh, Gary, I don't want to be cruel to her, I know she means well. I love your mom. I just don't know what to do."

"Well, we'll talk about this later when we have more time. I've got to run now, see you tonight." Gary plunked a sandwichy kiss on Sarah's lips and dashed off to brush his teeth.

"We can't tonight," Sarah yelled after him, " we have cards at Wilsons'."

Gary entered the kitchen from the little bathroom, toothbrush in his mouth, "Well, we won't be gone all night. Perhaps after." he mumbled, then dashed back into the bathroom.

Gary came back into the kitchen, grabbed his jacket and flung it over his shoulders. He opened the back door and stepped onto the back step narrowly missing the fresh apple pie that had been left there. He walked straight to his car, as did Sarah. Neither of them noticed the pie.

Meanwhile, back at her home, Louise sat and looked at her phone. Suddenly, she picked up the receiver and with her right index finger started to punch in some numbers. She was trying to get a hold of Jason Daniels, Pat's son.

Every fifth travelling day, the women took turns calling home to a friend or relative. Any news about any of the group was given to that individual, who was then responsible for directing it to the appropriate person. The reason for these calls was to inform everyone of their present whereabouts, what they had done since the last contact and a brief outline of their approximate route for the next five days. If there was an emergency, God forbid, the police would be able to track them down in short order. This message board worked both ways, if anyone at home wanted to send a message to an individual woman he or she could do so at the same time. Pat was the first to call home to her son, using his *Call Me Card.* After talking for over half an hour, she placed the phone back in its cradle and walked back to the van and was met with a barrage of questions.

"What took you so long?"

"Any news from home?"

"Is everyone okay?"

Pat looked at everyone and held up her hands, "Whoa! Just a minute. First, everyone at home is fine. No one has died, and no one is even the least bit sick. Everyone is still very worried about us. In other words, as Jason put it, 'They still think you're crazier than a lake full of fall loons.' We do have one thing to be a little bit concerned about. You know that spare seat where we keep our basket of dirty laundry and soaps, well, I'm afraid we are going to have to find another place for them."

The women all looked at each other, then back to Pat. "What's the big deal? Have to have some place for the dirty clothes."

"We'll figure it out because at 3:45 tomorrow we pick up Louise."

"Louise!" everyone yelled in unison.

"Yes, isn't it great? She had left a message with Jason. He talked to her and the arrangements are that he will drive her into the city to catch a flight out tomorrow afternoon. She should be landing in Thunder Bay at 3:45. So, by my calculations, we should be able to make it to Thunder Bay by 12:30, have time to grab some lunch, then still lots of time to run out to the airport. We can pick her up, and still drive an hour or so before we set up camp for the night."

"I wonder what changed her mind, and why is Jason driving her into the city? What's wrong with her own family?" asked Marie.

"I can't believe it. Imagine Louise leaving her family, who'd uv thunk it?" added Theda.

"I don't know, and I don't care. It will just be great to have her here with us," giggled Gwen. "Louise is lots of fun, and

I really felt sorry that we had to go away without her in the first place. Hope she remembers to bring a sleeping bag."

"Oh, she found one. Her grandson left one at her house when he stayed over once. She doubts that he will miss it. Jason said she said to tell us that she's got a little surprise for us."

The next day, at approximately 4:30, the brown van, holding six occupants instead of five made its way along the Trans-Canada Highway. The comfortable, cozy atmosphere inside the van, due mainly to the six good friends' reunion was complemented by the mouth-watering aroma of Louise's sticky cinnamon buns. The same buns that had been slated for Sarah's bridge party.

"Louise, these buns are so fresh. They absolutely melt in your mouth. When did you make these, this morning?" asked Marie jokingly.

"Actually, yes, the dough sat out all night on top of the fridge, and I made them this morning before Jason came to get me. I gave him some to take home to his family and we got the rest."

"Louise, you old shit, tell us what changed your mind about coming with us?" Theda took another bite of her bun, "I'm sure glad you did."

"Oh, my family finally persuaded me that it was time I did something for myself for a change," smiled Louise.

Chapter Nine

Pat put her hand over her mouth to stifle a yawn. Louise, sitting beside her, saw her out of the corner of her eye, "Pat you look tired. If you want, I'll drive for awhile."

"I forgot that we gained an extra driver when you joined ship, Louise. Sure, that sounds good, just let me pull over to the side here and then you can take over."

"Another hour and we should be in Manitoba," piped up Marie, who was busy flipping through the pages of a *Rand McNally Road Atlas.*

An hour later, the van crossed the border from Ontario into Manitoba. Marie was leaning back in her seat, with her eyes closed. Pat was busy putting a new film in her camera. She had basically become the group's photographer. With both a camcorder and a still camera, she managed to record the women's progress from the start of the trip up until the present time. Her intention was on her return from the trip to compile the photos and video pictures into a tape of the journey. She wanted to present a copy to each of the women as a Christmas present. Theda was passing around gum, "Gum, anyone?" Suddenly a loud police siren wailed behind them.

Louise looked up in the rear-view mirror and pulled over to the side of the road in front of a sign that said "East Braintree."

"What are you doing?" asked Gwen.

"That police car behind me wants me to pull over."

"How do you know?"

"Uh… his siren is going, that's why."

"Oh, pooh," said Gwen.

A young moustached officer approached the driver's side of the vehicle. Louise looked and felt for the switch to open the window. The officer stood for several seconds waiting with his right hand posed over his gun holster. He tapped a couple of times on the window. Louise looked up at him. He signed for her to roll down her window.

"Louise, you have to use that crank on the door there. This is an old beast, not one of your modern streamlined beauties," instructed Pat.

Louise finally managed to lower the window and she smiled up at the policeman. "Hello, officer."

"Ma'am, you were going twenty kilometres over the speed limit. May I see your driver's licence and car registration? Is this your vehicle?"

"Just a minute. It's in my purse." Louise opened her purse and started to search for her licence. "I know it's here. Pat, hold this stuff for me." She passed several articles over to Pat and continued her search. It seemed to take an eternity. The police officer started to show his impatience.

"Perhaps, ma'am, you would like to give me your licence."

"I'm looking for it. It's here. Just a minute, there's one more place. I'm almost at the bottom, aha, here it is!" Louise triumphantly held up her licence.

"Just give it to me," the officer demanded, "and then I still need the registration. Also, you didn't answer my question, is this your vehicle?"

"Registration, registration, okay, we'll just have to start over again," Louise started to rummage through her purse again.

"Louise, it won't be in your purse. It's in the glove compartment. Here, just a minute, I'll get it for you." She reached over, popped open the glove compartment, removed the registration from a black booklet, and handed it to Louise, who in turn gave it to the officer.

"Okay, ma'am, I see you're from Ontario. How much further do you intend on travelling?"

"I don't know, as far as this baby will take us, and then back, or until we run out of money," Louise said, grinning up at the serious young man.

"This car is registered under another name, can you explain this?"

"Well, of course, the car is my friend Pat's. This is Pat."

The officer leaned down and looked through the window at Pat, "Is this true, ma'am?"

Pat looked back at him and stated matter of factually, "Yes, yes it is."

"All right, look, I'm going to let you go this time, since you're a guest in our province. What I suggest is, use your cruise control. If you set it about five kilometres over the speed limit nobody will stop you. Okay?"

"Well, thank you officer, that's very kind of you."

"Fine then, ladies," he tipped his hat ever so slightly, "have a nice time, and drive carefully. You want this baby to get you home in one piece," he said as he patted the hood of the van.

Louise quickly stashed all her belongings back into her purse and then fastened her seat belt. She carefully signaled, glanced up into the rear-view mirror and pulled out onto the highway. The officer pulled out right behind her. Louise drove carefully, making regular checks in her mirror for the police car behind her. Pat started to talk to her and it wasn't long before she had completely forgotten about him.

"Louise, you didn't get around to telling us how your family is. Gary, Sarah and the kids. Okay?"

"Yes, yes, they're all fine."

"Good. You can be honest with me, Louise, did anything happen to change your mind about joining us?"

"Nope," Louise said, tongue-in-cheek, "no, just guess the spirit finally hit me. You know, wanderlust, something like that."

Pat looked at her friend doubtfully, "Okay."

Suddenly, the siren sounded again. Again, Louise pulled over to the side of the road. The police officer strode to the door.

"Ma'am, you were speeding again! I thought I told you to set your cruise control."

"I'm sorry, but this car doesn't seem to have any cruise. I was looking for it when you started yelling at me. I must have sped up unconsciously when I was trying to find the control."

"I never yelled at you!"

"No, you're right. You didn't, but your siren digamahoofie did."

The officer stepped back, looking at the van. "What year is this vehicle?"

"Year?" Pat tried to think. "I don't know. It should say on the registration." She took the registration out of the glove compartment and looked at it again. "Here it is, '82, that could explain why there's no cruise."

The officer took a deep breath, "Forget about the cruise control, but you must pay attention to your speedometer and to the speed limits posted on the side of the road. I'm going to forget about this again because I don't want to spoil your trip. Please, don't make me have to stop you again."

"No, no, you won't have to, that's for sure."

Again Louise pulled out, and again the officer followed close behind her.

Theda glanced back at the police car trailing them, "God, wouldn't you just die to be thirty or forty years younger? These young cops nowadays look so darn good in their smart little uniforms, their cute little moustaches and cute little asses."

"I don't know how you can possibly see their asses since they're covered with so much gear from around their waists. Guns, flashlights, writing pads, handcuffs, and a few other things I don't even know what they're for," laughed Pat.

"I remember once," laughed Theda, "I must have been close to twenty years old and there was this cute cop who came to town. So I took my dad's car out to where the cop was sitting in his patrol car and I drove up and down that street five or six times trying to get him to notice me. Nothing. So finally, I went about twenty kilometres over the speed limit. I thought for sure he would come after me. He didn't, but a couple of blocks down the street his partner did. Old Stewart McRoy. Remember him, girls, old goat with the triple chin, and a belly the size of a pregnant cow?"

"Do you think they all just seem young because we're just that much older now, or are they really as young as they seem?" queried Gwen.

"A little bit of both, I'm afraid," suggested Marie.

Louise peeked up at her rear view mirror, "Gee, I wish he'd pass us or something." She glanced down at the console, "Pat, I hate to say this, but I don't think the speedometer is working. When I press down on the gas, the needle doesn't move at all, look!" Louise pressed her foot down making the van lurch forward.

Pat undid her seat belt and leaned forward to check the indicator. "What are you talking about?"

"Look, I'll show you, now watch." Louise pressed the gas pedal down farther. The siren sounded again. This time it seemed louder than ever.

Louise pulled over to the side of the road this time. The police officer pulled up in front of her. He got out of his car and purposely strode back to the driver's side of the van. Louise, by this time used to the procedure, already had the window rolled down, her driver's license and the car registration clasped in her left hand. "Do you know how fast you were going?" he demanded.

"No, officer, I don't, you see…"

"I'm sorry, but I'm going to have to ticket you this time lady, not just for speeding, but also for not wearing a seat belt while the vehicle is in motion."

Louise looked at the officer in disbelief, "I had my seat belt on all the time!"

"Not you, lady, your friend took hers off. See she's not wearing one now."

"We're not moving now, so she doesn't need to have her seat belt on when we're not moving."

Pat leaned as far over Louise as she could, "Excuse me, but before you start to write up that ticket, could I just explain something to you?"

"Certainly, go ahead."

"Well, you see my friend had just informed me that she didn't think the speedometer was working properly and she was just demonstrating that it wasn't. Working that is. The only way that I could see the figures on the speedometer was to lean over, and the seat belt prevented me from doing that. As soon as I looked at the speedometer, I was going to move right back into my seat again and do up my seat belt. I NEVER sit or drive in a car without my seat belt."

Gwen piped up from the back of the van, "Yes, and if you were out catching real crooks instead of harassing us by driving behind us all the time, you wouldn't have caught us speeding and we wouldn't be having any of these problems right now!"

Pat covered her eyes, with her hands, "Oh, Gwen, please, not now." She turned and put her finger in front of her lip to shush Gwen.

The officer opened the door to the van. He put one polished boot up on the step, "Ma'am," he addressed Louise, "would you move into another seat, please. I'm going to take this van for a little ride, and see if we can find out what the trouble is."

He sat in the driver's seat and tried to adjust the seat to his height. The seat wouldn't budge. Pat looked at him and grinned, "Sorry, there's stuff right behind the seat. It won't go back any further. Afraid, you'll just have to make do."

He glanced back at Louise and then over at Pat. "Hope you two were telling me the truth."

Pat crossed her fingers and muttered a silent prayer, "Please don't work, please." She had just realized that the gauge that Louise thought was the speedometer wasn't the speedometer at all.

The van pulled out onto the highway and the officer quickly accelerated by pressing firmly on the gas pedal. Pat looked out of the corner of her eye to see what the speedometer gauge was doing. She opened her eyes wide and moved closer to get a better view. The gauge hadn't budged. The officer glanced down at the gauge and pushed his foot down farther. The gauge arrow fluttered slightly, but didn't move. Suddenly, he applied the brakes, and after looking both ways did a U turn in the middle of the highway, drove back past his own car, did another U-ey and parked a few feet behind the police car.

"Okay, ladies, you do seem to have a little problem here. What I want you to do is get it fixed. Any gas station should be able to help you. It's probably just a loose cable. It shouldn't cost much to get it fixed and it shouldn't take a mechanic very long to do it. Even if they don't have a mechanic, one of their service men should be able to do it."

The officer got up from the seat, turned to Pat, "If you can drive, and have a licence, I suggest you take over the wheel for awhile. I think your friend is just a little over anxious right now. It will give her a chance to settle down."

Pat moved over to the vacated driver's seat. Louise moved to Pat's seat. They both made quite a production out of buckling their seat belts. When they were finished they looked up and smiled at the officer. He acknowledged them with a nod and a pat on the hood again. Then he walked back to his car, got in and this time immediately drove off.

"Oh, sure," Louise said disgustedly, "now that you're driving, he takes off. Be careful, Pat, he's probably camouflaged in that stand of trees up ahead, or when you least expect it he'll come roaring out from behind that big sign over there. I think what he did was very close to harassment, don't you?"

Pat laughed, and stepped on the gas. The gauge raised steadily upwards, a little more pressure and the gauge raised accordingly. Smiling, she looked upwards and whispered, "Thank you!"

Chapter Ten

Parked in front of a huge sign in Dauphin, Manitoba, advertising a festival, Gwen turned to Pat and asked, "I've never been to a Ukrainian Festival before, what do you do there?"

"Actually, I've never been to one either, but from what I've heard, they're supposed to be fun. There's lots of good food and dancing. I don't know what else. I suppose what you'd do at any festival, sit around a bit and talk and visit with people."

After Pat parked the van outside the festival grounds, she and her friends pushed their way through several huge throngs of noisy people. Slowly, they managed to make their way over to the huge fairground. The party-like atmosphere buzzed with activity. Rows and rows of booths, each packed with delicious looking foods or interesting colourful crafts lined the narrow aisles. Delectable smells wafted over the grounds. There was steaming hot *varennyky*, little dumplings stuffed with potatoes and cheese that you could dip into dollops of rich sour cream. This was followed by roasting pans full of mouth-watering *holubtsi* (cabbage rolls). There was also all kinds of fish mixed with sliced raw onions. If you wanted just a snack to tide you over until supper, kettles of *yachminna zupa* (barley soup) or dark pink *borscht* sat bubbling gently on Coleman stoves. *Nalysnyky* (rolled pancakes filled with fruit or meat) or toasty brown onion rolls tempted you as you wandered among the booths. At the end of the walkway tables were piled high with sweets to die for: tortes, honey cakes, puff pastries of every shape and size. Louise walked along behind the others licking her lips and smiling as her eyes danced with anticipated pleasure as she eyed all the delicacies around her.

They kept walking, past a gypsy fortune teller. “I didn’t know Ukrainians were gypsies,” said Gwen.

“I don’t think they were or are,” replied Pat

“Well, what’s with that fortune teller?”

“I suppose we’re just surmising that she’s a gypsy fortune-teller. I’m sure you have fortune tellers in every race or group of people. I know my grandmother used to talk about this old lady back in Ireland. I don’t think she was a gypsy, but she could see the future. Everybody in the village used to go to her for advice.”

“Oh, listen, there’s a band of some kind over there.” Gwen, who was short, strained her neck up and stood on her tiptoes to see over the crowd. “And oh, look at the dancers. How pretty the girls look in their outfits. Let’s try to get closer.”

The women pushed their way through the crowd to watch as several young male Ukrainian dancers spun out onto stage. They were immediately followed by a long line of nimble-footed young girls wearing white blouses trimmed with bright red, black and yellow embroidery. Colourful garlands of flowers perched on their heads like hats and streams of multi-coloured ribbons flowed and swirled around their shoulders. Several of the men, wearing high, red leather boots and white puffy sleeved shirts, also covered with intricate embroidery around the collar and down the front of the shirt, stepped and twirled to the beat of the music. Their *shumka* or waist sashes flowed with their young vibrant bodies. The girls took quick, dainty, synchronized steps while the boys performed a more vigorous form of the dance that entailed high leaps in the air. Their arms and legs sailed through the air as they performed the intricate twists and turns before finally ending up on their haunches where they balanced on one foot while the other foot extended straight out, then they quickly changed feet in mid-air. The dancers smiled, white teeth flashing as they quickly moved their feet rapidly back and forth. The dancers and most of the audience clapped enthusiastically; a black moustached musician swayed rhythmically to his unrestrained accordion music.

Pat leaned over to an older gentleman who was clapping

to the beat of the music. "This dance that these boys are doing, is there a special name for it?"

The old man looked at her, ran his fingers over his pepper and salt moustache and smiled. "What they are doing, that is called *prysidy*."

Pat tried to repeat the name. As she did so, two of the young men separated from the main group, their twirling bodies doing cartwheels in mid-air. At no time did their hands touch the ground. The old man poked Pat in the ribs. "Ah, see. There they do the *kruzhlauchi pidskoky na odnu nohu*. I told you. I could also do that when I was young. Long time ago, I was young. I was very good at this. Now, you watch, they do the *viterec*."

Pat laughed as the same two men grasped each other by the arms and, as one man's legs flew up into the air, the other's remained on the ground. Just as the flying man's feet touched the ground, the other man's legs flew up in the air. They propelled themselves around and around the stage as the audience cheered and clapped its encouragement.

When the dancing ended and the clapping had subsided, Pat turned to thank the old man. "Thank you so much…"

Before she could finish her sentence, the old gentleman grabbed her in a bear hug and planted a big slobbery kiss on the side of her cheek. "You say, *diakuyu*. That means, thank you!"

As soon as he released her, Pat stood trying to catch both her balance and her breath, "Ah, die a you what?"

"*Diakuyu*."

"Oh, *diakuyu*."

"Good, good, you make good Ukrainian. Now I say, you are most welcome, pretty lady and please have rest of day a wonderful time."

"Thank you, oh, I mean, *diakuyu*."

"You are most welcome and maybe *do pobachennia*. That means see you again."

The crowd soon broke up and Pat looked around for some of her friends. Most of the people that had been watching the dancing were making their way over to the food tables.

Theda, who was bouncing up and down so she could see over some of the heads, finally spotted Marie, "Marie, over here. Where's Pat?"

Pat could hear her so held up her arm as high as she could. "I'm here, guys."

Theda and Pat came up behind her and both shouted, "Boo! Come on lady, let's go push our way over to those tables. I'm starved."

"Sounds like a good idea. The sign, over by the door where we came in, said it was all you could eat for $10.00. Sounds like you can have anything on those tables, anything but the desserts. They're sold separately. Tea or coffee is also included with your meal. If you want a beer or soft drink, you have to pay extra. That's a pretty good deal." Pat pointed over to the edge of the crowd. "There's Gwen and Edna, but where's Louise?"

They all stood together searching in different directions for their lost friend. "I don't see her anywhere. Where could she have gotten to?" asked Gwen.

Just then, Louise popped out from under a large man's elbow. She was moving towards them with a plate in one hand and a beverage in the other. The plate was laden with a huge mound of food. There must have been twenty *varenyky* covered in sour cream, five or six cabbage rolls, a huge chunk of fried chicken, a large bun, a cabbage salad of sorts. The plate looked like a huge tower that could collapse or tip over at any moment. Louise was smiling from ear to ear. She smacked her lips as she came close to them. "Oh, you guys, hurry up, and go get some food. I'm going to buy some desserts when we leave so we can have them on our trip."

"Louise, it was so nice of you to get enough food for all of us. Where should we sit?" laughed Pat.

"Keep your miserable hands away from my food. Go get your own. There's are no tables left, so I'm just going over there where those benches are," Louise pointed with her head and nose, "that's where I'll be if you want to join me."

An hour later found the group completely and uncomfortably full, all of them except Louise who had gone back for seconds. Theda looked at her and shook her head, "Lady, you take one more bite and you're going to burst and I don't want to be around when it happens."

Gwen laughed, "It would be like that marshmallow man in that show the *Ghostbusters*, except we'd be all covered with cheese and cabbage roll stuff."

"Oh, yuck, not a good thought," said Pat.

Theda turned to the people sitting beside her and said straight-faced, "You'd better get ready to move because our friend is going to burst any minute and spray you with cheese and rice."

A pleasant looking young lady, with a hint of freckles across her pert little nose, looked at her seriously, "Pardon me?"

"My friend has eaten so much food, she's going to burst."

The lady laughed, and repeated this to her friend who in turn repeated it to an old lady sitting in a collapsible chair near them.

The old lady leaned forward and looking in the women's direction, grinned a toothless smile and said, "You eat. You eat lots. Grow up nice and fat. Men like you. You have good times, make lots nice babies, eat. Eat!"

Theda looked over at the old lady and laughed, "I think we're way past having any more babies."

Louise looked down at her empty plate, "Ohhh…and I bought all those lovely desserts. They looked too good to pass up. I couldn't possibly take another bite of anything."

"Put them in the cooler. There must still be a little ice in it. We can have some of them for breakfast," suggested Marie.

Louise started to drag her body in the direction of the cooler. Suddenly she stopped, heaved a big sigh and turned back to her friends. "The cooler is in the van, and the van is way out to hell and gone."

"Never mind, just set them down. We won't be that much longer. We'll take them when we leave. Now come on back here and sit down. I want to show you all something," offered Marie.

The women all gathered around Marie as she withdrew a package from a white plastic bag she had been carrying. "Look, how beautiful! They call them *pysanky*. They are supposed to be a symbol of rebirth. Aren't they pretty?" Marie held an elaborately decorated egg up to the sun. She handed it to Pat, who showed it to each woman and then handed it back to Marie to repack.

"They are beautiful. Someone has devoted a lot of time to make this lovely little creation. Hope they don't get broken before you get home."

Marie had no sooner repacked the fragile egg in its container when two young girls bounced past their group. One of them a slim, pretty little thing, anywhere from thirteen to fifteen, separated herself from her companion and leaned down and hugged the old lady. "Hi! Baba, how are you doing? Did you eat anything yet?" Then she turned to one of the other ladies, "Mom, Sue and I want to go over and watch a ball game over at the other side of town. Can we go?"

"It's a long way over there. How are you getting there?"

The girl smiled, "Oh, we have a way to get there. One of the guys from school has a car."

"I don't like the idea of you bumming around with a bunch of guys in a car all day, young lady."

"I won't be the only girl. Sue's going to be with me. Please, Mom."

"If you drive straight over there, get out of the car and watch the game in the stands."

"Okay, that's what we'll do, right Sue?"

The other girl smiled at the mother, "Oh, yes, definitely. That's what we'll do."

"Fine then, away you go. Oh, and make sure you're back here by seven tonight, understood."

The young girl hugged her mother, "Thanks Mom." As she turned to go her mother suddenly reached over and plucked a magazine from the back pocket of her daughter's jeans.

"Whoa! What's this?" asked the mother, flicking through the pages of the magazine.

The girl whirled around and made a grab for the magazine, "Hey! Give that back, that's mine."

"Just a minute, let me have a better look." The mother read the title out loud: *Titillate your Mate in Ten Easy Ways.* Hm, what else do we have here?"

The girl stood with both hands on her hips, "Are you going to give me that book back or not?"

The mother looked at her with steely eyes, "Not!"

"Moth-er," she emphasized the *'er* part of the word, "it isn't even my book. It's Sue's and she wants it back, don't you Sue?"

The mother turned to look at Sue, "Is that right? Is this your book?"

"Well, uh," stammered poor Sue, "yeah, I guess so. Yeah, it's my book."

"Okay, fine then, I'll just keep it for the rest of the day. And don't worry, I'll return it to your house later on, you know, when your mom's home. That okay?"

The daughter stamped her foot and turned, "Fine, come on, Sue, let's go."

As the two girls walked away, the mother started leafing through the magazine, "My God, they're only thirteen years old and just look at the trash they're reading already." She stopped at one page, whistled and turned the page sideways. "Oh, my, isn't this quite something. Talk about letting it all hang loose."

Her companion got up quickly and moved over to get a better view, "Don't keep it all to yourself, girl." She turned to Pat's group and laughed, "My sister always was the selfish one in the family." She playfully grabbed the magazine away from her sister and had a good look at the page in question. "Here, do you guys want to have a look?" She passed the magazine towards Pat.

All of Pat's friends moved to peek over her shoulder. All except Edna who sat with her arms folded with, as Theda called it, her prissy look painted on her face. The first comment came from Theda, "Oh, just look at all his bits and pieces!" Theda, catching Edna's look change from prissy to disgusted, handed the magazine to her, "Here, Edna, want a peek?"

Suddenly, the old lady, who was supposedly sound asleep, sat up straight as a ramrod. "*Chekai*! *Chekai*! I look for you, girl. Let you know if all right to see."

"Oh, Baba, I don't think you'd care to see this. Here, I'll put it away." One of her relatives took the book and tucked it into her large handbag.

The old lady moved forward slightly, holding her hand out, "Give! I look. Maybe you shouldn't look either. For me, it's okay. I old." She turned to Pat and Theda, "Older even than you. I get to look," she said authoritatively.

One of the girls handed the book to the old lady and as she was doing so she whispered to her sister, "Maybe she won't be able to see anything without her glasses."

The old woman grabbed the book, "I eighty-seven this year past. Nothing wrong with my eyes. I don't need glasses. Nothing wrong with my ears, either." She started to leaf through the magazine. Finally she came to the picture that the rest had been ogling. She held the picture up in front of her face. Then she turned it sideways and squinted at the picture of a young man laying on his side propped up on a pillow with nothing on but a pair of black socks and a black bow tie. His pride and joy flopped over his tanned thigh. "Oy! So, that what it look like. I never know, hm…"

Theda not being able to help herself started to giggle. The whole group started to laugh with her. Finally, one of the sisters looks at the old lady in disbelief, "Teta, you were married for over thirty years. You had five kids for God's sake! Surely you must have seen what a man has between his legs?"

The old lady rolled her lips over her gums, and started rocking, back and forth, "I know there something there. I thought it like big stick, go poke, poke." She looked at the picture again, "This not so great. What for everyone get so 'cited? Look like old chicken neck and gizzards I throw in the soup. Oy! Now, I glad I don't see it much. Humpf!"

"Teta, you haven't answered my question. You and Uncle Harry, I mean five children?"

"I never see it before. We live on farm till Harry die. We not have snap lights. Always, I in bed before Harry come. He blow out lamp, undress, get in bed. Never see it," Baba shook her head and continued, "So, that's what Harry had, oy!" She put her hands on both sides of her head and started to rock back and forth. "Oy!"

Edna frowned thoughtfully and then interjected "Don't feel badly, Baba. I must confess, that I've never seen one either."

"One what?" asked Gwen.

"You know, a winkel."

Theda looked at Edna and exclaimed, "A what? Do you mean a winkie? You mean you never saw a guy's dick. Edna, I don't believe it!"

"Well," said Edna defensively, "I never had any brothers to grow up around, never had any children, didn't date all that much, and certainly not guys that wanted to show off what they had."

"Didn't you ever watch movies?"

"Not that kind of movie, no, I didn't!"

"Well, Edna, maybe you should have. Weren't you the least bit inquisitive?" Theda persisted.

"No, not really," Edna shirked her shoulders. "It's never bothered me before. Really could care less."

Theda looked at Edna and shook her head. Then she turned to the others. "We have a virgin travelling with us ladies. It isn't Sister Edna at all. It's even better. It's Virgin Edna."

"Excuse me, Edna, but you were married. What were you doing in your spare time?" asked Pat gently.

Edna looked around at her friends. She appeared very embarrassed. "Yes, yes I was. Right after the wedding, Ed and I went to a hotel for our honeymoon. We did it then, but…" she looked down at her feet.

Theda prodded her further, "Did what? Come on Edna, you can say it."

Pat turned to Theda, "Leave her alone. Can't you see she doesn't want to talk about it?"

Edna looked appreciatively at Pat. Then she closed her eyes and continued. “We fornicated. All right, does that make you happy?”

“Fornicated?” Theda repeated in disbelief. The old lady swivelled her head on her old chicken neck and looked at Edna. “Oh, that nice. Harry and I try that one time, too. Lots of hard work.” Then she nodded her head up and down as she looked off into the distance.

One of the granddaughters patted the old lady on the shoulder. “Oh, Baba, you don’t even know what the word fornicating means.”

“What for you think I don’t know this word. I do. It when you make to get happy before you do it.”

Everyone looked at her puzzled. The old lady paid them no heed and kept right on talking to no one in particular. “We not have time for that number party thing you young people do now in bed. Work hard all day, too tired at night, want just to sleep.”

Theda looked at Pat, “Number party?” Then she turned to the old lady. “Teta, honey, what are you talking about?”

“You know, number one, two, three, four, then have fun.”

“One, two, three, four, have fun? Ah! I think I have it. She must mean foreplay!”

The old lady clapped her hands together, “Yes, yes, you know, Harry like that fast bunny, how you say, *Boom, boom, thank you lady.*”

Theda covered her mouth with her hand and whispered out the side to Marie, “What the hell is she talking about now?”

Marie laughed, “I think she means, *Whiz Bam, thank you, ma’am.*”

“Yes, that’s how you say, *Fizz Boom, thank you, lady.* Little bunny say that.” The old lady smiled a satisfied toothless grin at everyone, crossed her hands over her stomach and then closed her eyes.

One of the old lady’s granddaughters reached over and gently touched the old lady’s arm. “Baba, Baba, are you awake?” There was no answer.

Pat looked at the girl and asked, "Excuse me, but half the time, you call her Teta, and the rest of the time, you're calling her Baba. I don't understand."

The girl laughed and looked over at the old lady. "Baba is my grandmother, but she's Elena's aunt, hence, Teta."

"Okay, I think I have it now."

The girl touched Pat on the arm, "I know it's very confusing sometimes. Some of my aunts are almost the same age as I am. So I just call them by their first names. Then she turned to her aunt, "Elena, sweetheart, go get the *vyshniak* and there's some plastic glasses right next to it. Bring those, too."

Elena trotted off to the edge where a huge basket was tucked under a tree and returned shortly with her arms wrapped around a good-sized bottle. The plastic bag that held the glasses dangled from her teeth.

"Here you go, Sophie, just what the doctor ordered."

"Good, good. Quick, now pour half a glass for everyone, and some for our new friends, too." Sophie turned to Theda, "How many are you?"

"There are six of us. What is this, wine?"

"*Vyshniak*? It's cherry liqueur, very sweet. You won't want a lot." She turned back to Elena who was busy filling and lining the glasses up on the edge of a bench. "Here, everyone, help yourselves."

Marie moved forward and passed the glasses on to the others in her group.

"Hurry, Elena," Sophie whispered, "before Baba wakes up. You know what she's like. She'll want to drink the whole bottle all by herself."

As soon as the last glass was passed, Sophie stood up, "Good, everyone has a glass. Now remember this is a sipping drink, not to be chug-a-lugged." She raised her glass, "*Nazdorovla*!"

"To old friends and new," Theda clinked her glass against Elena's. To her dismay, her plastic glass cracked up the middle. The red liquid started to leak out all over her hand.

"Oh, I guess these plastic jobbies aren't made for clinking." Theda lifted her glass and let the liqueur drain directly into her mouth.

"Quick, Elena! Give her another glass, before it all leaks out."

Theda accepted the new glass and immediately poured the remaining liquid from her cracked one into it.

Sophie laughed, "Not to worry. We'll top your glass up for you again."

Theda smiled as she licked her lips, "I thank you and no more clinking."

"Yes, no more clinking. Here hold your glass steady while I pour you a little more."

Theda passed her glass over in front of the old lady and Sophie poured until the glass was almost full again. As Sophie tipped the bottle upright, Theda started to withdraw her glass, but before she could do it, the old woman opened her eyes and quick as a wink grabbed for the glass. "Oh, good, wadka! I want some wadka, too!"

Theda turned sideways pulling her glass away from the old woman's grasp, "Not my wadka, Gran, sorry!"

"Baba, Baba, *chekai*! I'll get you some. Elena, go. Get her some of Uncle Pete's *horilka*. Just a small glass." Sophie turned to Theda, "My husband's whiskey, hardly anyone drinks vodka any more, at least not around here."

Elena passed the old lady a glass. "Here, Teta."

"Oh, good! Good wadka!" The old lady lifted the glass to her lips, tipped it and the bright, yellowy-orange liquid disappeared quickly down her wrinkled old throat.

Two hours later, the women were all busy setting up their tents in a tidy little campground not far from where they had attended the festival. Gwen pushed one of the tent pegs into the ground with her foot. "Well, at least we don't have to get the stove going tonight, we all ate enough at that festival to last us a week."

Pat threw two sleeping bags into the tent and then sat

down on the nearest sitting place which happened to be an old log. "Did you put your goodies in the cooler, Louise, and was there any ice left?"

"Yes, to your first question and not much to your second, but it should last the night," replied Louise.

Theda smacked her lips. "I quite enjoyed those pretzelly things Sophie came up with at the end there."

Marie laughed, "*Krendel'*, you mean?"

"Yeah, yeah, whatever. How in God's green earth can you remember all those weird names?"

Edna returned from the public washrooms just then. She was putting her toothbrush and paste away. "I liked everything about today, but I think I enjoyed the dancing most of all."

Theda bent down to untie her running shoes, "I like the Ukrainian dancing all right, but one thing really bothers me. Did you ever notice in a lot of those ethnic dances the women really don't get to do very much? They just sort of join arms and prance around looking pretty with flowers stuck all over their hair, like little goody two-shoes. I think they should try some of that whipping around and a few of those jerky little leggie things the guys do when they're sitting on their haunches. I know all kinds of girls who could do that just as well as the men, if not better."

Marie closed the book she was trying to read, "Probably. Since the girls in the old days were only allowed to wear skirts, I don't think it would have looked too good if they had tried all those kicks and stuff with a skirt on, sort of a Ukrainian Can-Can. I don't think the old babas would have liked that too much."

Theda laughed, "Oy! I never thought of that, but you're probably right. I don't think the old Baba we met today would've cared one way or the other. What a card she was!"

"She certainly was a character. Did you see how she put that glass of whiskey away?" laughed Pat.

"I know. She did all right for an old dolly. Well, on that note, think I'll turn in," said Theda, yawning. She walked slowly towards her tent and when she reached it turned and yawned again, "Night all you people, see you in the morning."

Chapter Eleven

Louise's son, Gary, flicked the morning newspaper to straighten it. He spread it out on the table to the left of his bowl of cereal sitting directly in front of him. Eating with his right hand and using his left, he traced down the page to the corner where the lottery numbers were printed. He always used the same number year in and year out, so he didn't have to check his ticket stub. He chewed his Cheerios and made a disgruntled sound.

Sarah, who had been running back and forth from the fridge to the kitchen counter, making her lunch for work and trying to tidy up at the same time, knew by this sound that Gary's ticket had not been one of the lucky ones.

"Better luck next time, sweetie."

"Yeah, you know Dad, if you had all the money you've spent on those stupid lottery tickets, we could go on a trip or a vacation with it," spoke up Paul who had just tipped his cereal bowl up to his mouth to slurp up the last of the sugary milk.

"Paul, I want you and Sarah to finish tidying up this kitchen. I have to run now. There are cold cuts and buns in the fridge for your lunches, lots of fruit, too. Oh, and don't forget to make your beds," his mother reminded.

Paul sighed, "Sure, sure, what a pain! Wish Grandma was still here. We didn't have to make our beds then because she always did it for us."

"Your grandmother did too many things for you kids. It's time you learned to do for yourselves," replied his mother.

"Charlie's mother works, too, and she makes his bed for him. I don't see why you can't do ours, too." Paul plunked his bowl on the table and started to leave.

His mother smiled at him and signaled that the dish belonged in the dishwasher.

Sarah Jr., catching the last of this conversation as she entered the kitchen, spoke up, "Yeah, and Mel's cleaning lady does her's for her. I have a good idea. Now that Grandma is gone, why don't we get a cleaning lady? We can afford one with you working full-time, Mom."

Gary folded the newspaper, left it lying on the table, and stood up in front of his family. "You kids have had it too good for too long with Grandma around all the time picking up after you. I think you're on to something, Sarah," he affectionately patted young Sarah on the head.

"Really, Dad?" she looked up hopefully.

"Yes, I think we should get someone to clean the house. In fact, I think we should get two cleaning persons."

Sarah had begun to smell a rat, "What do you mean cleaning persons?"

Gary laughed, "Exactly that– two people, young people – in fact, two young people that are both standing in our kitchen right this minute."

Both Sarah Jr. and Paul groaned.

"I agree with your father. It's way past the time that you two learned to pitch in and help out around here. In fact, we're going to sit down tonight after supper and have a little discussion about this very thing." She turned to Gary, "Thank you, sweetheart."

"I can't. I have baseball practice right after supper," said Paul.

Sarah Jr. hastened to add, "And I can't either, I have to go over to Mel's tonight. She's taking math as a summer school course and I promised to help her."

Sarah looked at her two teenagers. "That's fine, but you won't be playing baseball all night, and you," she pointed directly at her daughter, "don't need to spend more than an hour with Mel. We're doing this tonight, I don't care if it takes us to midnight to figure this out, understood?"

Both children nodded. Paul picked up his cereal bowl, opened up the dishwasher and placed it in the bottom rack. "Boy, I wish Grandma was back. Why did she have to go with her stupid old friends on that dumb old trip?"

"First of all, Grandma deserves a chance to get away once in awhile, and secondly, I don't want you referring to her friends as old in that tone of voice. You make it sound like being old is the most horrible thing in the world to be. They are Grandma's friends and that's that."

"But, Mom, they are old and face it you two, you're old, too," Sarah Jr. retorted teasingly.

Sarah flashed a smile at her impish daughter, "You little bum, just wait until tonight. We're going to think of so many chores for you, you won't have any strength left to use that mouth of yours. And don't either of you forget this: you'll be old one day yourselves."

Paul laughed good naturedly, "Yeah, but not before you and Dad, Mom."

Sarah Jr. put her arm around her father's waist. "I miss Grandma. Don't you miss her at all, Daddy?"

Gary kissed the top of her head and pulled her closer, "Of course I do. I also think her being away has made everyone in this house a little more responsible and independent, which is good. We really took Grandma for granted. I certainly don't want her to stay away forever, but…"

"A few more weeks won't bother me, that's for sure," interrupted his wife.

"Aw, Mom, you don't mean that," cut in Paul. "You know what I miss most of all is Grandma's cooking. Nobody can cook like Grandma. No offence, Mom. Boy, what I wouldn't give for a plate of her spaghetti right about now."

"Paul, don't get me wrong, I know your Grandma does a lot of lovely things for us all, but I'm sorry, I just feel she does too much. Since she's been gone I feel like I can, I don't know, breathe easier. Like this is finally my house. I feel that I can do what I want without somebody telling me that I'm doing it wrong."

"I never heard Mom criticizing you about anything."

"She never actually criticized me in so many words. She didn't have to. I mean when somebody comes into your house when you're gone, makes your beds, cleans your bathrooms, and tidies the kitchen up for you, that in itself speaks volumes. Christ, she even waters my plants. Half the time, I don't even have to cook supper. When I get home from work, I open the fridge and there's a dish of something or other with directions on how to cook it. If she's not trying to tell me something, then I guess I don't know squat."

Gary shook his head, "Boy, I know people who would die for those services, and you're complaining about them."

Sarah's shoulders fell. "Oh, I don't mean to complain. I love your mom Gary, and I know she's very good to us. But I'm sorry, she's just around too much. She might as well live here."

Gary lashed back, "Well, she's not here now so you should be happy."

"Look, Gary, let's not fight over this. I really hope Louise is having a great time. We'll try to discuss this rationally tonight. Come on, kids, hurry up! Paul, don't forget your bed! Look, I've got to run. See you all tonight." Sarah grabbed her jacket from the back of a chair, picked up her car keys in one hand, her purse in the other, and flew out the back door.

Chapter Twelve

"My Lord, it's hot. I wish there was someplace where we could pull over and dive into a nice cold lake," declared Edna.

Theda gave Louise a poke, "Did you hear that? She said, Lord. I'd say that that's pretty darn close to taking the Lord's name in vain."

"On a day like today, you sure miss air conditioning. We're lucky this old clunker hasn't heated up on us," commented Pat.

"Even if there was a clump of trees someplace where we could park under or get out and sit in the shade for awhile," said Marie.

The temperature had soared to 32° Celsius by noon hour. There wasn't a cloud anywhere in the vast prairie sky. Every window in the van had been opened, but even the breeze created by the movement of the van felt hot as it wafted over the women's bodies. They were nearing Anerley, Saskatchewan.

"A nice cold beer, that's what we need," insisted Theda.

"Oh, you and your beer. What's wrong with lemonade or pop?" responded Edna.

"Nothing, but it's a well-known fact that a beer quenches your thirst better than pop any day. If you don't believe me, ask Marie. I'm sure she's read about it at some point or other," stated Theda.

"Pat, when are we going to get to your friend's place? Are you sure that she lives out here? For that matter are you sure anyone lives out here?" asked Gwen,

"All I see is kilometres and kilometres of roads, but hardly any houses."

"And the houses that you do see look abandoned."

"It shouldn't be long now. I was out here with Earl, oh, gosh, it must have been fifteen years ago. I remember we drove and drove, and then suddenly the road disappeared. Absolutely disappeared! Felt like we'd come to the end of the earth. Then we went just a little further and suddenly the road dipped way, way down, like a roller coaster track and it ran through this magnificent valley. And smack dab at the very bottom of this huge depression sat my friend's farm. Probably years ago that huge old hole was a gigantic lake that some big sucker of a glacier ground out of the rocks, but right now the poor old lake's almost dried up to nothing. This all used to be buffalo country. When we get down to the bottom of the valley you'll be able to see the old trails the buffalo wore around and around the hills as they grazed on the grass.

Pat had no sooner said this, then the road in front of them did disappear and before they could catch their breath the picturesque valley she had described unfolded in front of them. She pulled the van well over to the side of the road and turned the motor off. Everyone started to cough as the huge billows of dust stirred up by their tires engulfed the van and made its way through the open windows.

"Close the windows, quick!" yelled Pat. The cloud of dust soon swept past them settling on the grasses and low growing shrubs on the side of the road. It wasn't long before the dust cleared and they could appreciate the vista below them.

"There, isn't that pretty?" Pat said waving her hand in front of her. A long road, straight as an arrow, split the ancient lake bed in two and then went straight up the other side of the valley to disappear like a little ribbon into the seemingly endless prairie. Out of the little dips and hollows sprang countless trees, and tucked into one corner of the valley fairly close to the road, was a little house with a farmyard consisting of a large barn, a few granaries, and other buildings bunched together. The small bit of lake water on either side of the road appeared blue and dazzling in the hot sun.

"Oh, look, water!" Theda's tongue hung out.

"Don't get too excited. That's an alkaline lake, not the greatest to swim in. It won't hurt you, they say. Fran, my friend, said they used to go on all kinds of picnics when they were kids and everybody swam in it then. It just doesn't taste that great."

Pat sat for a minute, leaning over the steering wheel, looking out over the valley below. She soon straightened up and said, "Well, guess we'd better get rolling. That's Fran and Bob's place right down there."

Pat turned the van back on and pulled out into the road. The hill was huge and long. Pat lowered her speed considerably. They could hear the loose gravel hitting the side and under portions of the van. All along the edge of the road large, sharp rocks had been flung by the road grader. Pat stayed in the middle of the road to avoid these.

"Wow, wouldn't this be great to have a toboggan or sled here in the winter! Man, you could probably get enough speed up to almost make it all the way up the other side." Theda had rolled down the window on her side and the whole upper portion of her body hung out of it. As long as the van was moving, dust didn't pose a problem.

"At least the road is straight now. Years ago when my friend was growing up, it twirled and twisted its way back and forth around the hill until it reached the bottom. Those were the days of the old gear shifts. I remember her dad taking us out for a drive once. We were so frightened. That year there had been quite a spring run off and the water had washed a huge section of the road away. The farmers had laid big wooden railroad ties across the opening. They were just wide enough for your car to straddle them. I remember her parents made us get out of the car, walk across the ties to stand there and wait at the side of the road for the car. Then Fran's mom stood and directed Fran's dad across the wooden ties, moving her hand this way and that to show him which way his tires should be going. Then when he made it to the other side, he didn't even stop to pick us up. He just charged up that hill, twisting and turning, changing gears right and left until he made it to the top. When he did, that was our signal to start walking to the top. On a hot day it was quite a climb. There was another road that they could use instead of this one, but it tacked a lot more kilometres onto your destination. I think every farmer around had to do Suicide Hill as it was called way back then, at least once a year. It sort of had bragging rights attached to it. No one ever got killed on that horrible road, but it was still quite exciting. I remember when the adults said that they were going to go down Suicide Hill you just dreaded it, but at the same time absolutely relished the idea. It was a heck of a lot better than standing on a bridge waiting for a truck to run over you."

Theda had pulled herself back into the van and heard most of Pat's commentary. "Oh, man, that sounds neat. Wish I'd have been around then."

Pat looked at her friend, "Ah, Theda, you were around then, you just…weren't here then."

"Oh, guess you're right. Is this the turnoff to your friend's place?"

"Yes, siree, this be it. Soon be there." The van bumped over Texas gates.

"What kind of a stupid roadie thing is that?" demanded Theda. "Surely they could have made it a little smoother. Even that gravel that was on the road was better than that."

Marie laughed, "That's called a Texas gate. It's a gate with rows of metal bars laid along side each other. A vehicle can drive over it, but most animals won't try to walk on it. It feels unstable to them. That way the farmer keeps his animals in and doesn't have to hop in and out of his truck to open or close a gate all the time."

Pat drove the van up close to the rustic farmhouse scattering an assortment of ducks, chickens, and other birds that dashed and squawked in all directions trying to avoid the van wheels. Feathers flew in all directions. One big goose stood his ground, opened his wings wide, extended his long neck and hissed at the van. Seconds later two large dogs ran out from the side of the house and jumped up at both front doors of the van. The first on Pat's side was a huge black lab. Its big nose pressed hard against her window. It left a trail of gooey, slimy saliva that dripped down the glass. Pat looked at the creature head on. One of its eyes was the brightest blue, the other a bright grey. Each eye was gorgeous on its own, but together they represented quite an oddity. On the other side of the window was another large dog, part collie, part whatever. He was a hairy creature, light beige in colour with the biggest floppy ears any of them had ever seen. His black eyes reflected out of his long fur like two little shiny-black marbles. He kept moving back and forth in front of the car window. He reminded Pat of a huge mop someone was using to clean the window.

Theda laughed, "Feels like we're in a car wash. The only thing missing is the water."

"Don't worry, these dogs won't hurt you. They're just a little bit over exuberant."

Theda looked at the big mop, "And how do you know that for sure?"

"Fran has written me countless times and told me all about these fellows. Besides, I know Fran and Bob wouldn't keep a really dangerous animal on the place."

The barking and yapping continued when the women got out of the van. A short plump woman suddenly came bustling out of the porch clapping her hands, "Goliath, Beauty, sit! Behave yourselves."

The two rambunctious dogs immediately responded to their owner's command and dropped down to all fours. "Come on, you two, into the house. Give these people time to stretch their legs before you pounce all over them." She opened the porch door and the two dogs charged into the house. As soon as she closed the door, she turned back and ran towards Pat, enveloping her in a huge hug.

"Oh, Pat, it's so good to see you!"

"That goes double for me, lady. I knew you had dogs, Fran, but you didn't tell me that they were vicious guard dogs."

Fran laughed, "Guard dogs? These two? If an intruder came to rob us or murder us in our sleep, the worst these silly things would do is lick the villain to death."

Pat stepped back to get a better look at her old friend. Fran hadn't changed much. She wasn't any heavier than usual. She had always been a tad on the plump side. Maybe her hair was a bit greyer than the last time she had seen her. She still had that wonderful smile that could win anyone, friend or stranger, over in a few seconds. It pleased Pat to see that Fran still seemed to be that bubbly, vivacious girl she had known years ago.

"Gosh, Pat, you made it. I didn't believe it when you phoned and said that you'd be here this summer. I still can't believe it, but here you are. Did you have a good trip?"

Pat wanted to introduce Fran to her other friends, but Fran kept chattering away, "Is that the thing you came here in? What is it? Whatever, I'm sure it's lovely. We'll find a better place to park it later. Someplace where no one will see it. I'm just joking. Oh, Pat, it's so nice to see you."

Fran reached down and grabbed Pat's hand and then hugged her again. "Oh, Pat, it's just so good to see you. I just said that, didn't I? Isn't she lovely?" she asked Pat's friends.

Theda snorted and Pat slightly embarrassed, laughed.

"No, you can laugh, but she really is. Anyway, come in, come in. Listen, everybody, I'm Fran. I've known Pat forever, and any friend of Pat's is a friend of mine."

Fran held the door while Pat and her friends filed into the cozy house. As soon as everyone was in she came into the house and pulled the door closed behind her.

"Don't mind the dogs. They won't hurt you."

Fran had no sooner said this than the big black dog came over and thrust his nose deep into Theda's crotch. Theda jumped. "Oh! Thank you, I needed that," she laughed.

Fran grabbed the dog's collar and pulled him back. "Sorry, they don't have very good manners. Once they get to know you better they'll settle down."

"I think that fellow already knows me as well as I'd want anyone to know me," insisted Theda giving the big dog a stare. "Oh, my God, look at his eyes. He's got two different coloured eyes! No wonder you're such a weird-acting dog, you are weird."

Fran laughed, "That's the reason Bob bought him. We went to a sale of strange and unusual animals. You know, they sell snakes, iguanas, and exotic birds. Well, that's where we found this fellow. Bob thought he was beautiful, hence the name Beauty. The one with all the hair is Goliath."

As soon as Gwen entered the cozy little house, she walked over to a massive, comfortable looking old brown leather couch. She stood looking at it for a long time then sighed. Fran immediately came over and took Gwen by the arm. "Please, if you're tired, just flop yourself down on it and rest for awhile. I'm going to fix us some drinks. Everyone, make yourselves at home."

Gwen had no sooner plopped herself down in the couch when a cute little red and white kitten pounced on her stomach. Gwen felt the little creature light on her and she jumped slightly then squealed with delight when she saw what it was. "Oh, you dear sweet little thing!" She reached down and gently grabbed the kitten. It protested with a small meow. She rubbed the kitten gently under its soft little chin, and then pet its tiny head. Contentedly snuggling down in the crook of Gwen's arm it started to purr softly. Gwen looked at the kitten and then up at her friends and smiled radiantly. Pat had her camera in hand, so quickly snapped a photo of Gwen and the kitten. No sooner did the kitten settle down and another one poked its little black head out from around the corner. It took one look at all the newcomers, raised its little back and hissed before it ran back behind a large wooden box.

"Never mind them," said Fran. The house and barn are full of them. We had two sets of kittens born this year. One thing we don't have many of on this farm is mice.

Louise happened to glance out the back window near the kitchen. "Oh, look, on that shed there."

Everyone turned in time to see a shimmering greenish blue peacock strut across the roof of the shed. When it reached the edge it turned and spread its iridescent tail feathers down over the end of the roof causing everyone's mouth to drop open. Even Gwen abandoned her kitten and comfortable seat to get up to see the spectacle.

"Did you see that? Looked just like a model, strutting her stuff on a runway," said Louise.

Fran laughed at the women's enthusiasm. "Well, it was modelling all right, but it's not a she, it's a he. Come on, ladies there's lots of chairs in the kitchen and if you want something a bit more comfortable you can sit in here. Just make yourselves at home. We don't stand on ceremony out here."

Fran noticed several of the women start to take their shoes off near the door.

"No, no, don't take your shoes off. Please, I mean it. This is a farmhouse. We're always running in and out, and if we had to stop and put our shoes on and off every time we went outside, we'd never get anything done. The only time we take the shoes off is if it's a muddy day, or you're pretty sure you've stepped in turkey shit. We haven't had rain for over eighteen days, and as far as the turkey shit, well, we'll just hope you missed it this time."

"Fran, is it always this hot here?" asked Louise.

"No, not always, when you get out into the open more there's usually a nice breeze, but tucked down in this valley like we are, especially where this house is situated, we don't get much in the way of wind. Fortunately, the evenings usually cool down considerably. In fact lots of times, it can be as hot as this and by evening you have to throw on a sweater or jacket if you're going outside for any length of time. We always leave our windows wide open at night, and then close them as soon as we get up. Manage to trap some of the cool air inside the house for a few hours. By noon, the temperature on the inside equals that on the outside so you fling open the windows again, hoping to get a touch of a breeze. I have to keep the ones on the east side closed all the time, because of the dust that the traffic makes when it goes by on the road."

"It really is dusty out here. I'd forgotten just how dusty it can get. We all noticed it coming in off the highway. Good thing our van is brown. It hardly shows the dust at all," commented Pat.

"Well, we haven't had a drop of rain for such a long stretch, so I guess we can't expect much else. Speaking of vans, is that the same old van that you and Earl came out in eons ago?"

"One and the same," laughed Pat. "Charlie – you remember him – Earl's nephew twice or thrice removed, teacher at school. He and his class fixed it up and he told me it was roadworthy. So far it hasn't failed us. It's really quite a comfortable old thing, like an old shoe."

"Of course I remember Charlie, who wouldn't? Is he married yet? Such a cute little guy, but I digress. Before we do any more talking, what can I get everyone to drink? Pat, I know you and I will have a beer, anyone else? I can get you anything you want: pop, tea, coffee, iced tea, lemonade, a mixed drink. We've got gin, vodka, whiskey, scotch. I have wine too, but I'm saving that for supper."

Everyone named their pleasure and Fran turned to go out to the kitchen. Theda immediately bounced up and yelled after her, "I'll give you a hand, Fran." As soon as she started to follow Fran out to the kitchen the black dog got up to follow her.

Theda whipped around and gave the dog a wicked stare, "Don't even think of coming close to me, you mangy cur. See this," she pointed to her knee, "it's kneed better males than you, fellow."

The dog lay back down. A final heavy wheeze emanated from its body as it flopped back down onto the hard floor.

Fran laughed, "He listens to you better than he does me. Anyway, I'll be glad of some help, follow me."

Theda followed Fran into a cute little alcove off the kitchen. It was in this alcove that Fran did all her kitchen work.

While Fran and Theda were making and arranging drinks on a tray, Pat poked her head into the alcove. "Fran, do you still have all those Indian relics and old bones that you used to keep upstairs?"

"Sure do. Do you think your friends would want to look at them? I don't offer all the time, because you never know who is interested in that kind of stuff and I hate to bore people with it. If you think they'd enjoy, please take them up. You know the way. We'll bring the drinks upstairs."

Pat quickly returned to her friends, "Come on people, Fran said that I can take you up to show you Bob's and her collection."

"Collection? Collection of what, more animals?" asked Gwen.

"No, Gwen, not animals; well I shouldn't say that. There's probably a few old bones of animals up there." Pat opened the door that led up a long narrow staircase. "Careful, it's a little dark here, and speaking of animals, if you think you've seen animals now, wait. You ain't seen nothing, yet."

They reached the top of the creaking old staircase and stepped out into a bright spacious room. The focal point of the room was a huge open acorn fireplace. The chimney ran up into the ceiling, where some gifted carpenter had created an intricate pattern out of hundreds of pieces of pine. Built all around the fireplace and around the periphery of the room were glass-covered cabinets. Displayed inside the cabinets were Indian native artifacts, arrow-heads, stone and bone tools, scrapers, awls, tomahawks, broken cooking utensils, bison jaws, ancient pronghorn bones, and on and on it went. Each item had been carefully labelled. Large windows surrounded the outside of the room. Before the women got down to the serious business of studying each inscription on the artifacts, they stood and looked at the panoramic vista the large windows afforded them. Pat panned her camcorder through the windows, took a few close up shots of the artifacts and then changed to her still camera to snap a few of her friends.

As they took turns moving from window to window, they each marveled at the different view each window presented. Marie pointed outside, "What is that or was that old building down there, across the road?"

Pat walked over beside Marie and looked out, "Oh, that used to be a general store, years and years ago. Then later on someone turned it into a little museum. Now it's nothing but an old building, its tired old bones bleaching in the sun."

Marie shook her head, "Look, it even has hitching posts in front of it. We'll have to get some shots of that old place before we leave. Almost makes you feel like you're in the Wild Old West."

Someone else commented, "Look at the sky, and the clouds. That's one thing I've noticed here on the prairie—the sky. It's so big and so beautiful."

"Oh, look, down there in the barnyard. You should see all the animals walking around down there. There's thingies down there that I don't even know what they are. What do they run here anyway, a zoo?" Several cows and horses lounged under the shade of a row of maples. There were a few spruce trees in the small pasture with all their lower trunks rubbed bare of branches where the bigger animals had used them as scratching posts. Straight out and down the middle could be seen the long stretch of road that they had just travelled down. Rolling, soft hills framed the farm, protecting the pasture land from the strong winds that were part of prairie life.

Pat pointed over to the hills, "See all those dark things on the sides of the hills. I can't tell from here, but I bet they're buffalo."

"Do they still have buffalo out here?" asked Marie.

"Not wild ones. Fran and Bob raise them, along with llamas, which I know you'll all love. I hope they have had some baby ones. They are so cute," replied Pat. "Come on, let's take a look at some of the artifacts in these cabinets."

"Where did they get all these?" asked Marie, ever anxious to learn all she could.

Pat waved her hand to the windows, "Just out there, on their property, mostly up, on and near the hills. Remember I told you this used to be hunting grounds for the buffalo, so Indians probably camped around here every year just before the hunt. The place is filthy with deer, and probably was in the old days, too."

"This is really so interesting. Imagine, walking along on your own property and finding something like this." Marie pointed to a tomahawk head, "And then being able to pick up something, that someone, maybe someone who lived thousands of years ago, made or worked with. It must make you sort of feel at one with the universe. You know that we're all tied together somehow."

"You're getting too deep for me, Marie," commented Pat. "Ah, good, here are our drinks."

Fran and Theda entered the room. Fran carried a large tray, which held several glasses and a small dish of crackers and cheese. Theda had a bottle of beer with its cap still on tucked under her one arm and each hand held two others. Dangling from her pinky fingers, which were crooked into the handles were two large beer mugs. Fran started to pass the drinks to everyone, "Didn't know if you people are hungry or not. If you are, you can snack on these cheese and crackers. Hopefully this will hold you until supper. I've got a deer stew cooking in the crock pot."

"Oh, I'm sorry, I should have said something before, but we don't expect you to provide supper for us, Fran," Pat said apologetically. "We just wanted a place to pitch our tents for a couple of days, rest up a bit, and I wanted the girls to see your spread."

"Oh, don't be silly, it's only deer meat. It's free, sort of. I hope everyone likes it. I never used to be able to cook deer meat very well. I tried it every which way. Tried soaking it in salt water over night. Then I tried wrapping bacon over it and cooking it on a very low heat in the oven. Finally Bob showed me how his mom used to cook it, and it was good. Much better than my other feeble attempts," laughed Fran.

"I've never eaten deer meat, so this will be a first for me," admitted Edna.

"I'm not that fond of it, but I'll eat it, if that's all there is," said Marie.

"Oh, pooh, I hate it, had some one time that one of George's friends cooked up at their cottage one year. Ugh! It tastes so dry or wild or something. I'm sorry, I'll just fix myself a sandwich, even peanut better. Anything will be better than deer," added Gwen, shivering in distaste.

Fran ignored Gwen's bad manners and passed around the rest of the drinks. She handed Edna the last beer and mug from the tray. "Here's your beer. There, everyone have something to drink?"

Edna accepted the bottle in one hand and the frosty mug in the other. Then she stood and proceeded to look at both with equal distaste. Finally she spoke, "I, uh, I didn't ask for a beer. I don't drink anything alcoholic," she added emphatically, "ever!"

"Oh, come on Edna, just this one time. It won't hurt you. Besides it's already open. It will just go to waste if you don't drink it," volunteered Theda.

Edna insisted, "No, I don't want it. Besides, I'm sure it won't go to waste if you're around."

Theda glared at her, "Well, thank you, very much sweetheart," then added to the aside, "mealy-mouthed bitch!"

Fran jumped in to the rescue. "It's okay, really. It was my fault. I'll go down and get you something else. What would you like, Edna?"

Edna smiled at Fran and said, "A soft drink of any kind will be great. Just tell me where they are and I'll go and get it. You don't have to be running after us."

Fran smiled back at Edna appreciatively, "Okay, they're in the fridge. The little fridge on the porch. The rest of you come over here to this window. See that little place down there by that clump of trees? It's really quite pretty there. You can pitch your tent there tonight. I thought you'd rather be a little ways away from the house. That way, you'll get the full effect of the stars and the moon. The mosquitoes shouldn't be very bad. We haven't had any rain or moisture so they haven't had any place to hatch their eggs. You can drive your van right down to the trees. There's a little road, right where your van is now. Just turn right and you'll be on it. Maybe three or four of you could go set up your tents now, and the rest of us will throw the supper together."

"Pat, you stay and help Fran with supper, that way you two can do some catching up," Theda suggested.

"Thanks, I will."

Edna also decided to stay to help with the supper. The rest cheerily chattered themselves out the side door.

"I have some cold cuts and fresh home-baked buns here, too, for anyone who doesn't want to try the deer stew. I'm going to throw together a small salad. If either of you want another drink, help yourselves. I might warn you that I do have a magnum of wine on ice for supper."

"I think I've had enough, especially if we have some wine while we eat. What can we do for you, Fran?" volunteered Pat.

"Edna, you can rip up some lettuce, put it in this bowl, and chop a few of these vegetables up to throw in, too. I don't care how you do it. Just anyway at all, okay. And you Pat, drain those potatoes in the sink there, and there's milk in the fridge. Would you mash them for me? When you're done, you can put them in this bowl." Fran handed Pat a large brown bowl. It had yellow baby chicks painted all around the outside of a huge rim.

Pat took the bowl, turning it around in her hands to admire the paintings, "Ever cute!"

"A neighbour lady made those for me, right from scratch. She uses clay that she finds from around this district, molds the various articles, fires them in a kiln, paints them, glazes them and fires them again. A lot of work when you consider you can go and buy a Pyrex dish for nine dollars."

Fran reached over and grabbed Pat's hand. "Oh, Pat, it's so good to see you again. You look so good. You really do. Oh, we mustn't forget Edna. You look real good, too, Edna, even though I never saw you before and don't know if you ever looked better than you do now. Oh, silly me. Just ignore me, Edna. I do go on sometimes. Oh, good, the others have come back. I call that perfect timing."

Fran ran to the back door and opened it. "Bathroom is right here to the left. You can wash up if you want. Supper will be on the table by the time you finish."

Fran turned and went back into the kitchen to join Pat and Edna. She started to spoon the deer stew out of the crock pot into a huge bowl. As she did that, Pat filled the salad bowls and handed them to Edna who passed them on down the table. The hot steaming stew was placed in the middle of the table. Delicious onion and meat smells spread through the kitchen. "Some people like to eat their salad first. In this house we eat it with the meal, but you do whatever you want. Please, dig in."

Edna quickly bowed her head and said her own private grace. Everyone else at the table ignored her and started to serve themselves.

"Oh, this smells so good. I wasn't going to eat any, but think I'll try just one little piece," Gwen decided.

"Give me your plates, and I'll serve it for you, save everybody getting up," suggested Pat as she started to spoon a small piece of meat onto Gwen's plate.

"Just a minute, I want my potatoes first, and then you can put some of that gravy and meat on them."

"Yeah, Pat, let us get our potatoes first."

"This is delicious, are you sure it's deer meat?" asked Gwen. "I think maybe I'll have just a little more, please Pat."

"Oh, yes, I'm sure. It's deer meat, all right. I cook it really, really slow and the other secret is to put lots and lots of celery in with it. Something in the celery must break down or help tenderize the meat. Oh, I almost forgot, there's a loaf of fresh bread that I made this afternoon just before you folks came. Marie, it's right behind you. Would you grab it for me please and the knife, too, it's right beside it? Oh, I almost forgot the wine. I'll be right back. I put it in the deep freeze to chill."

After Fran retrieved the ice cold wine and when all the plates and glasses were full, Theda lifted her glass. "I'd like to propose a toast to our hostess. Thank her for the lovely meal, and here's to continuing friendship." She glanced sideways at Edna, "At least until after this trip."

"Hear, hear," was followed by the clinking of glasses.

Later that evening, after the kitchen had been cleaned, everyone sat outside. The sky was very dark and illuminated by millions of twinkling stars. The Big Dipper stood out brilliantly among all the other stars. Fran had been right. It seemed that the mosquitoes would not pose a threat that night. Even though the house felt like an oven, the outside air hinted at a coolness to come.

Fran tipped her chair back on its legs as she gazed around at the night sky. "Look at that, not even a hint of a cloud. Boy, I wish we'd get some rain. If it doesn't happen soon, it will be too late to do any good for this year." She let the chair fall back down, "Listen up, everyone, tomorrow you people can do whatever you want, but Bob…"

"Speaking of Bob, where is he anyway?" interrupted Pat.

"Oh, I forgot to tell you. He was helping one of our neighbours, who lives over across the valley closer to town, with their cattle today and Betty phoned just before you rolled in to say that she would feed him. He probably won't be home till elevenish or so. Anyway, as I was saying, tomorrow, Bob and I and another of our neighbours, Harold, have to go up to the west pasture and herd some cattle back into a closer pasture. The water supply has dried up where they've been grazing, so it's time to move them closer to the main farm buildings. After that's done, I'll be free to show you the rest of the farm, the animals and some of the countryside. Now, it's going to take us several hours to herd the cattle, and before we even think of doing that, we have to feed and water all the animals here. So here's the proposition. If you all help me with the watering and feeding, we'll get done faster and then we can drive out later and join the fellows. By the time we get out in the pasture, Bob and Harold should have worked the animals a couple of kilometres closer to the farm."

Pat looked around at the others, "Why not? Always wanted to be a farm hand."

Everyone else nodded assent, except Theda. "What time do we have to get up to do these chores?" she asked warily.

Fran laughed, "When the sun comes up."

Theda pressed on, "And just exactly when does the sun come up in this country?"

Fran mumbled, "About five thirty."

"Five thirty! Like early? That kind of five thirty?"

"I was just kidding, actually if we get up at six that will be okay."

"Well, that's more like it! Six sounds just so much better than five. Okay, we'll be up, won't we girls?"

"Yes, and since we have to get up so early, I think maybe

this old broad had better hit the sack and get some rest," said Marie.

Fran stood in the porch doorway waiting for Beauty to relieve himself against a lilac bush. She could see the battery operated lanterns flickering down where the tents were pitched. One went out as she watched and soon the other followed suit. She could hear a frog chorus drifting over from the shores of the lake. Then she heard Theda's voice, "Good night, Marie."

Marie replied, "Good night, Theda."

Someone else chimed in, "Good night, Gwen."

Theda giggled, "Good night, Pat."

"Shut up, Theda. Go to sleep."

"Party-poopers."

Morning found Marie and Pat taking turns working the barnyard's old creaky hand pump. As fast as they filled the large water trough, the other women emptied it. Pail after pail dipped into the metal trough, and pail after pail was drawn out and carried dripping to the separate animals' and birds' water containers. Fran wielded her own pail and only stopped long enough to issue orders to everyone else on who to water, how much and where.

Pat pushed down on the arm of the pump and signaled for Marie to take over.

"Here, it's your turn. Are we making any headway? They seem to be taking it out faster than we're filling it."

Pat, standing back to let Marie replace her, wiped the perspiration from her sweaty brow. She looked up at the cloudless sky. "Whew, already you can tell it's going to be another scorcher of a day. It's not even seven o'clock yet. What's it going to feel like by noon?"

Before the morning was over, they had been introduced to Harve, a miniature pot-bellied pig; a pair of massive water buffalo that plodded around a small pen throwing up dust with their hooves; two miniature donkeys that nonchalantly dipped their heads into their feed bags when Fran filled them with feed; and, with long necks extended and wings spread wide, several geese that chased and hissed at them when they came too close to their goslings.

They were almost finished feeding the animals in and around the barn, when Fran suddenly bent down and plunged her arm under one of the cow's feed troughs. "Aha, got you, this time! Thought you'd get away from me, didn't you?" She stood up with what appeared to be a rather large rodent cradled in her arms. "Pat, hand me those gloves over there. You'll have to put them on me one at a time because I don't want to drop this character."

Pat grabbed a pair of heavy leather gloves lying on an old wooden sleigh propped against the barn wall. "Here, this hand first. What is that thing? And why do you need gloves?" She struggled to get Fran's thumb into the glove. "This is worse than dressing a kid in winter. Push! There you go. Now, the other hand."

Fran gently stroked the creature's head. It was still shivering, but seemed to have quit trying to escape. "Okay, okay, calm down now. You're all right. That's a good fellow, now. This, ladies, is a silver fox. This one we raised since he was a baby. He'll calm down in a bit, but as soon as I let him go, he'll revert back to his wild state, which is good. Come on a little closer to get a better look. He's really rather pretty. Just don't try petting him or get your fingers too close. You're strangers to him, so any show of affection may be misconstrued as an attack. Normally he won't bite Bob or me if we handle him, but sometimes he nips a bit and he has very sharp little teeth and if he uses them it can be quite painful— hence the leather gloves. I took a chance grabbing him like that. Normally, I wouldn't do that, but it might be the only chance you'll have to see him."

The highlight of the morning was going to view the llamas. There were over thirty of them, from almost-newborns to full-grown creatures who strutted regally around the small pasture. Each stately animal sported a halter. A young chocolate brown llama attracted most of the attention.

"Isn't that just the richest colour you've ever seen? You almost feel like you could eat him. Looks like a great big giant Easter...llama. Oh! I could take you home with me," cooed Gwen.

The instant the women entered the llama enclosure, several of the creatures raised their heads as high as they could and peered down their noses at the intruders. They started to slowly walk over to the girls who were all bunched together by the gate. Several of the animals started to run. Louise grabbed Pat's arm. "Oh, my God, it's a llama stampede. We're going to be trampled!"

Everyone started screaming and backing away towards the gate. Fran laughed. Then she started to walk straight towards the ringleader, her right arm extended as high over her head as it would go. She yelled back to the women, "Just stand where you are. They won't hurt you. Put your hand up in the air, as high as it will go. What you want to do is try to get taller than the llama. That's your way of letting him know that you are the dominant one. Marie looked over at her friend Louise who was still clutching Pat's arm. Slowly, Louise let go and took a couple of steps forward. Then she raised her arm. A huge llama came up to her, and pushed at her head with his chest. Then a second llama came over to her, soon three of four more were making their way over to poor Louise, who stood stoically, arms raised high in the air. Unfortunately, she was so short and roly-poly that even with her arm raised she didn't seem much taller than she really was. Fran pushed her way up to Louise. The llamas backed away slightly. "We're going to have to get you a pail to stand on or something," laughed Fran.

Soon, the llamas and the women started to get used to each other. Everyone had to take a turn posing in front of or beside one of the llamas while Pat snapped photo after photo. Gwen approached Pat, "Pat, would you mind coming over there and getting a picture of that one over there by the fence? I want a real close-up of his face. He has the most gorgeous eyes."

Pat handed the camera to Gwen, "Here, you can use the camera. You take the picture."

"Oh, thanks." She took the camera from Pat and started to walk over to her subject. "Yes, you little sweetie, you have the prettiest eyes I've ever seen. Stand still, okay? I just want a pretty picture of you." She was only two or three yards from the llama when she yelled over to Fran, "Do you have names for all of them? What's this fellow's name?"

Fran looked at the llama, "Yes, we do, and that one is Herman and I wouldn't go too close to him, he sometimes…"

Gwen had already turned back to the llama, "Herman. That's a nice name." She lowered the camera to carry on the one-sided conversation. Just as she did, the llama turned his head and spat right in her face.

"Arghhhh! Did you see what he did? Arghhhh! Oh, pooh and double pooh!"

Fran laughed, "I was trying to tell you not to get too close to him. He's a spitter. They all will spit, but Herman's the worst one."

Everyone looked over at Gwen who was trying to wipe the glistening llama spit off her face. Suddenly, the llamas didn't seem quite as cute as they had when they were first introduced to them. From then on, the llamas were quickly fed, as were the huge ostriches and some smaller emus.

Fran lifted an ostrich egg from a pile of straw in the corner of the ostrich pen. Theda, who was right beside her, touched the egg gently with her pinky finger. "Just imagine if you wanted scrambled eggs for breakfast, all you'd need was one of these suckers and you'd probably feed everyone here. What do you do with the eggs, eat them?"

"Actually, we sell most of them to a couple who live in a little town not far from here. They drain them, she traces designs on them and her husband carves them with a miniature electric drill. The end result is a huge lacy egg. They're quite an attractive piece of art and they do very well selling them."

An hour later Fran, Marie and Pat sat in the cab of an old farm truck, bumping and jerking their way along one of the pasture trails. The other four were in the box of the truck, huddled as close to the cab as they could get. They were trying hopelessly to avoid some of the dust the truck wheels were throwing up into the air. Everyone was hanging on for dear life.

Fran suddenly pulled the truck off the beaten trail a few feet and stopped it.

"There's Bob and Harold over there to the left. We'll stop here and walk the rest of the way. Have to see where they want us. I don't want to create a big cloud of dust on this side of the cattle because it might spook them and they'll start running in the opposite direction. Come on everybody, let's go."

It wasn't that far a walk to join the men, but being close to noon it didn't take long for the walkers to feel the effects of the sun as it beat down on their backs.

Pat licked her lips and turned to Fran, "Did you bring anything to drink? I don't know whether I'm going to die of thirst or choke to death on this blasted dust." She coughed and spit out some of the grit caught in her teeth.

Fran looked at her, "Are you all right? There's water back in the truck. Make sure to remind me when we get back to it."

"Don't worry, I won't forget."

A stocky man and the dog Beauty came from behind the truck. All Pat could see of him were his eyes and the inside of his lips when he opened his mouth. The rest of him was covered in dust. He took his hat off and whacked it on his thigh causing greyish brown dust to fly all around him. He walked over to stand in front of Pat. Beauty bounded over beside him and started to sniff at her. The man quickly pushed him away with his knee.

"Down Beauty, get down! Patty, good to see you, girl! Oh, but you're looking good." He shook her hand first and then grabbed her in a big bear hug. Puffs of dust flew off his clothes as he lifted her off the ground and swung her around.

Once she was back on the ground, Pat laughed, "Well, Bob, I really can't tell whether you look good or not with all that dust on you. But your voice sounds good. Come over and meet my friends."

Bob strode over to the newcomers, "Hi, ladies. I'm Bob, Frannie's main squeeze. I didn't get a chance to meet you last night. By the time I got in off the fields you were all sawing logs."

An older man, accompanying Bob, sauntered up beside

him. "Oh, and this young man here, ladies, is our neighbour, Harold."

Harold doffed his hat, "Pleased to meet you all, ladies. Bob hasn't told me a thing about you. Just like him to save you all for himself."

The women all laughed. Fran put her arm around Harold's back, "One good thing about Harold is his eyes are both the same colour." She gave him an affectionate kiss on his dirty cheek.

Bob looked over at Harold, "That's about the only good thing you can say about him." Bob quickly side-stepped Harold's playful punch. "Harold is a straight grain farmer; doesn't have any livestock of his own, so likes to volunteer his help when we need it."

Harold grinned mischievously, "If the truth be known, these two wouldn't be able to survive if it wasn't for me."

Bob laughed, "You old bugger, you've eaten enough meals and drank enough beer at our place to more than pay for the paltry hours you've put in for us. All right, enough chit-chat, you ladies ready to earn your keep?"

Bob noticed that the several "We guess so's" were not too enthusiastic so he laughed and continued, "I want you two," he took Marie and Theda by the arms, "to stand on either side of this gate, and when the cattle come this way I want you to stop them from getting through said gate. *Comprenez*? I want them to turn left and go down towards the lake. Once they get there, there's fencing all the way to the pasture that we want them in. If you have a spare jacket or shirt, use that to wave around. If not, use your arms." He looked at the two women that he had picked and laughed reassuringly, "Don't look so frightened. There aren't that many of them, so it's not like there's going to be a huge stampede or anything."

He drew Fran slightly aside. "Frannie, I think maybe you had better stay here with these two. This is the only place the cattle can get out and if they do, we'll have hell to pay trying to get them back in here again."

Finished talking to Fran, Bob turned to the rest of the women and Harold. "Everybody else, into the truck. Come on, hustle your butts. Beauty! Up, boy, in the back of the truck. Now!" The big dog immediately turned, gathered himself and with one giant leap, landed in the back of the truck. He turned and looked at the humans on the ground below him, his big tongue hanging out, saliva dripping out the corners of his mouth as if to say, "I'm ready, come on you slow pokes, hurry up!"

There was much grunting and groaning as each person hoisted herself into the box of the truck, and even more as it bumped and jostled over the rough prairie pasture. Suddenly, Bob slammed on the brakes near a rather stately stand of huge elm trees. He waited a few seconds for the whirls of dust to settle and then rolled his window down. He poked his head out the window and yelled back to the women in the box, "I forgot that there is one other place that the cattle can get through. Highly unlikely, but just in case, one of you can go down in those trees there. The fence runs right through them and there is one small space that a cow could get through, so all you have to do is stand right in that space. If you're there, they won't try to push past you. I'll leave Beauty here with whoever stays. He'll be company for you. Who wants to go?"

Gwen started to climb over the box of the truck. "I'll go." Placing one foot on the bumper and holding on to the box of the truck, she used the wheel as a step to lower herself to the ground. She walked up to the front of the cab and pointed to the trees, "Those elms, where did they come from? They wouldn't be native to these parts, would they?"

Bob answered her, "No, probably one of the early homesteaders brought them with them from the East when he settled here.You'd be surprised how many elms there are in Saskatchewan. We're really fortunate that the Dutch Elm disease hasn't reached here, yet. Anyway, we shouldn't be more than fifteen minutes, so just get under the shade of those trees and watch for us to come over that hill there. You've got a few minutes, so relax."

Gwen looked at her watch, nodded to Bob and, as the truck pulled away, she walked over to the trees. Standing under the huge branches, she managed to peer up through them and caught a glimpse of the sun flashing through the canopy of leaves. Then she walked over and easily found the opening into the other pasture. Bob was right. It was very small, but she supposed that a calf or a determined cow could easily push its way through the opening. After strolling around under the trees for what she thought was fifteen minutes, she stopped and checked her watch.

Yes, fifteen minutes have gone by, she said to herself. She looked up at the hill, no cattle yet. She resumed her walking, and while she did so sang a couple songs from *The Sound of Music.* After that she sang a few more songs.

Oh, pooh, where the heck did they go? It's been a half an hour already. She started to think that maybe she should start walking back to the farmyard. Maybe they had changed their minds and had taken the cattle by a different route. But what if she left her post and they eventually did come this way, no one would be here to protect that opening. *Oh, goodness, it's hot.* Her clothes, wet with sweat, stuck to all parts of her body. She tried to pull them away from her skin to let some air reach it, but as soon as she let the cloth go, her body just seemed to suck it back like a huge suction cup. Gwen looked back up into the tree branches. Through the leaves of one of the huge elms, she noticed a lovely crook in one of the branches. She also noticed that the leaves farther up the tree were moving.

There must be a breeze of some kind up there. A person could sit on that branch and lean against the tree itself and at the same time have a pretty good vantage point. "You can probably see for kilometres from up there," she said. The problem was how to get up there. She looked at the ground around her and spotted two rather large branches that had fallen from the trees at some earlier time. She went over and pulled them both under the tree where the inviting crook was. She laid them against the trunk and started to climb them using the huge trunk to steady her. She laughed to herself.

Not too old, yet, to scramble up a tree. She was always good at climbing things when she was young. Once up on the huge branch, Gwen was glad that she had made the effort to climb the tree.

Oh, isn't this lovely! I was right, I can see to the end of the earth up here. I still don't see any cows, not even any dust anywhere. Where could they have got to? Gwen's panties kept travelling up the crack in her bum and her shirt clung to her skin. Her bra, which she hated at the best of times, kept digging into her shoulders. It felt unbearable. She slipped easily back down to the ground.

Maybe they just forgot about me, and where is that silly dog Bob said he was leaving to keep me company? Gwen started to take her perspiration-laden clothes off. One by one, she hung them on the wires of the nearby fence. Once she had stripped down to her birthday suit, she negotiated the climb back up into the tree. The second time was a little more difficult because, this time, there were bare things that hurt when they rubbed against the rough bark of the tree. Once she made it back up into the crook, she settled down and rested her back against the trunk of the tree.

This is nice. There was even a little offshoot of a branch where she could rest one of her legs. The other, she let dangle over the opposite side of the big branch. A soft little breeze caressed her naked body. She turned slightly and glanced down at her clothes hanging on the fence. She stifled a yawn and decided not to worry. As soon as she saw someone coming she could be down in a flash and get dressed before they even got near these trees. Gwen looked out across the prairie searching for the place where the sky met the earth, but she couldn't find that spot. The land seemed to go on forever, and the sky seemed the same way, as if the earth and the sky were one.

"Heavenly," she sighed. Everything seemed so clean, if you forgot about the dust. The one good thing about the dust, she thought, was when you saw it you knew that there was another living, breathing creature stirring it up. Yes, it smelled quite fresh up here and there was nothing, nothing except the noise of the odd insect and a gentle snoring as Gwen slept. Her clothes fluttered gently below her on the fence.

"I don't see her, you guys. This is the exact spot that we left her. Right under those elms over there," insisted Bob. Harold slowed the truck down and steered the truck closer to the stand of trees. Fran was sitting snugly in the front seat between the two men. The rest of the women were in the box of the truck. "You'd think Beauty would come out to greet us."

Fran looked at him questioningly, "Beauty! What are you talking about, Bob? Beauty's in the back of the truck with the girls."

"Oh, shit. I told Gwen that I would leave Beauty with her to keep her company, and then I must have forgotten. I hope she didn't start to walk back to the house. It's quite a distance for the old dolly."

Fran stuck her tongue out at him, "What do you mean, old dolly? She's only a couple years older than Pat and me."

Bob looked at her and smiled, "Exactly."

Fran gave him a sharp dig in the ribs. "Well, let's get out and look around, she's got to be somewhere around here."

"Who would have thunk that those beasts would have taken that high trail so easily?" Bob wondered, half to himself. "Every other year, they always turn off and come down here, always!"

When the truck came to a complete stop, Beauty was the first out. He ran straight for the trees. Everyone else followed. Grasshoppers sprang up, criss-crossing in front of each footstep.

"Well, looks like her clothes on the fence, so she's got to be around here someplace," commented Marie. "Oh! Oh! If her clothes are on the fence that means…"

"Gwen! Gwen, where are you?" hollered Pat.

Beauty stood with his front paws propped against the trunk of one of the big trees.

Gwen yawned, stretched and suddenly realized where she was. She sat up, swung her one leg over the big branch she was sitting on and peered down through the leaves at her friends on the ground. Everyone is here, how nice, even Fran's husband and their neighbour Harold somebody or other.

She waved at them, "Hi, everyone. It was so hot, and I got so tired. Guess I fell asleep for awhile." Gwen stretched, hands over her head arching her back as she did so.

Theda who was directly below the tree shook her head. “Oh, God! Gwen, get your ass down here right now. What do you think you’re doing, up that damn tree, with nothing on but your birthday suit?”

Gwen glanced down at her body, then down at Theda. “Oh, forgive me, but it was so hot. I thought I was going to die. There was a little breeze up here and my clothes were all wet, so I left them down there. I thought I could get down and into my clothes before anybody came. I didn’t count on falling asleep.”

Gwen turned and shimmied down the tree. Her bare bum and back were heavily imprinted with the bark of the branch that she had been sleeping on. Bob and Harold turned their backs to Gwen and smiled at each other.

Pat gathered Gwen’s clothes off the fence being careful not to snag them on the barbed wire. She handed them to her. “Here, lady, just carry your bra and panties, put them in your pockets or something. It’ll be faster that way. You can do a better job when you get back to the farm,” suggested Pat.

Gwen smiled at her and proceeded to struggle into her slightly damp clothing.

“One thing, I want to know, Gwen, did you spit when you were up there?” laughed Theda.

“Oh, pooh, no, I forgot. I’d better go back up and spit before I go.”

“Forget it. Move your butt into that truck, lady!” ordered Theda.

The next morning, with the van loaded, good-byes made, hugs and kisses all around, dogs and cats given a final pat or rub, the friends pulled out of Fran and Bob’s driveway. The van bumped over the gravely road, spewing dust out behind it. In less than a half-hour, they approached the paved main highway. Marie was jostling a map in front of her, trying to fold it so that only the immediate area that they were travelling in would show. “We must remember to stop off at the next decent place we see and grab a post card to drop Fran and Bob a little thank you note.

Gee, Pat, your friends are really super people. I enjoyed them. Hope we weren't too much bother."

Pat looked over at Marie, "Yeah, they are nice and I imagine they enjoyed our visit, too. They like to show off all their pets." Pat looked up into the rearview mirror and yelled back to Gwen, "Gwen, did you get all your clothes?"

Gwen rolled her eyes and smiled, "Yes, I did, but I didn't get to spit."

"Never mind, in a couple of days or less we'll be in the mountains. We'll find a good place for you to spit," reassured Theda.

Pat turned onto the highway. "Would anybody be against spending a night in a motel for a change? We've been travelling quite a while now. I could stand a decent bath and a real bed. I didn't want us filling the bathtub at Fran's because I know they don't have much spare water this year. What do you all think?"

"No objections from the back of the bus."

"Or the middle either. You're right, I think we deserve a treat," replied Edna, who was busy refilling her pill containers.

***

Gwen's daughter-in-law Karen came to the back door and yelled through the screen to her husband who had just stopped the lawnmower. He bent down to release the grass catcher that was attached to the back of it. "Phil, Jason just called. He'd just heard from the ladies. Thought you'd want to know that everything is going well. Your mom is fine and is enjoying herself."

Phil dumped the grass into a large garbage pail, then pulled off his gardening gloves and threw them down next to the lawnmower. He walked over to the steps leading to the door. Karen opened the door, "Phil, did you hear me, I said that Jor..."

"I heard you! I heard you, for cripes sake." Phil flopped down on the top step leading up to the little back porch.

Karen stepped out onto the porch, pushing the door closed behind her, and eased down beside him. "Want something to drink?"

"Nope, I'm fine, just taking a little break. So, that old bus is still in one piece. I still don't know what possessed that idiot Charlie to fix that old dilapidated van up for Pat. All he did was just encourage those old women. If it wasn't for him they never would have gone on this crazy trip. Now, the rest of us are the ones that have to sit and worry about them."

"Maybe. They're really having a great time, Phil."

"Yeah, sure. Mom's not in that great a shape as it is. At least when she's around here we can watch out for her."

"That last picture your mom sent of her at that festival outside Winnipeg was really cute. She looked pretty good. I didn't know your mom could even dance. I've never seen her do it around here. She hardly ever goes to any of the family weddings and if she does she usually just sits in a corner watching everyone."

"That's exactly what I mean. She shouldn't be doing anything too strenuous, like dancing. That's a heart attack just waiting to happen."

"Oh, well, she's gone now, and it's not like she's off travelling on her own someplace. She's with her friends and I'm sure they wouldn't let anything happen to her."

"You get back on that phone and talk to that Jason character. You tell him that the next time those old sods phone to give them a message. I want my mother home. Tell her I'll even send the money out for a ticket home. She can take the bus."

"Phil, maybe your mom is enjoying this. It's something different. She's never gone anywhere before. Besides what are you so concerned about? You hardly ever go over and visit with your mom when she's here. You don't even call her on the phone."

"Listen, you, I didn't ask for any comments from the Peanut Gallery, did I? This is my mother, not yours, and you don't know what the hell you're talking about anyway, so just keep quiet. Now go and make that call." Phil got up and strode back to the lawnmower, reattached the grass catcher and yanked viciously at the starter cord. The machine started on the first pull. Phil went back to mowing the lawn. His wife sighed and went back into the house.

Chapter Thirteen

The rodeo had been in progress for two days when the van and its occupants pulled into the campground near Medicine Hat, Alberta, early Saturday morning. Tents and trailers of every size and description lined the grassy field adjacent to the rodeo grounds. Before the weekend was done, every blade of grass would be trampled into oblivion. Truck and car wheels, people's shoes and horses' hooves would all contribute to its demise.

The only place the women could find to pitch their two tents was at the rear of the camping compound. Today was the last day for what Pat referred to as cowboy type events, and by late afternoon the championships would be determined. After setting up the tents and organizing their campsite, the friends set out to try and find a good vantage point to view the remaining events.

Theda and Marie soon split up from the rest and pushed their way into a large boisterous group of onlookers who were watching a bucking bronco event. Louise talked Edna into taking off to find a place to buy some food, and Pat and Gwen relaxed as they sauntered around enjoying the sights.

"Look, Gwen, there's some empty places up there in the bleachers. Let's move on over there and get those seats before someone else does."

Pat grabbed Gwen's arm and pulled her along. They excused themselves as they pushed their way through what seemed like thousands of denim knees. Finally they made it to the empty area. They both looked down in despair. Someone had been sick recently and had barfed all over the seats.

Gwen looked down at the disgusting mess, "Oh, pooh! Some poor person had a really bad tummy ache."

Pat looked at her, "Well, they shouldn't have one now, looks like they got rid of everything that was in it. Come on, let's go. God, I don't know how these people can even sit here that close. It stinks to high heaven. Quick, before I start to gag."

Once back on the ground, Pat looked around and spotted Theda in the stands. She had some stranger's huge cowboy hat on and every once in a while Pat would see her jump up in her seat, take the hat off and wave it around in the air. "Look, Gwen, there's Theda." She pointed up in the direction of the opposite stands. "She looks like she's having a good time."

Gwen laughed, "When does Theda not have a good time? Let's go over there, maybe there's some spare seats."

When they reached the bottom of the bleachers, Theda spotted them before they had a chance to even call up to her. She immediately started waving and yelling at them. "Hey! You guys, up here. Come on up."

She turned to her new friends and started to push them down the wooden seats, "Here come my friends, let's smunch over some more and make room for them? Here, Pat, Gwen, sit here. Pat and Gwen, I want you to meet Hilroy and Perkins. Hilroy is from England and Perkins lives on a farm a few kilometres from here."

Perkins, who didn't look a day over ninety, nodded over at Pat and Gwen. "A ranch, not a farm, I live on a ranch. I was a rancher, not a farmer."

Theda looked down her nose at him, "Well, I am sorry, truly. I didn't really know that there was a difference."

Perkins wiped his tongue around the inside of his mouth, "Quite a difference, quite."

Pat sat down beside the old gentleman, who really looked quite spiffy. His neck sported a fresh blue bandanna that accentuated his alert blue eyes. He had on a pair of worn but clean jeans, a rather sharp cream-coloured shirt with blue trim, scuffed but serviceable cowboy boots and on top of his wrinkled old head sat a grey Stetson with a tiny red feather tucked in the band.

"So, you're Perkins. The man with you, a friend of yours?" asked Pat.

"Nope," replied the old man.

"Oh, a relative?"

"Nope."

"Do you even know him?"

"Yep."

"Well, maybe it's none of my business, but who is he?"

"Yep."

"Yep, what?

"Yep, it's none of your business."

Pat looked a bit undone, "Oh, all right, then. Just forget I asked."

"But I'll tell you."

"Tell me what?"

"You're the one who asked, you should know." The old man had a mischievous grin on his face. He laid his hand gently on Pat's shoulder. "I'm just yanking your chain, hon. He's the undertaker for these here parts."

Pat looked at him, "An undertaker! I thought he was supposed to be from England?"

"Oh, yeah, forty or fifty years ago, he came from England. He was about two years old when his parents came across the pond. The last ten years, all he's done is follow me around, 'spects me to croak at any moment, and being the cantankerous old bugger that I am, I refuse to accommodate him." Perkins laughed and slapped his knee.

Perkins turned and sniffed the air. "Mmmmm. Something sure smells good. Someone's frying onions, probably for a burger. If they're as good as they smell I surely wouldn't mind one of those. Hil, old boy, how about a burger? Here's a ten spot. Get yourself one, too." He turned to Pat, "You want one, too, hon?"

Pat smiled back at him, "Oh, no thanks. But here, give me your money and I'll run down and get you a burger if you want. Anything else I can get you while I'm there? A drink, maybe?"

"Come to think of it," Perkins wiped his mouth with his sleeve, "I might like a Pepsi or Coke, whichever one they have. Don't worry, I'll save your seat for you, and if I'm not here when you get back, I'm probably dead. And even if I am here, I still could be dead. So hurry up, 'cause I don't have a lot of time to waste."

Pat laughed and started making her way down the bleachers. Perkins turned to Gwen who had been sitting beside Pat. "Hello, there. You're even better looking than your friend. What's your name, hon?"

Gwen smiled, "I'm Gwen, and what's your name?"

"Wilt Perkins, been a rancher in these parts for over seventy five years."

"Where did you come from originally, Mr. Perkins?"

"Come from? Nowheres in particular."

"Then you were born here," stated Gwen.

"Nope, I was one of those people who just happened. One minute I wasn't here, the next, I was. Hope I die the same way. Wish your friend would hurry up with those burgers, I'm starved. Makes me think of the time my friend and I were out on the prairie looking for cattle. We didn't have any food with us, and we got so danged hungry we trapped us a couple of gophers and cooked them over a fire and ate them."

Gwen shivered a little and looked at Perkins, "What did they taste like?"

"What did what taste like?"

"The gophers."

Perkins sat thinking for a few seconds then replied, "They tasted like…like gopher."

In a few minutes Pat came back with Perkin's hamburger, drink and his change. "Here you are, Mr. Perkins."

"This was much appreciated, little lady." Perkins patted the seat beside him.

Pat declined his invitation with a wave of her hand. She remained standing and managed to attract her friends' attention. "Gals, I saw Louise and Edna down there. We're all going back to the campsite and rest up a bit. There's a dance or a party tonight in that big old arena over there. We thought we'd try to go fairly early and get a table for our bunch. That way, we can have a couple drinks while we watch the locals in action."

"A little catnap sounds good," said Gwen. She turned to Perkins, "It was so nice to meet you, Mr. Perkins. I hope you have an enjoyable time at the rest of the rodeo, and you leave those gophers alone, hear?"

Perkins with a mouthful of hamburger, nodded amiably. Setting his soda drink down by his feet and clutching the hamburger in his left hand he tipped his hat to the ladies. Once he had finished swallowing his burger, he yelled after them, "The pleasure was all mine. Take care. Don't take any wooden nickels." Then he took another bite of his burger. Fresh hamburger juice rolled down both sides of his chin.

Theda and Marie had walked over to the arena early to try to get a table for their group. The bar was set up along the back of the rink surface and they found a table quite close to it. "This should do nicely. I wish the rest of them would hurry up and get here. I hate saving seats for anyone. Here let's put our jackets and purses on each of these other seats. Then if we sit down on a chair each, it'll look like we're expecting someone."

"Which we are, you silly goose. I dare anyone to come and try to take our places," stated Theda defensively, throwing her jacket over one of the chairs. "Here give me your jacket. I'm going to go and get us some drinks. You keep watch over our table."

"Oh, don't leave me here all by myself."

"Look, Marie, just put on your tough-girl act. Anybody comes anywhere near this table, scowl at them. I won't be long. Remember, no one gets our places."

Marie had to tell two or three people who approached her about her table and she surprised herself by politely, but forcibly telling them that the table was saved. In less than five minutes,

Theda came back with two drinks in her hand, and two rather handsome cowboys walking on either side of her. “Marie, this is George and Pete. They were both competing in the rodeo events. Imagine real cowboys! Sit down gentlemen, Marie has been saving these chairs for just the likes of you.”

George shook Marie’s hand, and held one of the chairs out for her. “It’s not quite as glamorous as your friend makes it out to be. We were competing in the Senior’s events which is quite a bit tamer than the real thing. It’s still lots of fun, though.”

Marie sat down and as she reached for her drink from Theda she whispered to her, “I thought I was saving these seats for the rest of our gang?”

Theda looked at her threateningly, “Marie, hush up! Look, you don’t find guys like this every day. Come on, be a sport. They’re real nice fellows. Neither of them is married. At the moment.”

“How do you know that?” Marie said between clenched teeth.

“I don’t know how I know it, I just do. When you’ve been around as much as I have you get to know these things. Now, sit back and enjoy. Besides, we’ve got two extra chairs here, plenty for the rest of them when they come.”

Before the half-hour was up, Marie and Theda had learned the complete rodeo history of the region. Their new men friends turned out to be quite entertaining. George had just finished telling a hilarious story about one of Pete’s adventures when he worked as a rodeo clown. All four of them had tears in their eyes as he skillfully related the story. “Poor Pete was standing there, the goddamned barrel had splintered in two, his pants and underwear had been ripped off by that bloody bull. All he had on were his boots and half a shirt. They’re both standing there, the bull at one side of the circle and Pete at the other. It looked like it was a contest to decide who had the bigger one, the bull or Pete.”

Pete cut in at that point. “Christ, there was no contest. The bull won hands down. I was scared shitless, and anything I did have to boast about at one time was so shrivelled, you’d have sworn I was a girl.”

"Then what happened?" coaxed Theda, taking another drink and setting her glass down. "Oh, here are the rest of the girls. You've got to meet them first. Then you can finish your story. Come on you guys, hurry up. You're missing all the fun. Gwen, Pat, Edna, Louise, this is Pete and George. They have just been telling us a story. Let them finish and then we'll get you some drinks. Go ahead, guys; the bull, what did it do next?"

George quickly recounted the story for the other women and then continued. "That bull, God he was a big son of a bitch! Remember, Pete?"

Pete looked over at George, laughing, "How could I forget since I'm the one he stuck his bloody big horn into, or did you forget?"

"Anyway, that bull charged at Pete, who fortunately – or unfortunately however you look at it – turned at the last minute to try to get away. One of those big horns caught him right in the side of his ass. The bull threw his head up and kept running around the ring. Poor old Pete was spinning around and around on that horn, like one of those windmill toys that kids run around with at fairs. I thought for sure he was a goner."

"I did, too. The one good thing, after the initial stab of the horn I lost all feeling. But it was still a weird sensation. Finally, that bull put on the brakes and I just sailed off that old horn like someone shaking a piece of chicken off a fork. Fortunately, I rolled right to the edge of the fence. That old bugger took one look at me, and charged over to finish the job. Fortunately, two old-timers standing near the fence grabbed me by my feet and dragged me under the fence just as that old bull got within two inches of my head."

"Pete's got so many scars, and has had so many bones broken, we call him the Evil Knievel of the rodeo circuit. Pete, show them your scar from that bull."

"I think not. The ladies don't want to see that."

George laughed, "Before the night is done, he'll show you, don't worry." He elbowed and winked at Edna who was now sitting beside him.

Edna crossed her arms in front of her and gave George the dirtiest look she could.

George leaned over to her and touched her arm, "Listen, sweetheart, you don't have anything to drink. Come on, I'll get you something. What's your pleasure?"

Edna shook his hand away from her and glared at him. "I don't drink, and please don't touch me again, and my name's Edna, not, sweetheart."

George reached for her arm and then caught himself in time. "I'm sorry. I promise I won't do it again. I sure didn't mean any harm. Look, one little drink won't hurt you. You say you don't drink. Why, health reasons?"

Edna looked at this man and decided that he wasn't a threat. "No, I just never have. I grew up in a house of total abstainers, no alcohol period."

George took his hat off and set it on his knee. Edna looked at him. *Good Heavens!* she thought, *With his hat off, he could pass for Paul Newman. He even has the same blue-blue eyes, and that funny cute little thing he does with his top lip.*

George leaned closer to Edna and practically whispered, "There's nothing wrong with a drink or two, sweethear…. Ah, I'm sorry, what's your name?"

"It's Edna, and there most certainly is something wrong with drinking. Look at all the people who wouldn't do some of the horrendous things they do if it wasn't for drink. Our Lord would not like it and I'm a good Christian."

"Well, Edna. Pretty name, it suits you. Edna, I consider myself a good Christian too, and I do have the odd drink. Edna, our Lord drank wine. That has alcohol in it and he drank it all the time. At lunch and supper and probably when he was just plain thirsty. Didn't seem to hurt him none. That's 'cause he didn't go overboard with it. Same as anything if you do or take too much of something, it ain't good for you. I think singing is great, but I wouldn't want to be around someone who sang twenty-four hours a day; same goes for eating or smoking. Now they make the nicest Singapore Sling here. It's just perfect for someone who has never drank a lot before. In fact, if you want, I'll get them to only put half as much alcohol as they usually do. Come on Edna, I'm really sure the Lord wouldn't mind, just this once."

Edna looked over at George, then down at the table. She sighed heavily then proceeded, "All right, just one, and make sure they only put half as much alcohol in mine as they normally do."

George jumped up from the table and went over to the bar. In a few minutes he returned with a tall glass of red liquid topped with lovely foam. A red cherry, with a cute little paper umbrella stabbed into it, floated on top of the drink. Two tiny straws had been poked down between the glass and the ice. Another little umbrella, stuck through an even redder cherry, hung over the edge of the frosty glass. George set it in front of Edna.

"There you go, Edna. Try this. I'm sure you'll like it. And there's not enough alcohol in there to harm a grasshopper."

George sat down next to Edna. Before he helped himself to his own drink, he removed his hat again. Edna gasped and thought, *What is it about this man? When he has his hat on, he looks like, well, like George, but as soon as he takes it off, he just instantly becomes Paul.*

Edna ventured a sip of her drink. *Ooooo my! That does taste very good*, she thought. She took another longer drink this time.

George had turned and was talking to Marie and Pat. Pete was up dancing with Theda. When the music stopped and Pete and Theda returned to the table, Pete wiped the sweat from his brow as Theda kept dancing to her own tune. George turned back to Edna. Her drink was empty. He smiled over at her and he was surprised to see her smiling back at him. Then she winked at him.

"Edna, that looks like it went down pretty good. Want another?" he asked.

"Oh, I shouldn't really, but…oh, no I shouldn't, but, oh, all right, just one more shouldn't hurt." Edna looked over at Gwen and Louise and smiled, her head bobbing from side to side.

Theda gave Pat a push with her foot, "Would you look at that? Edna looks like she's having quite a time of it. George looks like he's quite taken with her. Who'da thunk?"

An hour passed quickly. Theda and Louise were on the dance floor taking turns grabbing Pete by the arm and whirling him around and around in a boisterous butterfly dance. Pat and Marie had run off to the little ladies' room. Gwen had wandered over to another table to visit with some people who she had discovered, via the grapevine, hailed from her dead parent's home town. She was pleased that they both knew quite a few people in common.

Edna yawned and leaned her head against George's shoulder, at the same time running her hand up and down the glass of her empty drink. George took his hand and turned Edna's face to his and gently kissed her. It was a short kiss. Then he stood up, reached over and took her hand in his and pulled her up beside him. With his other hand, he grabbed his large Stetson and placed it on his head. He put his arm around Edna's shoulder and guided her out the side door of the arena.

Later, when all the women happened to be at the table at the same time, they decided they were tired and ready to call it a night.

Theda picked Edna's jacket off the back of the chair. "Where is Edna?

Louise thought for a second or two and then replied, "Come to think of it, I haven't seen her for quite awhile."

"She was visiting with George for the longest time," commented Pat. She turned to Pete, "Pete, your friend George, do you know where he went?"

"Nope, he left with your friend about an hour ago and they never came back."

"Look everyone, we'll split up and each of us will check a different side of the arena. Theda, you go check in the bathroom. Everyone, we'll meet back here in five," commanded Pat.

Five minutes later, the group reassembled at their original table. Edna was nowhere to be found. "Let's go back to the van, maybe she got tired and went to rest there," said Gwen.

"She wouldn't have walked all the way back to the tents would she?" asked Louise.

They all made their way out to where the van was parked. Pat started to put the key into the lock, but noticed that the front door was slightly ajar. She tested it first and the door opened.

"I swore I locked this thing when we left it. God, I hope nobody broke in and robbed us, or anything!" Pat opened the door wider, stepped up the two little stairs and using her flashlight peered into the back of the van. Curled up on top of the small storage area that Charlie had built against the windows at the back of the van was Edna, sound asleep. Her body was wound up in the small blanket that the girls used if anyone felt cold or sleepy. "Well, I found our Sleeping Beauty. She looks okay, just tired I guess."

Theda came up beside Pat and laughed, "Probably a little hung over, too. For someone who doesn't drink, she managed to finish off quite a few of those Slings tonight. She's gonna have one H of a headache tomorrow."

Louise poked her head in, "Is that Edna sleeping in the back there? I wonder why she didn't come and tell us that she was tired. We could have left earlier. Oh, well, might as well leave her as is. No sense waking her now."

"Well, at least we're all here and accounted for. Let's get back to the tents and grab some shuteye. I wouldn't mind pulling out of here half decently early tomorrow morning, before everyone else gets the same idea. It would be nice to beat some of this traffic. We can stop and have breakfast later after we've driven for an hour or so. What do you guys think?" asked Pat.

"Sounds okay by me. You're the driver tomorrow, Pat, so you're the boss. If anybody is still tired they can sleep in the van," replied Theda.

As everyone vacated the van, Theda turned to take one last look at Edna. Then she grabbed Pat, who was right in front of her, by the arm. "Look, at Edna. Look at her face, how she's smiling," she giggled, "must be a good dream she's having."

Pat looked and laughed quietly along with Theda. "I'd better check on the windows. The mosquitoes will eat Edna up if they're left open. Just that one over there can stay open. It's the only one with a screen. We don't want her to suffocate, do we?"

"Sweet dreams, Edna, see you in the morning." Theda closed the door to the van.

The next morning, everyone packed and settled into the van as well as they could without disturbing Edna, who was still dead to the world. "We're going to have to do a little rearranging here. Some of that stuff will have to just go in the aisle until Her Majesty gets up," suggested Theda as she tried to make a spot for her sleeping bag.

"What did she say, couldn't hear her?" asked Louise.

"She said that the old adage–a place for everything and everything in its place–will have to be shelved. With Edna sprawled all over that shelfie thing that's in the back, there's not enough room for our stuff," replied Gwen.

"Some of you might even have to hold something in your laps for awhile." Pat sat down in the driver's seat. She had just come from checking on their campsite.

The van pulled out of the still slumbering campground, bumping over a rather large metal rail that the rodeo committee had placed across the road at the entrance of the campgrounds to help slow vehicles down.

"Look, the sun is just peeking up over the hills there. Isn't that pretty? You can almost watch it coming up, isn't that amazing? It's been so long since I've seen a sunrise, you know, an actual right-from-the-beginning sunrise," observed Gwen.

At the next intersection they pulled out onto the main highway. Pat drove the car about a half a mile down the road and then pulled into an all night car wash.

"Going to get the van washed. It's all covered with dust from that field we parked in last night."

Quite a few big rigs whined by as they were getting the van washed. Their drivers had probably been travelling all night. In less than ten minutes the van was washed and they were back out on the road. Suddenly, it was daylight.

Without warning a huge tractor-trailer suddenly loomed up behind the van. It tooted it's horn. Pat glanced sideways at the outside rear-view mirror. She checked the road in front of her. Nothing. The truck's horn sounded again.

"What the hell is his problem? There's all kinds of room here to pass." Pat looked back in the mirror and caught the truck driver's image. He had a huge smile on his face. "Well, go ahead and pass, you stupid bugger. I'm not stopping you. To hell if I'm pulling right off the road for you."

The truck continued to keep right on Pat's tail for several more kilometres. "This is too dangerous. I'm not going to play this game any longer." Pat signaled a right turn, all the time hoping that the truck driver wasn't so close to her vehicle that he would miss seeing her signal lights. The truck driver did slow down and allowed some space to form between himself and the van. Pat pulled over to the side of the road. The truck roared past giving a couple more toots on its horn.

"Guess he's saying thank you. What an idiot!"

The truck's horn woke up everyone in the van who was trying to grab a couple more minutes of sleep. Everyone but Edna, who hadn't moved a muscle since the van took off. She looked quite peaceful and cozy in her little bunk at the extreme back of the van. Her blanket was tucked under her chin and she still had a big smile on her face.

Pat pulled back out onto the road humming softly to herself for awhile. Then she remembered something.

"Louise, would you check that my little camera is in my fanny pack? It should be right beside my jacket. I was taking pictures at the bar last night. I'm sure I brought it with me, but we'd better check. I'd hate to lose that camera. Not that it's expensive or anything, but it takes really good pictures."

Louise searched through the pile of jackets, found Pat's and the fanny pack with it. She opened the pack, and found the camera. "Yes, not to worry. It's here."

"Good, that makes me feel better." She glanced over at Theda, who was yawning. "The next decent place we come across, we'll stop for a coffee. Might even get some breakfast."

"That sounds like a good idea; might wake a few of us up. It wasn't that late when we got to bed last night. Don't know what's the matter this morning. Feel like I never slept at all."

"Could be eight or nine beers have something to do with it?" Pat laughed.

Theda looked at her, "Ya think?"

Pat glanced up in time to see a small green truck pull up close to the back of the van. It started to pull out to pass, then seemed to change its mind and pulled back into Pat's lane and stayed behind them. Pat looked down the road in front of her. The road was clear of traffic. "Good God Almighty, another stupid bugger who doesn't know how to pass!"

Theda bent down to look through the side mirrors at the truck. "There are three yokels in it, and," she laughed, "they're waving and blowing kisses at us. Do you think it's someone we might have met at the party last night?"

Pat peeked in her side mirror, "They look a little young for us. My bet is they probably haven't even started shaving yet."

Theda giggled, "Maybe they're just coming home from a bash and they're still hung over."

The truck continued to follow the van for several kilometres. Finally, it pulled out and passed the van. The young chap on the passenger side hung his body precariously out the side of his open window as he drummed with both hands on the outside of his truck door. When the truck moved into the lane in front of them, the driver whose window was also open gave them the thumbs-up. Pat appeared slightly exasperated, "Boy, this is the last time that we ever start out this early again; seems it's the time for all the loonies to take to the road."

"There's a car coming up on us pretty fast. Nice to see a car for a change," commented Theda.

Pat looked back, "Looks like an older couple. Really zipping along for old codgers, aren't they? Okay, bud, the road's clear ahead, away you go. Keep driving like that and they'll reach heaven sooner than they expect."

The driver of the car signaled a left turn, and started to pull left, but then suddenly touched his brake, and fell back into Pat's lane. The woman in the passenger seat grabbed the driver's arm and pointed at the back of the van. He nodded and smiled.

The woman took off her glasses, blew on them, and wiped them on the corner of her shirt, then put the glasses back on and stared at the van.

"Pat, somebody must have written something on the back of our van during the night because everyone who comes near us seems to be getting quite a charge. It can't be good, 'cause that old biddy behind us looks like Santa Claus crawled up her ass, reindeer, sleigh and all."

"We just had the van washed this morning. Oh, look, they're finally going to pass."

"Oh, good, you guys, wake Edna up. She's missing all the fun."

"No, don't do that. She had a few drinks last night. She's not used to that, so she probably needs her sleep. Leave her be," ordered Pat.

"Yeah, you're right," agreed Theda, "besides, with her asleep I can swear to my heart's content and not have that scowly old face of hers sitting here judging me."

"There goes another car and look at those fools waving at us. This must be some of that Western hospitality you hear about all of the time. What do you think?"

"I really don't know, but I do know there's a gas station right over there, and it has a restaurant. We can grab that cup of coffee."

"Looks good, and I'll fill up while we're here."

Pat pulled the van up to the gas pumps. Turned the ignition off and pulled out her wallet. "Okay, guys, anybody want breakfast, or do you just want coffee?"

No one wanted breakfast yet, but everyone wanted a coffee, so Theda volunteered to get it. While Gwen and Louise went off to find the washrooms, Pat walked back to open the gas tank. A gangly young man sauntered out of the station and dragged the gas line over to her before she managed to get it open.

"Here ma'am, let me do that for you. We have full service here so you might as well take advantage of it." He finished undoing the cap to the gas tank and shoved the gas nozzle into the opening, then went back to pick up a squeegee to wash the windows.

Pat watched as the young man whacked the squeegee on the side of the container to get the excess moisture off of it. "You probably don't need to wash the windows. We just had the van washed just a few kilometres back."

The young man looked down at the squeegee, "Like I said, full service. Traffic has been light this morning so far, and doing this helps keep me awake."

Pat threw up her hands in defeat, "Oh, what does it matter. Go ahead finish cleaning, and by the way, did you happen to hear any weather reports this morning?"

The young man finished both sides of the front of the van, then walked back to dip the squeegee in the pail again. "Don't think it's going to rain or anything. Sounds like it's going to be another hot one. This close to the mountains you never can tell. We could get a shower later on, or not."

Just then the gas pump clicked to signal that the tank was full. Pat went over and took the cleaner away from the young chap. "Here, you go attend to that, and I'll finish this job. Like I said, we had the van cleaned this morning, so the windows aren't that bad. I'll just go touch up the back ones a bit, they're the only ones that seem to gather dust. Here's the money for the gas."

Pat walked to the back of the van and lifted the squeegee up to the window to give it a couple of swipes. She watched the young man extract the gas nozzle and replace the cap. It was then that she happened to glance up at the back window. "Oh, my God!" she exclaimed. She rubbed the cleaner across the window once more and then let it drop towards the ground, "Oh, my God!"

Theda returned to the van with Styrofoam cups full of coffee and set them in the van. She yelled back to Pat. "Pat! While you're back there, check to see if anyone wrote something stupid on our van. It might explain some of the crazy looks we've been getting."

Pat couldn't move for several seconds, her mouth hung open, water from the sopping wet squeegee ran down the side of her clean blue jeans. Finally, she composed herself long enough to yell, "I think you'd better come here and see for yourself. You really won't believe this. Oh, and bring my camera." She shook the squeegee to rid it of its excess moisture and laughed to herself, *Oh, yes, definitely, bring the camera.*

Marie and Theda rounded the corner of the van at the same time. "I have your camera. What is it?" said Theda.

"I brought mine, too, anything the matter?"

Pat pointed to the back window, "Look."

A few seconds later, Louise and Gwen returned from the bathroom, and seeing the others gathered at the back of the van, joined them. They all stood, in a row, mouths agape staring at the back window of the van. Gwen broke the silence, "My Lord. Did you ever?"

They all shook their heads simultaneously, "Never."

Pressed against the back window of the van, for the whole world to see, was the backside of Edna's ass.

"Jesus, no wonder all those silly buggers on the highway were acting so stupid. One view of this, and it's enough to rattle anyone's brains," laughed Theda.

"Maybe the windows were dirtier then, and no one could see," said Gwen hopefully.

"No, I think they could see all right. Remember we pulled out onto the highway and it was only minutes later that we pulled in and had the van washed."

Theda grabbed Pat's camera, "Holy Christ, just imagine, she mooned half of Alberta. This is fantastic! Move out of the way. I've got to get a picture, before she moves." She snapped a couple of pictures.

Marie squinted through her viewfinder. "Do you all want to kind of move over beside Edna there and I'll take a shot of everyone?"

The women all looked at her in disgust, but immediately assembled around the window. "Okay, squat down a bit, Gwen, I can't see Edna. Pat, shove over just a bit. Good. Now everyone, SMILE!"

Chapter Fourteen

Charlie finished sorting the quiz papers that his class had handed back to him at the end of the period. He glanced out the window of his classroom. It was Friday and the weather man had promised a glorious weekend.

He quickly shoved the papers into his briefcase and snapped it closed. He grabbed his jacket from the back of his chair, flung it over his shoulder and walked out of his classroom, down the hall and outside into the fresh air. He wanted to pop in and check Pat's house before he started the weekend. He usually went over once a week, just to check things. So far, he had received about five postcards from her and it sounded like the girls were having a ball. "Good for them," he thought.

"Charlie, wait up!" It was Greg Stoppard, a history teacher for over twenty years. Greg caught up to Charlie. "What you got planned for the weekend, young fellow? A bunch of us are going out to Peter Hansen's place on Cloud Lake. Do a little fishing, play some cards. Want to come?"

"When are you going?"

"Right now. Jake's driving me over to my place. I want to change first. We could come over your way and pick you up about five-thirty."

Charlie thought for a moment. "I'm sorry, but I have a couple of things that need taking care of, so why don't I just drive myself up when I'm done. That way, I'll get there when I get there. What do you want me to bring?"

"Well, your own booze, some munchies. Jake's old lady made up a big potato salad, and Peter is grabbing some salad stuff at the store. I picked up some buns at the bakery. We're hoping to catch our supper. If we don't, we'll have to eat hot dogs. What do you have to do? Like, is it going to take you a long time to do it? We could wait a few minutes for you."

"I have to go over to Pat's, check on her house. Then I hope to get to the bank before it closes. Actually, maybe I'll reverse my schedule, that way I'll make the bank on time. It doesn't matter when I get to Pat's."

"God, Charlie, why the heck did you let yourself get tied down looking after Pat's house? Are those old broads still trying to get to the other side of the world or wherever the hell they're trying to get?"

"Pat's my friend, Greg. When I first moved here to take up my teaching job, she and Earl put me up for over three months while I adjusted and looked for a new place. Then when I did get a place, Pat was the one who cleaned it for me. I've eaten more meals at her place than I dare try to count. So, I think I owe her the odd check on her house while she's away."

"I was talking to Gwen's family – well actually it was just her son Phil – and he sure isn't too pleased with his mother taking off like she did. He says all those old broads coaxed her into going, and she really shouldn't have. Says she has a heart condition, or something."

"Greg, I'd appreciate it if you'd quit calling them old broads. They're women. Wome, who want to do and see something different. I think it's great that they went on this trip. Even if they fail, at least they are trying. To me the trying is more important than the actual accomplishment and I wish them all the luck in the world. And as far as Phil missing his mother, the man hardly has anything to do with her when she's here. I'm afraid Phil's more like his old man than anyone would like to admit. I heard that he was a real grump box. Never smiled a day in his life and that he used to get sloshed every weekend and beat the hell out of Gwen. I seem to remember hearing about a few times that Phil came to school with both eyes blackened, and bruises all over his body, too."

"Yeah, you're probably right. He was a scary old bugger that's for sure. You must have met him, or were you even teaching here then? Managed to drink his whole paycheck up every weekend. The only thing he left Gwen and the kids when he croaked was that little house. Fortunately, there was a little bit of insurance too. That helped some. You're right. She's had a hard row, that's for sure."

"I was here about a year before he was killed. The few times I saw him around he didn't impress me too much. It's funny, you'd have thought that having to go through all that abuse from the old man would have drawn Phil and his mom closer together. Phil seems to have inherited his father's temperament. At least he doesn't seem to touch the booze like the old man did. Poor Gwen, she seems like such an unhappy little lady. I've heard Pat and her friends discussing her and apparently the only time she seems to get out from under that cloud of darkness is when she's singing at church. Then she seems and looks moderately happy."

"Gwen is a terrific singer, no doubt about that! The wife and I heard her in the Christmas Cantata a few times. She was quite impressive," reminisced Greg.

Pat says she never misses a Sunday. Oh, there was one time when George had apparently beaten her so badly, he cracked a couple of her ribs, so she couldn't sing for over a month. She couldn't sing, but still made it to church on Sunday, cracked ribs or no."

"Probably singing was the one thing that helped maintain her sanity all those years when she lived with George. Funny, people say he never made a fuss about her going to church, ever."

"He was probably so hung over Sunday morning that he never even missed her leaving the house. No, I hope Gwen has a marvelous time. I don't know what crawls up Phil's ass but he can be a real cantankerous bugger sometimes. His wife told Pat that when she tried to invite the old lady over for Easter supper one time, Phil wouldn't let her. Said he had better things to do with his time. Then he went fishing."

"I heard that he blames his mother for all the abuse they suffered from his dad."

"Why would he blame her? It was the old man who was doing the beating!"

"He thought his mother should have stood up for herself. That she should have taken him and his sister and got away from the old boy."

"Well, yes, she probably should have; but in those days, there weren't many places to run to. It's hard enough today getting away from an abusive situation and there's more help out there now for victims than there used to be."

"Well, whatever, our standing here yakking isn't letting you get the things done you have to get done. Anyhow, there's Jake. Sure you don't want us to wait for you?"

"Naw, it's okay. Who knows what I'll find at Pat's, and if I take my own car I'm free to leave tomorrow whenever."

"Suit yourself. See you when you get there."

Charlie gave Jake a wave as he turned to join Greg. Then he drew an envelope out of his back pocket and slipped a letter out of it. He had glanced at the letter briefly when he picked the mail up today, but didn't have time to really savour its short contents.

Hi! Charlie,

Have a couple free minutes now to drop you a line. I'll keep this short. We're having one hoot of a time. So far I think it's the best thing we could have done, this trip. Everyone's well, so far.

We stopped in a small town in Alberta and Marie bought two new outfits, got her hair cut and streaks put in her hair- she looks fab. Theda and Edna speak to each other once in awhile and I don't mean just spiteful stuff back and forth. The other day, I actually heard them discussing something in normal tones. Probably won't last. Louise had to go buy a new pair of track pants. The ones she brought with her are too big. Can you believe it? She's lost quite a few pounds- we all seem to be eating lots- try to go for walks and such whenever we stop. Oh, and Edna, has stopped taking about three of her thousands of pills. She had told us the other day, she was running low on them, so I offered to stop at a drugstore to pick them up- she already has the prescriptions for them- She said, no, she thought maybe she'd try to get along without them for awhile.

And Gwen, you should see her, Charlie, smiling all the time, now. She's having a wonderful time. She has moments. Sometimes I'll see her when she's sort of off to herself, and she doesn't look very happy then. But when she's participating in whatever we're doing at the time, she seems really happy. I hope she is. God knows, she deserves some happiness! And me, well, of course I personally don't think there's much difference in the way I act or look, but I'm sure my friends will all say I've become more open to fresh ideas, willing to take a chance more often. Certainly, I'm more accepting of other people's actions and habits. I'm trying really hard not to think that I'm always right (even though deep down, I know that I am).

Can't wait until I'm home to show you the pics and tapes. You're not going to believe some of the stuff we've seen and done. Going to make a huge pot of spaghetti sauce, and we'll sit and gorge ourselves on it while we watch the tapes.

Love, Pat.

Chapter Fifteen

Gwen reached up and pulled the rear view mirror down slightly. "There, that's better. I can see you guys better. All I could see before was a little bit of the road."

Louise, sitting in the passenger side while Gwen drove, looked over at her, "Gwen, you're supposed to see the road, not the people in the back seats."

"Well, I can see the road through the side mirrors, so what do I need to see even more road through this mirror in front."

Louise, keeping her eyes on the road in front of her, shook her head.

Edna yelled up to Gwen, "Gwen, let's sing something. We haven't done that in a long time."

Gwen yelled back over her shoulder, "I'd really rather not. Not while I'm driving. I'm one of those people who can only concentrate on one thing at a time."

"Okay, then, I'll lead us in a song. Everybody ready? Here goes, a one, a two, a three*:* On an old rugged cross, where...."

"Jesus H. Christ! It's bad enough that you want to sing, but why the hell do we always have to sing hymns. I'm sick of hymns. You'd think we were some travelling bible group. Don't you know any other kind of songs? I'd even be happy singing some kids' songs instead, how about *Farmer in the Dell*?"

"There's nothing wrong with hymns. There's some lovely modern music that can trace its roots back to old sacred music. Besides it wouldn't hurt you to sing or listen to something else besides that crappy country music you're always tuned in to."

"What do you mean crappy? There's no music around that, that…demonstrates man's sentiments towards himself and others as much as country music," Theda stated defensively.

Edna lashed back, "Sentimental claptrap is all it is. Pinch your nose and mumble the first thing that comes to mind. That's country music."

"Claptrap! Well, it's a sight better than that stupid, raise your eyes to heaven and look down your nose at the same time music. You and your holy, holy, holys!"

"Maybe if you tried the odd hymn or two once in awhile it would help to clean your mouth out," hissed Edna.

"I'll have you know, Miss Holier-than-Thou, no group of singers sing more hymns than country and western singers."

"Well, I can't argue with you there. But they only do it to make money. I can assure you that if they didn't make a mil or two cutting a few religious records they wouldn't do it. Half of them have probably never even set foot in a church in their lifetime."

"So what. I don't believe you have to go to church every week to have a good rapport with God. Half of the people that I know who go to church every week are some of the biggest hypocrites in the world. They wouldn't do a thing for anybody or anything, unless you pay them to do it. Oh, sure, they might donate some time or money for some worthwhile cause, but very few of them will get down and dirty to help someone. You'd never catch them going out in the street and helping someone who had fallen down drunk or was sitting in a corner, high on a drug trip. As long as they don't really have to see or touch the victim, they'll help."

"Are you finished?" asked Edna sarcastically. "Do you mean to tell me that you, you of all people, actually believe that there is a God?"

"Of course I do. Well no, to be honest I don't know what

I believe. When I said a rapport with God, I didn't just mean God, I meant the whole ball of wax, you know—nature or whatever turns you on."

Gwen turned briefly to Louise, "Oh, those two. Listening to them bicker all the time gives me a headache."

Louise laughed, "They aren't birds of a feather, that's for sure. It would be fun to throw them both in a bag and shake them up good. See if some of their traits would rub off on each other a bit."

"I'm afraid it would be a losing battle. You could sprinkle them both with the same icing sugar, but you'd always have a different doughnut on the inside."

They both laughed when they heard Theda scream, "Put on your bloody headphones and you can listen to all the freaking hymns you want to, but just leave me out of it!"

A few kilometres from Pincher Creek Gwen started to slow down. "Look, up ahead, it looks like someone has broken down. Should we stop and see if there's anything we can do?"

Louise put her hands on the front dash in anticipation of a quick stop. "Oh, be careful. Maybe we shouldn't stop. It could be a hatchet murderer. Just before I came out to join you guys, I watched a movie on TV about a family that picked up a hitchhiker in the desert somewhere. He ended up stabbing them all to death and then stealing their car. Every time he ran out of gas, he'd stop another car. He stole cars and killed people clear across three states before they finally caught up with him."

"Well, it looks like there are only two of them. What do you think Pat, should I stop?" asked Gwen.

"Sure, go ahead. There are six of us so that makes it three to one in my book. I think we could take them," replied Pat.

Louise looked worried. "What if they have a gun? It won't help us any if we're three to one then."

Theda had unfastened her seat belt and was standing up behind Louise trying to peek past her head to see what the people in distress looked like. "Hey, they're cute little buggers! Besides we may be old, but we're not helpless. Anyway, if they get out of hand, Edna can sing hymns at them. She can sing them to death."

Edna retorted, "Oh, and just what would you do to protect us if the need be, line dance around them until they pleaded for mercy?"

"Well, it's a sight better than…."

"Okay, you two, put a cork in it for awhile. God!" Pat looked slightly exasperated. "Pull up in front of them, Gwen."

As the van came to a stop on the side of the road, Steve gave his friend, Bruce, a nudge. "Hey, Brucie boy, looky here. Someone's actually stopping to help us. Maybe if we're lucky it'll be a van load of sweet-looking babes."

The other young man's body was hidden under the hood of a little red Spitfire. As he pulled himself out, he ducked his head to avoid hitting the hood. Once both feet were on the ground again, he straightened up. His blond hair fluttered in the breeze. He had on a bright blue shirt that as Theda put it, "Did wonders for his blue eyes." The shirtsleeves of his shirt were rolled up to his elbows showing off his well-tanned arms. He squinted slightly to avoid the sun as he looked over at the van. The doors slid open and five "babes" tumbled out. Steve turned and leaned against the front of his car as five of the women bailed out of the van and advanced on him. "Right. Babes. Shit! First we break down in this God-forsaken part of the country and now this. You'd think we could expect one miracle at the very least, but what do we get instead, a van load of what…grey power?"

Pat stopped for a second and yelled back at Gwen, "Gwen, aren't you coming?"

Gwen finally stepped down from the van and proceeded to lock her door. She quickly caught up to Pat. "I just made sure all the doors were locked, and I hid the keys." She shook her blouse slightly. "I tucked them down here between my boobs. No one would ever think of looking for them here. Better not to take any chances."

Theda nudged Marie, "Look at that one in front. My God, he looks just like Robert Wagner used to look when he was young, and the little blondie one with the blue shirt is nothing to shake a stick at either." She walked right up to the first young man, "Two young studs in distress! Hi, guys, what happened? Need any help? I doubt if we can mend anything ourselves, but we'd be glad to drive you to a service station or send somebody from a garage out to help you. You guys got names?"

The man in the blue shirt pointed at his friend. "This is Steve, and I'm Bruce."

Marie poked her head under the hood. "What's wrong with the car?"

"Lady, if we knew, we wouldn't be standing here in the middle of nowhere."

Theda circled the taller man with the red shirt. She looked appreciatively at his tight jeans and wide shoulders. She turned to Pat and whispered, "Hasn't he got the cutest little buns you ever did see? I could just...."

"Theda, behave yourself! They're a little young for you."

"How old would you say they are, twenty, twenty-five?"

"I'd say early twenties, whatever. I repeat, they're too young for you."

Marie was already stretched over the front bumper wiggling the connecting wires to the battery. Steve was the first to notice her. "Hey, lady, be careful there. Don't make matters any worse than they are."

Marie ignored him. "Tell me, when did you find that your car wouldn't start? Were you driving along and it just died on you, or did you stop and turn it off for any length of time?"

"What difference does it make. We stopped for a lea..., I mean we just stopped."

Theda had been listening to Steve and Marie. "It's okay to say that you stopped for a leak, a piss, a pee, to relieve yourself or whatever. I assure you it's really no big deal. We all do it. Now, my friend asked you a question before and I don't think you gave her an answer. She wants to know when did your car conk out on you?"

"Sorry lady. While we were," Steve paused, "relieving ourselves by the side of the road, we spotted a whole herd of horses coming out of that ravine over there." He pointed off to the West. I went back and grabbed my camera and we started walking over to get a better look at them. They're no fences or anything around here, so we figured that they must be wild horses.

I suppose we were gone a little over a half an hour. I tried to start it, and there was nothing. It was dead as a doornail. Couldn't have flooded it, because I didn't turn the key long enough."

Marie looked up at Steve, black grease marks were smeared across her forehead. "Your battery connectors are pretty corroded. Listen, you wouldn't happen to have an orange soda pop? If you don't, we might have one in our cooler."

"Orange pop? No, are you thirsty? Sorry, we don't have anything. We had a few beers in the car, but we finished them. That's why we stopped to take a… to relieve ourselves."

Marie laughed, "No, I'm not thirsty." Then she peeked out under Steve's arm at Gwen. "Gwen, could you go check and see if we have an orange pop in the van. If we do, bring it here, please. Oh, and a couple pieces of paper towel. too."

Bruce was sitting on the side of the road. He had taken one of his running shoes off to shake out a pebble. "Ladies, maybe you could just give us a lift to the nearest town? We can find a garage and get some help."

Steve started to close the hood on the car. When the hood touched Marie on the head, he gently reached over and tried to pull her back out of the way. Annoyed, Marie looked down at his hand on her arm, then up at Steve's face. "What do you think you're doing?"

"Lady, I'm sorry, but I'd rather you leave our car alone. What do you know about cars anyway? Please, don't make a fuss, just move."

"What do I know about cars? Well, for one thing, I know your car won't start, and I pretty much think I know why it won't start. Of course, if you don't care if you get the thing going, or you don't care it you have to have it haul-assed into a garage, where they are going to charge you an arm and a leg, to do basically the same thing I'm going to do for free, by all means then, hop into our van. We'll drive you to the next town."

Theda grabbed Bruce by the arm, "Good idea. Come on handsome, you can sit beside me." She was already steering Bruce over towards the van.

Marie dove back under the hood. They could hardly hear

her as she said, "Listen, I think I might be able to help. Just let me try, and honest, if it doesn't work, it's not going to hurt anything in your car, I swear. All I'll need is fifteen minutes to half an hour."

"Did she say fifteen minutes or a bit more?" asked Steve. He shirked his shoulders as he looked at Bruce. "Oh, what the hell. We've already been sitting here close to three hours now, so what's another half an hour?"

Theda giggled, "Oh, goody, come on." She tugged on Bruce's arm. "I forget your name, I'll just call you Mr. Blueshirt. Come on Mr. Blueshirt, we can go over and wait in the van."

Bruce smiled down at Theda. "Let me introduce ourselves, again. This is my good friend Steve, and I'm Bruce."

Theda looked up at Bruce, "Just how good a friend are we talking about here?"

"My very good friend," he said emphasizing the very. Then he smiled at Theda.

Theda let go of his arm. "Oh, shit! I should have known it. Just our luck, travelling across no man's land and the only two eligible men we meet are gorgeous and they turn out to be pansies."

Pat's mouth dropped open, "Theda! What a thing to say! They hardly look like pansies to me."

Theda quickly walked over to Bruce, "I'm really sorry for what I just said. That was uncalled for. Please forgive me. It's just that you both are two of the greatest looking fellows that I've seen in a long time, and when you said that you were, …you know, I just thought that if I was a twenty-or-so young girl again and I met you two and you turned out to be—that way—what a bloody disappointment it would be." Just then she saw Gwen coming with the pop. She was happy to change the subject. "Ah, here's Gwen with the orange pop."

"Here you go, Marie." Gwen handed the pop to Marie who again disappeared under the hood. They could all hear the loud fizz as Marie pulled the tab back on the can. Then she gently poured the whole can over the battery connectors. The liquid immediately foamed and bubbled.

Edna poked her head under the hood across from Marie. She looked up at Steve who was beside Marie. "Where are you young men from?"

"Bruce and I are both from Sturgeon Falls," he said never taking his eyes off the bubbling mess on top of his car battery.

"Sturgeon Falls. My sister used to live there. Perhaps you know her family, Jensen?"

"Jensen? Hmm, nope, don't know any Jensen. Could be it was before my time."

Edna laughed, "Probably was. It was twenty years ago when she moved so, if it wasn't before your time, you would have been pretty young."

Steve looked at Edna and laughed, "You're right, I was about one year old then."

Edna persisted, "What are you doing way out here?"

"Bruce and I both finished a carpenter's course. Neither of us could find work back in Ontario. Everyone told us that there was a building boom in Calgary, so we thought we'd try our luck."

"If you're on your way to Calgary, I think you kind of missed it, didn't you?"

"Well, it's kind of silly, but neither one of us has even been this far West before and we wanted to at least be able to say we stuck our big toe into British Columbia. So that's where we were headed. The border is not supposed to be very far from here. Where are you ladies headed?"

Marie, ignoring Steve and Edna's conversation, stood intently watching the foam on top of the battery. It didn't take long for the bubbles to start to die down.

Pat, who was on the other side of Steve, answered for the group, "We really don't know. I guess we'll stop when we topple off into the ocean or run out of money, whichever comes first. We just want to see as much of the country as we can. You know, widen our horizons."

Steve smiled down at her with a gleam in his eye. "And have you done it?"

"Done what?"

"Widened your horizons?"

"I think so, yes, actually quite a bit."

Marie wiped the connectors with a piece of paper towel. and then re-connected them to the battery. She pulled herself out from under the hood. "All right, young fellow, put the key in and let's see what this babe can do."

Steve inserted the key in the ignition, crossed his fingers on his left hand, held his breath and turned the key. The car started on the first try. Everyone cheered and patted Marie on the back. Bruce went over and stood by the open driver's door and looked at Steve. Steve looked up at him. "Do you believe it?"

Bruce laughed and gave him a high-five, "No, I don't. Just listen to this kitten purr."

Steve left the car running, slipped out of the driver's seat and walked over to Marie and gave her a big hug. "Don't know where you learned to do that, lady, but thank you so much." He planted a big kiss on one of her cheeks.

Marie blushed slightly then reached up and gently touched the cheek where Steve had kissed. "Well, thank you. It wasn't anything, really. Orange pop counteracts the acid on the connectors. It has to be orange pop, colas just add more acid."

Theda quickly ran up beside Steve. "Excuse me! Marie just poured the pop on the battery. I'm the one who got the pop for you so I think I deserve a kiss, too."

Gwen quickly asserted herself. "You did not. I'm the one that got the pop."

Steve and Bruce both laughed. Bruce held out both arms. "Come here, all of you, we'll give you all a kiss. You deserve it." Theda receiving her kiss on the forehead rolled her eyes in mock ecstasy. Gwen hardly came up to Bruce's armpits so her kiss was delivered to the top of her head.

Pat waved off both Bruce and Steve's attempts to kiss her. "Come on ladies, back in the van. Let's let these young chaps get back on the road so they can do whatever young chaps do. Okay, Gwen, give up with the keys."

Gwen smiled, reached down the front of her blouse and extracted the keys and handed them to Pat.

Theda giggled. "Good luck on your job hunting, guys."

"Thanks for everything, especially you," Steve grabbed Marie's hand. She blushed.

Bruce was already opening the door of the red Spitfire. He turned and raised his clenched fist in salute, "Yeah, ladies, here's to Grey Power!" To himself he said, *And I mean that in the nicest way.*

"Oh, pooh, I don't know whether I like this Grey Power thingie. Do we really look that old? I don't know about the rest of you, but I don't feel old," pouted Gwen.

Pat smiled as she commented, "Oh, I suppose we do. I remember when I was in high school thinking all our teachers were really over the hill. After I was married for a couple of years, I met one of them and was shocked to find out she was only a few years older than I was. We were all seventeen or eighteen in our final year, so even if these teachers went to university, some of them in their first year of teaching were only twenty-two or twenty-three. I always thought of that particular teacher as old, and still do."

Fifteen minutes later, Bruce and Steve had tacked on close to ten kilometres on their little Spitfire. "That was a piece of luck," commented Steve, "running across those old broads."

Bruce laughed, "You're telling me. At first when I saw them all pile out of that van like they did, I thought they were a bunch of old grannies who were going to smother us to death with hugs and kisses."

"Speaking of hugs and kisses, what did you say to that one old dolly? Jesus, for a minute there, I thought she was going to Shanghai you into her van there and do all kinds of unmentionable things to you."

Bruce blushed, "Right. Well, I sort of let her think that we were an item."

"We...***us***...an item? What do you mean an item? Did you tell her we were gay?"

"No, I didn't tell her we were gay. I just let her think we were."

"There's a difference?"

"Oh, what the hell, we'll never see them again. And anyway, as soon as she thought I was gay, she backed off right away," laughed Bruce. He couldn't help noticing out of the corner of his eye, Steve moving as far away from him as his seat belt allowed.

***

The phone rang three times before Charlie managed to get to it. He quickly picked up the receiver and said, "'Lo, Chuck here."

"Hey, Charlie, how's it going? It's Pat."

"Pat, it's great to hear from you. Everything going all right? Everybody's fine, I hope?"

"Yes, we're all alive and accounted for. There's some beautiful country out here. Really different. The girls are enjoying it, especially Louise, Gwen and Edna. I don't think they'd ever been out of Ontario before this trip."

"So where are you now?"

"We're sort of south and east of Banff. Hope to make it to Banff, tomorrow. Some of the girls want to try whitewater rafting, maybe take a couple of nice hikes, and just plain relax."

"Whitewater rafting! Wait 'till I tell the folks here about that!"

"I'm hoping it will be fun. We'll probably spend a couple of days there and then head on through the mountains. I won't bother calling again 'til we head home. I won't keep you, Charlie, because I'm calling from a pay phone and they charge an arm and a leg even with my card."

"Okay, Pat, good to hear from you, however short the conversation. I'll let the others know that everything is fine with you all. Bye then."

"Thanks, bye chum."

Chapter Sixteen

"So this is Banff," declared Theda, as she maneuvered the van down Banff's main street. The city, tucked cozily amid tall rugged mountains, was a destination that attracted thousands upon thousands of tourists annually from all over the world, all eager to get a first hand glimpse of its natural splendour.

"My God, have you ever seen so many tourist buses in your life. And I swear over half of them are full of Japanese."

When the van came to a stop at the first red light Pat opened her window and watched a group of people who were obviously tourists standing near the intersection. "Good for the economy. Imagine they drop a few bucks here and there when they come."

"When you talked to Charlie last night, what did he have to say about Banff?"

"Oh, nothing much, said it's pretty. Pretty crowded. Said not to bother trying to get a motel room here, or buy anything for that matter. He claims they charge exorbitant prices for everything here."

"I can believe it. Hey, I just saw some huge leggy creature standing in the middle of that last side street. Looked like a big moosey cow or something."

Pat laughed, "Probably an elk. I've read that they run wild in the city. Apparently, it's common to find one munching on your flower bed in your front yard at any given time of the day."

"What a silly old thing. It's a good thing we inquired about campgrounds way back when. We were lucky to cash in on a cancellation. Otherwise we'd be out of luck."

"How much farther do you think before we come to the campsite? Do we have to go through the whole city?"

"Yes, that's what that attendant said. The city's not that big, so it shouldn't take us long, provided we don't come across any more elk in the middle of the road."

In fifteen minutes they had passed through to the outer limits of the city. "The campground should be around here pretty soon and the office is supposed to be on the right hand side of the road." Pat squinted through the windshield. "There, there it is. See the sign? Next turn, just pull in there right up to the office."

Marie snapped her seat belt open. "Oh, good, there's a restroom. I need to go in the worst way."

"Me, too!" declared Edna.

Pat turned and looked back into the van. "Anybody else, have to go? I'll run in and register, do what needs to be done."

Theda pulled the keys from the ignition. "Think I'll come in with you. I need to stretch my legs a bit. If you other two aren't going into the restroom, will you keep an eye on our stuff, okay?"

Marie and Edna ran for the restroom. Theda and Pat stepped out of the van. Both of them stretched their arms and shoulders, hitched up their jogging pants and at the same time tucked in their shirts. Theda rocked her head to and fro several times and then both women disappeared into the building marked Office.

When they returned to the van a few minutes later, Marie and Edna were already back. Both of them were leaning against the side of the van. Pat handed Marie a large envelope. "Here, Marie, put these somewhere where we can find them. There's a whole bunch of pamphlets in there with maps of hiking trails and information on other fun stuff we may want to see or do while we're here."

Theda held up her envelope. "And I have our fire permit, some trash bags and a map of the campground. Okay, everyone, let's load up and be on our way. Want to drive for awhile, Pat?" Theda handed the keys to Pat.

Pat waved them off. "No, you're doing great. Not unless you're getting tired?"

"Nope, I'm fine. Come on everyone, hop in. We're off to find our camping spot."

The doors of the van were hardly closed when Gwen started to sing to the tune of *The Wizard of Oz*, "We're off to find a camping spot, a wonderful, wonderful spot! I wonder where, I wonder where, I wonder where it will be."

Twenty minutes later the group of six was standing by the edge of a turbulent river. The blue-green water smashed against the rock walls of the river bed creating large frothy white waves. "This is our camping site?" wondered Gwen out loud.

"Sort of noisy, isn't it?" yelled Louise above the sound of the water pounding over and against the rocks.

"It's beautiful. I love it!" yelled back Theda. "Where can we pitch our tents, Pat?"

"The attendant said there should be a pole around here with a number on it. Sixteen is our number," Pat glanced around the site. "There it is. He also said that we can go across the road and set up camp back in those trees over there if we want."

Theda stood by the water and took a deep breath. "Oh, just smell that! I never knew anything could smell that fresh." She turned to her friends, "Come on you guys, let's pitch the tent right here. It'll be great."

Edna stayed well back from the water. "I don't think we should stay so close to the water."

Theda snorted at Edna, "Why not? The river isn't going to overflow its banks and sweep us away in the middle of the night."

"I'm not worried about that, but what if we have to get up in the middle of the night to go to the bathroom, and let's face it, we all do, and we take a wrong turn and trip into that mad torrent of water."

Theda looked at the rest of the group imploringly, "Oh,

come on you guys. Just listen to that water. Doesn't it give you the most marvelous rush? Besides that, I guarantee you it'll lull you to sleep as soon as your head hits the pillow and it'll be such a deep sleep that your body won't even think about peeing in the middle of the night."

"Do you always have to be so vulgar?" sniffed Edna.

Theda looked at her surprised. "Vulgar? What are you talking about? Do you mean when I said, peeing? Good God, Edna, what's wrong with the word, pee? We blow our noses, we burp, we fart, we sniff, and yes, believe it or not, we pee, all common body functions, even for you, Miss Priss."

Louise poked Pat with her elbow, "Oh, oh, here we go again."

Gwen pushed her way into the middle of the group. "Well, I'm for putting the tent up right here, like Theda says. I was just glancing at some of that literature Pat and Theda picked up and I think this is the river where they do the whitewater rafting. Maybe we'll be able to watch a few rafts go by, and see if we'd like to try it ourselves."

"You're right, I think this is the river, but I doubt if this is exactly the spot that the rafts travel. It's probably farther down. Like this is really fast water, but there's not many rapids."

"Whoa, wait a minute. What are you talking about, try it ourselves?" interrupted Marie.

Theda laughed, "We mean, we're going whitewater rafting. It will be terrific!"

Marie looked doubtfully at her, "I don't think so! Count me out. The rest of you can go if you're that crazy, but me, I'm staying right here. It'll give me a chance to relax and catch up on my reading."

"Ah, come on, Marie, don't be such a loser. You'll never get another chance. It's not supposed to be that bad. Nancy Hardwick did it when she came out here to visit her son last summer, and she's seventy-two years old," volunteered Louise.

"Nancy Hardwick is crazier than a loon at the best of times," retorted Marie.

"I kind of think it might be fun," said Edna.

Theda looked at Edna, "What you know about fun I could put in a thimble."

"What are you talking about? I enjoy life as much as the next person."

Theda smirked and gently jabbed Louise on the arm. "Right, I forgot. You are the only one who has had any fun on this trip if I remember correctly. Who among us can forget the rodeo?"

Pat laughed to herself. "Come on people. Let's cut the gabbing and get these tents up. Then I'll take the van over to the woodpile and get our wood. The ranger guy said that we can have a small campfire tonight. They've had lots of rain here in the last few days so all the fire restrictions have been lifted. After I drop the wood off, I'm going over and ask about the whitewater rafting. The times and prices are in these pamphlets, so look them over while I'm gone."

Pat left in the van. The women were getting quite proficient at setting up their campsites so the tents went up in less than ten minutes.

Theda came up to Louise. "I'm going to set our stove up on this rock. When we go to use it, we'll have to put it on the table. Nice and quiet here, other than that water. Except for those two guys over there under those trees, there's hardly any other people around. I wonder if they're gay."

Louise looked over at the two young men. One was busy cleaning his shoes, and the other was sitting on his haunches stirring a small pot on a tiny stove. "Just because a couple of young men are camping together doesn't make them gay, Theda, and so what if they are, they're not hurting you any."

"Well, if they're gay, I won't waste my time on them."

Louise looked at her friend in disbelief. "Heavens, Theda, they're all of maybe twenty or twenty-five, don't you think they're just a little young for you?"

Theda sighed, "You're probably right, I keep forgetting I'm as old as I am. I don't know which is worse: being old and not feeling your age, or being old and feeling it. I never feel as old as I am, and then I'm disappointed when somebody points it out to me that I am getting old. Bugger."

An hour passed before Pat pulled the rustic van up in front of the two bright gold and blue tents. Half-secured window and door flaps flapped in the breeze. Theda and Marie were sitting on a couple of logs they had moved near the picnic table. Louise's head was buried in one of the coolers searching for something. They all looked up as Pat drove up. "Hi, girls. Well, I found the wood. It's on the passenger side on the floor. They don't give you a heck of a lot, but I guess it will be enough for half an hour or so. Also, I got the lowdown on the trip tomorrow. Sounds pretty good."

"Thought you were going to drop the wood off first, then go and inquire about the rafting."

"That was my plan, but I had to pass right by an info centre so went in. Thought it would save some time. Anyway, I take it everyone's going. I didn't hear any dissenters."

Marie's hand shot up, "Not so fast there. Major dissenter here. I am not going. The rest of you go. I don't mind sitting this out."

"Well, there's a bit of a problem. You see if all six of us go, we go as a team. The guide travelling with us makes a full boat. We get quite a hefty reduction on our fares if we take that route," reported Pat.

"I really don't care how the rest of you do it, but there's no way I'm setting foot in one of those flimsy rafts. You guys all know I can't swim a stroke. Look I'll pay the difference of whatever the increase in cost will be. Just leave me out of it."

"Come on, Marie. They give everybody a life jacket and a helmet. There's no way you can get hurt or sink or anything. Please!" begged Theda.

"Yeah, Marie, you hardly ever hear of anyone getting hurt on these excursions," said Louise.

"Exactly, you hardly ever hear about it, but it does happen, and I don't intend on being the one that you hear about or don't hear about."

Pat looked at Marie. "Louise's right, you know. I talked to one of the guides and he hasn't seen anyone carted away on a stretcher in all the time he's worked here."

"Ha! That doesn't prove anything. This could be his first day of work. Anyway, I've made my mind up. So don't even think of changing it. I'm staying right here."

"Okay, okay. Anyway, we've got until eight o'clock tonight to decide. That's when I have to reserve the raft and pay our deposit. So, think about it until then."

Shortly after supper, Louise and Gwen tidied up the eating area. "There," said Louise wiping her hands down the side of her jeans. "I'm going to go for a short little walk. I'll be right back, Gwen."

As Louise walked past the van she could hear someone rummaging around inside it. "Who's in there?"

Theda poked her head up to one of the windows, "Oh, hi, Lou. Just looking for a little surprise that I've been saving for just this moment. Where are you off to? You don't want to miss the surprise."

"Don't worry, I won't be gone long. I'll be back before you can say *Surprise!*"

Theda found what she was looking for and walked back to the table where the rest were sitting. She plunked a huge paper bag in the middle of the table and tried to anchor a tube of plastic glasses next to it. "Gang, I've got a treat tonight. Mama picked you all up some vino. It'll go real nice with the roar of that water." Theda popped the cork. "Grab some glasses, and I'll do the honours." After pouring four glasses, Theda looked over at Edna. "Sure you don't want a little drinkie pooh, Edna?"

"No, thanks, you know better than to even ask me. You know I don't drink, and if the rest of you knew what was good for you, you wouldn't either."

"Okay, sweetie, just don't say I never offered you anything." Theda took a good healthy sip from her glass then refilled both hers and Marie's. She recorked the bottle and then turned to Pat, "Can you believe the woman? She honestly believes that she has never had a drink. What does she think she was doing the night of the rodeo?"

Marie drained her glass and kept it tipped up in the air trying to get the very last drop. When she was finished she turned to Edna. "Actually, Edna, it's a well-known fact that a drink or two of either beer or wine is really quite good for you. Helps control all sorts of ailments, like heart attacks, high cholesterol, strokes. I just finished reading about it in a rather interesting and enlightening article in a health magazine. The magazine's in the van. Remind me to give it to you tomorrow to glance over."

Edna looked at Marie skeptically.

Marie continued, "I've read it in lots of other places, not just this one magazine, and on top of that my doctor actually recommended that I have a glass of red wine every day."

"Right on Marie," Theda smacked her lips, "and this is red wine!"

Marie smiled around at the group. "It definitely is red wine!"

Theda swept around refilling the glasses. "Here's to red wine! Marie, hand your glass over here closer, 'cause it looks pretty empty. Besides if one glass is good, two have got to be better, right?"

"Oh, I don't know. I've had my quota. I think two is quite muchly plenty. No, I mean plenty much, oh, I've had enough."

"Oh, come on, Marie, don't be a party-pooper. There's enough for everyone to have one more glass. Be a sport, there's a good old girl," Theda insisted. She held the bottle up in front of the little Coleman lantern to see its contents then reached over, picked Marie's glass from the table and refilled it. "There you go, old Mariesy Peasy." She handed the glass to Marie who accepted it.

"Hate to change the subject, ladies, but when are we going to light our campfire?" Gwen asked.

"Well, sweetie, I seem to have a full-time job as our chief wine steward this evening," Theda grinned at Gwen. "Why don't you get it going, that's a good girl?"

Gwen looked pleased that she would be trusted with the monumental task of starting the campfire. She had never done it before. It didn't take her long to gather up some scraps of paper and small twigs to use as kindling. "Who piled these stones right in the center of the fire pit? They weren't here when we came. Guess they won't hurt anything." Once she got the fire started, she added a couple pieces of larger wood, and then a bit more kindling. "There, isn't that pretty and cozy?"

They all agreed that it was indeed cozy, but the small pile of firewood that the park service had allowed them looked rather dismal. In a matter of minutes the little fire started to crackle and the dry wood popped. As the flames grew higher it wasn't long before the fire outshone the light given off by the little Coleman lamp. Just then Louise returned carrying a huge armload of branches that she dumped unceremoniously beside the existing pile of wood."Girl, what you doing?" demanded Theda, still dancing around with her huge wine bottle. "Louise, you haven't had a drink yet. Here, Theda will get you a glass, honey."

"Oh, Theda, I'd love a glass, but I just took some medication right after supper and you're not supposed to mix business with pleasure, so I'd better not this time, thanks anyway."

Theda smiled at her and then turned to Marie. "We might as well finish this since there's not enough to save. Hand your glass over."

Marie held her glass out to Theda, "Oh! I really shouldn't have any pore," she said, and then tried to correct herself, "more, more pore."

"Oh, just one more and then we can have a toast to our whitewater rafting trip and the river, to the river!" Theda raised her glass high in the air.

Marie did the same, "Yes, sir, absolutely. To the river! Forward, ladies. To the river. March, one-two, one-two." Marie started to march toward the river.

Pat and Theda grabbed her and turned her around.

Pat glanced at her watch, "Holy smokes, people, it's a quarter to eight! We have to get on over to the booth and register for our trip tomorrow. Hurry up, everyone in the van! We all have to sign the waivers. You can't have someone else do it for you."

Marie and Theda were walking with their arms around

each other's shoulders. Marie looked up at Theda, "What's a waiver, Theda?"

"I don't know, sweetie, something we have to sign. It's easy, you just watch me and do the same thing, okay?"

"Good idea. Let's go sign that wavy thingamajig."

Two young men stood talking beside a white minibus while they waited for their boss and the rafting patrons to arrive. Emblazoned on each side of the minibus was a scene, a close-up of two young people – a boy and a girl – big smiles on their faces. They were sitting in a huge yellow raft and one assumed that the huge white waves that surrounded their vessel were propelling them around the dangerous looking rocks. Bold black printing, *Devil's Own Whitewater Rafting at its Best* completed the scene. The taller of the two men turned as another man exited the building where Pat and her friends had registered for their outing the night before. He walked over and stood in front of the young men. "Yo, Randy, Sammy, you two can take the first trip this morning, together."

Randy looked at his boss, "Why together? We usually just ride one of us per raft."

"You'll see in a minute. I have a rather interesting group lined up for you two. Besides, we don't have another booking 'till ten, so Randy, you might as well go along for the ride. Anyway, back to the business at hand. Last night just before closing, six really classy dames signed up for a trip, and from what I understand they're all single, too!"

Sam's ears immediately perked up, "Six broads, no dates or significant others? Great!"

"Right on, Sammy, and here they come now."

Sam and Randy turned to watch six matronly figures making their way carefully down the narrow stairs leading from the building to the parking lot where the company's equipment was stored.

"I'm sorry Marie, but last night you signed your name and paid your money to go on this trip, so you have to go." Theda continued, "Besides nothing terrible is going to happen to you because people do this every day and no one gets hurt. Trust me, you won't drown. With that life jacket on you couldn't sink if you wanted to."

Marie looked back at Theda who was walking right behind her, "Well, last night I didn't know what I was doing."

"Yeah, and whose fault is that, Miss I-Usually-Only-Have-One-Drink?"

"Come to think of it, it was yours. You were the one who kept filling my glass."

"And you don't know how to say 'no'."

Marie laughed, "Actually, to you, it's pretty hard. Oh! My head is splitting. I really don't think I can go through with it. I might barf on you all when I'm in the raft. Actually, I'd like to barf on you. Think I'll sit right behind you and when we go over a big wave and the back end goes up, watch out."

"You can't be that sick, you only had three glasses of wine. Anyway, give me your hand and Theda will fix you up."

Marie put her hand on Theda's shoulder, "What do you want with my hand? You want to hold it?"

"Turn it over silly. I've got a pill for you. Take it and in no time you'll feel right as rain."

"A pill! Have you been raiding Edna's stash?"

Theda dropped a pill into Marie's hand. Marie clasp her hand shut and then opened it in front of her. "It's a pill all right. And how am I supposed to get this monster down me. I don't have any water."

"Oh, for Christ's sake, fifty million gallons of water flowing through this chasm every second and the woman wants more water. Just pop the pill in your mouth when we get out on the raft, and then open it when a big wave comes along. Trust me, it'll go down."

Sam and Randy stood with arms akimbo watching the group advance on them. "Hey, check out the little one in the middle."

They watched as a large orange ball propelled by two quick

little feet moved towards them. Two fat little arms stuck straight out both sides of the ball, and there was a little blue helmet perched on top of it. Louise had lost quite a bit of weight on the trip already, but still couldn't fit into a medium life jacket so she had had to use a large one which came well below her knees.

"Good morning, ladies, I want you to meet your guides for your upcoming adventure. This is Sam and the hunk to the right is Randy."

"Gee, they both are rather hunky," observed Theda.

"Theda, behave!" remonstrated Pat.

The boss laughed at Theda's remark and then apologized. "Sorry, Sammy, of course you're a hunk, too. Now ladies, I'll leave you all in the capable hands of these two…hunks…and have a good trip."

Randy stepped forward, "Good morning, ladies, as our boss said, we will be your guides for this morning's trip. Trust me when I say you are going to have the ride of your lives. Now, it's extremely important that your life jackets and helmets are secured properly. My partner and I will go around now and check your gear."

The two men pulled and tucked at the various life jacket and helmet straps making sure that everything was secure. Sam wiggled Theda's helmet, then pulled hard on her chinstrap. He tried moving the helmet again. Satisfied that it was sitting on her head snuggly, he stepped back.

"Holy freaking helmets, do they have to be that tight? I'm going to choke to death. If the water and rocks don't get me, this bloody helmet will." Theda stuck her tongue out as far as it would go and rolled her eyes.

Sam laughed, "Ladies, your helmet, on a trip like this one, may turn out to be your best friend. It can save you from bashing your head against a rock or another person's head. If they are loose, the water will just pull them off your head, and they'll be of no use whatsoever. If everyone's all set, into the raft."

Sam stepped over beside the mildly bouncing raft and lent his hand as each woman climbed into the raft. In short order, actually faster than Sam had expected, everyone was in and seated — everyone but Marie. He turned and waved for Marie to hurry up. While he was waiting for her he turned again to the other women, "Now, listen up, ladies. There are paddles, so if you feel comfortable enough to paddle once in awhile, do so. If not, just hang on. Randy and I will do the navigating, so don't worry about a thing. Just enjoy. We've never had a raft not make it to the end yet."

Marie edged up beside the bobbing raft. "Rafts maybe, but he didn't mention people."

Randy, who was holding the raft steady, overheard her. "Actually, we haven't lost any people either, unless, of course, you count that raft load of Scandinavians last week."

"Oh, and those other two groups from…where were they from…Germany and Switzerland, wasn't it?" added Sam.

"Yes, that's right, Germany and Switzerland." Randy winked at Theda.

Marie stepped back on shore. Everyone else sat on board waiting. Sam left the raft and went up to Marie and touched her arm gently, "We're only joking, ma'am. It's safe, really it is. Randy and I make this same run four or five times a day, and I swear, we've never had a mishap yet. Come on, I'll help you get in."

Marie finally gave in and climbed into the raft. After she was seated she made sure to anchor her feet under some ropes, and then she held on with both hands, one to a handle on the side of the raft, and the other to the edge of her seat.

Randy and Sam both swung their lithe bodies into the raft. Randy made his way to the extreme back where he grabbed two long oars that jutted out each side of the raft. Sam took a seat near the front.

"Okay, ladies, are you all ready? If the raft does happen to upset, don't panic. Just try to push off any rocks with your feet. You'll float downstream into calmer waters, and we'll pick you up there. So, ready Sammy? Ready to rock and roll, ladies?"

Everyone cheered in unison, everyone except Marie, whose hands were turning purple from hanging onto the raft so tightly.

The huge yellow raft bounced gently as the first waves carried it farther out into the river. Suddenly, the main current grabbed it. Randy quickly adjusted his stance; legs spread out in a big V to anchor himself, the ends of the oars were placed under his elbows so he could use the full force of his arms against the powerful water. As the current grabbed the raft and pulled it down the river, the water soon became quite rough. The raft lurched against the first huge wave. Most of the wave broke over the front of the raft, drenching all of the occupants with ice cold water. Theda gasped, "Oh, my God!" She looked over at Marie who was using both her hands and feet to hold on to everything it was possible to hold on to. She yelled at Marie, "Didn't I tell you? Just keep your mouth open and you'll have enough water to take fifty pills if you want."

The raft bucked and dipped into and under waves, barely missing the huge rocks that stuck treacherously out of the rushing water. Several times, it did nudge a rock or the side of the ravine and when it did its occupants were jostled roughly about in their seats. In seconds though the strong current yanked the raft about and soon pulled it in a new direction. Each time the raft dove down into a depression in the water and then sprang back up into the air, Theda screamed with delight. Louise, who sat in front of Theda, tried to shift to a more comfortable position. Her life jacket was so huge that, every time the raft went down, the life jacket moved up until it completely covered her eyes so she couldn't see. Then when the raft went up, she felt like she was going to pop right out of her jacket.

About the sixth or seventh time that the raft dipped into the water she lost her grip completely and was lifted right off her seat into the air. She landed down in the bottom of the raft by Theda's feet. Theda reached down and grabbed a corner of Louise's life jacket. A second later, Sam happened to glance around to see how everyone was doing. He saw Theda struggling with Louise. He turned and reached over and managed to grab the bottom of her life jacket. He signaled with his eyes for Theda to let go and with one mighty pull, he had Louise back in her own seat. He watched as she grabbed for one of the ropes of the raft.

Louise tucked her feet under her own seat, and mouthed a quick "Thanks" in Sam's direction.

Each time the raft rose and fell, Edna, sitting at the back of the raft, almost in front of Randy, felt like she was going to be flung from her seat. No matter how hard she tried, she just couldn't seem to get in sync with the ups and downs of the raft. As it plunged into the water, she seemed to be going up, and when the raft came up, her bottom whacked down hard onto the seat below her. She knew that Randy's legs were stretched out behind her. They looked so much more substantial than any of the ropes attached to the raft. She wanted desperately to turn around and grab one of them.

As the front of the raft dove into the water, the back, where she and Randy sat, rose high into the air riding the crest of a huge wave. The rest of the raft and its occupants disappeared from Edna's view. All she could see in front of her was a huge wall of white water. She screamed at each rise. As the raft approached the next section of the white frothing maelstrom, she tensed up and then screamed louder and harder than she had ever screamed as the raft undulated through and over the waves like a giant fat snake. "Oh, God, Oh, God!" The back end of the raft rose again and Edna felt her body rise into the air. She clung desperately to the handles on the raft to keep from being thrown into the white churning mass of terrible water.

Suddenly, they were in a narrow gorge where huge, wicked, glistening, grey rocks lined the frothy waterway. The raft hit one of the impenetrable walls and started to turn to the side. Randy tried to use his oars to turn the raft, but the right oar was caught between the raft and the hard surface of the wall. The back end of the raft rose sharply into the air. Edna and Gwen looked sideways at each other. Theda glanced back and saw the look of terror on Edna's face just before the back of the raft disappeared into the mass of churning white water.

As the front end of the raft emerged through the waves followed by the back end, Edna rose above the waves, water draining from every portion of her body.

She gasped quickly and yelled above the roar of the water, "Holy shit!!"

Edna turned slightly to see how Randy was managing at the back of the raft. Then she turned to face the front again and prepare for the next onslaught of waves. Suddenly, she turned back. Something was wrong. Randy was gone. His oars were slapping haphazardly against the side of the raft.

She thought quickly to herself. *Maybe he's still there. Just fell out of his seat.*" She made sure she had a good grasp of the side of the raft with her left arm and freeing her right one, reached behind her to see if she could feel Randy. There was nothing. She leaned as far back as she could just as one of the handles of the oars flipped up and whacked her across the side of her head. Her body immediately slumped down and she slid to the bottom of the raft.

Theda sensing that something was wrong turned her head just in time to see the oar strike Edna on the head. Each time the raft plunged down into the water, Edna's body floated to the top of the raft. Theda's immediate concern was that Edna's body, with one of the plunges, would float or be carried right out of the raft. She managed to poke Louise to signal to her to poke Sam who was busy trying unsuccessfully to direct the craft away from the sides of the rocks.

Theda turned completely around in the raft and grabbed Edna's legs, ducking to avoid the handles of the oars that were still swinging sporadically around the back of the raft. She managed to hook her own legs securely through the ropes lashed to the raft. With each dip of the raft, the water would tug mercilessly at Edna's inert form.

Theda's grasp was starting to weaken. Just when she thought she couldn't breathe in another mouthful of water, the raft suddenly hit calmer waters. Sam made his way expertly to the back of the raft and took over the oars. With several strong swipes, he maneuvered the raft to a flat outcropping just past the rapids. When the raft bottom scrunched against the gravely shoreline, Sam grabbed a long yellow rope attached to the front, jumped off the raft and pulled it up as far as he could onto the shore.

Theda sat in the back of the raft cradling Edna's ashen head in her arms. Blood trickling from a small gash in the side of Edna's head made its way down Theda's arm and finally pooled on the bottom of the raft. Theda screamed, "Oh, my God, guys, come and help me. Edna's been hurt!"

Sam ran around to the other side of the raft to get a better view of the water. He walked down the shoreline a few yards scanning the water behind the raft's previous path for any sign of Randy. Much to his relief he spotted an orange life jacket bobbing in the water a little to his left. Sam cupped his hands around his mouth, "Randy, are you all right? Do you need any help?"

Randy raised his hand over his head signaling that he was fine and could make it to shore on his own steam. Sam watched as his friend took a few strokes towards the shore. Suddenly, Randy started to make frantic gestures towards the shore. He frowned at his friend's antics. This was no time to fool around. He turned to see what Randy was pointing at and when he did his mouth dropped open.

The raft was floating back out into the water. He ran as fast as the gravel and rocks would let him. If he could only get a hold of the rope before the current picked the raft up. It was obvious that all of the women had made their way to the back of the raft to help their friend. Their combined weights had caused the raft to sink deeper into the water lifting the front end away from the land. Just as he reached for the rope dangling from the front of the raft, the river's current pulled the raft around pulling the rope out of his reach.

Sam dove into the water and tried desperately to catch up with fast moving vessel. His life jacket hindered his progress rather than helped him. Sam realized that any further attempts to try to rescue the raft and its occupants, were futile, so he turned and swam back to join Randy just as he emerged from the water. The men, standing side by side, breathed deeply as water streamed from their bodies. The raft moved rapidly downstream with five little heads gathered at one end of the raft.

"What the hell happened, man? Shee-it! What are we going to do? We can't even radio anyone, the damn phone's on the raft."

"Jesus! I only turned my back on them for a second. I should have tied the bloody thing down. I never dreamed that they'd all move to the back of the thing at the same time."

"Well, old bud, I think we can kiss this job good bye."

"Aw, I feel so bad. It's bad enough losing our jobs, but those poor old broads. Christ, if the raft doesn't swing over when they round that next bend they'll be heading straight for the Devil's Dropoff. Let's just hope they have the sense to hang on for dear life."

"Another raft should be coming through here in a few minutes. We'll have to Shanghai it, and go after them. As soon as it lands, we'll radio for help. Shit! Shit! Shit!" Randy kicked a rock into the water.

In less than five minutes a second raft broke through the white water. The oarsman in the back expertly directed the raft towards the gravely shoreline where Randy and Sam stood, waving frantically. Randy grabbed the front of the raft as it hit the shore near him. The raft belonged to another company, but Sam recognized the guide. He rushed to the side. "Paul, we need your radio for a few seconds. Have to make an emergency call."

Paul reached over and undid a large packet near his feet and reached in to retrieve a phone. He handed it to Sam, who walked several steps away from the group to place his call. When he returned, Randy was already in the raft. He had filled Paul and his friend in on their predicament. "Hop in, Sammy. We've got to find our raft. Hurry up!"

The turbulent ride that followed through the foaming, churning mass of water was exciting for the paying passengers, but not so for the dour-faced Sam and Randy. Horrible pictures of old ladies, their bodies dashed and mangled against the huge sharp rocks jutting up through the rushing water, kept flashing through Sam's mind. Randy kept thinking about the job he wouldn't have after this episode, and where he was going to get the money to finish his education.

It wasn't long before the second raft broke free of the swirling madness. Randy and Sam helped Paul and his partner paddle the raft to a small island that seemed to protect what looked like the mouth of a huge cave in the side of the mountain.

Randy reached over and tugged on Sam's jacket, "Look, over to the right, there, the raft!"

Sam shaded his eyes with his left hand, "Oh, my God, you're right!"

The raft was pulled well up on shore and five bodies lay stretched out in various positions. Three were slightly propped up against rocks, and two were spread-eagled on the gravel shore. A round yellow ball rolled back and forth along the shoreline.

"Oh, my God, they're all drowned!" yelled one of Paul's passengers.

Just then one of the drowned lifted her head and poked another one of the victims who instantly sat up and started waving. Soon there were five individuals dancing and waving. The yellow ball suddenly bounced into the water, but was immediately retrieved by two of the other women. One body remained propped up against a log.

"How many people did you have in your raft, guys?" asked Paul.

"Five, no six, yes, it was six," replied Randy.

"It looks as if all are well and accounted for. Maybe we shouldn't use the word well. It looks like you have one casualty. Not bad considering."

The raft pulled up right where the women were standing. Randy and Sam immediately jumped out and inquired, "Are you women all right? Your friend, is she hurt badly?"

Edna peered out as the troops approached her. She had a massive bump on the side of her head and when she tried to sit up, a bit of fresh blood trickled down the side of her face. Randy knelt down beside her, examined the cut on her face, applied a bandage to close the wound, checked her pulse, and turned to her friends who were watching the procedure. "I think she's going to be fine. Her pulse is good and strong. They'll probably put a few stitches in that cut, and she'll be right as rain."

Sammy added, "We've got a chopper coming in to airlift you ladies out. It should be here shortly."

"A chopper, no less! Man, wait till they hear about this back home!" Theda yelled giving Pat a good pound on the back that sent her stumbling forward.

Randy and Sam had expected that they would have to contend with six frightened, hysterical women, so they were very surprised when they were greeted instead by six seemingly happy and excited women. Even the one who was hurt wanted to get up to be with the rest of her friends. Randy and Sam both encouraged her to stay prone until the helicopter came.

At one point, while Randy was checking her bandage to see if it was still secure, Edna grabbed him by the front of his life jacket, "Young man, I was just that far," she held her thumb and forefinger a smidgen apart, "from God's doorstep, but He told me it wasn't time yet. Isn't that just wonderful?"

Randy gently helped Edna release her hand from his jacket and patted her on the side of the arm, "It certainly is, ma'am. It certainly is. Now, just lie back and try to rest. Everything's going to be all right."

***

Charlie was asleep when the phone rang. At first he thought the sound of a phone ringing was coming from the television. It took him a few seconds to realize that it was his own phone. Still groggy from sleep, he reached over and lifted the receiver. "Hello, Chuck here."

"Charlie, is that you? Doesn't sound like you. Hope I didn't wake you up. I didn't, did I?" asked Pat.

"Pat, no, I wasn't sleeping. Well, guess I was kind of… dozed off in front of the boob tube. How ya doing, gal? Good to hear from you."

"Charlie, you won't believe what happened to us yesterday. We all signed up for whitewater rafting and…" Pat recounted the entire trip for Charlie.

Near the end of the story, Charlie interrupted her. "How did you girls manage to get the raft steered towards the island?"

"Well, I was just getting to that. When we realized that our raft was floating back out into the middle of the river, you wouldn't believe it, but Louise of all people yelled at us to try to move to the front of the raft. I took over Theda's job of holding Edna and she managed to make it to the front with the rest. Then while we were doing that, Louise actually sat herself down in Randy's place, grabbed the two oars and started to maneuver us down the river. I guess she kind of inspired the rest of us, because all of us who could, grabbed a paddle and started to use it. When we made it through the bad section, which was relatively short, we managed to land smack dab in the middle of the island. We weren't going to let the same thing happen to us again that did before, so Theda and Marie grabbed the rope on the front of the raft, jumped out and pulled the raft up as far as they could. Gwen and Louise helped me get Edna out and then the five of us pulled the raft up on the shore until it was completely high and dry."

"Well, if only Edna was hurt, why did they lift you all out by helicopter? Is there something you're not telling me, Pat, you're not hurt or anything?"

"No, no. At first they were just going to lift Edna out because of her injury, but then I heard one of the boys radioing that since all the rest of us were old dollies, it might be best to take us all out. I guess they were afraid we'd all have heart attacks or something worse. Anyway, we were all lifted out by helicopter. Oh, Charlie, what a sensation! If you haven't done it yet, you've got to try it sometime. We were hanging in midair just by an iddy-biddy skinny string. The girls are waiting for me Charlie, so I'd better run. Contact you later. Bye."

Before Charlie had a chance to make a comment or even say good-bye, the receiver on the other end clunked in place.

***

Pat lifted the corner of the tent flap and peered outside. Sometime during the night a light greyish fog crept in, snuggling around the trees and tents. She checked her watch and saw that it was only six-thirty. She yawned and then rummaged around the end of her sleeping bag until she found her battered old running shoes. Since it was a bit nippy in the mountains at night, she'd slept with her socks on, so all she had to do was shove her feet into her shoes. Grabbing her jacket that was underneath her shoes, she eased her sore body out of the tent entrance trying not to disturb anyone who might still be sleeping.

Once outside, she quickly put on her jacket and then took a couple of steps towards the water. She looked around to see if anyone else was up. No one was. Pat shivered a couple of times and then yawned lifting both arms up slowly into a lovely big stretch. *Good. Everything still seems to be working,* she said to herself. *It was a wonder* she thought, *after that bone-crushing ride down the river*. She looked at the river surging along beside her. It was hard to imagine that they had actually come down this exact part of the river. What she wouldn't give for some film footage of that trip. They had advised her not to take her camera on the raft, and they had been right. It would have been soaked through and through, or worse yet, lost. It was unfortunate that no one back home would believe what she and her friends had been through. She reached into her jacket and found the ticket that they had issued the women for the ride. At least she had it to keep as a souvenir. She smiled as she glanced down at the ticket. "Bearer of this ticket is entitled to one ride on the *Devil's Own Whitewater Rafting at its Best.*" Underneath in small print she read, "A video of each thrilling ride, only $20.00."

Pat poked the ticket back into her jacket pocket. "I've got to get one of those," she said out loud to herself. She checked her watch again. Too early for the rafting place's booth to be open yet. Probably have to wait until after breakfast.

The flap of the other tent rustled and then swung up. Louise poked her head out the tent opening. "Oh, good, thought I heard someone out here. Morning, Pat."

Pat smiled over at Louise and yawned again before she replied, "Good morning, lady. Have a good sleep?"

"Oooo, brrr. I've got to get my jacket. Just a minute." Louise reached back into the tent to retrieve her jacket.

"What the hell? What are you trying to do?" yelled Theda.

"Sorry, Theda, I'm trying to find my jacket." Louise's large rump protruded from the tent as she poked her head and shoulders into the tent.

"Here's your bloody jacket. Now get out of here! God, you'd think you had a foot fetish or something."

Louise backed out, bending her head to avoid the tent flap falling on her hair. She laughed, "Boy, that one sure wakes up miserable," then she turned to Pat, "You guys were right about the sound of the water helping you sleep. I really do think I fell asleep before my head hit the pillow. Want to help me start breakfast? By the time it's ready, the rest of this crew should be up."

"Sure, I'm going to walk over to the restroom first. You have to go?"

"Might as well. Wait a sec while I tie my shoes."

"How's Edna doing?"

"Not bad. I think she spent a fairly comfortable night. Those pills they gave her for the pain probably knocked her out. Remember what the doctor at that clinic said. He doesn't want her taking any more pills today. Just to make sure everything is working all right."

"Yes, I heard him, but he said if there was still pain tomorrow she could take a couple more."

"The nurse said that because the skin was broken, the wound probably wouldn't swell as much as it normally would. I doubt if we can go for our hike today. She's not going to feel much like it." Louise reached over and grabbed the large coffee pot sitting upside down on the picnic table, "Might as well get some water while we're over there."

They had no sooner crossed the road to take the path to the kitchen and restroom area, when a black compact car flew by their campsite. Suddenly the car screeched to a halt. The driver backed the car up and parked directly behind the van. An agile young man jumped out of the car and started walking after Pat and Louise. Neither of them recognized him at first. He was carrying a parcel in his right hand.

It was Randy from the rafting company. "Morning, ladies. I know it's awfully early, but I start work at seven, you know, checking and setting up gear. Didn't know if any of you'd be up yet. How are you doing? How's your friend?"

"Fine, come to take us for another ride?" Pat smiled at the younger man.

"Uh, no, but I do have something for you. Don't know whether you were aware or not, but videos are always taken of our customers on their rides. Not the whole ride, mind you, just portions. It's about ten to fifteen minutes long. I think you'll be pleased with it. Unfortunately, it doesn't show you girls coming through the second run all by yourselves."

"Actually, I was just looking at my old ticket and did notice the little insert about the video. Just let me go and get my wallet. It's twenty dollars, isn't it?"

Randy waved his hand back and forth in front of him and shook his head, "Never mind. It's okay. This one is on the house. Company decided that you deserved a free one, so they made a copy for each person in your group. We hope you enjoy it."

"Are you trying to buy us off or something? Because if you are, it's working! Thanks ever so much. I know the girls will love this."

Randy handed Pat and Louise a medium-sized plastic bag.

"They're all in here. You can give them to your friends. Oh, and I hope you won't take exception to this, but the guys down at the raft company sort of, well, we admired your spunk. Also, we understand that none of you registered a complaint against us, not even your friend who was hurt. So we just want you to know that we appreciate that. Sammy and I saw this little thing in one of the souvenir traps down the road and it made us think of you people. Remember, we don't mean any disrespect by this. It's in the bag with the tapes. I've got to run now. It was great meeting you all. Bye."

Randy turned and ran back to the car where Sam sat revving the engine while he waited. The two boys waved as they drove away. Pat and Louise walked over to the restroom, and on the way back Louise stopped to fill the coffee pot with water from a little tap. When it was full, she set it down on the ground. "Here, Pat, you can help me carry it back. It's pretty heavy."

Pat walked over and took a hold of the handle closest to her. She waited while Louise bent down to grab her side. "And away we go. Coffee coming right up!" sang out Louise.

When they came back to their campsite, Theda and Edna had strung a string from one tree to another and were busy hanging their sleeping bags over the string. Theda turned as Louise and Pat placed the coffee pot on the table, "Thought we'd air these out for a couple of hours. I have another piece of string if anybody else wants to hang their bag up, too."

Pat came up and put her arm around Edna's shoulder. "How are you feeling this morning, Edna? Does your boo-boo hurt much?"

Edna looked at her and laughed, "Actually, no, it doesn't. I'm quite surprised. I feel really good. I'm so thankful. God certainly watched over us that day. He saved me." She looked heavenward, "Thank you, God."

Theda, who was shaking out her clothes from her duffel bag, muttered to Louise, "God be damned!"

"Now, now, Theda, be a good girl now." Louise pulled the Coleman stove out and shook it gently to see how much fuel was still inside it. "Sounds like there will be enough. Just pump a little air in here, then I can put the pot on and we'll have coffee before you know it."

"Be careful near that little pit there. I was pushing some rocks and stuff around over there, and they're still really hot from last night. I couldn't believe it," Theda warned.

Louise laughed, "That's not from last night…well, it is sort of. Remember all that wood I gathered yesterday? Anyway, I came out regularly last night to keep our little fire burning."

Theda looked at her in disbelief, "Why in the world would you do that?"

Louise looked over at her and said, tongue-in-cheek, "Oh, never mind. I just couldn't sleep, so it gave me something to do."

"Whatever turns you on, honey."

Louise looked over at the tents and yelled, "Hey, Gwen and Marie, get your lazy bones out here. Breakfast is ready and we have a surprise for you, hurry up!"

It wasn't long before the last two women, yawning and stretching, joined the group around the picnic table. Marie sat down at one end and immediately jumped up. "Yikes, that seat is wet!"

"You want that we should dry it off before you plunk your royal rump down, your majesty?" teased Theda.

Marie looked over at her and replied, "Well, actually, yes, it would have been appreciated." Then she turned to Pat. "What's the surprise? But before you tell us what it is, I wish to file a formal complaint. I distinctly heard someone say that breakfast was ready. I don't see or smell any breakfast. Where is the big fat liar?"

Louise popped up. She was busy whipping eggs together for scrambled eggs. "That was me. I'm the big fat liar. I just wanted you to get up. Randy popped over on his way to work and left us something. Pat has it."

Pat pulled the six videos out of the bag and handed one to each of her friends explaining about them as she did so. When she was finished, she took one last look in the bag, reached her hand in and drew out a large rolled piece of heavy flannel-like cloth. It was tied with a red ribbon.

"What do we have here? Randy said there was something extra."

Theda was bouncing up and down like a small child yelling, "Undo the ribbon and let's see what it is. Hurry up!"

Pat undid the ribbon and slowly started to unwind the scroll. After a couple of rolls it became obvious that it was a banner and by the time she opened it up completely, it stretched about three feet across. The words GREY POWER, emblazoned in bold red across a soft grey background, jumped out at her. She smiled and turned the banner for the rest of them to see. Everyone laughed.

Pat looked at the sign again, "You know, if anyone had given me one of these signs a month or two ago, I'd have been so insulted. Now I could care less. If you want to know the truth, I'm kind of proud of it."

Theda grabbed the banner and looked at it more closely. "You damn well right we should be proud of it, after all, we survived Devil's Gorge."

"Yes, and we did it on our own," added Marie.

Theda held the banner over her head. "I think that deserves a place in our back window. People can look at that instead of Edna's ass."

Everyone laughed when Edna blushed. Then she walked over to Theda and held out her hand for the banner. "And since it was my ass, I think I should have the honour of hanging the banner."

Theda raised her eyebrows at Edna's request. The rest of the group stood with their mouths open.

Edna took the banner and turned to Theda, "Think you can find something that I can stick this on the window with?"

"Oh, my lordie, my bacon, it'll be burned to a crisp!" yelled Louise jumping up to attend to her smoking frying pan.

Edna and Theda went to hang the banner while the rest ran over to the little stove where the strips of bacon snapped and crackled. "Oh, thank goodness, it's all right. I'll just turn them over, before they start to stick." Louise expertly grabbed the corners of the bacon and flipped them over, patting each one to flatten it out.

"Oh, that smells good," offered Marie, "but why are we having bacon? Not too good for the old cholesterol levels."

Louise kept flipping the bacon, "I know, but I just couldn't resist. Here by the water, the fresh mountain air. This will be the last time, I promise."

Marie laughed, "You're right, it is lovely here, so I won't argue about it. Anything I can do to help?"

"You can get the bread out. This bacon will soon be done, and then I can do the eggs. The rocks in the campfire should still be hot enough to toast bread."

After the delicious breakfast, Pat and Gwen washed the dishes while the rest finished tidying up their campsite. Edna came over as Pat and Gwen were finishing tidying up the dishes. Pat was placing the clean pans back into their containers.

Gwen gave the tea towel a sharp snap and threw it over the line. "Hi, there, Edna. Head still all right? Pat and I were just talking about you. We think maybe it might be a good idea to wait until tomorrow to take that hike up the mountain. You'll feel better by then."

"Oh, don't be silly! Don't delay it on account of me. I feel fine, really. It's such a gorgeous day out, so nice and sunny. Who knows what it will be like tomorrow? It could be all cloudy, or even worse, it could be raining. Cook while the pot's hot, or maybe it's the stove, or the fire, I don't know. Guess the blow to my head has done something to my thinking process. Anyway, what I'm trying to say is, let's go today."

Pat looked at her crew. "All right, we'll go, but only if you promise, Edna, to tell us if you don't feel well. Promise?"

"I promise. Don't forget to bring your camera, Pat. I heard that the scenery is breathtaking."

"Yes, and if we get up high enough, I'll get to spit off the edge of a cliff," piped up Gwen.

Three hours later the fearless six-some were trekking over a rough rocky trail. It started in a heavily wooded portion of the mountain, but soon changed to a pathway surrounded by rocks and boulders. The path was well-used and they had met several other parties who had made the climb earlier in the morning and were now returning. Twice they had moved to the side of the trail to let younger sets of hikers pass them. It was reassuring to know that there were other people around if they needed help, but not too many that it took away from the feeling of being alone in the wilderness. The women had moved slowly up the mountain and had taken several rest periods in which they either perched themselves on an available rock or flopped against the nearest tree to catch their breath. The fourth time that they stopped they found themselves overlooking a fairly wide valley with a ribbon of river running through it.

"Oh, isn't that gorgeous! What a view!" proclaimed Marie. "Pat, take a picture of us all together with that magnificent backdrop. It's too bad someone wouldn't come along now so we could get them to take the picture and we'd all be in it together."

Pat slipped her camera over her head. "Well, maybe we don't need anyone." She slipped the lens cover off her camera and tucked it into the back pocket of her jeans. Then she peered through the viewfinder for a couple of seconds. "Help me pile some of these flat rocks on top of each other. Probably need about three feet of rock to hold the camera, and I can tip it the rest of the way with a tiny stone or a coin."

In less than three minutes the rocks were stacked and the women posed by the edge of the large overhang. Pat peeked through the viewfinder. "It's perfect. Don't need any more. Make room for me someplace. I'll just press the timer, and...here I come!"

Theda and Marie had left a space for Pat who ran and jumped into it. Everyone smiled as the little red light on the timer continued to blink for several more seconds and then finally the camera clicked. Pat went back to retrieve her camera.

"This looks like as good a place as any to stop for our lunch. I doubt that we'll get a better view than this," suggested Louise.

Theda eased her knapsack off her back and let it drop at her feet. "I can't think of a better suggestion," she wheezed.

"Just watch yourselves if you start wandering around, guys. That's a cliff over there, and it's a mighty long ways straight down from the looks of it," reminded Pat.

"Oh, good. I can spit," declared a happy Gwen.

"Don't you dare go near that edge, Gwen," demanded Theda.

Gwen smiled at her and walked over and gingerly peeked over the edge of the cliff.

"Gwen, please get away from that edge. You're giving me the willies," said Marie.

"If I start to fall, don't worry, I'll just grab a hold of this branch here, see." Gwen grabbed in mock desperation at a branch from a gnarly old tree. A loud crack echoed against the surrounding rock walls and the branch broke away from its parent tree. Gwen quickly righted herself and stood at the edge of the cliff with the broken branch in her hand.

"Oh, pooh!"

Everyone gasped, then Theda yelled at her, "There, see, you'll kill yourself before you're done. Get your white ass over here, now! Sit down and behave."

Louise snickered, "Not only that, but if she went over the edge she'd have taken half our lunch with her. It's in her knapsack. Hurry up, Gwen, come over here and let's open up lunch. I want to see if it worked."

Theda looked at Louise, "What do you mean, see if it

worked? I'm famished. Whatever it is, it damn well better have worked. Don't tell me you're experimenting on us. If it didn't work, you're in big trouble, lady."

Louise helped Gwen slip her knapsack off her shoulders. Gwen sighed as the weight left her back, "Well, I'd sure like to know what I've been carrying around, it's starting to get darn heavy. What's in here anyway, rocks?"

"Actually, come to mention it, yes."

"The woman's finally flipped. She's going to try and feed us rocks."

Louise set the knapsack on the ground, opened it, and slowly withdrew a large bundle of newspapers.

"No, she's not going to feed us rocks. She's going to feed us newspapers," laughed Marie.

Pat slapped Marie on the back, "Well, at least you'll have something to read."

Louise proceeded to unwrap the newspapers and then carefully tucked them back into the knapsack so that they wouldn't blow away. Finally, she pulled out an ovalish piece of aluminum foil and quickly transferred it to a flat rock next to her.

"Ooooh, hot!" Louise blew on her fingertips. "This will be our table, ladies. Sorry, I didn't bring any knives and forks. You'll just have to use your pinkies."

As soon as she opened the top of the aluminum foil the tantalizing smell of roast chicken wafted through the air. She pulled the aluminum foil down on all sides to display the mouth-watering roast chicken. The meat fell away from the bones when Louise touched it. She took a small piece, blew on it, and then popped it into her mouth. She chewed a couple of times and closed her eyes, "Mmmmm, that is so good. Help yourselves, girls. Careful though, it's very hot."

Everyone reached inside the bowl Louise had created with the aluminum foil and took a piece of the chicken. Theda smacked her lips, "Oh, boy. You really outdid yourself, Louise. Who woulda thunk? Good, good, good!"

It wasn't long before all that was left of the bird was the carcass. Louise jumped up and reached for her own knapsack.

"Don't worry, girls, I have one more here. Also, Theda, you and Pat have the juice in your sacks, and someone has the bread. I think it's Marie. I didn't make the bread, but when I ran down to that little market this morning to get the chickens, there was a lady there selling buns and bread, fresh-baked this morning."

"We didn't have enough wood to do this, did we?" asked Gwen, her mouth full of tasty chicken.

Louise laughed, "Don't you remember, when we got here I went out and gathered wood. I wanted lots so I could get a couple of those stones in the fire really hot and keep them hot. All through the night, I kept going out to stoke it and throw a couple logs on it each time."

Gwen giggled, "I thought you just had a bad case of the runs or something and had to keep going to the bathroom."

"No, just keeping the home fires burning. Anyway, this morning when I picked up the bread, I also picked up a couple of chickens that I had asked the manager of the little store to save for me. Brought them back here. I had to whack the stones a couple of times to get rid of any soot and then I pushed a couple of them into each cavity of the chicken with a sturdy little stick. Then all you do is throw some spices on the chicken, wrap it in aluminum foil, then a few layers of newspaper around for insulation, and presto! While you're walking along, the stones cook the chicken. I think it's the neatest thing."

Pat reached over and pulled a wing off the last chicken. "It's delicious, Louise, and don't think I don't appreciate your effort, but that's exactly it, an effort. It really seems like a lot of work. You know, keeping the fire burning, and finding a chicken in the first place. Like, if you were really camping, who would have a couple of chickens in their food arsenal?"

"I guess if you were really out in the wilds, you would have caught a couple of grouse or something. No, I agree, it was a lot of work, but I had read about it somewhere or maybe I saw it on television, I forget. I just wanted to see if it worked."

"Well, it certainly did. Your experiment with stones and chicken can only be classed as an all-out success," offered Theda.

Gwen stood and looked at the little pile of stones and

bones, then at Louise, back to the stones and bones, then at the rest of her friends. “You mean to tell me that you made me carry rocks up the side of this mountain? No wonder my knapsack was so heavy. Excuse me ladies, but I’m going to go spit.”

The women all smiled as Gwen walked over to the edge of the cliff. “God, I hope she’s careful,” whispered Marie.

“What’s with that woman and spitting off of high places?” asked Pat.

They all watched as Gwen leaned over and spit out a globule of liquid. She leaned just a little farther out and watched until her shiny glob of spit disappeared. Then she turned back to the others with a big smile on her face. “There, I spit!”

Theda drained her glass of juice and tucked the plastic glass into her pack, “I’m so glad. I hope you’re happy now.”

Louise jumped up, “I think I’ll try it, too. Have to see what the big thrill is.”

“Oh, no, please dear God. Not another one,” protested Theda looking up to the sky.

Louise walked to within six or seven feet of the edge of the cliff and then got down on her hands and knees and crept slowly to the edge. Finally when just her head peeked out over the opening, she spit. Then she slowly crept backwards until she felt safe enough to stand up, “She’s right. It is sort of fun. You guys should try it.”

“No, thanks, I think two weirdos per van is about all we can handle right now,” protested Pat.

Louise turned to face the group, hoisted her track pants up, then walked back to help tidy up the remnants of their lunch. Pat watched Louise as she moved around the temporary campsite. Louise’s sweat pants were getting quite loose and she had to keep pulling them back up to her waist. Also, when she knelt down to retrieve anything off the ground, her big tummy that practically used to drag on the ground before had almost disappeared. She used to have to take a big breath before she stood up, but now she was going up and down with the best of them. Her little feet still looked like they had little wheels attached. Pat laughed to herself because she still resembled a little ball rolling along the surface of the ground, but the little round ball was turning into something more like a little football.

She thought back to a time when Theda was describing Louise as "Just a big happy face. No body. Just a big happy face rolling along the ground."

Pat looked at Louise once more and said out loud to herself, "You can't say that about her any more, with the fat disappearing from her face, you can actually make out some of her features and damn if she isn't becoming quite a pretty lady."

***

Gary, Louise's son, came into the kitchen via the back door. He took off his suit coat and flung it over the back of the nearest chair. Then he walked over to the little desk by the phone and leafed through the mail: three bills, two advertising leaflets, and a letter. Recognizing his mother's writing on an envelope he picked it up and tried to make out the smudged postscript.

"Ah, news from Mom, good." Gary opened the envelope, left the letter on the table in front of the chair with his coat on and went to the fridge to grab a can of pop. When he came back to the table, he pulled the tab on the pop can, waited a few moments for it to stop fizzing, then sat down and started to read.

Dear Loved Ones,

It's been quite awhile since you heard from me. I know you've heard indirectly from Charlie and some of the others like Jason, but I think it's time I sat down and told you some of my feelings. I know I left rather quickly, but I was really hurt when (I must confess) I overheard your comments the day I brought the pie over to your house.

Since then, I've done a lot of thinking about my relationship with you all. First of all, you must know that I love each and every one of you more than I can possibly describe, and I know you love me, too. Some of us, I'm talking about me really, have a tendency to think that we have to devote every waking hour to the people we love to show them that we love them. I've been away from you all a few weeks now. I've been occupied doing quite a few rather exciting things, seen countless wonders and I've found that I still have time to think of you and care for you. The only difference is I'm just not there to physically do anything for you. I miss that.

What I'm trying to say, is I think a person can do both, so when I get back home, I hope to see lots of you, but not too much. I'm going to spend more time with my friends who have become like a second family to me. I'm going to enjoy them, you, and someone who I think I have been neglecting for years, someone very important to me, myself.

Love you all to bits,

Mom and Grandma Louise

Chapter Seventeen

Windshield wipers screeched against wet glass as they laboured against the heavy snow. As fast as the blades pushed the white sticky stuff to the side of the window, the snow covered it again. Pat leaned over the steering wheel. She had her sunglasses on. Even though there was no sunlight to speak of, the dark glasses seemed to help cut through the falling snow. The headlights, which she had turned on a half-hour ago, didn't seem to help her see the road any better, but perhaps they would help an oncoming car to see their vehicle. "Listen, people, we're going to stop here in Golden for the night. I know it's early, but I'm really not comfortable driving on these mountain roads under these conditions. Only the devil and his cronies would be out on a day like today. I don't think the weather is going to get any better any time soon."

Theda used the edge of her sleeve to wipe the frost from the side of her window. She held her breath while she peered through the little hole she had created. "Pat, Pat, right over there. See to the right, that's a motel. We can stay there."

Pat drove on a few more yards ignoring Theda.

"Pat! That was a motel, right there. What's the matter with you?"

"Theda, I'm going to pull in right by this little store here. I'm going to go in and ask if this is the only motel in town. No sense staying in a dump if we have a choice. It will only take a minute. You might want to crank your window down just a smidgen, 'cause I'll leave the motor running to keep you warm."

Pat pulled her jacket collar as far up around her head as she could, opened the van door and high tailed it over the sidewalk and into the little store.

Theda rolled her window down a bit and then turned towards the back seats, "I didn't think that motel looked like a dump. Oh, well, whatever, I just hope wherever we go the rooms have showers, or better yet, a bathtub. What I wouldn't give for a real bath."

"I'm hoping there's a bank in this town. I'm getting pretty low on cash. Wouldn't mind restocking," said Marie.

"Oh, and just think, a real meal for a change," volunteered Gwen.

Louise looked over at her, offended. "Well, thank you very much!" Since Louise had joined the group, she had almost single-handedly done all the grocery shopping, and all the cooking for everyone. Any offers of assistance were usually turned down.

"Oh, pooh, I'm sorry, Louise. I didn't mean what it sounded like. I think your cooking is wonderful. I meant that for a change it will just be so nice to sit at a regular table, with regular glasses, knives and forks, on a regular chair and eat a regular meal." She looked over at Louise, "You notice that I said it would just be a regular meal, not a wonderful, scrumptious, yummy meal that you had prepared. Am I forgiven?"

Louise chuckled, "Yes, you're forgiven," patting Gwen on the shoulder, "and I think it will be nice to sit down to a regular meal, too. Oh, here's Pat. Back already."

"Good news and bad news, girls. The bad news is that that is the only motel in town with a vacancy and the good news is that the proprietor of that store said that it's really quite a half-decent place. There is another motel, but it was out on the highway. We must have passed it coming in, and there's one on the other side of town, too, about the same distance. Also, there is a bank in town and right across the street from here there's a tavern," she turned her head and looked at the sign across the street. See it's called *The Bear Facts*. You're supposed to be able to get an excellent meal there. So, what I'm proposing is, why don't you all go over and grab us a table while Gwen and I drive back and book us a couple of rooms. If we're lucky, we can get adjoining ones."

Theda was the first to get out of the van. As soon as her feet touched the ground she pulled her collar tightly around her neck. The others soon followed. As soon as the four women had crossed the road and entered the tavern, Pat backed the van up and drove over to the motel.

The second Theda opened the door to the tavern loud raucous laughter and gay, tinkling piano music wafted out to meet them. It took a few seconds before any of their eyes became accustomed to the dark.

"God, they sure don't believe in wasting any electricity in this berg," muttered Theda under her breath. "Brrrr. Cold out there." She blew on her cupped hands and then stood rubbing them together trying to restore some circulation.

"Gee, wonder if something is going on here, seems to be a lot of people in town," observed Marie.

"Maybe a rodeo, what do you think, Edna? Maybe you'll get lucky again," added Theda cattily.

Edna's first instinct was to ignore Theda's comment, but she changed her mind and retorted, "Jealous, are you Theda?"

Louise and Marie exchanged looks. Louise patted Edna on the back, "Good one, Edna." Then she turned and did the same to Theda. "Think she got you that time, Theda."

Clattering dishes and clinking glasses accompanied a tinny piano as it rolled out a tune from the far corner of the huge tavern. A pert young lady approached the women. She grabbed several menus from a large waist-high table, "Hi, ladies, welcome to *The Bear Facts*. How many? Going to need menus?"

Theda looked at the little girl in front of her, with her little fringed shirt, the bottom of which was tied up tight beneath her boobs, exposing a perfect little bare midriff. She had the usual Western accoutrements, cowboy hat and boots. She also sported a pair of hip-hugger shorts. The whole ensemble made her look more like a high school cheerleader than a waitress. Theda smiled at her and replied, "There will be six of us, and yes, we'd like menus."

The girl turned and stood on her tiptoes to look out over the crowded room. She bit her bottom lip lightly. "We're so busy. Just a minute, I'll be right back. I'll go see what I can rustle up for you."

She turned quickly on her little boots, the bottom of her little bum cheeks showing beneath her shorts. She disappeared into the maze of tables and thick smoke that hung over the room. It wasn't long before she bounced up in front of them again all smiles, "You're in luck, ladies. That is if you don't mind sitting with a couple of gentlemen that are already at this particular table. They said they don't mind if you join them."

Theda looked back at the other women. They all agreed that they didn't care where or with whom they sat as long as they could do just that, sit. "You do remember that there will be two more joining us soon. Will there be room for them, too?"

"Oh, I don't think there will be any problem. It's a pretty big table, and it's just a matter of stealing a couple more chairs from some other table. Just follow me." The little cowgirl led the women to a good-sized table on the other side of the room. She added, as she placed the menus on the table, "The group that was here before just left to join their friends. They have a place closer to the stage. These, ladies, are the two gentlemen that are letting you share their table. I'll leave you to your own introductions. Be back in a sec to take your orders."

The women all smiled and nodded to the two men. Theda walked over and drew out a chair beside the one closest to her. He sat with both elbows on the top of the table; hands supported his chin and a wide black cowboy hat graced his head. A fresh draught of untouched beer sat in front of him.

"Hi, how you doing, guy? Name's Theda and this is Marie, Edna and Louise." She pointed at the women as she said their names.

The man lifted his pointer finger of his left hand in greeting, "'Lo, ladies. My name's Lester, and the good-looking son of a bitch to my right here is Furball. Say, hello to the ladies, Furball."

Theda leaned around Lester to greet his friend. She looked him over quickly and then scanned the room. Furball seemed to be the only person in the entire room who wasn't wearing either a cowboy or a sports cap. Theda looked him over and thought to herself, *He's either bald or has recently shaved his head, because it's as smooth as a billiard ball. Doesn't have any eyebrows or eyelashes either. No sign of a moustache or even a four o'clock shadow. He's got the bluest eyes, though, really beautiful. For a guy with no hair, he's really quite attractive.* Furball smiled angelically at each of the women in turn and nodded his head.

"It's so dark in here I can't make out anything on this menu," Marie complained as soon as the introductions were made.

Lester slowly extracted a lighter from his shirt pocket and reached over and lit the little lamp in the middle of the table. When he was sure the wick had caught, he pushed the lamp over to Marie. "Perhaps this will help somewhat."

Marie looked up, "Oh, thank you." She pulled the lamp closer and peered at the menu again. "Yes, it definitely helps. This is great! Oh, and look on the back of the menu, some interesting *Bear Facts*. Isn't that cute?" Marie read quickly and then looked up, "Listen to this. It says here that an adult Brown Bear can increase its weight by 40 percent over the summer."

Louise clapped her hands together, "Ha, that's nothing! I can easily do the same thing over Christmas holidays."

Marie smiled then continued reading out loud. "And, listen to this. There's a bear called the Sloth Bear found in India and Sri Lanka, and oh, there's even a Spectacled Bear that has big white, circle patches around its eyes. That one is from South America. Also, did you know that the adult Grizzly Bear can weigh as much as 860 pounds and the babies at birth only weigh eleven to twelve ounces?"

Theda reached over and grabbed the menu away from Marie, "Here, give me that damn thing. Enough about bears, okay!"

Marie giggled and picked up Louise's menu. "Also, there are no bears in Prince Edward Island. That's interesting, I didn't know that."

Theda shook her head in disgust. "I really could care less how many or how few bloody bears there are anywhere in this world."

"You'd care if one of them happened to visit our campsite some night. They are quite the nocturnal animal I understand."

Theda closed her eyes and shivered, "Don't tell me that."

Their waitress returned. "Back again, ladies, ready to order, yet?" she asked enthusiastically.

Marie looked up at her and grinned, "I'm sorry, but I think we'll wait until our friends come to order our meal, but could we get a round of drinks while we're waiting. We'll get a couple of drinks for them, too."

"Sure thing, whatever you want. Go ahead."

After everyone ordered drinks, Edna added her order of a beer. She had read several of Marie's medical articles on the effects of minor quantities of alcohol on the body so didn't feel as if she was abandoning her principles by having one beer a day. *After all,* she thought to herself, *it was just what the doctor ordered.*

Theda pushed her chair back, and stood up. "Gotta find me a restroom, guys. Don't go away, I'll be right back." Marie bent over the vacated chair and touched Lester on the arm. "Hope you don't mind me asking, but why is your friend named Furball? You know…like he doesn't seem to have any, you know, fur or hair."

Lester put both hands around his glass and played with it for several seconds, then he snorted softly, "Oh, you know, people always seem to get hung up on opposites."

"Opposites?"

"Yeah, you know, sometimes they'll call someone who is fat, Slim, or someone who is tall, Shorty or someone who is bald, Curly. Opposites, like…." Lester started to stroke his black moustache, then he leaned over to Marie, "like, your nickname would be Ugly, Real Ugly. Do you see what I mean?"

Marie giggled nervously, "Yes, yes, I think I do."

Lester pushed his glass over into Theda's spot, and then

stood up and sat down behind his glass. He smiled at Marie, "Thought I'd just move closer. No sense us having to yell ourselves silly. Hope you don't mind."

Marie smiled, and glanced over at Furball. He smiled back at her. Goodness, how could someone with no facial or head hair at all be so attractive? Granted, he was far too young for her. Actually so was Lester for that matter but, like Theda said, it never hurt to look. She began to wonder if Furball had any hair on any other part of his body. She felt her face redden and then laughed out loud, embarrassed at her thoughts.

Lester looked over at Marie and laughed with her, "What's so funny?"

"Oh, nothing, Lester uh...we're just travelling through and I was wondering, do you fellows live around here?"

Lester took a sip of his beer and let the cool liquid sit in his mouth for a few seconds while he thought over Marie's question. Then he swallowed and replied, "Yes, and no. We have a place farther up in the mountains. We do a little hunting. The odd time we take hunters off the beaten trail to do a little hunting. Yanks, mostly. They like to hunt bear and the odd goat. We do enough to keep ourselves alive."

"Couldn't you find some work down here? Living back in the mountains must be rough."

"Yeah, it's rough all right, but we both like it away from the hustle and bustle of town life. Besides, my buddy has a few problems. He doesn't do too well in civilization. Or we could say civilization doesn't do too well with Furball in it. He has a bit of a medical problem. Something just a bit wrong in his head. Gets a bit mixed up with what you can and cannot do. I bring him out once in awhile. We pick up a few staples for our cabin, buy a little ammunition, and then come over here for a couple of drinks and a good meal. Tomorrow we'll head on back, quite happy to do so."

"How does Furball manage out in the bush?"

"Seems when he's back up the mountain, he's just fine. Normal as pie. There's no one I know that I could trust with my life if I was in a pinch as much as I would Furball."

Marie glanced back over at Furball. No one was sitting near him at the moment, but he was talking and laughing, looking like he was having a great old time. She smiled at him, and turned back to Lester, "What specifically is wrong with him? Couldn't he get some help with his problems, medication or something?"

Just then, Theda returned from the restroom. "Look who I found wandering around the place." Pat and Gwen were right behind her. Theda looked at the table. "Our drinks not here yet? What's the holdup? Pat and Gwen, don't worry we ordered you drinks, as well. Grab a seat." Theda walked around Lester and leaned over to Furball, "Heh, cute thing, want to get up and shake your bootie a bit?"

Marie looked at Lester, "Oh, should she? Maybe she shouldn't bother him?"

Lester watched as his friend stood up, adjusted his belt and followed Theda to the dance floor.

"Oh, don't worry. He won't get violent or anything. He likes to dance. He's really quite a good dancer. Besides, he's on medication. There's a bit of tranquilizer in it. You were asking about medication; well, he's on it, but mostly just when we come down here, though. He and lots of people usually don't mix too well. The sooner we're out of here, the better, for him and everyone else."

By this time everyone was listening to Lester. "Last time I brought him out he was outside waiting for me over at the post office. They have a sort of bulletin board there and he spotted a poster that told about an upcoming Turkey Shoot. I think the Legion or some such group was sponsoring it. He asked me if I thought it would be okay if he went to that Turkey Shoot. I thought, why not? He's one hell of a good shot. The man could shoot the tongue off a snake at fifty paces. If he could manage to win us a frozen turkey or a big juicy ham, that would be great. We could cart it on up to the hills with us and not have to worry about fresh meat for a few days."

"Anyway, we parted company, and I don't know, an hour or so later I'm coming out of the grocery store and this police car goes roaring by me heading out of town. Just about ran me over. Stupid cop! At the time, I didn't think too much about it. Maybe there was an accident out on the highway."

"A few minutes later, I was heading on back to the post office 'cause I had a letter I'd forgot to mail. And didn't that same police car come barrelling down the road at me again. This time though the police fellow puts on his brakes and stops right in front of the R.C.M.P. building. The officer gets out, opens the back door and reaches in and bedamned if it isn't Furball that he pulls out of that car. He's got handcuffs on and everything. I ran over right away to see what the hell was going on."

Lester plucked a cigarette out of the band of his hat, popped it into his mouth, leaned over the candle and puffed on it until the end glowed red. Then he leaned back in his chair and proceeded to take several long puffs.

Gwen was sitting on the edge of her seat by this time, her empty glass still in her hands, "Well, don't stop there. What happened?"

Lester reached over and patted one of her hands. "Just be patient, sweet thing, I'm getting to it. Anyway, I ran over and the officer was shoving Furball ahead of him into the R.C.M.P. office so I followed right behind the two of them.

"He threw Furball into a cell and then turned to me, 'Now, McTavish,' he says. I told him 'That's my name,' and he says, 'Okay, McTavish, don't get smart with me. Your friend just told me that you told him to go out to McNally's Turkey Farm and shoot all his turkeys. I just came from McNallys and every last one of his two hundred prized White turkeys has been shot dead. I'd advise you both to find a lawyer. I'm going to have to arrest you, too, until we can get to the bottom of this.'

"He proceeded to shove me into the clink with Furball, who's just sitting in the corner mumbling to his own self. I have to give the officer credit, though, because he sat down just outside our cell door and listened to everything I had to say on the matter. I told him about Furball's problem and also gave him the name of the doctor that Furball had been seeing for a number of years. He phoned him and within an hour or so he came back and said we could leave the jail as long as we left town right away. He let me pick up our groceries and anything else I'd needed and then he personally ushered us both right out of town. Advised us that the longer we stayed away the better it would be for us. Seeing as how we didn't have hardly any money between the two of us to pay for all those dead turkeys, it was either keep us in jail or send us on our way. That's why we can't stay more than a couple of days when we come to town. We're not too welcome. People remember those turkeys. I heard later that McNally donated all those dead birds to local churches and groups. You know, like the Elks or the Legion, for them to put on suppers. There was nothing wrong with the birds, just they were dead. Then the organizations, from the profits they made, gave McNally enough to buy a new crop of young turkeys later on in the season. Hey, waitress, sweetie, bring us another round for this table, would yah, hon?"

Edna started to protest, "Oh, thank you anyway, but no more for me, if my friends want…"

Lester reached over and grabbed Edna by the wrist, "Hey, whoa on just a minute here. You too good to drink with us, is that what it is? Here we are two damn good-looking guys that were good enough to make room for all of you at our table and now you won't even have a drink on us." Lester turned back to Marie and gave her a wink.

Edna protested, "No, really, that's not the reason I don't want another drink. I've already had my quota for the day."

"Quota? What's with this quota business? We're not talking about wheat or barley or oats. When you're drinking with friends, there is no such thing as a quota."

"Yes there is. One drink a day of wine or beer is supposed to be good for your health."

Lester, who had his glass up to his lips ready to take a drink of his beer laughed, spraying beer all over the table in front of him. He started to wipe it up with his shirtsleeve. "Oh, dear me, I do beg your pardon, ladies. I don't usually do that." Then he leaned over to Edna, "Well, dear lady, what I deduce from this little pertinent bit of information that you've given me is that if I give you a dollar, you'd like that, wouldn't you? Well, then if I dip into my pocket one more time and trade you your one dollar for a two that I have, then you'd like that even better, am I right? Do you follow me, sweet thing?"

Edna nodded, "Yes. No. I think I do. No, it's still only one dollar, not two."

"That's just picking at straws. Now in this case two is better than one. Therefore if one drink is good for you, it only goes to follow that two will be better than one. Do you agree?"

Edna shook her head.

Lester took off his hat and gently reached over the table and placed it on Edna's head. "That's to keep you from shaking your head and disagreeing with me. Now, when I leave and take my hat with me, you can disagree with me all you want 'cause I won't be here and I won't care. But right now I am here, and I'm ordering you a drink, understood."

Edna started to shake her head again. "It's still only one dollar, not two."

Lester held up both of his hands in protest, "No, no, the hat's on your head. You can't do that when the hat's on your head." Then he laughed. "Bring a whole round for the table, Jennie."

Jennie, the waitress, laughed back at Lester, "Sure thing, Lester," then she turned to the ladies, "Doesn't pay to even try and argue with Lester, ladies. Better to just go along with whatever he says."

"Thank you, Jennie, you are a true friend and a lady to boot," he patted her on her bum as she turned to go and get their order.

She turned as she was walking, "Lester, you stop that. You know I don't like that. The next time you do that, I swear, I'll beat you over the head with my tray, and don't think I won't do it."

Lester yelled after her retreating figure, "Jennie, dear, I'm sorry. I truly am, can't you see how sorry I am? If you'd wear some clothes that covered a bit more of that sweet little ass of yours, a fellow wouldn't be tempted to whack it every now and then."

Theda stood up and put her hand out to Furball, signaling that she wanted to dance again. Furball smiled, pushed his drink back on the table and rose to accept Theda's invitation. Lester watched as his friend took Theda's hand. "Furball, you old bugger, you going to trip the light fantastic again? Now, Furball, when you get back, I have a little job for you. I want you to make sure that lady here," he pointed to Edna, "is never without a drink, you got me? We have to look after our friends."

Pat gave Marie a little nudge, "Watch our friend there. We don't want Edna pie-eyed again, and have a repeat of the rodeo."

The rest of the evening passed pleasantly. Lester was good company, regaling the group with story after story of Furball and his escapades. Furball hardly had time to sit down. Every woman at the table danced with him several times. He was an excellent dancer, and aptly maneuvered his partners through rowdy polkas, and he could waltz better than anyone on the floor. The whole table got up once to try their hand at line dancing, and giggled and laughed through the whole dance. They always seemed to be going in the opposite direction to the rest of the dancers who tried vainly to turn them around to face the right direction. Soon everyone on the dance floor was laughing as hard as the women were.

When they came back to their table and sat down, puffing from the exertion of dancing and laughing, Pat glanced at her watch. She tapped Marie on the shoulder. "It's past eleven. What do you think, should we call it a night? We don't have to hit the road real early tomorrow, but I'd like to get gone from this place around noonish at least."

Marie yawned, "You're probably right. This is fun, but I'm tired. Probably should tell the rest."

Pat signaled for their waitress, "We'd like our bill, please."

Jennie quickly flitted over to their table, watching Lester out of the corner of her eye. "Okay, I'll be right back with it." She was back with their bill in less than five minutes and handed it to Pat, "I put all you ladies' stuff, your meals and your drinks on one bill. Is that all right? If, it isn't I can go back and work it out and make six separate bills. It will just take me a while that's all."

Pat took the bill, "No, no, this is fine."

Jennie practically curtsied in her little shorts, "Fine then, hope you had a good time, ladies. You can just pay your bill over there by the door where you came in."

Theda and Pat looked over the bill. "Seems okay. Ladies, can I have your attention for a minute? Here's the damage. We owe $223.80, split that six ways. What does that come to?"

Marie didn't even take the time to calculate before she yelled back, "That's $37.30 each."

Pat grinned, "You sure, Marie?"

"I'm sure."

"Okay, and you'll each be responsible for your own tip. You can leave whatever you want, so fork over your share, chums."

Gwen and Louise looked at each other, then at Marie and Pat. "Oh, pooh, what do you mean, fork it over? I don't have a penny to my name. I was going to stock up tomorrow at the bank," protested Gwen.

"I don't have much either, a couple of bucks and a few odd cents," added Louise.

Marie looked at Pat, "I'm afraid that I'm in the same boat."

Pat held the bill in her hand, "Oh, never mind, I'll just use my credit card and then you can all pay me back tomorrow. Make sure you all take your jackets, purses and so on. We don't want to have to come back here tomorrow because we've forgotten something. Edna grabbed Lester by one arm and Furball with the other. The rest followed as they made their way to the checkout counter. Pat greeted the cashier, an older lady, behind the desk. "Hi! Want to pay our bill. Here's my credit card."

The woman looked at her, "I'm very sorry ma'am, but we don't accept credit cards here, only cash. There's a sign right on the door when you come into the tavern."

Pat stood with her mouth open then mouthed, "No credit cards, oh."

Edna, now being supported by Lester and Furball started to sing, "Oh, we don't have a barrel of money, maybe we're ragged and funny, tee hee." Then she started to recite in a deep voice, "Oh, we ain't got no cash, and we just had a bash." She smiled up at Lester and started to sing again, "If we don't have much money, honey, what we gonna halva do, do, do what you do to me."

Lester leaned over to Edna, "Heh, sweet thing, you've got a great little voice there, you know that?"

Edna blushed and turned her head into Furball's shoulder, "I am a pretty good singer, aren't I? Don't you think that I'm a good singer, Furbull?"

Furball nodded.

It was less than a minute before a man walked over to the counter, "Good evening, ladies, I'm the manager here. Do we have a problem?" Before they had time to answer he turned to Lester and Furball, "What's your problem, Lester?"

Lester held up his hands, palms facing the manager, "Me, us? We ain't got no problems. I've got money to pay for our bill, don't worry none about that. It's the ladies here. They don't have any cash money to pay for their bill. Seems there has been a misunderstanding as the ladies thought they could pay with their credit card, but since you don't take credit cards, they can't pay. And me and Furball, we don't have that much cash on us to help them out." He turned to Pat, "Sorry, ladies, if I had any, I'd be the first to bail you out of this predicament."

Pat put her hand on Lester's arm, "I know you would, Lester."

"Pat, you had some money when you went over to the motel. What happened to it? We could use it to pay for some of the bill," asked Marie.

"I haven't had a chance to tell you about that yet, but over at the motel, they wouldn't accept credit cards either, so I had to pay for our room in cash."

Theda pushed her way up beside Pat, "Excuse me, but did I hear correctly? You did say, room?"

Pat smiled awkwardly, “Yes, you heard correctly. The place was almost booked up, and there was another couple right behind us ready to take our room, so I had no choice. I had to take it then and there. We all have to share this room, tonight. I didn’t tell him that there are six of us. He thinks it’s just Gwen and me. I didn’t even think about supper and drinks. Thought if the worse came to worst, we’d just use our credit cards.”

“Maybe we could sing for our supper,” hiccuped Edna, “I’ll be right ba….ck.” She hiccupped again. “I just have to sit down for a little bit,” and she walked away.

“Maybe we’ll have to wash dishes to pay for our meal?” said Louise.

Pat turned to the manager, “Listen, we do have money.” She held her credit card up under his nose. “Tomorrow we can go to the bank as soon as it opens. We’ll get the money for you and come right over and pay you. We’re staying right at that motel across the street. Look I’ll give you my watch to hold as collateral.” She took her watch off and handed it to the manager.

The manager took it from her and turned the cheap Timex watch over in his hand. Smiling, he handed it back, “No, thank you.”

Pat looked around at her friends. “Maybe two watches, then. I know, here, my ring. It’s worth a couple of bucks. Take these. We’ll write this all down and tomorrow we’ll come back and trade you for them.”

Suddenly, a voice drifted out over the loudspeaker— a familiar voice. Pat and her friends looked back at the front of the room. There, standing at the edge of the small stage, clutching a standup microphone was Edna. “Ladies and gentlemen, it seems that my friends and I are a little eensie bit short of cash and the funny thing is, because we’re a little eensie bit short of cash we can’t pay for our supper. So, gentlemen and ladies, I’m going to offer myself in payment.”

Hoots, cheers and eardrum breaking whistles greeted Edna’s statement. Hats of all description sailed into the air. “Take it off!”

Edna looked down at the crowd, “No, no, silly, not like

that. I'm going to fing a fong for you all. You might know it, and if you do, just seel sree to join in. Oh, I'm sorry, I got my f's and s's mixed up a little there."

Pat put both hands over her eyes, "Oh, Edna, no!"

Louise jumped up on a chair to see the stage, "Hey, it is Edna! Oh, dear, she's going to sing a hymn, I just know it. This bunch is going to appreciate that."

Gwen jumped up on another chair beside Louise, looking and yelling at Edna, "Edna Banting, you come on back down here, right now, before you make a fool of yourself." The fact that Edna was daring to get up in front of an audience and sing perturbed her more than she cared to admit. She was the singer in the group. It should be her up there on that stage.

Someone a few tables over stood up and turned to Gwen, "Aw, lady, leave her be. If she wants to serenade us, let her."

"Yeah, jeez the poor old broad can hardly stand," yelled someone else.

"Better go up and help her out."

Edna stood with one leg and both arms wrapped around the microphone looking out at her audience. Suddenly, she unwrapped herself, stood up straight, tipped her head from side to side as if she were doing exercises. When she was finished, she turned to the small band, "Gentlemen, could I have a little reggae beat, please?"

"You got it lady." Reggae music filled the Western bar. Edna pranced up and down the stage then put her mouth to the microphone and sang, "*Moo-van, Moo-van, in our big crap van! Pain-teed brown 'cause there weren't no tan. 'as one headlight, three tires good-one not so, such a pain. Crap van go'n' take us there and back again...*"

By the time Edna finished, she had given one of the best renditions of *Big Crap Van* that anyone, including Theda, had ever heard. The building erupted when she finished, as the crowd cheered, whistled and stomped its feet on the wooden floor. Everything short of taking the building down. Edna bowed low.

"My God, she wasn't half-bad," someone said.

"What do you mean half-bad? She was terrific, how 'bout another one, lady?"

Edna leaned into the microphone again. "I had a lot of inhibitions when I came up here, but those," she hiccuped, "my 'bitions, seem to be all gone now. Funny thing is I'm getting really really sleepy, so maybe I'll just get ready for bed instead, you won't mind, will you?"

She turned to the band, "I need some going-to-bed music, gentlemens, please." The band started to play a lullaby and everyone thought Edna was just going to sing, but slowly she reached up and started to undo the buttons on her shirt. The audience started to cheer again. Edna leisurely turned her back towards the tables. As soon as the band saw what she was doing it quickly switched to some bawdy striptease music. Her blouse dropped to the floor. Edna bent down and soon a shoe flew out into the audience.

Pat grabbed Gwen and Marie's hands, "Oh, my God, she's stripping. Come on girls, we've got someone to rescue. Let's move it!"

Pat pushed her way through one group of onlookers, "'scuse me. Coming through." She grabbed one of Edna's shoes from a man's hand.

Gwen managed to retrieve her belt and hollered, "Marie, get her other shoe. That guy in the red shirt over there has it."

By the time Pat reached the stage, half of Edna's clothes were either in the audience or strewn over the stage. She took the stairs up to the stage two at a time yelling as she went, "I'll try to get her shirt on the stage and take her out the side door. You guys salvage as many of her clothes as you can."

The five-some managed to usher an unresisting Edna out the side door. The six women stood outside the tavern, ankle deep in soft snow. Heavy snowflakes drifted softly in front of the street lights. Marie and Pat held Edna between them. Louise had thrown her jacket over Edna's shoulders. Edna was singing softly. "Just a closer walk with thee, grant it Jesus is my plea, ohhhhhhh…"

Gwen kicked at a mound of snow, "Oh, pooh, guys. I just thought of something. They probably think that we rigged this so we could run out without paying our bill."

Theda stuck her tongue out to collect the big snowflakes that drifted lazily down around her head. Then she looked down at Gwen. "Well, didn't we?"

Gwen's mouth dropped open.

Theda gave her a soft jab, "Just joking, Gwennie. Well, gang, I suggest we take Strip-Tease-Nellie here back to the motel. Gwen, you might as well come with me. The rest of you give us a few minutes to get her into bed. The way she looks, she'll conk out as soon as she hits the pillow.

"What about our bill?"

"Never mind about it now. We'll get the money in the morning and take it over to the tavern. Come on Edna, let's put you to beddie bye."

Edna rolled her head and looked at Theda, "Hi! Theda, how you doing, old thing? You want to know something. I really like you. I really, really do."

Theda laughed, "And I really, really....I guess you're okay."

"Blessed moments like these, oh God, are meant to cherish..." Edna's head plopped to her chest.

Marie threw back her covers. She looked over at Edna who was gently snoring. The two of them had shared the only bed. She yawned softly and then pushed the button on the side of her wristwatch that illuminated the face. "Eight-ten" she whispered to herself. She looked down at the floor and the various lumps and bumps of the sleeping bags that covered it, trying to determine where she could step without stepping on someone. She swung her feet out of the bed and placed them on the worn carpeted floor. It was warm at least.

She made her way over to the edge of the window and pulled a corner of the curtain back to look outside. It was sunny and bright. The fresh layer of snow that had fallen last night covered everything. Each tree branch was delicately trimmed with white. The pines cradled soft white bundles in their wide dark branches. All the wires that crisscrossed the streets were laced with puffs of snow. Marie opened the curtain a bit more. The cars and trucks were tucked cozily under a huge blanket of snow. Someone stirred behind her. It was Pat. "Oh, Pat, come on. Get up and take a peek at this. It's absolutely breathtaking."

Pat pulled herself out of her sleeping bag. She stood up and stretched, "What time is it? Must be later than I thought." She walked over to stand beside Marie. "Okay, what's so breathtaking?" She looked out the window.

"The snow. It's everywhere. Isn't it pretty?"

"We may not be able to travel today. Guess it depends on how many inches we got last night and how fast they get out with the plows. You're right though, it sure is pretty."

Marie let the curtain drop back into place, "Imagine all this snow now and it's just the end of July."

Pat walked back to her sleeping bag. She yawned and bent to pick it up, "Don't forget we're in the mountains now. Anything is possible up here, snow being one of them. I'm going to go take a shower now. I'll leave the door unlocked so if anyone needs to use the John while I'm showering they can."

By the time Pat came out of the shower everyone was up, even poor Edna. Edna sat up on the edge of the bed. "Oh, my head. What happened? Oh, I must be getting the flu or something." She stood up and walked into the bathroom.

As soon as the door was shut, Marie whispered, "Psst…you guys…I don't know how much Edna will remember about last night, but maybe we won't mention, you know, the strip tease or the song. Let's just say that she got up on stage and sang quite a lovely song and leave it at that." Everyone agreed and promised not to enlighten Edna on her behaviour the previous evening.

Edna stuck her head out the bathroom door, "I'm going to take a shower. I won't be long. Anybody bring a hairdryer? I'll need one."

Pat handed her the hair dryer and, while Edna was showering, the rest of the girls tidied up the room. They roughly made the bed, repacked clothes and rolled up their sleeping bags. "We're lucky we have these bags. They sure came in handy last night.

Have to figure out how much money to get out of the bank when we go. What did our share of the motel and food come to, Pat? Did you figure it out yet?" asked Marie.

Pat laughed, "Well, actually, you don't owe me anything. I paid for the motel out of our general funds so all you need is money for the bar and the food. Then we have to start a new general fund today to pay the bill we owe, and don't forget any monies you might need for your personal use."

Pat threw her sleeping bag on top of the ones piled on the bed. Then she walked over to the window and started to draw the curtains open. "Mind if I open these? No one is running around in their birthday suits are they?" She wiped some of the frost off the window and looked across the street at the bar. Then she checked her watch. "It's almost ten o'clock. The bank should be open soon. Once we get our money, we can go over and pay our bill. Did anyone notice if that place we were at last night served breakfast?"

Marie tucked her makeup bag into the side of her duffel bag and zipped it up. "Yes, they do. It wasn't on the menu they gave us last night, but I remember seeing a breakfast menu on one of those big blackboards near the bar."

"Good, as soon as Edna's ready we can go," Pat said, turning her attention to two men across the street. She watched as a man leaning against a car watched another man whack at the ground with what, from where Pat stood, looked like a broken hockey stick. The taller of the two men would come up to the one leaning on the car, say a few words to him, then walk away. He would take two or three steps and then suddenly lift the stick high in the air and hit at the ground with it. Then he would quickly pivot, pulling snow up into the air and whack at the ground again, narrowly missing his friend with the stick. Pat thought at first that he was playing hockey with an imaginary puck.

"You guys, isn't that Lester and Furball over there? What the heck is Furball doing?"

By the time everyone managed to crowd around the lone window to see what Pat was talking about, Furball had swung the stick over his shoulder and was busy talking to Lester.

"What are you talking about, Pat? They're just standing there by a car, talking."

"Just wait, maybe he'll do it again."

They stood for several minutes while Lester and Furball continued their conversation.

Pat looked out the window disgustedly, "Oh, never mind. Maybe I was seeing things."

Just then Edna came out of the bathroom, with her panties, bra and socks on. "Just be a couple seconds. Have to grab my shirt and jeans." She rummaged for several minutes through her bag. "That's weird, I brought two bras with me, and I'm wearing one, and the other's nowhere to be found. Plus, I'm missing my shirt with the blue polka dots. You know, the one I wore yesterday."

Pat quickly stepped in, "Ah…Edna, maybe one of us packed it in with our clothes by mistake. Just put on another shirt and we'll find your stuff later." While Edna picked out a T-shirt, Pat turned to Marie and whispered, "I forgot, I must have dropped her shirt when we were getting her outside. I thought I stuffed it into my jacket pocket, but it's not here," she said as she checked in both of her pockets.

Marie laughed softly and whispered back, "She's damn lucky she's got as many clothes as she has after last night."

By ten-thirty everyone had been to the bank and money for the bill at *The Bear Facts* had been gathered. Edna folded her money and tucked it into the front right pocket of her blue jeans. Everyone was surprised at how good she looked after the experiences of the night before.

"You feel all right, Edna? You didn't look all that good last night when you went to bed," asked Marie.

Edna looked at her sweetly, "Didn't I? I feel just fine. That shower made me feel right as rain. Listen, are we going over to the bar for breakfast?"

Pat looked at Edna, "Actually, I was just talking to Marie and Theda and we were kind of thinking that maybe we'd just pack up the car and drive for an hour or so and have a late lunch. It's past ten-thirty already and by the time we're packed and ready to go it will be elevenish."

"That sounds good. I'm not very hungry. Have a bit of a queasy tum. Don't know why. I'm really thirsty too. Do you think I'm coming down with some kind of flu?"

Theda patted Edna on the back, "Maybe you are. I think when we get out on the road you should take your blankie and pillow and just rest."

"I think that sounds like a good idea, but first why don't you let me take our money over to the bar and I'll take care of our bill while you folks load the van."

Edna would usually help if she was asked, and she certainly did her share, but this out-of-the-blue offer to take on an added responsibility was quite rare. Pat, slightly taken aback and looking rather surprised, handed the money over to her. "Okay, here's the money. We also put in enough for a tip for the little girl who served us last night. So, that's good, you go do that, and we'll meet you back here. Thanks, Edna."

It didn't take long for all the women to gather up their possessions and load them and themselves into the van. Theda ran back inside the motel room to check that no one had forgotten anything. Pat had started the motor before the van was loaded so it was toasty warm and the heat from the vents had melted all the frost off the windows.

As they sat waiting for Theda to return, Marie poked Louise, "Let's run over and say goodbye to Lester and Furball. They're still outside the bar. Edna just finished talking to them and she's just gone inside *The Bear Facts*, so we've got a few minutes before she comes back out."

Louise and Marie turned to Gwen who was cuddled up under a blanket behind them, "We're going out to say bye to Lester and Furball, want to come? What about you, Pat?"

Pat, sitting in the driver's seat perusing a road map of the area, looked up, "Sure, just let me fold this creature back up."

Gwen yelled after them, "I'll be there in a few seconds."

The snowplow still hadn't come by and there was very little traffic on the streets, so the snow was quite deep in spots and still lovely and white. The women were barely half way across the street when they saw Furball running toward them. Everyone smiled and thought he was coming over to meet them and exchange pleasantries. Not more than seven feet in front of them, he suddenly stopped dead, swung his stick high in the air and brought it down barely missing Pat's toe. Furball kept watching where the stick had landed and then suddenly turned and whacked his way all the way back to Lester. The women, leery to proceed, came to a dead stop.

Lester yelled over to them, "Ladies, come on over. It's okay. Furball won't hurt you." He saw the hesitant looks on their faces. "Really, I swear. It's good to see you all looking so chipper. I was just talking to your friend, what's her name? Edna. She looks real good, considering." He turned to Furball, "Furball, why don't you take your stick and go get some of those buggers over by that fence there, while I talk to the ladies."

Furball nodded, turned and walked over to the fence. Upon reaching it he proceeded to strike the ground with his stick. With each swing he grunted and you could hear him every once in awhile saying, "Got you, you slimy bugger, you!"

Pat walked over to Lester. The other women crowded close to the two of them. Everyone but Gwen. She looked like a statue that someone had dropped in the middle of the road. It was obvious that she was not going to move, not even for a snowplow if it happened along. Gwen yelled to Lester, "What in heaven's name is he doing?"

Lester laughed, "Oh, don't mind Furball. He's just after snow snakes."

"Snow snakes!! Oh, pooh!" shrieked Gwen.

"That's what I said. Come on over here. Honest, he won't hurt you. Come on." Lester put out his hand and beckoned to Gwen.

Gwen slowly placed one foot in front of the other. Before long she had successfully made her way across the street and thankfully grabbed Lester's outstretched hand. Gently he led her to a snow covered park bench and with his gloved hand swished away enough snow so she would have a place to sit. "Here, sit down on this bench." Gwen sat placing her hands on the bench on either side of her thighs."Careful though where you put your hands," Lester cautioned.

Gwen looked up him warily, "Why?"

"Snow snakes."

She quickly drew her hands up under her chin.

"Yeah, the trouble with those damn things is they're white just like the snow. You can be right on top of one and you can't even see it. That's why they call them snow snakes. The place is crawling with them, especially after a summer snow like this one. A snow snake bites you, too bad. There's nothing you can do. It's the end, zippo dippo-pwit!" Lester turned and spat into the snow.

Gwen, face the colour of the snow, sat on the bench immobilized. Pat turned to her, "What's the matter, Gwen? Are you feeling okay?"

Gwen looked up at her like a sad little child who had lost her mother, "No, I'm not and I'm going to go back to the van as soon as I can make my feet move."

"Gwen, are you afraid of snakes?"

"Yes," Gwen shivered.

Pat put her hand on Gwen's back, "Gwen, there's no snakes here. Lester's just pulling your chain, aren't you Lester?"

Lester put his gloved hand over his mouth and started to snicker, "Oh, sweet thing, I was just teasing. There's no such thing as a snow snake. I can't believe you thought they were for real. I'm sorry, I truly am." Lester held out his hand to Gwen, "Come on, there's nothing to be frightened of, really."

Gwen looked up at Lester's hand suspiciously, "If there aren't any snow snakes why is Furball killing them?"

"Because, he thinks there are."

"Well, maybe he's right. How do you know there aren't any snow snakes? You said yourself that they are white just like the snow and that's makes them almost impossible to see. They could be out there and we just can't see them. In fact there could be one right behind your foot there."

Lester glanced back behind him and then laughed. "Oh, you got me there little lady. You sure did."

Just then, Edna came out of *The Bear Facts* and joined the group. "Hi, Edna. Everything taken care in there?" asked Pat.

"Yes, all paid up, sort of. Our slate is clean, so to speak."

"What do you mean, sort of?"

"Well, when I asked to speak to the manager, he quit what he was doing and came right over, a great big smile on his face and he says, 'Good morning, young lady.' Imagine, he's half my age and he's calling me a young lady. I just thought he was being a sarcastic little sh…, anyway, I told him that I was here to pay our bill from last night and he says, 'The bill? There is no bill.' I told him, that yes there was a bill, and I demanded that he give it to me. I told him that we take care of all our debts and then he said the strangest thing. 'You people provided the best entertainment this joint has had in a long time and in payment for that the drinks and meals are on the house.' "

Pat stifled a grin and asked, "What did you say then?"

"Well, I told him that he must be mistaken, that we left early and went over to our motel and went straight to bed," declared Edna.

"And what did he say to that?" prompted Theda.

"Nothing. He just smiled and said, 'Whatever.' Then he handed me this bag." Edna held up a medium-sized brown paper bag with its top folded down. "He thought this was probably mine. I really don't know what he's talking about. I don't remember asking for a doggie bag. Did I?"

"I don't remember you asking for one, but maybe you did and we just didn't hear. Why don't you take a peek inside, Edna?" offered Louise. "Maybe it's doughnuts."

Edna waved the idea away and pushed the bag under her arm, "Oh, later, when we're on our way."

Pat turned to Lester, "Well, Lester, we're going to hit the road. Just want you to know that we had a great time with you and Furball. We won't soon forget you two."

Lester removed his hat and held it down at his side, "Well, ladies, I believe the pleasure was all ours. I thoroughly did enjoy your company. I doubt if we'll ever run into each other again, and maybe that's for the best. We'll just have this one good time to remember each other by." His rapscallion eyes sparkled.

The women took turns hugging Lester and then they waved to Furball. He neither heard nor saw them. He was still busy attacking his snow snakes. He reminded Pat of a dog chasing its own tail. Theda watched him fondly and then turned to Lester, "How long are you going to let him chase after those snakes, Lester?"

Lester's hat was back on his head. "Oh, I'll let him run around for a couple of hours. You see, once we come into town, he quite likes it and doesn't want to leave, so I have to let him do something that just wears him out. In a little while, he'll be too tired to object to me loading him onto his horse and leaving with our supplies. Once we're on the trail, he'll be fine."

"What happens up at your camp in the winter when there's snow every day? He must go absolutely crazy. No pun intended," asked Marie.

Lester lifted his chin and laughed, "We don't have any snow snakes up in the mountains, just in town here. Anyway, I better let you ladies get your show on the road. Once again, it was a pleasure meeting you all. It will give me something to think about all this winter. I'll remember you all for a long time, 'specially you, Edna." He took off his leather glove and touched her gently under the chin with his curled forefinger.

"Take care, sweetie. I hope you didn't catch cold last night." He lowered his hand and winked over at the others.

Cozy places were soon created in the van as each woman made herself comfortable. Pat was in the driver's seat. Marie was riding shotgun.

Marie looked up from the map and said to Pat, "Do you think we should be heading out with the roads in the condition they are?"

Pat looked in the rear-view mirror and expertly backed the van out into the road, "While you guys were finishing up in the bank, I came outside and ran into a police chappy. I asked him if he knew anything about the roads. He told me that the snow just fell in this valley yesterday and last night. He said the main roads outside of town have been plowed and once we get over that summit, which is twenty to thirty kilometres away, it's clear sailing."

"You mean this is the only place it snowed?"

"Guess so. He says this happens all the time in the mountains. It can be raining cats and dogs on one side, and on the other the sun will be shining. Same goes for snow. He says it's not unusual for sections of the mountains to get a snowfall in the middle of summer, especially at the higher elevations."

Edna picked up the brown paper bag that she had placed between her feet while she was arranging her pillow behind her shoulders. She leaned back against the pillow.

"There, that feels good," she yawned."Oh, goodness, don't know why I'm so tired. Still think I'm coming down with something. My tummy feels just a little suspect. Remind me to give you people back your money for the bill that we didn't have to pay."

She started to open the bag, "I hope you're right, Louise, and these are doughnuts. They could be our breakfast. Feels too light for doughnuts though. I'll just take a peek."

She stopped opening the bag and looked up, "What did Lester mean when he said he hoped I didn't catch cold? Why would I be any more likely to catch cold than any of you?"

Finally Edna peeked inside the top of the bag, and reached in. Slowly her hand came out of the bag, withdrawing first her bra, and then her blue polka dot shirt.

***

"Mom, Dad, anybody here? We've got a letter from Grandma." Louise's grandson Paul dumped his back pack on the floor near the kitchen table and plopped himself in the nearest chair. Sarah, Sarah Jr. and Gary came out of the living room where they had been discussing their day. Sarah rushed over to the table and sat down. "Good, come on everybody, sit down. Go ahead, Paul, open it. You can read it to us."

Paul sat down at the head of the table, and Gary and his daughter took the other two chairs. Paul had the letter in his hands. He looked around the table, "Ready?"

Dear Family,

This will just be a short note to you. I'm trying to write this as we drive along in our van and the roads aren't that great this morning, lots of ice and snow. No, I haven't lost it, yet. Imagine that, yesterday, the end of July and we went through a snowstorm and had to stop at a motel for the night. We are still having a wonderful time. We're making our way down to Vancouver and once we get there, our intention is to turn around and start heading for home. Might pop in and out of the States the odd time on the way back home. We don't want to go too far into the States. In case something happens to one of us, we want to be able to get back to the Canadian border as fast as we can. Good old Medicare won't cover us completely if we get sick down there. Seeing lots of new things, but I am starting to get excited about getting home and seeing you all. Paul and Sarah, you should see some of the ski runs we've driven past, I hate to say it, but they make our Ontario ones look like anthills. Maybe someday the two of you can take a trip out here and try your luck on them.

It didn't take long to get out of the snow. I couldn't believe it when we came over this one little pass in the mountains and turned to go down another valley and there was only a dusting of snow. Now there's none. We're not making great time today not because of bad roads, but because the first twenty or so kilometres, the scenery was so beautiful, the trees and rocks all covered in snow. Pat was driving and she stopped practically every five kilometres or so to take photos. We've been lined up so many times in front of some view or other that I've lost count. Something Pat wants to do, she said, before we head home is stop and have our lunch right beside one of the countless rivers or brooks that come tumbling and gurgling out of the mountains. I'm with her there. We might even do it to-

day. Must run, hope you can make out my writing. See you all soon.

Love Mom and Grandma Louise

Chapter Eighteen

Pat slowed the van down to a crawl to negotiate a speed bump. The campground they were in, approximately fifty kilometres south of Revelstoke, was almost full to capacity. Pat drove around the park a couple of times and finally Marie pointed out a spot between a green and beige trailer and a small igloo tent. It wasn't an ideal spot but would have to do. As soon as the van was parked, each of the women jumped out and attended to her separate chores. The main one, setting up of the tents, was done by Marie and Gwen. The two of them always worked well together and the tents were set up in no time. A large aspen tree on the corner of their site afforded some shade so the girls moved the picnic table directly under it. Gwen found a brush and started to clean the top of the table.

"Do you need any help with anything? If not, I'm going to flop in the tent and read for awhile." Marie asked Gwen.

Gwen didn't answer, so Marie presumed that that meant no. She walked into the tent she was sharing and pulled a thin book from her duffel bag. She glanced at the cover, *Insects of Your Garden:Friend or Foe*. She flopped down on her sleeping bag and stuffed her pillow under her stomach and started to read. Soon she could hear the other girls talking outside the tent. At first she could only make out the odd word, but soon the voices raised a couple of levels and she was hearing more than she wanted.

"Listen, Miss Holier-Than-Thou. What's with you anyway? If I feel like cussing the odd time. I can. Nobody's mother, least of all you, is going to tell me I can or cannot."

"It has nothing to do with thinking I'm holy. I just don't like being around people that use rude, coarse language all the time. Wait! Before you say anything, hear me out. Tell me this: you don't like it when someone lights up a cigarette in the same room that you're in, do you? If they light up, you're the first person that will ask them to butt out, right? Well, it's the same thing. I don't like it when someone swears around me, and I'm going to tell them I don't like it."

"May I talk now? It's not the same thing at all. Smoke hurts and pollutes your lungs and body."

"Well, as far as I'm concerned your mind can be polluted in just the same way."

The voice levels kept rising. Marie tried to cover her ears so she could concentrate on her reading, but the voices filtered easily through the thin tent walls.

"Well, if my vile mouth is so damaging to your poor precious mind, stay away from me."

"Oh, that's easy to say, isn't it? Where the he…where am I supposed to go? We're all stuck in this van together day in and day out. I should never have come on this trip when I knew you'd be here, too."

"Ahhh, don't you see how bad I feel for you, Miss Goody-Two-Shoes."

"Yes, it is too bad. All you think about is yourself. What's best for Theda? What makes Theda happy? Will Theda like this? Theda, Theda, Theda!"

Marie sighed and rose from her comfortable position and went outside the tent. Pat was walking past the doorway just then. "God, they sound like a couple of old washerwomen going at it," grumbled Pat.

Theda and Edna stood noses apart, with both their hands on their respective hips.

Theda finally stepped back, "Fine, if that's how you feel.

Well, let me tell you this. I've had enough of you and your Miss Perfect attitude." She then pursed her lips, stuck her nose up in the air, one hand down to her side and the other bent at the elbow and wrist and started to walk away taking tiny little perfect steps. "Look, I'm Little Miss Perfect and I'm going for a walk." Ten or so tiny steps soon transformed into mighty strides as Theda left the campsite and charged down the road.

Pat and Marie came and stood beside Edna. The three of them watched Theda go down the road.

"Boy, you two, I think we should just give you both a pair of boxing gloves and let you duke it out," said Pat.

Edna was still shaking, "Oh, that woman, I absolutely detest her!"

Pat laughed, "Well, from the looks of it, the feeling is mutual. It would be nice if you could be a little quieter when you argue. Goodness, Edna, I think the whole campground and half of British Columbia for that matter, heard the two of you."

"I'm sorry. I guess I shouldn't let her get under my skin. We're just too different from each other. So you can't expect us to get along."

Just then, Louise returned from the laundromat. Her arms were ladened with a large load of clothes that she had just washed and dried. "There you go girls, fresh towels and undies for another week. Is the table clean enough to put these on?"

Gwen popped her head out of one of the tents, "Clean and ready."

"Good, I'll just set them down and you can pick out your own stuff. I already took mine out. Say, I just met Theda coming barrelling down the road and she wouldn't even say, Hi. What's with her?"

"Edna and she had a few words just before you came back," said Pat.

Louise shirked her shoulders, "What's new?" She tugged up her bagging sweat pants, and flipped her T-shirt over the top of the pants.

Marie watched as Louise performed these minor tasks and

then commented, "Gee Louise, have you lost more weight? Your clothes are starting to look pretty baggy on you."

Louise looked pleased with herself. "I was wondering when you people were going to notice. If those scales in the laundromat are right, I've lost over thirty pounds this whole trip. I haven't been starving myself either, but the old fat is slipping away for some reason. I think the next town we hit, I'll run in to a mall and buy myself a new track suit. Maybe I'll even spring for a pair of jeans. I haven't been able to fit into any for years. It'll be nice, for a change, to buy a large and not an extra large."

Marie was pleased for Louise, "Good for you!"

Just as Louise was about to say thank you, they were interrupted by a loud male voice coming from the adjacent trailer. A rather heavy set man, balding and wearing sandals and not much else, kicked the small trailer door open and started down the flat narrow steps. He was carrying a rather large, flat, boxy object. "Goddamn, piece of crap!" e turned back to the trailer and tried to close the door with his foot, but in the process hit his big toe on the edge of the door. Marie winced in sympathy.

"Goddamn it all to hell! Shit and more shit! Damn stupid piece of junk. Never should have bought it in the first place. Damn the stupid book they give you with it too. Good riddance!" He turned the box sideways and tucked it under his arm so he could lift the lid of the large garbage pail that was placed at the front of each campsite. Then he flung the box into the pail. He replaced the lid and lifted it again to fling more verbal abuse at the discarded object, "There! Right where you belong, you piece of crap!"

He was already halfway back to his trailer before he noticed the women watching him. "Oh, excuse me, ladies! I'm sorry."

Instantly his grumpy face transformed into a very pleasant one with an amiable smile that spread from ear to ear. "I just bought that VCR. It doesn't work worth a damn. I guess I shouldn't complain. It's just a cheap thing, should have known better than to buy something like that. A few days ago, I taped a couple movies that were on late at night. They taped all right, but all the characters look like they are skooshed sideways and down, like those mirrors in a carnival show. Not only that, but the picture is really blurry. I thought I was doing something wrong so the wife suggested I go and rent a movie, so I did and it was just as bad. Has to be the machine, piece of crap! Oh, well, easy come, easy go."

Marie glanced over at the garbage pail, and then turned to the man, "Why don't you return it for one that works?"

"I bought the damn thing in Edmonton at a flea market no less. Didn't pay much for it, so guess it doesn't owe me anything."

Marie smiled and then asked nonchalantly, "Do you mind if I take a look at it?"

The man looked her up and down and snorted, "You? Well..." He snorted again, "Why not, go ahead. I threw it in the garbage, as far as I'm concerned once it's in the garbage it becomes public domain."

Marie walked over and retrieved the VCR from the garbage pail. As she started to walk towards the table, her hands started to slip from the bottom of the apparatus. She turned the VCR over and found the bottom covered with something red and slimy. She looked at her hand. It was covered with the same reddish slime.

"Yuck." She held her hand up to her nose and sniffed, probably pizza sauce.

"Hand me a couple pieces of that paper towel over there, will you, Gwen?"

She wiped her hands clean first and then carefully balanced the VCR on its edge and wiped it clean, too.

"There, that's better."

Marie set the VCR on the table and began to scrutinize the front buttons. She kept nodding her head, and muttering, "Uh...mm... Humm...Okay. Yes, that should be that, I wonder?"

While Marie fiddled with the VCR, the four other women congregated at the other end of the table. "When are we leaving tomorrow?" asked Louise.

Pat, with a *Chatelaine* magazine in front of her, looked up. "I don't know. We made decent time this morning. What do the rest of you think? It's very pretty here. The facilities are good and it's pretty cheap compared with some of the campgrounds we've stopped at."

Louise opened a plastic container and plucked out a slice of carrot. "Here. Anyone else want one?" She set the container in the middle of the table. "Help yourselves. I agree. It is a nice campground. Has good clean showers, a place to wash your clothes and they let you use as much wood as you want and I especially like that little kitchenette place that has a roof right over it." She pointed across the road through a large stand of firs.

Edna, sitting right across from Pat, lifted the *Chatelaine* magazine up to see the cover. "Excuse me, Pat, just wanted to see if I've read that one or not. May I read that after you're finished with it? I think it will be nice to just relax here, take a few little walks. Maybe, if we get energetic, we could even all wash the van today. You know, spruce it up, a bit. If we all pitched in it wouldn't take very long." she suggested.

"What about you, Marie? What do you want to do?" Pat bent down so she could see Marie on the other side of Louise.

"Mmmm...whatever, makes no difference to me."

Pat returned to her Chatelaine. "Agreeable lady isn't she?"

Gwen yawned and laughed as she tried to cut the yawn short. "I was wondering if we have a destination? Every trip should have one, don't you think?"

Pat chuckled, "Well, I'm just presuming that it will be Vancouver. Vancouver is pretty much the end of Canada, unless we take the ferry over to the island, which I wouldn't object to, if the rest of you were game."

"I say," Edna hesitated, then continued, "I say, we get to Vancouver first, and then make our decision about continuing on to the island."

"Yes, good idea. We should take a vote on it. Maybe we'll be the font of democracy," said Gwen.

Marie laughed in her corner of the table. "I wouldn't call us the font. Font means the beginning, or source of something, in this case democracy, and democracy has been around for quite a while."

Gwen not to be deterred said, "I thought a font was like a basin, or big jar that held water, you know, like in a church. I thought we could be the big basin that held democracy."

Marie looked at Gwen, "You're right there. It also is what you said. Okay, if you want to be a font you can be one. It's okay by me."

Pat held up her pointer finger, licked it and made an imaginary mark in the air, "Mark one up for Gwen. Way to go, Gwen!"

Everyone laughed, including Marie.

Pat finally folded her magazine and handed it over to Edna. "Here you go. Gee, Theda has been gone for a long time. She must have really been pissed off."

Louise finished off the last carrot. "Oh, she's probably met someone and is in the middle of a gabfest. I wouldn't worry about her too much. She's one lady who can take care of herself."

Marie stood up, the VCR in her arms, and walked over to the trailer next to them. She managed to reach up with her foot and gently kicked at the door. It was only a few seconds before the door was opened by a gentle looking lady with pouffy strawberry-red hair. Soft brown freckles covered the woman's pale face and arms. She smiled down at Marie and started to say hello, but before she could get a word out the man who had thrown his VCR away came up behind her. "Oh, hello there. Give up on it, did you? Just throw it back in the garbage."

Marie stood with one foot on the bottom stair leading into the small trailer, balancing the VCR on her knee. "Well, no. I haven't given up on it, not yet anyway. I'd really like to try something, with your permission of course. The only problem is we don't have a TV, so if I could use yours I doubt if it will even take five minutes."

Marie saw the dubious look on his face, as he looked first at Marie and then at his wife. "Oh, what the hell, what can it hurt? Here let me help you in with that thing. My name is Fred and this is my wife Jesse."

Fred grabbed a corner of the VCR and, by pulling on the VCR, managed to pull Marie into his trailer at the same time. He pointed to the corner of their cozy neat trailer. "There's the television over there. You got time for a coffee? We always have a pot brewing, don't we, Jesse?"

Marie looked over at the television set then back to Fred and Jesse, "Oh, that sounds really nice. Just let me try hooking this up first. We'll see if we can get it working and then I'll join the two of you."

Fred fished glasses out of his shirt pocket and sat and watched with interest as Marie inspected and fiddled with some wires. Finally she sat back on her haunches. "Do you have a remote for your TV and VCR or do you just turn them on manually?"

"Yeah, there's one here somewhere. Look under that cushion there on the couch. It's always hiding under something on that couch. If it's not a pillow, it'll be the newspaper."

Marie lifted the edge of a quilted pillow and immediately spotted the remote.

Fred smiled, "See, what did I tell, ya. It's always somewhere on that couch, like it's alive or has a mind of its own."

Marie looked the remote over quickly and pressed a couple buttons. After a little space of time and the odd soft snap the TV screen lit up. Marie turned to Jesse, "Do you have an old tape with something on it, a movie or show? Then we can put it in and see if this works."

Jesse opened up a little cupboard beside the kitchen and came out with a tape. "Here, try this one."

Marie popped the tape in the VCR and turned it on. The sound was clear, but the picture was distorted and sporadic dark lines covered the screen. There was no way you could make out the features of the characters.

Fred pointed at the screen. "There, what'd I tell you, piece of crap! Throw the damn thing back in the garbage."

Marie leaned forward and turned one of the dials. Suddenly, a clear bright picture sprang onto the TV screen. Rhett

Butler was walking up the huge staircase to meet Scarlett O'Hara.

"Gone With the Wind, good movie," said Marie, as she moved away from the front of the TV set.

Jesse stood behind her, clasping her hands together like a little girl, "Oh, Fred, look at that. It's perfect! Whatever did you do to fix it?"

"It wasn't anything much, just the tracking was off. Here, I'll show you, because sometime you might get another tape that the tracking could be quite different and all you have to do is adjust this little button right here. It usually improves it a bit, and in this case, a lot!"

Fred stepped back, arms folded in front of him, and nodded. "Yes, that's good, very good. Hurry up with that coffee, Jesse. This little lady deserves a reward." He patted Marie on the shoulder.

"It's almost ready, Fred. Perhaps you should offer her something besides coffee for fixing your VCR. Well, if the truth be known I guess it's not really yours any more, is it? I heard you tell her she could have it when you threw it in the garbage."

"Oh, lord, you're right, I forgot!"

Marie laughed as she got up from the floor and started to sit on the couch. "Oh, don't be silly. I didn't take it because I wanted it. I just wanted to have a look at it. Thought this might be the problem and it was. I do have one favour that I would like to ask in return, if it's all right with you?"

Fred crossed his arms in front of him again and stood looking at Marie. "A favour, well, I guess. What do you have in mind? I won't say yes, and I won't say no, until I hear what it is."

"Well, my friends and I just recently received a tape of our whitewater rafting excursion and we haven't been able to see it yet. I'd love for them to be able to watch it. I don't think it's very long, so it would only take up a few minutes of your time."

Jessie poured Marie's coffee and reached over for another cup. "I don't see anything wrong with that request, Fred. How many friends do you have? I'm sorry, I don't even know your name."

Jessie handed Marie a cup and Marie gratefully accepted it. "I'm sorry, I'm Marie, and I have five friends that are travelling with me."

Fred looked at Jessie again and then shirked his shoulders, "Okay, by me. It will take a bit of doing to squeeze eight people in here, but it's not impossible. You go get them, Marie."

Jessie looked pleased, "And I'll throw another pot of coffee on."

"Oh, please don't go to any bother."

"It's no bother at all and besides, it's kind of fun to be able to visit with someone besides old grumpy puss there."

Fred laughed, "Well, thank you, and you're always Miss Joy-of-the-World."

Marie went back to her campsite to find the others, retrieved her film from the van and then they all sat waiting for Theda to return. Ten minutes passed.

Finally Marie spoke up, "Listen, Theda could be gone for another hour or so, I really don't think there's any sense waiting any longer for her."

Everyone agreed with her and they all traipsed over to Fred and Jessie's trailer. Fred greeted them at the door and with some neat maneuvering they all managed to cram themselves into the little space of the trailer.

Jessie handed coffee out to anyone who wanted it and placed pretty pink-flowered containers of cream and sugar on the table next to the teaspoons.

"I'm sorry I don't have any real cream. Milk will have to do," said Jessie as she tried to edge her way around her guests.

"Milk will do just fine," said Louise as she reached over to help herself to the small pitcher of milk. She poured a minuscule amount of milk into her coffee and stirred it with one of the spoons Jessie had provided and then looked up, "Oh, but there's no place left for the two of you to sit."

Fred waved his hand, "Doesn't matter. We've been sitting all day. Jessie and I will just stand here in the kitchen. We can see the screen from here. Don't worry about us."

"Okay, Marie. You can turn it on. Let's see this cinematic masterpiece," said Pat.

"Well, don't laugh, but with all the academy award actresses in it, what else could it be," joked Gwen.

"Wait, wait," yelled Fred, "let me close this curtain over the sink. It will make it a little darker."

As the room darkened, someone yelled, "Where's the popcorn?"

All eyes watched as a large yellow raft plunged up and down, up and down, through raging whitewater. Each time the front end rose above the water it would sit precariously on the top of a huge wave, and then it would disappear into a large depression left by the swirling current only to rise again, undulating up and over each new onslaught of waves. Huge outcrops of hard grey rocks poked up at irregular intervals in the violent thrashing water. Massive sprays of water splashed over the entire raft and its occupants, many times hiding them from the camera's view. Suddenly, Marie yelled, "There, that's where we lost our guide! Oh, and there's where you got conked on the head, Edna."

The room fell silent as they watched Theda lunge over to where the Edna's unconscious body was being tossed from side to side on the bottom of the raft. They saw her grab Edna with one hand and ward off the swinging oar with the other as she tried to stabilize her own body by hooking her feet through some straps that hung from the side of the raft. The raft plunged down into one last depression in the water and when it surged up to the top again a lazier current grabbed it and pulled it over to the quieter side of the river. The raft spun around once and the last thing the camera caught was Theda leaning back against the side of the raft, with Edna's head cradled against her shoulder. Then the screen went fuzzy, hissed a bit and then turned bright blue. No one spoke for several seconds. Edna sat with her mouth open, clutching her coffee cup between her hands, starring at the blank screen.

Fred broke the silence, "Boy, was that something. I can't believe that you old dolls actually went down that river!"

"Fred!" exclaimed his wife, "For heaven's sake watch your

tongue. Besides, if it comes right down to it, I doubt that these women are any older than you are."

"I know, I know. But I'll tell you one thing: you wouldn't catch me on one of those rafts."

Fred tried to bow as gallantly as he could in the cramped quarters, "I didn't mean to insult you, ladies, I have only…admiration for you."

Marie started to rewind the tape, but before it went back very far, Edna put her hand on Marie's arm, "Wait."

"You mean stop it?" Marie pushed the stop button.

"Thanks, just leave it on. I want to watch it once more, by myself. Please, I'll bring the tape back to you as soon as it's done."

Pat tried to stand up and clunked her head on the edge of a little cupboard that jutted out from the top of the trailer. She laughed as she rubbed her head. "Well, thank you, Jessie and Fred. We really appreciate being able to see that tape, and thank you again for the coffee, but I think we'd better get moving."

The women got up one at a time and left the trailer.

Marie stepped down from the last trailer step and spotted Theda coming out of one of the tents, "Hey, Theda, where've you been, lady person?"

Theda looked up smiling, "There you bums are, been looking all over for you. Thought you all took off on me and left me with this pile of junk." She patted some of the chrome on the front of the van.

"I resent that," yelled Pat, running over to put her arms around her van protectively. She leaned over and kissed the front of the vehicle, "Did that mean old lady say nasty things about you?"

Louise laughed at the two and then looked around for Edna. "Where's Edna? She was right behind me."

Jessie and Fred waved goodbye and returned to their trailer. When they stepped up into their little living room, Edna was still sitting in front of the television. The VCR was set on pause. The screen showed a close-up of Theda holding Edna.

Edna turned to Jessie and Fred with tears streaming down her face, "Oh! I'm sorry. I just wanted to see it one more time.

Hope you don't mind."

Jessie walked over and put her hand on Edna's shoulder, "Is anything wrong?"

"No, I'm fine, thank you. Just feeling a little, I don't know…maybe just a little sentimental. I'll get out of your hair." She reached over and pushed the eject button, grabbed the tape and made her way past Jessie and Fred. At the bottom of the stairs she turned and waved, "Thanks again."

Edna, clutching the tape to her chest, walked over to her group of friends who were joking about Pat's van fetish. Edna came up behind Theda and tapped her gently on the shoulder. Theda turned and seeing that it was Edna gruffly asked, "Yeah, what do you want?"

Edna threw her arms around Theda and gave her a huge hug. Theda looked over at her friends in complete surprise. Edna had Theda's arms trapped in her hug, but Theda still managed to hold her hands palms up out to the side of her body in a questioning gesture as she mouthed, "What the hell?"

***

Charlie had just come in from outside. He grabbed the phone on its second ring. Before he had even said hello, the person on the other end started talking, "Charlie, hi. It's Pat. Didn't know if I'd catch you at home or not? Won't keep you long, just thought I'd keep you informed. How are you?"

"Good, good. What are you up to and when are you coming home?"

Pat laughed, "Probably soon. We're only a day from Vancouver. We have had absolutely terrific weather, the whole trip, except for that one snowstorm. Well the odds were that one of these days we were going to hit some crappy weather. It's been raining for two days straight now. We're starting to get pretty waterlogged and tempers are getting just a little short. We try to leave as much of our stuff right in the van so it will stay dry. One of the tents sprang a leak last night, so we have everybody crowded in one tent. Marie finally went and slept on the floor of the van which gave us a little more room. A few of us go and sit in the van every so often. We caught the weather report at noon. The rain is supposed to let up sometime in the next couple of hours. We're hoping that the sun comes out with a vengeance to dry some of this stuff before we have to pack it."

"Don't you have one of those little propane heaters? Turn that on for a while and it should dry out the inside of the tent at least."

"Yes, we do. We've never used it yet. Don't know why I never thought of that. I'll get Marie on that as soon as I go back to our site."

"What time is it there?"

"I called you just before eight, to get the cheap rates."

"Okay, it's elevenish here. So, you'll be in Vancouver in a day."

"We don't know for sure. We could be, because we're not that far away. But we've been stopping and enjoying anything and everything, so who knows how long it will take us to get there. Also, we haven't decided yet, if we're going on to the Island or not. I think today probably put a damper on that prospect, no pun intended. You get a couple crappy miserable days and it makes home look pretty inviting."

"Oh, well, you got to take the bad with good.Your tune might change when the sun shines. Might as well see as much as you can while you're out that way."

"We'll see. Think I'd better go, I'm starting to steam up this phone booth pretty good. Can't even see out any more. Take care Charlie. See you when we see you."

"Wait, Pat, the van, any problems with it yet? Nothing has broken down on you, has it?"

"No, Charlie, but keep your fingers crossed. The old girl's still holding her own. About the only thing she's lacking is extra pep when you're going up a hill. You know, if you want to pass someone when there's a passing lane and you're travelling up hill, well, in a lot of cases, it's just best to stay behind. Other than that, she's been great, thanks to you. Really have to run now. Bye, love.

Chapter Nineteen

The heavy rainfall had managed to wash most of the dust and grime off the van. Pat and Marie had taken rags out and wiped the worst of the streaks of dirt off it. Shortly after noon, the clouds moved up and over the mountains and the sun came out bringing with it better humours and cheerful banter.

Gwen laughingly commented, "Isn't it nice, the two g's, griping and grumbling, have been put on hold for the time being?"

The women were surprised at how fast the hot sun dried the tent canvas. The brown van sparkled in the welcome sunlight and seemed to take on a new personality as it twisted and turned up and down the mountainous highway. Marielooked out the window as the tall lush green spruce hugging the mountainsides sped by. Several times pleasant waterfalls, spurting from the sides of cliffs or tumbling down and around rocky outcroppings, sprayed the van. A soft mist floated through the trees and the mountains, settling on the windshield like delicate dew.

Marie wiped a corner of the window on her side and peeked through the little hole she had created. "Pat, I think we'd better get some air moving through this vehicle, or else tell everyone to stop breathing. The windows are all foggy. Can you believe how green everything looks? I never knew there could be so much green!"

Pat looked quickly to the side of the road. "Just flick that little switch there, and then turn the fan on a few notches. Hopefully that should help. I'll open my window a crack, too. Don't bother with your side, 'cause that's where all the waterfalls seem to hit."

Theda poked her head up between Pat and Marie. "I never knew anything could look so lushy-lush. Almost makes you want to try and eat it. Did you see those berries on those trees where we stopped to go to the bathroom? My Lord, they're twice the size of the ones we get at home."

"Yeah, what were they exactly?" asked Pat.

"They were a type of raspberry," said Theda.

"No, they weren't," volunteered Marie.

"Well, what were they then? They sure looked like raspberries."

"I haven't a clue. They didn't taste like raspberries. They were good though."

Theda yawned, a short little yawn. "Well, I think this is just about as close to paradise as you can get."

She turned her head to look out the side of the van. As she did so, a giant bird swept out of a patch of fog and soared right alongside the van for a few seconds. As suddenly as it appeared, it just as suddenly disappeared.

"Oh, my God, did you see that? What a magnificent bird! He was so close. I could see his eyes. He was huge. Do you think it was an eagle? Maybe it was a bald eagle."

Marie and Pat had both seen the bird, too. Marie kept glancing back through the window hoping to catch another glimpse of the creature. "It was definitely an eagle, but no, it wasn't a bald eagle. Trust me, you'll know a bald eagle when you see it, big white head. Wouldn't that have been something to have gotten a picture of that?"

Theda stuck a stick of gum in her mouth, "I think that we should stop the next chance we get. Set up camp, sit back and appreciate everything: the climate, the scenery, even the birds."

Pat closed her window. "Well, just remember how depressed we all were with all that rain pelting down on us yesterday and this morning. And this mist, as lovely and idyllic as it seems, is still wet. Our tents and everything would be sopping wet before we even got them up. From what I remember, as we get closer to the Grand Forks area it gets quite a bit drier, and I know there's a campground or two there. There are also motels where we can always spend the night if this mist keeps up or if it starts to rain again."

Gwen passed the magazine she was reading over to Edna, "Here I'm finished, you can look at it now. I hope we can find a nice high spot so I can spit."

Edna took the magazine and smiled, "You and your spitting, Gwen. I'm sure we'll find you a very nice place to spit from."

Theda turned around and looked at Gwen, "I think that in your other life before this one, you must have been a hockey player."

Gwen looked at her questioningly, "Hockey player? Why do you say that?"

"Ever watched them on TV? They're absolutely the spittingest bunch you ever did see. When the TV camera pans the players' box every last one of them has to spit. I'm sure that they are given a signal. 'Okay, guys get ready. The camera is going to pan on you in five, so be ready to spit.' "

"Imagine having to sleep in bunk beds with Gwen in the top one," someone mentioned.

"Yuck!"

"Oh, pooh, you wouldn't have to worry, I don't spit on people."

"No, just cars with people in them."

"Could we change the subject?" Louise begged, "This is beginning to gross me out."

Three hours later, the van pulled into a campsite just a few kilometres outside of Grand Forks. The site was within walking distance of an attractive lake nestled in between the mountains. Louise, as usual, was in charge of getting the little Coleman stove running, and before the tents were up she had a big pot of beans bubbling on top of it. "Good thing I sent this old clunker of a stove with you guys. It's come in handy more times than I care to think about. Hope it lasts to the end of the trip. You don't know how close I came to tossing it in the garbage a couple of years ago. I noticed that they have pits and barbecue places over in that closed in kitchen area. It's okay to use them, isn't it, Pat? What did the manager say about that?"

Pat was busy tying a rope between two poles so she would have someplace to air out the sleeping bags for a couple of hours. "Yes, you can cook on those stoves or on the barbecue they provide. Just can't have any open camp fires. He said that the fire index is very high through this corridor."

"Funny how the climate can change so quickly, from soaking wet to this tinder-dry area in a few hours."

Marie started to scrub down the picnic table and stopped midway when she saw Gwen come out of the large bathroom situated down and across the road. She waved at her and Gwen waved back. Gwen was walking very slowly, with none of the usual spring in her step. "Probably just tired," Marie thought. "Gwen's no spring chicken any more. She's got twelve years on some of the rest of us, so actually Gwen's doing extremely well to keep up with us." Marie went back to scrubbing the table.

Gwen came up beside her and watched as she finished the chore. "Isn't it nice here? And look, Mr. Sun has put on his happy face for us." Gwen turned to face the other women, "By the way, ladies, there's a sign in the restroom that tells where the building is that has shower stalls, and I also saw an advertisement about a coin-operated laundry in town."

Marie acknowledged the information with a nod, put the pieces of paper towel she had been using to clean the table with in the garbage and walked over to where Pat was hanging up the sleeping bags. "Mind if I take mine from you? I'll hang it up myself when I'm done with it."

"Not in the least. Here. Yours didn't make it up on the line yet anyway," Pat kicked Marie's bag towards her. Marie bent down and tried to undo the knot on the drawstrings of her sleeping bag case. "Darn, did I do this thing up? If I tried to tie something up this tight, I wouldn't be able to do it." She bent down and grabbed a piece of the knot with her teeth and yanked it. A little piece of the knot seemed larger, and Marie managed to get enough of her finger under it to pull it loose. She pulled the bag out and laid it down on the ground near the tent. Then she flopped down on her back, arms stretched out to the side, eyes closed against the sun's glare. "Oh, that feels so good, just as if I've died and gone to heaven. If I fall asleep, don't wake me up until it's time to pack the van and hit the road again."

Pat spooned herself a small plate of beans, grabbed a piece of bread, making sure to close the bag it came in and sat down cross-legged beside Marie. "Want some beans and bread? I'll get you a dish if you want."

Marie opened her eyes for a second, then closed them again, "No, thanks. Maybe I'll get some later. I just want to lie here for awhile and enjoy."

Pat waited a bit until she had finished chewing, "Speaking of heaven, I can think of better places than this that I'd rather be."

"Oh, I don't mean this place exactly. I really mean my body feels so good. Tired, but a good tired. That's a good feeling, good tired. Sort of therapeutic, like sharing in a good belly laugh once in awhile."

Pat smiled at a memory. "I know what you mean. I had a cousin once who was a year or so younger than me. She was so much fun. She was always laughing and getting other people laughing with her. She'd start to tell some story or other, and she'd hardly get a quarter of the way into it and she'd start to laugh this most marvelous infectious laugh, and before we knew it, everyone in the room was laughing along with her and when we were done, none of us even remembered what the story was about in the first place. I don't think she even did."

"What happened to her? You said you had a cousin once."

"She died a few years back, breast cancer."

"I'm sorry. Here's Theda with her bowl of beans. Suppose she'll want to share my sleeping bag."

Marie sat up and laughed, "This is so ironic, people. I cleaned the table off so you could sit down and eat your meal, and here you all are, slumming it out on my sleeping bag."

"Don't get up. I only want a teensy little corner of your bag. What did I interrupt?" Theda dipped her chunk of bread into the bean sauce to soak up some of the brown liquid.

"Pat was just telling me about her cousin who died of breast cancer a few years ago."

"Was that the girl who came to visit you one Easter? You had us over for a meal and there was this girl from down south visiting you? I seem to remember her being a cousin."

"Yeah, that was her."

"She was a riot. Such a lot of fun! I didn't know she died, that's too bad."

Pat balanced her fork with several beans on it in front of her mouth and then set the fork back down on the plate. "I wonder what happens after you die. Do you think there's life after death?"

Theda took another bite of bread and talked through chews. "What happens? You die. You rot and that's that. Just like a bug. We're really no better or worse than a bug, you know. We just think we're special." She swallowed and then took another bite, "We take a bit longer to rot than a bug because of all the crap they shoot into us, but eventually the worms get us too."

Gwen, Edna and Louise had joined the group by this time. Louise shivered, "Oh, how morbid! Let's change the subject."

Edna put up her hand and started to wave it in the air, "Oh, oh, I'll change the subject. Have any of you made your burial plans?"

Pat reached over with her foot and gave Edna a kick on the foot and laughed as she said, "That's really changing the subject, Edna. What were we talking about before? Dying. What are we talking about now? Dying. Good change."

"Well, regardless, just before we came on this trip, I went down to the funeral parlour and made all my plans, so that my family won't have to worry about anything when I pass."

"When you pass what, gas?" Theda lifted her plate up to her mouth, licked the last of the bean juice from it and looked around at the others and then started to giggle. "I know, I know, it's very rude to do that, but I'm camping and I'm in the bush, so it's accepted. I promise I'll never embarrass you by licking my plate at an Elk's banquet. I won't even do it at the company picnic."

Gwen went around gathering up the plates. "I don't think

I want a funeral. I think they're barbaric. Everyone says a funeral is closure for those people you leave behind. The closure is, you're dead, and that's that. I especially hate sad funerals."

"Most funerals are sad, I'm sorry to say," said Pat.

"No, but they shouldn't be. When someone is over eighty and they've lived a full good life we should be celebrating that life and that we were fortunate to know him or her. It seems so silly that most churchgoers profess to believe in a wonderful place called heaven, so why wouldn't it stand to reason that if that person is going to heaven, we should be glad for them, not sad?"

"Maybe the people who are so sad know something about the dearly departed that we don't. You know, something that just might prevent them from entering those old pearly gates or even worse maybe they're afraid they're going to hell instead," Theda said digging a toothpick around her teeth.

There was one piece of bread left in the wrapper. Louise reached for it, then thought better of it and took it out and ripped it into several pieces. She tossed it to a big chattering brown squirrel that sat perched on a log several feet away. "Here, you silly old thing, take this and be quiet. I think that most of the sadness that we feel is not that we feel sorry for the person that has died. It's just that we're just going to miss having them around."

The squirrel ventured down from his perch and picked up one of the pieces of bread that Louise had tossed to it. The little creature rotated the bread several times in its little paws, sniffed it and then dropped it. Then he ran over and proceeded to do the same to the other pieces. Finally, he ran off leaving all the pieces of bread on the ground where he had dropped them. Gwen stood and watched him, "Well, aren't we the fussy one!"

She continued, "I think so many funerals are hypocritical. I've attended quite a few that when the dearly departed was alive no one had a good word for him or her. Then as soon as he or she's dead, my goodness, there never was such a saintly or beloved person in all the world."

Theda snorted, "I know what you mean. It's all such a bunch of crock!" She leaned over and grabbed Marie by the foot. "And what are you going to do at your funeral, milady?"

"Me? I'm going to be cremated, but I'll probably still have a memorial service. I'm one that thinks a service of some kind is closure for the family and good friends."

Pat stood up and walked over to the red cooler and opened it. "I'm going to have a beer. Anybody else want anything? There's lots of pop in here, too, if you'd rather have that. I think I'll be cremated too. It seems cleaner that way. I can't stand the thoughts of waking up in a coffin with the top sealed shut." Pat shuddered.

Theda glanced up at the sun for a moment. "I'll have a beer, too, Pat, and would you mind handing me the suntan lotion. It was right on top of the cooler, so it's probably on the ground behind the cooler, now. Yeah, having the top sealed down on you and, years down the line, worms crawling through your eyeballs and out your nose is pretty gross."

"I wouldn't mind being cremated if I knew it wouldn't hurt," offered Edna.

Everyone stopped what they were doing, looked at her, and started to laugh. As Pat handed Theda the lotion and a beer, a drop of moisture fell on her arm. She wiped it away with her free hand. "I felt a drop of rain. Surely it won't rain now. The sun is out and I don't see a cloud in the sky."

Marie looked up at the sky. "I felt a few spits, too, but I thought I must be mistaken."

"Well, when I die, I'm going up, up in the air and every time you feel a drop of rain fall on you, you'll know it's me, standing up there, spitting down on you all," giggled Gwen.

"Oh, yuck," protested Marie, "and when it pours rain we'll know that Gwen is up in heaven teaching a bunch of her new friends how to spit on the people on earth."

Edna pursed her lips and raised her eyebrows. "I'm never going to enjoy a walk in the rain again."

A few hours later, Pat and Marie returned from a short trip into Grand Forks where they had restocked their beer and grocery supply. While there, they also refueled the van. Pat backed the van into their parking space and then leaned out the window, "People, the guy at the gas station told us about a neat trail. He gave us the directions. Said there's an old logging road that's still in decent condition that we can use. It will take us almost halfway up the mountain. Then he said at the end of it there's a wide part, almost like a lookout where we can park the car. From there, he said, we will only have to walk a little over a half an hour before we reach a viewing area. The way he talked, the view from there is supposed to be something else. We've got a full tank of gas, and a couple of hours to spare, so what do you say? Think you'd like to go?"

The road going up the side of the mountain was like the gas attendant had said, in fair condition. There was a bit of winding and a couple of hair-pin turns that taxed the nerves, but the ascent itself seemed quite gradual and at no point did they feel like they were going to topple off the mountain. The road gradually snaked its way up through trees that sprouted out of the rocky crevices. Suddenly it opened up into a large clearing where most of the larger trees had been cut.

"This must be the spot where the attendant said we could park. Now all we have to do is find the walking trail," said Marie. "The ground looks pretty firm over there to the side, Pat. Park right beside that gnarly old tree."

Pat brought the van to a stop where Marie had indicated and, as an added precaution, pushed down on her emergency brake. She wasn't even sure if the brake worked, but it made her feel better just to put it on. "Someone remind me to release this brake when we leave."

The women tumbled out of the van and split up in twos to try and find the path that the gas attendant had described. It wasn't long before Gwen yelled, "I bet this is it."

Everyone came running over to the direction of Gwen's voice. Pat and Marie stood turning in circles. "Gwen, where are you?"

Leaves started to rustle, and then they heard some branches breaking. Before long Gwen poked her head out of a stand of bushes. "Here I am, in here."

Pat and Marie pushed the branches to the side and sure enough there were the remnants of the old logging road. The middle of the road was indented with deep ruts. The sides were grown in with small brush and trees, but it was still quite a well-worn path.

"I hope this path is worn down by people and not bears. Do they have grizzly bears in this part of the country?" wondered Marie.

"I don't know. Make lots of noise so we'll scare them away if there are any."

Marie laughed, "Don't we always? We're six chattering women going up the side of a mountain so I don't think we have to worry. I wonder if there are any mountain lions."

The women were forced to walk single file through the undergrowth. Half an hour later, the trees and shrubs gave way to solid flat rock. Stretched out below them was the valley, the lake and the town.

Gwen collapsed onto a rock and sat with her head bent down to her knees for several seconds.

Theda walked over to the edge of rocks and looked down. Then she breathed in deeply, "Ah, talk about fresh air! That guy was right, the view is really something. I feel a Picture Moment coming on, am I right, Pat?"

"Right! Everyone over there quick, line up and I'll set the camera up on this rock here."

The women arranged themselves while Pat set the self timer. As soon as that was done, she rushed to her spot at the edge of the group. The camera clicked before Pat realized that Gwen wasn't in the picture. She was still sitting on the rock.

"Gwen, are you all right? You're not in the picture. Come on over here and I'll take another."

Gwen got up and the women made room for her in the second picture. After it was taken, Pat and Marie tiptoed over to the edge of the big overhang and looked over the scene below.

"It's a long ways down, isn't it? I can see why Gwen wanted to come up here. Excellent place for her to spit." Theda snorted. "Gwen, come over here. You'll love this place."

Gwen was back sitting on her rock. Her right hand was pressed against her chest and she looked like she was concentrating on each breath she took.

Theda, looking slightly concerned, walked over to her, "Gwen, are you all right?"

Gwen immediately perked to attention, "Oh, yes, just a little winded from the climb. I can usually walk for kilometres on flat ground, but put a bit of an incline in front of me, and it wipes me right out. I'll be fine. Now what were you saying about this place, I'm afraid I was only half listening?"

Gwen stood up and walked towards the drop off. She looked out to take advantage of the view that the others had been admiring. "Oh, it really is pretty, isn't it? It was well worth the effort getting here." Gwen tried to absorb everything around her: the scenery, the view, the things her friends were saying to her. A strange sensation started to come over her. Like everything was happening in slow motion and every action and face were melting together. Then as quickly as the sensation came it disappeared and she felt fine again.

She heard Theda asking her, "Where are you going? Aren't you going to spit, Gwen?"

Spit. She should spit since she was up here. Maybe she wouldn't bother this time.

Next time she would. Really tired now. Gwen thought about her comfortable sleeping bag and wished that she could cuddle up in it right now.

The trip back down to the van was pleasant and uneventful. The women's carefree chatter rose above the trees and floated out over the valley as they made the effortless climb down the narrow path. Back at the campsite they stood around discussing the walk.

Louise started to bang pots and pans around, "What should we make for supper tonight?"

Marie looked up from the book she was glancing through, "Why don't we go out to eat tonight? Pat and I saw quite a few decent looking places where we could grab a bite, didn't we Pat?"

Before Pat had a chance to reply, Gwen stood up, "Listen, I'm game for whatever you people decide, but I'm really tired. I'm just going to go into the tent and lie down for a few minutes. If I fall asleep don't let me sleep more than half an hour.

I just need a little catnap and then I'll be right as rain."

Theda popped open a beer. The can hissed as air was released and Theda held it as far away from her body as she could. Then she bent over the open can to slurp its contents as it foamed over the side.

"Ahhhh, nothing like a cold one. Anyone else want one? Have to pick up a case tomorrow. I doubt if the beer store will still be open when we go into town to eat."

Pat sat down at the picnic table, "We picked up a case when we were in town today. Didn't I tell you?"

Louise took a sip of her diet soda, "Well, if we do go out to eat, I'm going to have something really outrageously sinful for supper tonight. Like a great big beef burger with cheese and bacon and a giant plate of French fries smothered in gravy." Louise stopped to lick her lips. "Then I'm going to top it off with a scrumptious cheesecake dripping with hot chocolate and whipped cream."

Marie looked up at Louise, "Oh, Louise, you wouldn't do that, would you? You've done so well on this trip. I've never seen you look better. You're probably one of the few people who can say they've changed three sizes of clothes in one trip."

Edna offered more encouragement, "Yeah, Louise, and you've gone down in size; most people go up when they're on a trip. You have done well. I do think you should treat yourself to something special tonight. Go ahead and order just what you described, but I'll half it with you. That way, we'll each only be half sinful."

Louise looked thoughtful for a few seconds and then smiled at Edna. "You just might have something there, Edna. Good idea, let's do it. Somebody had better go and wake Gwen up now. It's been over three-quarters of an hour since she laid down."

Edna stood up, "I'll go and get her." She walked over to the tent and ducked under the tent flap, "Come on, you old sleepy head, you're going to sleep your life away. Rise and be shiny!"

Theda started to squash the beer cans with her foot. "Hand me that little bag there, please. I'll put these cans in it."

As she bent down to place another can under her foot she heard Edna's yelling frantically. "Gwen! Gwen! Oh, my God, you guys, someone please help! Oh, hurry! Oh, my God..."

Everyone dropped what she was doing and raced to the tent trying to push her way through the small opening all at once. "What is it? Is it a snake or something?" yelled Theda.

With two women already in the tent only Theda and Pat managed to squeeze in beside Edna. The other two women poked their heads in the door. Edna was sitting on the floor holding Gwen's hand. "It's Gwen," she sniffed trying to hold back the tears that were already coursing down her face, "I can't wake her up. I shook her and everything. I think she's...."

Theda grabbed Gwen's hand, "Nonsense, you must be mistaken. She was just really tired, that's all. Gwen, come on, lady. Time to get up."

Pat reached over and shook Gwen's shoulder gently. Then she placed her fingers between Gwen's neck and chin just below the ear. "Oh, no...we'd better call an ambulance, right away."

"No! Let's all help get her into the van," Marie ordered. "I know exactly where the hospital is in town. It will be a lot quicker that way. Hurry up, everyone."

* * *

"No, Jason, I don't know. We didn't bother getting an ambulance. We just took her right over to the hospital. I'm sure the doctor wasn't with her more than ten minutes before he came out and told us. I've been trying and trying to get a hold of her family, but there's no answer. I didn't want to leave a message on their answering machine. That just seemed pretty cold, so all I told them was we have to talk to them, and I left the number where they can reach us. Do you think they might be out at the lake? Yes, please try to find them. You wrote down the doctor's number, too. They can call him instead of us if they want. The police here are trying to contact them, too, so surely in the next hour or so, one of us should reach them. Okay, thank you dear. Yes, okay, I'll phone you back in exactly one hour. Bye."

Pat put the phone receiver back on its hook. She leaned her head against the side of the phone booth and closed her eyes. She could still see the way the doctor had come into the waiting room. She remembered him asking, "Are you the friends of Gwen Perkins? I'm very sorry, but there was nothing we could do."

No one had moved. It was probably only seconds, but it seemed like an eternity to Pat. Then there was one soft little sob and then everyone seemed to be crying. Like a choir backing up a soloist. Pat was the only one who wasn't a part of the group. She felt like she was standing way off in the background watching a movie or television show.

The doctor was saying something again. He was talking to her. "Would you like to come with me? There's an office just around the corner where we can talk privately."

He gently took her by the arm and walked down the corridor with her to his office. Just as they started to turn the corner, she turned and looked back at her friends. They were all standing in the middle of the room, hugging each other. God, she would really like a hug now, but she couldn't, because she was following this strange doctor into a room. Gwen was lying on a table somewhere in this building, all by herself.

"Here, have a seat. Once again, I'm really sorry. You do know that your friend was already dead when she was brought into the hospital. It was a heart attack."

Why had this white-coated person singled her out to explain Gwen's condition? Was it because she was the only one not crying? Did he think she was the only one in control? Well, I'm not in control, doctor, not at all.

The doctor reached over and touched Pat on the arm, "Don't worry, I doubt if she even had any pain, and if she did, it was sudden and quick."

Oh, that makes me feel so much better, doctor that she didn't have any pain. She's dead and she's not going to feel anything any more. Pat just nodded. Why couldn't she cry or something? She loved her friend, and already she missed her terribly. Questions started coming from the doctor, about Gwen's family and how to contact them. Must remember to thank the doctor.

For what, she didn't know. He really hadn't done anything for Gwen.

Finally, she went back to the waiting room where she received several much-needed hugs. Still no tears.

A nurse came and asked, "Did any of you want to see the deceased?"

No, she didn't want to see her friend, dead. She wanted to remember her the way she had been before. The others followed the nurse dutifully down the long beige corridor. Pat had told them that she would meet them in the van.

Pat straightened up and pushed the door to the telephone booth open, sighing as a puff of welcome fresh air met her.

Chapter Twenty

The van, with now only five occupants, kept up a steady pace travellling east toward home. Gwen's body had been cremated. None of the five knew where or when. Gwen's family had arranged it. There would be a memorial service back home as soon as her friends could get there.

Edna was staring out the side window of the van, "Oh, I wish that we'd never come on this stupid trip. Gwen would probably still be alive if we didn't. I know her family feels the same way. I talked to Karen briefly last night and she said that her husband blames us for Gwen's death. Wish I'd just stayed home where I belong, where women our ages all belong, in our own homes, with people who know and care about us." Pat noticed that Edna's voice had reached an annoyingly hysterical pitch.

"Oh, God in heaven, woman, give us a break! We've been hearing this same crap from you for the last two days. You've about worn it to death," reproached Theda.

"Well, it was our fault that she died. She was sick and she should have been at home where her family could have taken care of her," sulked Edna.

"What are you talking about woman? Her family never did a nice thing for Gwen all the time she lived. Well, I shouldn't say that because I don't know much about Karen. But her son has always been a self-centered, miserable little piece of machinery. Hardly ever came near Gwen's place except the odd time to ask for a handout."

Edna sniffed, "She didn't want to come in the first place. If you people hadn't practically begged her to come, I know she wouldn't have."

Theda's hands tightened on the armrests of her seat. She turned back to face Edna, "Listen, if you don't shut up there's going to be another death and sooner than you think. Have you ever wondered what it would feel like to be choked to death? No? Well, you're this close to finding out." Theda held her hand up in front of Edna's face emphasizing her point by holding her middle finger and thumb a fraction of an inch apart.

Suddenly, Pat swerved the van over to the side of the road. She slammed on the brakes. A huge swirl of dust enveloped the already dusty van. She pushed the van into park, turned the key off and swiveled her seat around. Her eyes flashed dangerously. Everyone stopped and stared back at her.

"All right, I've had it up to here," she said pointing past the top of her head, "with this constant bickering. First of all, it was no one's fault, not yours, not mine, no one's. Gwen died because her heart failed her. The doctor told me she could just have easily died in her bed at home, or listening to the TV, with or without her family. Her time was up and that's that. Second, no one had to come on this trip. No one forced any one of you. You all had a choice. Now, up to a couple of days ago, we were having a wonderful trip, Gwen included. She told me umpteen dozen times that as much as she appreciated her home, she never knew she could have such a fun time, or thought she could possibly enjoy the comradeship she shared being with us. I know that she wouldn't have missed this opportunity for the world. She was already planning a trip with all of us for next year. Now, get a grip on yourselves, especially you, Edna. We all feel bad, and have to grieve in our own ways and I don't care if you sit there and say nothing. I don't even care if you cry out loud, but what I don't want to hear is anyone blaming anyone for what happened."

Pat's eyes glowed like two little red coals that come to life when air is blown on them. "Have I made my point?" She turned her back on her surprised friends, turned the key in the ignition and drove the rest of the way home to Trenton in silence.

***

A week later, Pat was in the shade in her back yard relaxing and visiting with Marie. The sun filtered gently down through the leaves of the large oak tree by the patio. A pair of gardening gloves lay beside a pair of clippers on the edge of a little brown wooden bench. A large garbage pail sat on the grass, brimming over with clippings of spent flowers and dead or overgrown branches. Pat took a careful sip from the cup of hot coffee she was holding, swallowed and then said, "I phoned Edna and Theda but couldn't get a hold of them."

Marie looked over at her friend and replied, "Oh, well, we'll probably see them both at the Legion card party tonight. They both said they were going." She held her cup out to Pat. "Could I have a little more of that coffee? It's really hitting the spot."

"Certainly, my lady, just let me get the top off this thermos." Pat refilled Marie's cup, put the top back on the thermos and tucked it down between her feet. "If you want any more just holler. There's lots."

The two women looked around at Pat's garden. It hadn't suffered too much in her absence. Some of the areas had become a little overgrown, but in the two days that she had been home, Pat had managed to whip it back into what she referred to as "a sort of respectable shapely state."

Marie continued, "Oh, Pat, I still can't believe that Gwen's family had her funeral before we got home. It just seems so mean."

Pat looked in her cup, then reached in and removed a piece of a leaf that had blown into her coffee. She wiped it off on the side of her jeans. "I know. You can blame Phil for that. I doubt if his wife had anything to do with it. It was a memorial service so it didn't matter when it was and we had told them we would try to make it back in three days, which we did. I don't know whether he blames us for her death or is it just his strange way of dealing with grief?"

"I'm wondering if he doesn't feel a little guilty about how he treated Gwen when she was alive. Phil certainly wasn't the best son in the world. And for some reason or other people sometimes have to blame someone or something for a death. Who better to blame than us. We're the ones in his eyes who took his mother away from him. He won't even acknowledge me if we meet in the street. I came out of Sears the other day and ran right into him and his wife. Karen said, 'Hi,' but Phil just grabbed her arm and jerked her away before she had time to say anything else. It feels kind of funny. I've never been in this position before."

"Well, it really makes me angry. I don't think any of us deserve this kind of treatment. If it was just Gwen's family that felt that way, I wouldn't mind so much, but Phil's big mouth has managed to influence quite a few other people. I was thinking of enlisting your help, Marie, if I can. Would you come over, maybe tomorrow sometime, and bring any pictures of Gwen that you might have tucked away in your house? I'll phone the other girls and see what they can dig up, too."

***

Three o'clock in the morning, a passerby walking past Pat's house that night would have noticed a flickering light in her family room and would have just thought that she was having trouble sleeping so had decided to watch television.

Pat stood up and stretched, "Want anything to munch on? They're some cookies and cakes in the fridge."

Marie yawned, "No, thanks, I thought we'd never finish this. You know, we could have waited and finished it up tomorrow instead of working so late."

"I know, but once I get on something, I like to finish it. Let's watch the whole thing through and then call it a night."

Marie pushed the VCR button. The first picture, the face of a rather sad looking lady filled the screen. The lady in question was standing between two other women, both of whom were smiling. That photo soon faded out and was replaced with the same lady, only a few years older and a few pounds heavier, sitting at the back of someone's wedding party. She looked even sadder in this picture than she did in the first portrait. Then a group photo flashed onto the screen. Everyone in this gathering was laughing or smiling, everyone but one lady—Gwen. This was replaced by a rather wistful portrait of Gwen, in Pat's garden, gazing down at a deep red rose.

The format of the tape changed to clips from the videos Pat had taken on the trip. The screen lit up, firstly, with Gwen smiling and singing in the back of the van, followed by Gwen's hearty laughter over Theda's rendition of her favourite song. Pat had turned the volume down in the clip, while Theda sang, as she didn't think the topic was too appropriate to send to a grieving family. Next came a photo of Gwen proudly standing in front of the portion of the Hoeflickers' garden that she had help clean. This was followed by an endearing one of Gwen and the kitten at Fran's house. As the trip progressed Gwen's face seemed to change as her smile got bigger and bigger. It was like watching a beautiful butterfly emerge from its dark heavy cocoon. The last picture on the video was one that Marie had picked. She had taken a frame from Pat's camcorder and put it on pause. It was a close-up of Gwen in the raft, water streaming down her face, hands clutching the edge of the raft as it dipped and sped through the swirling waters. It was the face of an enthusiastic and exhilarated person which made it hard to believe it was the same woman portrayed at the beginning of the little film. Suddenly the screen went blank, hissed and went blue. There was silence for awhile. Finally Marie reached over and pushed the remote to turn the tape off.

"Want me to rewind it? Boy, it's hard to believe, all that work and it was only what, eight or nine minutes long at the most?"

"Yeah, you might as well rewind it."

"Seven days and practically seven nights it took us. Feel a little bit like God must have felt."

"At least he got to rest on the seventh day. What did we do? Just kept on trucking. I think it's pretty good though, don't you? I'm going to give Gwen's kids this copy and then make one for each of us. It really made me feel good to watch it."

"Me too. Well, guess that's it." Marie stretched and

yawned, "Gonna head on home now."

"You're welcome to spend the night. There's a comfy bed in the guest room."

"Thanks anyway, Pat. But I prefer to flop in my own bed. Besides I have an appointment at eleven, so it's probably best that I go home. See you tomorrow, night."

"Good night, Marie."

***

The next morning, Pat waited until she was sure that Gwen's family would be at work, and then she walked over to their house. She opened the front screen door and inserted a small package between it and the main door. On the front of the package was a brief note, requesting the occupants to take the time to watch this short film. She didn't sign it.

***

Three days later, a cloudy, but otherwise pleasant day found Pat, Edna, Theda, Marie and Louise lounging in Pat's back yard.

Theda looked around at her friends. "Why do you suppose we always seem to end up in Pat's yard?"

"Well, it is a gorgeous yard," said Louise, "I certainly don't mind coming over and enjoying it."

"Maybe because it's central to all of us," suggested Marie.

Pat laughed, "I've given this a great deal of thought, and I think I know the answer."

They all waited for Pat to continue and when she didn't, Theda finally broke the silence, "Well, tell us, what is it?"

"It's very simple really. I'm usually the one who calls and invites you to come here."

They all laughed.

Theda yanked a piece of grass out of Pat's lawn. "Who cares where we are, as long as when we get to be our age we're somewhere?"

The friend's faces sobered and a few uncomfortable looks were exchanged. Pat looked around at each friend. "Oh, come on guys. We can't stay feeling all gloomy and doomy forever. Life goes on, and I'll tell you one thing, Gwen would be the last person who would want us to lose our sense of humour."

"Pat's right. Let's look on the bright side. We still have each other," added Edna, "and I truly believe that someday we're going to see Gwen again."

Louise looked up at the sky, "Looks like it might like to rain today. Oh, well, rain is better than snow. Almost the end of August already."

"You're going to miss puttering around in your garden, Pat," said Edna.

"Yes, I will. I still can't believe how well Charlie looked after the place while I was gone."

Edna pulled a letter out of her purse. "I hope you people don't mind, but I just have a letter here I'd like to open. I can't tell from the outside of the envelope who it's from. Hope it's not a chain letter."

"For your sake and ours, I hope it's not either. Go right ahead and read it," Pat said encouragingly.

"Don't want to change the subject, Pat, but back to Charlie. Have you seen much of good old Chuck?" asked Theda.

"Oh, yes. The first thing I did when I got home was…well, actually no, it was the second. No, it was the third thing. The first thing I did was drive out to Jason's for a visit, and when I came home from his place I walked out here and took a tour of my yard. Then I phoned Charlie and invited him over for spaghetti supper the next night. We had a great visit. It was good to be home. He manages to visit once a week or so. "

Pat turned to Louise, "Louise, those doughnuts are there for the taking, help yourself. I bought them especially for you."

"No thanks, Pat." Louise stood up and pirouetted gracefully in front of her friends.

"It took me a month to get myself looking like this. I don't intend on blowing this fantastic figure just for a few stupid doughnuts."

Pat smiled at her friend, "Good for you, Louise. I have to admit that you do look fantastic."

"Right on. Lay one on me lady!" Theda high-fived Louise.

"Oh! Oh!" Louise continued. "Have to tell you about my job."

"A job?" exclaimed Theda and Pat at the same time.

"Well, it's not really a job. I'm going to teach a cooking class two nights a week. Right now, there are nine women and one man signed up. The high school is letting me use the home economics room, and I'm getting paid for it."

"If you're getting paid for it, I'd call that a job. Way to go, friend!" Marie leaned over and patted Louise on the back. "I don't want to change the subject, but since we're doing show and tell. I have some news, too."

Marie stood up and, with a turn of her head, flipped her hair back from her face. Pat laughed to herself. It was hard to believe that this was the same Marie that used to sit out here with her friends a couple of months ago. The Marie with the long greasy grey hair and sloppy clothes. Marie now sported a short pert bouncy hairdo. Her hair still had lots of grey colour, but now it was gently streaked with dark brown and auburn colours, shades that enhanced her natural grey.

Marie also twirled on the patio. "Notice the new duds, and I want you to know that there's more where these came from. No more track pants. This is the new me!"

Theda clapped her hands. "You look like a completely new person. I heartily approve. There's more though, girl, tell them the rest."

Marie sat back down in her chair and continued, "Yes, well, I went over to the high school and put my name in as a tutor. I have three students already. The school is letting me have a little corner in one of the study rooms. The kids meet me there. It's much better than having them come over to your home. Twenty bucks an hour. Nothing to sneeze at."

"It sure isn't," agreed Theda. "Cripes, you've read so many books and know so much stuff. I'm sure you'll be a great teacher."

Theda crossed her legs primly, "Now for my news. Don't get excited. I don't have a job, and I'm not making any money, but I'm trying something new, too."

Theda stopped and reached for a doughnut, then casually sat back and started to take a sip from her coffee cup.

"Well, don't stop there, woman, tell us. What are you going to do?"

Theda waited several seconds while she finished chewing then continued, "I've joined the choir at the church, with Edna."

All of Theda's friends mouths dropped open, "The choir? With Edna?" they all said in unison.

Theda laughed, "You guys are good, and all at the same time, too! Very impressive! Gwen would have been so proud of all of you."

"I think she would, but the choir, Theda? I know the churches have become very liberal in the last few years, but do you really think they're ready for *Big Crap Van?"* teased Pat.

"I know, I know. It sounds weird. But I really enjoy singing and the choir does lots of other things besides sing. They go out twice a year and clean up one of the streets in town. You know, the Adopt-a-Street thing. They've adopted a family in South America and raise money to support them. And they don't just sing in church. They sing all over.:old folks homes, schools, special occasions, you name it. I think it will be fun."

Pat grinned at Theda, "Well, one thing is for sure, if it's not fun now, with you in it, it soon will be."

She turned to Edna. "Well, Edna, you're the only one we haven't heard from, anything new and exciting in your life?"

Edna smiled as she bit her lower lip. "Well, ah, actually, ah…"

"Oh, for God's sake, Edna, whatever it is, out with it!" demanded Theda.

"All right, all right, here goes. Remember George, the man we met at the rodeo in Saskatchewan, or was it Alberta? It was Alberta, George was from Saskatchewan, that's how it went and he had a friend named Pete. Anyway, halfway through the evening, George and I left the party before you all did so we could have a little visit."

Theda snickered under her breath, "Visit? Is that what they call it nowadays. In my day, it was a tumble in the h...." She gasped suddenly when Pat jabbed her in the ribs with her elbow. Edna didn't seem to notice the mild exchange between Theda and Pat. Theda gave Pat the evil-eye and proceeded to take a sip from her coffee cup.

Edna licked her lips and continued. "Anyway, this letter that I just received is from George and guess what? He wants to come here to see me?"

Theda coughed and gasped a second time, spraying coffee down the front of her shirt. She quickly swiped her mouth and chin with the back of her hand and looked at Edna. "George! Wants to come and see...you."

Edna, looking slightly hurt continued, "Why would you think it's impossible for someone to want to come and see me?"

Ignoring Theda, she turned to Pat, "Do you think it would be too presumptuous of me to invite him here? What do you think, Pat? I value your opinion."

Pat, looking slightly embarrassed, smiled at Edna, "Well, thank you. First of all, I don't think it would be brash of you to invite him. He's already invited himself, so all you have to do is give him the okay. Of course that's just my opinion. What do the rest of you think?"

Theda shook her head from side to side, "Well, first of all, I resent that you don't value the rest of our opinions and secondly, Edna, I say, you go girl!"

Everyone laughed. Suddenly, Pat cocked her head, got up and started towards the house. "Excuse me, girls, but I think I hear the doorbell. Be back in a sec."

Several minutes passed before the women on the patio heard Pat and her visitors making their way through the kitchen to the back door. Theda and Edna watched three forms loom behind the large window in the door. One of the figures bent down as if it was tying a shoe. Then the door opened and Pat came out first, followed by Gwen's two children.

Pat put her hand on Phil's shoulder. "Ladies, you all know Phil and this is Gwen's daughter Emily. Emily left town many years ago. First she went away to University and when she finished her studies, she got a job in Toronto. It must be over twenty years or so, am I right, Emily?"

Emily smiled, "You're right, Pat. I still work full-time and have three children now so keep pretty busy. My husband and I tried and tried to get Mom to come down for a visit, but she never would. I used to think it was because she didn't care very much for me, but after we started settling Mom's estate we found out that she just didn't have the money to travel anywhere. Funny what you learn about a person when it's too late."

Pat took Emily's hand. "That's all right, dear. Now, ladies, Phil has something he would like to say to us. Go ahead, Phil."

Gwen's son bent his head, swallowed hard, and then stood up. He looked straight in the eye of each one of his mother's old friends in turn before he started to speak. "First of all, ladies, my sister has informed me that I've been acting more like a spoiled stupid kid than the man that I'm supposed to be. I might add that those weren't her exact words. Stupid ass was what she called me, or was it Royal Jackass. Whatever. I don't know what came over me. When I heard that my mother was leaving to go on that trip with you guys, I don't know, I think I felt like she was deserting me or something. Guess I was just jealous. I was pretty mean about the whole thing, and did some pretty nasty badmouthing. Then when Mom died and Emily came home, I lied and told her that none of Mom's friends could make it for the funeral so we might as well have it right away and get it over with."

Emily glared at her brother, "When I found out after, that you had actually rushed home to be here for her funeral, and we had held it early just to spite you, I could have killed Phil. I still could."

Phil kicked at the patio floor with his toe. "I know. I was

an ass. I didn't realize it until Emily and Karen forced me into watching that little video you sent over. We presumed that it must have been you, Pat, that put it together. Watching that video finally made me realize how happy Mom was when she was with you ladies. I'd never seen her so…I don't know what to call it—radiant isn't the right word I guess, but that's sort of how she looked. Radiant. She was never that way with us, and I suppose that was no one's fault but our own. She didn't have a whole lot to smile about when she was around us. We must have watched that same video fifteen or sixteen times last night. Practically wore it out. Anyway, what I came over here for was to apologize to you all. I'm sorry for the way I treated you, and sorry that we had Mom's memorial service before you could get back for it. I'm sorry that I was such a shit."

Theda jumped up and put her arm around Phil. "You are a shit, Phil, there's no denying that, but I think you may turn out to be a good shit after all."

Louise came over and linked her arms through both of Gwen's children. "Well, I say, let bygones be bygones and just know that your mother loved both of you very much regardless of how…"

"Regardless of how shitty you were," kidded Theda.

Pat put a restraining hand on Theda's arm, "Ease up, Theda, give the kids a break."

Emily wiped a few tears from her eyes and laughed, "I say keep giving it to him, Theda. The miserable little bugger deserves it. Anyway, we brought something over for you ladies. Phil, go get it."

Emily's brother turned, opened the back door, bent down and gently lifted out a small cream-coloured wooden box with a white lily engraved on its lid. Gently and reverently he handed the box to Pat. She took the box in her hands and looked at it, then up into Phil's eyes. Thinking it was a peace offering of sorts she asked, "What is it?"

Phil smiled, "They're mom's ashes. Both Emily and I are entrusting them to your care until next year when you go on your next trip. We'll leave it to mom's friends to spread them where you think fit. You'll know better than anyone where that should be."

As Pat held the box she glanced up at the dark overcast sky. A single drop of rain fell on the top of the box right near the lily. Then another and another. Theda laughed, "Remember what Gwen said about spitting at us from heaven when she got there."

Pat kept looking towards the sky. Several more drops of rain spat against her face. First she laughed and then she cried.

It rained heavily most of the evening.

As soon as Pat wiggled out from under her bedding, she reached over to peek outside to see what the weather was like. The sun was shining. Pat quickly made her bed, dressed and scooted out to the kitchen where she filled the coffee pot with coffee and water. After switching the coffee machine on, she walked over to the back door where she slipped on her old runners. Outside she went towards the garage at the back of the property, skirting her way around several large puddles that the rain had left in its wake. She pulled the garage door open and peered into the dark interior where the old brown vehicle was parked. She walked up to the front of the van and ran her hand across the hood, "Well, old girl, you done good, didn't you? Have a good rest, my lovely, you deserve it."

Pat laughed softly to herself as she walked along the side of the van. When she was just about at the garage door she stopped and gave the van a swat on the back bumper, "Just don't get too comfortable, lady. You don't know this yet, but we've already started to make plans for a trip down East next year. Think you'll be up to it?"